PRAISE FOR

SUGAR FORK

"Walt Larimore can write! He weaves a tale that will take you into the coves of the Great Smoky Mountains and introduce you to the hearts of its noble people. Pull up a chair, pour a glass of iced tea, and relax with a story that will capture you."

—Ruth Graham, author of *Fear Not Tomorrow,
God Is Already There*

"*Sugar Fork* takes a unique look back to a lost and almost forgotten era in the history of the industrial age of the southern Appalachian Mountains—a transitional period in the history of Western North Carolina. As the fictional characters of Sugar Fork interact with figures whose names grace the pages of both local and national history books, these characters come alive. I am delighted with *Sugar Fork!*"

—Judy Andrews Carpenter, director of the
Proctor Revival Organization

"The Randolph family could easily fall apart trying to survive in the Great Smoky Mountain wilderness. The captivating stories and colorful voices of these characters, their lives and struggles, will stay with you long after you reluctantly come to the end. A good old-fashioned novel."

—Julie L. Cannon, author of *Twang*

"Come hike with me through the virgin Smoky Mountain forest, along stream beds lush with trilliums, ferns, and orchids. Contrast this spectacular beauty with the simple life of an orphaned Southern Highlands maiden. See hope, faith, and love conquer hate and greed in a setting where good, simple folk wrestle evil in the bygone world of old Appalachia. Walt Larimore has done it once again in his powerful, heart-string-tugging page-turner, *Sugar Fork*."

—Eric Wiggin, author of the Hannah's Island series,
Bridge Over Coal Creek, and *The Recluse*

"Walt Larimore isn't just a great storyteller. He paints word pictures that linger like country wood smoke—so strong you can't get it out of your mind."

—Chris Fabry, author of ECPA Christian Book Award for Best Fiction winner *Almost Heaven*

"*Hazel Creek* stands right along with Catherine Marshall's *Christy* or Francine Rivers's *The Last Sin Eater.* This book will stir your emotions at a deep level, entertain, and open your eyes to a different time and world far back in the Great Smoky Mountains. I hated to see it end, and I'm thrilled to give *Hazel Creek* my highest recommendation."

—Miralee Ferrell, author of *Love Finds You in Sundance, Wyoming*

"A compelling story of courage and faith."

—Augusta Trobaugh, author of *Sophie and the Rising Sun* and *River Jordan*

"In *Hazel Creek*, author Walt Larimore tells a story woven through with timeless themes of family, friendship, and faith."

—Beth K. Vogt, author of *Wish You Were Here*

WALT LARIMORE

SUGAR
FORK

A NOVEL

HOWARD BOOKS
A DIVISION OF SIMON & SCHUSTER, INC.

New York   Nashville   London   Toronto   Sydney   New Delhi

Howard Books
A Division of Simon & Schuster, Inc.
1230 Avenue of the Americas
New York, NY 10020

First Howard Books trade paperback edition October 2012

HOWARD and colophon are trademarks of Simon & Schuster, Inc.

For information about special discounts for bulk purchases, please contact Simon & Schuster Special Sales at 1-866-506-1949 or business@simonandschuster.com.

The Simon & Schuster Speakers Bureau can bring authors to your live event. For more information or to book an event contact the Simon & Schuster Speakers Bureau at 1-866-248-3049 or visit our website at www.simonspeakers.com.

The author is represented by the literary agency of Alive Communications, Inc., 7680 Goddard Street, Suite 200, Colorado Springs, CO 80920. www.alive communications.com.

Designed by Jaime Putorti

Manufactured in the United States of America

10 9 8 7 6 5 4 3 2 1

Library of Congress Cataloging-in-Publication Data

Larimore, Walter L.
    Sugar Fork : a novel / Walt Larimore.
        p. cm.
    I. Title.
    PS3612.A64835S84 2012
    813'.6—dc23
            2012001040
ISBN 978-1-4391-4190-8
ISBN 978-1-4391-9685-4 (ebook)

To Gilbert Morris
With admiration, affection, and appreciation

PROLOGUE

Saturday, September 12, 2009

"**Y**ou look like a giant prune in a rucksack," I said, chuckling as I strode behind her. She was strapped to a carrying chair—a backpack used to carry feeble or injured folks in the wilderness—and was being carted up the precipitous mountain trail by a young, muscular national-park ranger. Sitting back-to-back with him allowed her to face our group as we struggled to keep up.

"It's rude calling someone a prune. Not nice at all." She scowled.

"I apologize, Mrs. Abbie."

"Accepted, but I cannot believe ya talked me into this!" she complained. "This is plumb foolish."

"You do look pretty funny," I said, laughing out loud. I was getting short of breath and felt the sweat pouring down my face as the climb became steeper and steeper.

"Ya best stop laughin' at me! The Good Book says respect your elders."

"You sure about that?" I asked, already knowing the answer.

"Are ya questionin' my Bible knowledge?" she scolded, as she cleared her throat. "Okay, here it is, and I quote: 'Rise in the presence of the aged, show respect for the elderly and revere your God.' That's from Leviticus, chapter nineteen, and the thirty-second verse."

"Well, I *am* honoring you, Mrs. Abbie."

"How's that? By calling me a *prune*?"

"I apologized for that. But I am honoring you by bringing you to Decoration Day at your family cemetery. And I'm showing my respect by coming back with you to your home place. You say you haven't been out here to Sugar Fork in what, about sixty-five years? Doesn't that count for something?"

"Harrumph," was her only reply.

Three months earlier, I completed my family-medicine residency at the prestigious Duke University Medical Center and was assigned to practice in Bryson City, at the far western end of the state, in exchange for reducing my considerable medical-school loans. Only about fourteen hundred folks inhabited the hamlet, known as the southern wilderness entrance to the Great Smoky Mountains National Park, but it sported a well-equipped forty-eight-bed hospital. I looked forward to practicing there for at least the next four years.

"Couldn't you have chosen a cemetery site that's a bit easier to get to?" I asked.

"I didn't pick it," she countered. "My grandpa chose the site. But I'll tell ya this: it's 'bout as pretty a family plot as there is in these here Smoky Mountains. And I've seen a bunch of 'em, Doc."

Suddenly the ranger's foot slipped, and he and Mrs. Abbie began to fall toward a precipice. Her eyes widened as her hands flew to cover her mouth and stifle a shriek.

I lunged forward and grabbed Mrs. Abbie, which served to stabilize them both.

"You saved us from a terrible fall, Doc. Makes me think back to when Gypsy Mary did the same thing when I was a young'un."

"Just glad you're as thin as you are, Mrs. Abbie," the ranger called over his shoulder as he repositioned the shoulder straps. "Thanks for the help, Doc. Should be at the top soon," the ranger panted. "Then we'll be able to rest a bit."

True to his prediction, in less than fifteen minutes we came to the top of the ridge, which was covered by a thick forest.

"Here," the ranger said, "let me put you down on this stump. Looks like this was a giant chestnut tree at one time."

"Pa said she were the crown of this ridge for at least two

centuries," Mrs. Abbie commented. "Stood over a hundred and twenty feet tall and her branches covered the whole ridge, including the cemetery. Had to have her cut down and sold after the chestnut blight hit in '27. Old man Calhoun had to pay me a pretty penny for her trunk. He hated handin' me even a single dime."

The other members of the party, including a reporter from one of the most prestigious papers in the county, all breathing heavily, crested the ridge. I suspected the editor of the local *Smoky Mountain Times* in Bryson City had tipped him off about our historic trip. The members of the party were too short of breath to say a thing, so they just mopped their brows as they inhaled water or sports drinks.

After the ranger unhooked Mrs. Abbie, I pulled out my handkerchief and began to pat the moist beads on her deeply wrinkled forehead. "Let me wipe that sweat off."

"Proper women don't sweat," she complained.

"Really?"

"It's true. But we can dew up a bit, like a honeysuckle vine in the early morning."

I laughed as I gently dabbed her forehead. Mrs. Abbie Randolph was one of my first patients at the Mountain View Manor Nursing Center and was my first centenarian. I quickly grew to admire her and found her stories about growing up during the early years of the twentieth century in the Hazel Creek watershed of what is now the Great Smoky Mountains National Park as fascinating as they were engrossing.

Besides seeing Mrs. Abbie during rounds at the nursing home once a month, I, along with my wife, would share lunch with her at the Fryemont Inn in Bryson City every week or two. What I learned about Hazel Creek captivated me; however, what I was finding out about the small creek on which the Randolph family farm was located, the Sugar Fork, was enthralling. Finally I suggested we make a visit to the site of her former home.

She had wavered about making the trip ever since I suggested it during one of our lunches. Even though she was initially reluctant, in the hope that she would eventually agree, I worked with the North Shore Cemetery Association and the National Park Service, both of which bent over backward to assist me in putting the trip together. It was not inexpensive, but I felt it was a worthy investment.

"Looky there! There it is!" she exclaimed in an excited voice, pointing with a small, crinkled, trembling finger in the direction of a stone wall.

I saw her little body shiver and wondered if it was with trepidation or anticipation.

"The rock wall used to be whitewashed, but I guess the paint's all chipped off over time."

She sighed as I offered her my arm, and we began to slowly walk toward the enclosure.

"It was certainly well built," the ranger commented, as he closely examined the moss-covered rocks. "Look, no mortar or grout at all. Just stacked stone with hardly any space between the rocks. And still standing after all these years."

"Over a century," she said, as she looked around and pointed to a narrow opening in the wall. "This here's where the gate used to be. When I was a little girl, this wall seemed *so* tall. Guess I was just a tad short," she said, smiling.

After walking in, Mrs. Abbie sat down on the two-foot-tall wall. The cemetery wasn't more than twenty by twenty feet and was surrounded by a thick forest fighting for a foothold among the large boulders strewn across the ridge. Several members of the party entered with rakes and flat-headed shovels. "Okay to begin cleaning up, Mrs. Abbie?" the ranger asked.

She nodded and pointed to the two white marble tombstones. "There are Mama's and Pa's stones. Dr. Keller bought 'em both and had Danya haul 'em up here after Pa died."

"This looks like a pretty rocky place," the reporter observed. "Bet these graves were hard to dig."

Mrs. Abbie nodded. "In fact, the crew that dug Pa's grave

musta been the strangest collection of gravediggers in history—two gypsies, two black men, and a Haint."

"A Haint?" the reporter asked, as he pulled out a notepad and pen. "What's a Haint?"

"That's all I'm gonna say 'bout that," Mrs. Abbie replied. "All the graves face due east. It was the tradition. That's so when the Lord returns, and the resurrection of the bodies begins, everyone is facin' the Lord hisself."

The men began to rake the ground, which was covered by a thick carpet of composting leaves and mast.

"Be careful when ya get to the stones," she warned. "Don't wanna scratch 'em."

Over the next few minutes, the men carefully cleared off seven stones and cleaned them with brushes and soapy water they retrieved from their backpacks. As the stones were scrubbed, the carved inscriptions appeared, as if by magic.

"Why don't most of the graves have tombstones?" the reporter inquired.

"They were just too expensive for mountain folks. So, we took plain ol' flat fieldstones, placed 'em over the graves, and carved the names and the dates. Sometimes a verse or remembrance."

"Who's under the four larger stones?" the reporter asked.

"That one is for Pa's ma and the other for his pa. They came over from Tennessee and staked out this claim back in the late 1800s. Pa's pa cleared the land and built the first cabin on the property. He was as fine a man as there were. They said he could shoot a fly off the ear of a bear at a hundred paces with his Winchester."

"And the other two?"

"Ya won't find an inscription on 'em," she said, as she looked suspiciously at the unwanted reporter, and turned to me. "The folks buried there didn't want one. But that's another story for another day." Mrs. Abbie was quiet for a moment and then said, "Them small stones is where my little brothers sleep."

I turned to look at her as her dark brown eyes misted.

"They represent three sad stories," she said, almost in a whisper.

I reached into my day pack and pulled out a clean bandana. "Here," I said, handing it to her. She took it and wiped her tears. The men were quiet for a moment, leaning on their rakes.

Truth be told, in the few months I had known her, I developed a deep affection and growing appreciation for this unique woman and the remarkable story of her family—a story worthy of being told: a tale of good battling relentless evil; a yarn of five young girls and their struggle against evil men and uncaring nature; a chronicle of faith, friends, and family; an amazing embroidery weaving threads of innocent affections mingled with heartbreaking events; a needlework composed of both love and loss, framed by the lyrics and melodies of ancient mountain songs that added a sweet touch of music to her chronicle.

Today I hoped I would learn a few more chapters of her family's extraordinary legend, most of which took place on the Randolph family farm and in the Sugar Fork valley, located more than a thousand vertical feet below this high, lonely ridge.

"Well," Mrs. Abbie said. "How 'bout we place the silk flowers we've brought, have Pastor Semmes lead a short memorial service, and then head down to the home place for our picnic and frolic."

A tall man with thinning hair, wearing a clerical collar, walked into the cemetery. He cleared his throat and began. "Mrs. Abbie, my great-grandfather married your ma and pa, and he proudly officiated at your very own marriage. Before that he baptized you and all seven of your siblings. He also baptized each of your children. He led every single service at this cemetery. The last one was a long time ago, so I'm honored to be asked to do this service for you today, and in the memory of Rev. Willie Neuman Semmes and your ancestors."

"Who'd you marry?" I whispered.

"Shh!" she cautioned. "We gotta pray."

"Tell me later?"

She said nothing, but clasped her hands and bowed her head as the pastor opened his great-grandfather's Bible and began. "Let us pray."

Part One

SATURDAY, MARCH 13

through

MONDAY, MAY 10, 1926

1

Wash

The hills looked barren and exposed, almost naked, as the biting cold March wind blew across the Randolph farm. During the bleak winter months, the views up and down the Sugar Fork changed dramatically. With the loss of its luxuriant and lavish leafy canopy, the forest revealed its normally veiled ridges and hollows, crests and gorges, vales and basins—a landscape carefully concealed during every other season.

Abbie Randolph gazed down the valley with her attentive dark brown eyes. The oldest of Nate Randolph's five daughters, she was tall for her age and considered one of the most eligible girls in the entire area. She was pleased that the curves for which she had prayed so long were beginning to blossom. Her dark brown eyes sparkled above a radiant smile and her thin, soft face, framed by glossy, shoulder-length auburn hair, neither exposed nor revealed the harshness of running a homestead in the wilderness. The arduous life of the highlanders often hardened and creased the faces, souls, and hearts of those less hardy than she.

However, of recent she had begun to worry that her facial features would begin to show the signs of the stresses from the responsibility of having to complete the myriad tasks previously accomplished by her mother. Added to this was the never-ending burden of her schoolwork. The combination of chores and study made her days significantly longer and more difficult, not to mention making her relationships with her younger sisters testier and increasingly strained.

It won't be long before we start seein' some spring weather . . . at least accordin' to the Farmers' Almanac, she thought. Her family had not kept up with the almanac in previous years, because their old friends Lafayette and Dove Faulkner intimately familiarized themselves with the entire publication and made sure their neighbors knew all the applicable particulars.

Mr. Lafe, as she and her sisters called him, though he was more than eighty years old, had been Abbie's ride to town to attend school for as long as she could remember. His passing that spring after a horrible bout of double pneumonia—an illness which killed the majority of those it struck in the mountains—was particularly distressing to her.

Premature death was a reality of life for the mountaineers of western North Carolina. Abbie knew women frequently died during or after childbirth, as had her mama a year and a half before. Children often went to sleep—permanently—long before they had a chance to grow up, as had been true with her three little brothers. *Tragical,* she thought, as she sighed. *No good lingerin' on the past. At least Mr. Lafe lived a good, long life.* She was trying to comfort herself. *But I still miss him in a powerful way.*

Dove, his wife of more than sixty years—they married when he was twenty and she only thirteen—died in her sleep only two weeks after her husband. "It were a broken heart what took her," Maddie Satterfield, the local healer and midwife, told the girls. "I'll miss 'er. We was the dearest of friends fer over fifty years. It took her that long to git me goin' back to church, at least once in a while."

Abbie used the back of her wet hand to brush her long hair away from her face. *What is it 'bout this time of year I don't like?* She felt her nose crinkle as she pondered the question. *Guess it's 'cause it's so blame gray and dull! But spring's not far off. Cain't wait to see the flowers and baby rabbits and newborn birdies.*

She stood up and extended her back to stretch out her cramped lower-back muscles. *That's what I like about spring: it represents new life and a new start. It's like washin' off the old. That's what I need!*

The morning air was crisp and cold, and from time to time Abbie would hold her hands close to the fire roaring underneath a huge black pot. A nearby wire held the bed linens and towels that had already been washed, while another wash line held one-piece underwear that looked like a family of ghosts swaying in the breeze.

Although Abbie detested washing clothes, as the oldest, she was responsible for the entire operation. It involved smearing the clothes with soft lye soap, then thoroughly boiling them in the wash kettle, which was hung above the fire on a tripod. Then the clothes would be laid out on a washing bench their pa had made from a huge virgin white oak trunk and pounded out with a paddle. After that, the clothes were smeared with the soap once again and plunged back into the hot water where they would be scrubbed vigorously. That boiling and rinsing completed the cycle.

Abbie looked longingly toward the forest. She could almost hear the trees calling her to come explore and play. *I'm too growed up for that now!* she thought. *Got to be the mama of this farm, like it or not.*

Usually her younger sisters helped with the washing, but their teacher, Miss Grace Lumpkin, was tutoring the two oldest, Whit and Corrie. Meanwhile, the two youngest were in the cabin, where Anna Katherine was caring for the baby, Sarah Elisabeth.

"Back to the wash," Maria commanded in her usual deep, husky voice, as she laughed and stood to her feet. Abbie had grown to love and admire the tall, full-figured gypsy woman who, along with her younger brother, Danya, worked full-time on the Randolph farm since before her mama's death. The siblings, in their late twenties, had emigrated from Russia and spent time with a traveling carnival until deciding to settle down.

With jet-black hair that nearly reached her waist, wide full lips, an olive complexion, high cheekbones, and black arching brows, Maria attracted the gawking of the men in the company town of Proctor whenever she journeyed the six miles down valley to go there.

Of course, the ogling had, to Maria's relief, become less obvious since she and the local deputy sheriff, Zach Taylor, one of the area's most desirable bachelors, began seeing each other. Then again, Maria's colorful dresses and scarves; long, dangling golden earrings; and rings she wore on several fingers would have made her stand out in *any* crowd of mountain women.

Suddenly Maria looked down the road. "You hear something?"

Maria's dark eyes joined Abbie's in gazing down the road leading away from the Randolph cabin. Abbie listened a moment, then shook her head. "Don't think I do." She then returned her attention to the loathed washtub.

"Bet your mama would have loved your sisters' birthday party last weekend," Maria said as she wrung out the items she had just rinsed. "It was so much fun. I can't believe little Anna is eight and Whit has reached fifteen."

Abbie bent down to continue the washing. "'Bout everyone came!"

"It appeared to me you were your gayest when Bobby Lee Taylor arrived."

Abbie laughed and nodded. "Of course. He's my beau. And ever since we started courtin', I cain't hardly get him off'n my mind. Every time I see him, at church or school or just anywhere, why my heart just flip-flops."

"Reckon he'll be setting a wedding date soon? You've been courting how long now?"

"Since my fifteenth birthday."

"I figure that to be a bit over eighteen months," Maria said. "I think a spring wedding would be fine. Over a year of courting is more than enough in my book."

"I agree!" Abbie responded. She stood to face Maria. "How

'bout we make it a double wedding? You and the sheriff, his son and me. Your brother could be the best man for us both."

Maria's guttural laughter echoed off the family barn. "I think Danya would be honored. He'd go down in the record books as the largest best man in the history of the Smokies."

Abbie smiled as she thought about the gentle giant. His six foot, six inch, 260-pound frame was massive, but his heart and demeanor were gentle and mild mannered. His olive complexion, fierce curly beard, and dark blue eyes surrounded a large bulbous nose. He usually wore a hat, to both contain his thick, wavy coal-black hair and cover his large ears, which tended to stick straight out from his huge head.

Abbie was surprised to feel her eyes begin to fill with tears.

"What is it?" Maria asked as she stepped toward Abbie and took the girl's hands into her own. "Are you all right?"

Abbie shook her head. "Mama loved you and Danya. I remember the day we all met you and when we all shared our first dinner together."

Maria pulled Abbie into her arms and gave her a gentle hug. "Your pa and mama, along with you girls, were kind to take us in. Otherwise we'd likely still be traveling with that vagabond troupe that brought us to this valley. The carnival life was very difficult. People can be cruel to carnies—that's what they called us. But your parents gave us work here on your farm. They invited us to live here and to become part of the family. Danya and me . . . well . . . we will be grateful forever."

"Don't know how Pa would'a kept the farm runnin' without you two," Abbie said as she sniffled.

"Initially we all worried about him, didn't we? After your mama passed, he seemed depressed for so long. We all feared for him. Then, last fall, our worrying increased when he turned over most of the farm management to Danya and spent long days away from here. Remember how we all fretted he had taken a job in the new Fontana Copper Mine just over the ridge in the Eagle

Creek valley? It seemed to explain the hours he spent away and the money he brought home to you girls."

Abbie nodded. "Not to mention the luxuries he brought us—the store-bought soap, scented candles, and even a nice set of towels for each of the girls. He ain't never been able to afford such things." She pulled back, reached into her pocket, and brought out a small handkerchief. "He even brought me this."

After wiping her tears and gently blowing her nose, she continued. "Pa dismissed my concerns 'bout him bein' away so much. I was a-feared for him. He told me not to worry. But I did, till ya told me the truth."

"Maddie let me and Danya know your pa was running her and Quill's moonshine over to Bryson City. She wanted us to know so we'd be aware of where he was. I told you because I didn't want you to be needlessly upset."

"But I was, Maria! It's the first secret he's ever kept from me; at least the first one I know 'bout." Abbie blew her nose again. "I was *so* a-feared 'bout his runnin' whiskey. I was powerfully bothered by it. Didn't seem right. Sure 'nough didn't seem legal."

"But Maddie told us that all the moonshine he was running *was* legal because it was labeled as medicine," Maria responded.

"I know," Abbie sighed. "Doc Kelly, the pharmacist, took the deliveries and stocked it. And Dr. Bennett, Doc Kelly's pa, was the one to write the prescriptions for his son to fill and dispense. Even the sheriff over in Bryson said it was all legit—"

"But you didn't believe it, so you checked with Sheriff Taylor down in Proctor, right?"

"Yep."

"And he said it was legal, right?"

"That's partly true, Maria. He's said *makin'* medicinal moonshine were legal. It's just the *transport* what worried him. Said it were a gray area under the law. But what bothered me the most was that I knew Mama would want Pa to depend upon the Lord and not upon some questionable activity."

"Maybe this is the Lord's way of providing for you girls, Abbie. After all, doesn't the Good Book say, 'God is able to make all grace abound toward you; that ye, always having all sufficiency in all things, may abound to every good work'? I'm thinking there's sufficiency here for you and the girls."

Abbie nodded. "But to be honest with ya, I was most a-feared 'bout what folks at church would say when they found out. Why, they'd likely shun us, I tell ya! Plumb made me lose sleep!"

"Your pa's a good man, Abbie. Remember how he and the rest of the men spent a full week raising and finishing our home?" Maria asked, looking at the small cabin standing at the edge of the meadow. "It was the first time Danya and I had a house of our own since we moved to America from the home country. A lot has changed for us."

Abbie sighed. "For us both, Maria."

Maria spun around. "I thought I heard something. Here they come."

"It's about time," Abbie said, dabbing the last of her tears.

A woman of medium height—her brown hair pulled up in a bun, her green eyes flashing above a radiant smile—expertly guided the handsome chestnut gelding pulling her carriage up the road. Grace Lumpkin, the teacher at the one-room school and the woman who seemed to have captured their pa's affection, let loose an infectious laugh as she pulled to a halt in front of them. "Okay, girls!" she called out, "playtime is over. Looks like you're just in time to help Abbie and Maria."

Darla Whitney, a thin girl whose heart-shaped face featured dark brown eyes and was framed by a wealth of thick brown hair, stepped daintily from the carriage. Abbie always thought of Whit as the most fragile of her sisters, both physically and emotionally. Of all the sisters, she had the greatest difficulty handling the death of their mama.

Behind her, the mischievous and irascible Corrie Hannah jumped out. Corrie had inherited the bright red hair and green eyes of her mother and was considered the feistiest of the girls, by far the most impulsive and daring, something of a tomboy, caring little for the things that proper young girls were supposed to care about, such as dolls, playing house, or combed hair.

"Good morning, Abbie, Maria," Grace called out.

"Top of the morning to you," Maria replied.

"The lessons went well, Abbie," Grace reported.

"We done good!" Corrie blurted out.

Grace laughed. "We did well," she corrected. "I think the tutoring is helping, especially for Miss Corrie Hannah. She's coming along. I may even be able to pass her on to the seventh grade."

"Will miracles never end?" Whit said, laughing as she poked her sister. "Come on, Corrie, let's start hepin'."

"Helping," Grace corrected. "Abbie, is your pa still out hunting?"

"Yes, ma'am," Abbie responded. "He took his huntin' dog, Lilly, and left before sunup to get some game. Don't 'spect him back till this afternoon at the earliest."

"He loves that Mountain Cur hound of his, doesn't he?"

"She's a good dog, Miss Grace."

"Well, I'm hoping to see you all in church tomorrow."

"Lord willin'," Abbie replied.

Grace reined her quarter horse and waved as she pulled around and down the driveway toward the Sugar Fork. Abbie felt her lips tighten as she thought about how Miss Grace and her pa had tried to keep their visits and budding romance a secret. However, one day Miss Grace did something that gave fodder to every gossip up and down the valley.

2

Hurt

The first time Miss Grace sat by Nate at church, it was *the* topic of discussion around the valley, especially from the loose lips of one Etta Mae Barnes, wife of the owner of Barnes General Store in Proctor. But eventually folks seemed to accept the budding romance.

This was especially true after Reverend Willie Semmes put out the word to the women to cease and desist the whispering. "I believe with all my heart that Callie Jean Randolph would approve of her husband seeing Miss Grace Lumpkin," he had told them when he dressed them down at a special meeting of the Ladies' Circle.

Abbie appreciated the pastor taking up for her pa and Miss Grace but just could not bring herself to accept that her pa might be having feelings for another woman. With his falling for Miss Grace and spending so much time away from the family, Abbie couldn't help but wonder if he was thinking as straight as he should be.

Pastor Semmes continued. "Y'all might wanna remember that Miss Lumpkin was born to the family of a Georgia farmer. Her pa, William Wallace, was a Confederate veteran who gave his children a strong sense of pride in our Southern cause. Her religious upbringing—even though Episcopalian, which I can forgive due to her devotion to our church—and her love of the Scripture, would all be approved by Cal."

Abbie would be the first to concede that Miss Grace, as all the children called her, was the only possible woman in the area who might have a chance of winning her pa's attention after the loss of his lifelong love. And Miss Grace had accomplished just that, winning not only his affections, but also the admiration and regard of Abbie's sisters. Nevertheless, and in spite of how much Abbie respected her as a teacher and liked her as a person, she just could not begin to imagine Miss Grace coming anywhere close to replacing her mama.

"Durn!" Corrie exclaimed, bringing Abbie's mind back to the present. "I'd just as soon wear dirty clothes!" She pounded several pairs of pants, then, as the wire was full, carried and pinned them to the lower limbs of the big magnolia tree that almost overshadowed the barn.

"You know what I seen in the Monkey Ward book?" Whit called out, referring to the annual Montgomery Ward catalog.

"What?" Corrie asked, as she returned to the washboards.

"I saw what they're a-callin' a washin' machine. You just throw dirty clothes in there, and it washes 'em all clean as anythin'."

"Maybe Pa bought us one over in Bryson City this last week," Corrie mused. "He drove over there a couple of times."

Abbie looked over her shoulder to see if he might be coming up the road, and she felt her mouth grow taut when she didn't see him. For some reason, an uneasy intuition had haunted her since he left that morning.

"Maybe he's hidin' it at Maria and Danya's cabin and is plannin' to give it to us for a present. Maybe tonight at dinner!" Corrie said, laughing.

Maria looked sternly at her. "Corrie Hannah, if there was a washing machine at my house, don't you think I might just be using it right now?"

"Then maybe he took it to Miss Grace's place down in Proctor for safekeepin'," Whit suggested.

"Or maybe Mr. Barnes has it at his general store in Proctor and will personally deliver it to us later," Corrie said. "A machine will fit better in his delivery wagon than in Miss Grace's carriage."

"Maybe Pastor Semmes or his wife, Maybelle, is hiding it at the parsonage," Whit said.

"And maybe when they come," Abbie mused, "they'll bring along their son, Rafe, to offer to court you, Whit. After all, you're fifteen now. It's time for you to begin courtin'."

"I still think Rafe's sweet on Corrie," Whit quickly responded.

Corrie stuck her tongue out at Whit, and then said emphatically, "I'm definitely gonna get me one of them when I get growed up!"

"What, a washing machine or a boyfriend?" Maria asked, laughing.

"You'll just have to wait and see. But I'll tell you this much, I'm gonna marry me someone who is as rich as—"

Suddenly a loud scream from the cabin startled the girls. Dropping a pair of pants that was hanging by one clothespin, Corrie sprinted toward the cabin with Abbie, Whit, and Maria right behind.

Bursting into the cabin, the girls found Anna sitting on the hearth, pale and crying, while sixteen-month-old Sarah Elisabeth was on the floor squalling at the top of her lungs.

"Whatcha done now, child?" Corrie shouted.

"I ain't done nothin'!" Anna exclaimed, squeezing her left pointer finger with her right hand. Her blond hair and blue eyes were striking. "I was crackin' walnuts on the hearth for y'all, and the hammer accidently squished my finger. It right made me yelp, I tell ya. And when I cried out, Sarah Beth let in."

Whit walked over and picked up Sarah. The toddler immediately began to quiet down. "Sarah girl, your curly hair looks like you went to town and paid for fancy ringlets," Whit cooed as she ran her hand through Sarah's wavy blond hair.

"Since all's well here," Maria said, as she turned to walk out of the cabin, "I'll go finish the wash."

Abbie reached out for Anna. "Here, lemme see, sweetie." She carefully examined her sister's finger, which was bright red and beginning to swell. "Can ya move it?"

Anna nodded and began to make a fist.

"Good news. It don't look broken. I think it'll be all right. Here, let's do Pa's magic healing recipe and make it well." She kissed Anna's finger. "May this kiss heal thy red-rose-pricked finger, Sleeping Beauty." She then cradled Anna's swollen finger in her right hand, while passing her left hand, palm down, in a circle above the puffy finger, and said, "Abracadabra, Cinderella, Rumpelstiltskin, get well!" The whole ritual caused Anna to smile.

Whit was walking the floor with Sarah, making comforting noises.

Corrie walked over and gave the baby a kiss on her forehead. "Now, now, Sarah Beth, you're all right. That mean ol' girl ain't worth dried spit for taking care of a little one like you."

"It weren't my fault!" Anna said loudly.

"Ya let the fire almost go out!" Corrie complained. "I swan, girl, you're as worthless as withered weeds!"

"I ain't worthless!" Anna shot back. "Pa says I'm beautiful."

"Well, beautiful, you've done run us outta wood!" Corrie scolded. "Why don'tcha take yer beautiful self out and get some more? Ya don't have two broken legs, do ya?"

Abbie was relieved that the crisis was so minor but bothered by Corrie's harshness. "Ya don't have to fuss at her so much, Corrie," Abbie scolded. "I think she's doin' the best she can."

"Well, her best ain't good enough!" Corrie exclaimed. "Anna, did you put the taters in the coals like you were told to?"

"I was just 'bout to do it," Anna answered.

"Just 'bout to? You had all day to do it! I've a mind to take a stick to ya, Anna Katherine Randolph."

Anna's face twisted up as she attempted to keep the tears back.

Abbie walked over to Anna and put her arm around her

shoulders. "Don'tcha cry, Anna." She turned toward Corrie and said, "It was *my* fault. I forgot to put 'em in the coals."

Corrie folded her arms and turned away from her sisters. "I think I might just run away!"

"Girls! We're supposed to be sisters!" Abbie said. "Look at what we're doin'. We're gettin' all over each other and bitin' each other like fleas on an ol' hound dog."

Whit and Anna looked at each other.

"And I'm likely the worst!" Abbie exclaimed. "I know that I am too hard on you'uns at times, and even too hard on myself. I blame it on stayin' exhausted all the time. And I think we're all a bit strained from the work of keepin' a house, 'specially with a little one, and goin' to school. Reckon we're all wore a bit thin."

She sat down in her mama's rocker. "But I'm wore down the most! I feel cheated. Gotta be the oldest sister *and* the mama to this whole group. And I gotta supervise all the chores and try to git my schoolwork done. It's just too hard! 'Specially with Pa bein' gone so much." She crossed her arms across her chest.

Whit walked up beside her. "Abbie, this ain't gonna last forever. Ya've got Bobby Lee as a beau. He loves ya and he's gonna care for ya. Ya've got Emily Rau, Maria, and Danya to help out anytime you ask. Ya've got friends, ya've got your family, and ya've got food and a farm. Despite the hard times, we got us a lotta blessing." Whit looked at her sisters. "We all need to git outta this pity party of ours . . . and now! 'Specially you, Abbie. We all need ya to be strong when we're not."

Abbie nodded as she took in a deep breath and slowly let it out. "You're right, Whit." Abbie thought for a moment as she tried to remember a verse from the Epistle of James. When it came to her, she slowly recited it. "Be patient therefore, brethren, unto the coming of the Lord. Behold, the husbandman waiteth for the precious fruit of the earth, and hath long patience for it, until he receive the early and latter rain. Be ye also patient; stablish your hearts: for the coming of the Lord draweth nigh."

Whit laughed. "Mama made us say that verse again and again. But I think it's easier to say than do."

"Remember the rest of the verse?" Corrie asked. "Mama made me say it anytime I'd complain about you girls or my chores." Standing up, she pretended to open a Bible and let it flop across her outstretched hand as she leafed through the imaginary pages until she found what she was looking for. Pointing to the unseen Bible, she began, "As the apostle James teaches us in the ninth through eleventh verses of the fifth chapter of his epistle, 'Grudge not one against another, brethren, lest ye be condemned: behold, the judge standeth before the door. Take, my brethren, the prophets, who have spoken in the name of the Lord, for an example of suffering affliction, and of patience. Behold, we count them happy which endure. Ye have heard of the patience of Job, and have seen the end of the Lord; that the Lord is very pitiful, and of tender mercy.'"

The girls all clapped as Corrie bowed.

"You could be a preacher!" Anna exclaimed.

"I just may one day," Corrie said, sitting down, "'cept it would have to be a rich church to pay me very well!"

The girls laughed as Corrie smiled and continued. "Well, I guess I need to apologize, Anna. I've forgotten those verses and hope the Lord won't judge me too severely."

"He won't," Anna reassured her. "I'm sure of it."

Abbie smiled as she took Anna's hands into hers. "I hope you girls won't pay me no never mind when I get too sharp." Abbie also suspected that her worry about her pa contributed to her bad mood, but decided not to say anything about it.

Whit, the sweetest tempered of the five, smiled and said, "That's all right. I'll go with Anna to get the wood right now." She turned to go, but as she did, she stopped suddenly. "Somebody's a-comin'! Maybe it's Pa!"

3

Walkingsticks

"He's a-comin' back!" Corrie exclaimed as she raced toward the door. "I hope he got us a deer."

"Maybe he got us a turkey!" Anna cried as she ran to follow Corrie. After Corrie threw open the door, disappointment tinged her voice. "It ain't Pa. It's the Walkingsticks."

Abbie felt her stomach knot. Her worry for her pa welled up in her soul like a pot of soup boiling over as she walked to the door. Two Cherokee Indians approached the cabin wearing white man's clothing. In the summer and fall they would wear deerskin chaps and moccasins, but now they wore insulated hunting boots and brogans. Abbie waved and tried to smile as she concentrated on quelling her fears.

Jonathan Walkingstick and his oldest son, James, had been close friends to the Randolphs ever since she could remember. They lived ten miles east of Bryson City, in the Qualla Boundary, part of the original Cherokee Nation, but often came by on hunting trips or when traveling to the Snowbird Mountains near Robbinsville, south of the Little Tennessee River.

"Greetings, girls!" Jonathan said. He was sixty-two years old and his face was lined from years of exposure to the elements, but his posture was straight and his hair still as black as a crow's wing. His son, forty-four-year-old James, taller and more muscular than his father, also had hair so black it shone, and his eyes were as dark as the darkest night. Abbie did not know two more considerate or compassionate men.

"Where's your pa, girls?" James asked.

"He's gone huntin'," Anna said, sticking her head around Abbie's waist.

"Well, I wish he hadn't done that." Jonathan shrugged as he unstrapped a large backpack and swung it onto the ground. "We trapped a bear last week, and we brought you folks a big chunk of it."

"That's wonderful!" Abbie exclaimed. She was partial to bear meat, especially when it was cooked just right, and at once changed her mind about the plan she had for supper. "I'll cook up a bunch of it if'n you fellows will stay and help us eat it."

"We'd be happy to," Jonathan said. "That is, if it's no trouble."

"None at all!" Abbie replied.

"How 'bout we slice some meat for the meal, and put the rest in the smokehouse?" James asked. "Then my father and I will chop some wood."

Abbie nodded. "And we girls will throw ourselves into preparin' the dinner."

After finishing with the meat and filling the wood box for Whit and Anna, the two men sat at the kitchen table as the girls worked.

"Our neighbor, Mr. Tom Rau, tells us the bear aren't as plentiful these days," Corrie commented as she peeled carrots.

"That's what most of the white hunters are saying," James said. "But my father can track and trap with the best. And we know where they are and how to find them."

"Unlike the elk and panther that I hunted when I was a child," Jonathan said wistfully. "Those are now all gone from these mountains. But bear meat, for those who like it, and most people in these parts do, is still my favorite game."

As the girls and the men talked, Abbie trimmed the fat from the bear meat, cut the meat into small pieces, and parboiled it for ten minutes in creamy milk from their springhouse. Then she browned the meat in bacon drippings in an old cast-iron frying pan on her mama's cooking stove before adding salt, pepper, branch water, and butter. She then put the meat and fixings in a big pot and hung it in the fireplace, adding wood to the coals. She planned to cook the stew for an hour and a half. She would also make dumplings and drop them into the simmering stew a half hour before it was done.

As the food was cooking and Sarah Beth napping, the younger girls took James to tour Maria and Danya's cabin and invite them up for dinner, while Abbie quizzed Jonathan about his family and the latest news from the tribal lands.

As Jonathan was sharing all the recent reports from the Cherokee community, Abbie found herself uncharacteristically silent as she stared into the fireplace.

"Your spirit seems glum, Abbie."

Abbie was quiet for a moment, and then looked up at the old man. "Mr. Jonathan, when I was lookin' across the valley this morning, I seen so many patches without forest, without trees, I plumb found myself gettin' so angry at the lumber company that my insides shook."

He nodded.

"They're destroyin' and wreckin' our woods. If it weren't for Pa, Mr. Rau, and Mr. Kephart, they'd have already clear-cut the entire Sugar Fork valley. It just seems so unfair."

After a few moments of silence, the old man said, "I sense that's not all, is it?"

Abbie continued to stare at the fire. For a moment she didn't know how to answer him. Finally, she knew what it really was and shook her head.

"What is it?"

She felt her eyes tear up. "I'm powerful worried 'bout Pa. He's gone more than I like." She looked back at the old man. "At times I feel guilty about being mad at him. It's wrong, ain't it, to be mad at Pa?"

The old man's eyes softened and he shook his head. "No, my little sister, it's not wrong to want the best for your family. It's not wrong to ache to have someone return who's away from you. Most people feel angry at times. I know I have."

"You have? When?"

He turned to look into the fire for a few moments. Finally, he said, "Abbie, I too have had anger for those who have taken much from me and my people."

"What do you mean?"

"We Cherokee have lived in these ancient mountains since the Great Spirit formed them. He gave this land to us. Then the white people came to *our* land nearly three hundred years ago. For two hundred years, my people extended hospitality to all of them. We've always been happy to help newcomers. Many of our peoples intermarried. White people had a written language and taught it to my people. As a result, my ancestor Chief George Sequoyah developed the Cherokee alphabet in 1821, and the majority of the Cherokee nation became literate."

"I heard the story at school."

"This is where the story turns sad. Land speculators wanted to take my people's land to sell. We Cherokees fought this in court, all the way to the great Supreme Court of the United States. Unfortunately, we lost, and in 1838, most of my people were forced to move from these mountains to Oklahoma; forced to walk over eight hundred miles. During the cruel march, many died of exposure, disease, and the shock of separation from our native homeland."

"That's why they call it the Trail of Tears, isn't it?"

Jonathan nodded. "All the Cherokee in western North Carolina today descend from those who were able to hold on to land they owned, or those who hid in the hills, defying forced removal. And then there were those who returned from Oklahoma on foot, like my great-grandfather. But he returned a man broken in heart and spirit, an anger-hardened man." Jonathan stared into the fire.

"Did he hate the white man for doing that?" Abbie asked.

Jonathan turned to Abbie. "I asked him the same thing when I was a young man. He told me that he did not hate any longer. I remember my anger burning as I said to him, 'Why not? After all they did to you . . . to our people . . . why not?'"

"What did he say?"

The old man looked back at the flames. "Abbie, he told me that hate destroys only the one who hates. Hate does nothing to those who commit injustice against you. But hate can demolish . . . it can decay your very heart and soul."

He took an iron poker and stirred the coals as he continued. "As I listened to him, I calmed down. He told me it was not easy for him to give up his anger, his bitterness . . . his hatred. He struggled with these feelings many times over many years. Finally he realized he had two wolves inside his heart: one was good and one was evil. The good wolf lives in harmony with all around him, and does not take offense when no offense is intended. He will fight only when it is right and just to do so, and only in the right way."

"And the other wolf?"

"The other, Abbie, is wicked. He is full of hatred, bitterness, lies, and anger. The smallest thing will set him off into a fit of temper. He is the evil one that fights with everyone, all the time, many times with no reason." He tapped his forehead. "That wolf cannot think straight because his anger and hate are so great. That wolf is the foolish one. He renders the person who embraces him just as helpless in his anger and hatred—he causes disease and disorder inside the heart and spirit."

Abbie also looked at the fire, letting the ancient wisdom seep into her heart.

Jonathan continued. "My grandfather said it was hard for him to live with these two wolves inside his heart, both trying to control and dominate his spirit. He finally realized only one could win the great battle."

Abbie looked intently into the Indian's eyes and asked, "Which wolf won, Jonathan?"

He smiled, looked back at Abbie, and quietly said, "The one he fed."

Abbie smiled back. "I like his advice very much."

"I do, too, Abbie," the old man said. "He used to say, 'Don't let your yesterdays eat up your todays.' He was wise."

Abbie nodded. "His counsel reminds me of something written in the Bible."

"Which is?"

"Saint Paul said, 'Let all bitterness, wrath, anger, clamor, and evil speaking be put away from you, with all malice. And be kind to one another, tenderhearted, forgiving one another, even as God in Christ forgave you.'"

Jonathan smiled. "It sounds like this Paul knew of the two wolves. I like his wisdom."

"Me, too," Abbie responded.

4

Amen

After dinner, everyone was sitting around the warm, crackling fire. The two Indians and Danya were smoking their pipes as the girls were sipping the hot chocolate Corrie and Anna had prepared.

"I'm a-feared somethin's happened to Pa," Whit said.

"He said he might be late, Whit," Abbie answered, trying to comfort her sister, but her heart continued to feel troubled.

James spoke softly. "Sometimes a hunter has to go a long way when he is tracking a large, muscular buck; they are mighty creatures and can run long distances. Your pa is a good hunter. My guess is that he probably got one but it was too late to bring it in. Did he take his horse with him to bring the carcass back?"

"Yep. And he always takes some camping gear with him," Abbie explained, "along with Lilly. That Cur would protect him from Satan hisself."

"He's probably all right," Maria said.

But Abbie could see the worried look on her face. This was even more bothersome to Abbie, as Maria was known to have the gift of prophecy.

"Maybe we should go look for him," Corrie suggested.

"It's too late today," Danya said, looking toward the window at the fading light.

"I agree," Jonathan said. "If he doesn't come back in the morning, my son and I will look for him."

"You'uns could stay in Pa's summer room across the dog trot," Abbie offered. "The chimney's good and you're welcome to our firewood."

"That's a kind offer, Abbie," Jonathan said. "But my son and I are more comfortable sleeping under the stars."

Corrie, thinking out loud, said, "Pa ain't never stayed the night out when he went huntin' alone. He's too good a shot. And there are still plenty of deer in the Sugar Fork valley. And it's gonna be below freezin' tonight. Something's amiss, I'm tellin' y'all."

Abbie thought sure she also saw worry deep in the old chief's eyes. Another chill came over her. Since the death of her mama, she had clung to her pa, perhaps more than she should have. "He'll be all right," Abbie said as confidently as she could. "Don't worry about him, girls. Let's get ready for bed."

"Jesus said, 'Let *not* your heart be troubled,'" Anna added as seriously as she could.

Abbie smiled and pulled her close. "Amen. Thanks for the reminder, little one. I think all that Scripture memory we're doin's makin' a difference."

Anna nodded. "And we need to say a bedtime prayer for Pa."

"Jonathan and James, would you mind joining us for evening prayer?"

The two men looked at each other, and then the older turned to Abbie and smiled. "Of course," he softly responded.

As they joined hands and bowed their heads, baby Sarah exclaimed, "Amen!" even before they began to pray.

"Well, I guess that ends that!" Whit said. Looking at the Walkingsticks, she said, "Sarah doesn't like long prayers and she's learned saying 'Amen' can stop a long one. Now I guess she's learned she can stop them before they start."

All of the older girls, except Abbie, giggled. She hoped against hope they couldn't sense how concerned and anxious she really was about their pa.

5

Wait

Everyone was up before dawn. Even Sarah Beth was awake and whining for breakfast. Nate had not come home, so the Walkingsticks brought in fresh firewood and stoked the main cabin fire before preparing to leave.

"We'll find him," Jonathan reassured the girls. "My son is a better tracker than even my father, a man who was renowned for his ability to trail a man or an animal even when all others had failed. My eyesight is not as good as it was when I was younger, but James can track a fly from here across the Little Tennessee River and all the way to the Snowbird Mountains."

"I hope so," Abbie whispered. "I'm a-feared somethin' bad a-happened to him."

James put his hand on her shoulder. "He's only been gone twenty-four hours. Men in these parts will often go hunting for days."

"I know that," Abbie said, "but that's only when the men go together. Pa's never hunted by himself and stayed out all night. I'm worried."

"We'll be back as soon as possible," James reassured her, "and we'll give your pa a hard time for worrying you like this."

"Are you girls going down to church?" Maria asked as she entered the cabin.

"We probably should," Abbie answered, "but if you don't mind, I think we'll just wait here for the men to come back."

Maria nodded her agreement. "Then I'll stay with you," she said as Danya entered the cabin behind her.

"Good morning, girls," he called out in his tenor voice. "James, Jonathan, greetings." He was wearing hunting trousers, which were stuffed into massive black boots. His loose-fitting shirt looked large enough to be a tent, and his head was crowned with a round cap of bear fur his sister had made for him.

Maria turned to the Indians. "Jonathan, teach my brother how to track, will you?"

The old man smiled and nodded. "He can track almost as well as my James. But he still has to learn how to stalk silently."

"It's hard in these boots," Danya said. "Maybe you should have James make me some moccasins. I could walk more softly in a nice pair of deerskins."

Jonathan looked at Danya's gigantic feet. "It would take an entire deer to make one moccasin for you, my friend."

Danya let out a laugh and slapped the old man on his back, nearly knocking him over, as the three men turned to leave.

All morning long the girls impatiently endured the wait. Abbie kept looking at their mantel clock, feeling that the second hand had slowed as if it was moving through a puddle of drying molasses. As she stared at the clock, she could almost see their neighbor, Sandy Rau, walking over to the clock, gently opening the front glass, reaching in, and stopping the pendulum. The loud ticking had ceased, preserving the moment of her mama's entry into eternity. One month later, her pa had removed the black cloth he used to cover the clock and restarted it, marking the end of their formal mourning, but not their sadness. She could only pray it would not have to be stopped again.

Maria played with Sarah until her nap time after lunch. After placing her in bed, Maria took the other girls to the porch and sat them around her. She opened a canvas bag and pulled out a wooden instrument with a triangular body and a neck with three strings. The base was painted red with a scene of horses pulling people in a carriage over a field of snow.

Abbie thought Maria's balalaika was a striking instrument—the most beautiful she had ever seen—and its sound was both sumptuous and unique. In Maria's expert hands it sounded like a rich combination of a harp, a harpsichord, and a banjo.

"I have an old Russian song for you girls. It's a story of how a beautiful young lass outwitted a young suitor who wanted to take advantage of her." She began to play the haunting melody as she sang:

> *A young lad stands, and he thinks*
> *Thinks and thinks a whole night*
> *Whom to take and not to shame*
> *Whom to take and not to shame*

"Here's the chorus. I'll sing it once and then we'll sing it together," Maria said.

> *Tumbalalaika, strum balalaika*
> *Tumbalalaika, may we be happy*

The girls were able to join in heartily. "Now, see if you can answer the young lad's riddles," Maria said.

> *Girl, girl, I want to ask of you*
> *What can grow, grow without rain?*
> *What can burn and never end?*
> *What can yearn, cry without tears?*

As Maria continued to strum her balalaika, she asked, "Anyone know the answers to these riddles?" The girls laughed as they all shook their heads. "Then listen."

Foolish lad, why do you have to ask?
A stone can grow, grow without rain
Love can burn and never end
A heart can yearn, cry without tears

The girls all laughed as Maria said, "So, he tries to fool her once again."

What is higher than a house?
What is swifter than a mouse?
What is deeper than a well?
What is bitter, more bitter than gall?

"Here's her answer," Maria said.

A chimney is higher than a house
A cat is swifter than a mouse
The Bible is deeper than a well
Death is bitter, more bitter than gall

Maria strummed the last chord and the girls cheered. Maria laughed out loud. "It's a good song, yes?"

"And even better riddles," Whit added.

Maria stopped her strumming and looked up. "Someone is coming!"

6

Down

The girls all turned as James Walkingstick emerged from the forest, trotting on Nate's horse toward the cabin. Quickly hopping off the horse, he ran up to the porch.

"Did you find Pa?" Abbie cried, fearing the worst.

"Yes, he has been . . . uh . . . . injured. His back is hurt."

Relief flooded Abbie. *He's alive!* That thought filled her mind for a moment, and then she ran to get her coat. "We've gotta go get him."

"Wait," James said quickly. He looked down, then up to Maria, as if uncertain how to break the news.

"I already know," she said, nodding. "You can tell the girls the truth, James."

James looked at Abbie. "Your pa's been shot. But he's alive."

Abbie collapsed into a rocking chair, too shocked to move. She heard her sisters gasp and glanced at them. Anna's lips began to quiver. Whit's eyes widened as she reached down and pulled Anna close as she began to cry. Corrie shook her head in disbelief and covered her mouth with her hand as her eyes misted.

Abbie turned to James. "Shot? Did he have an accident? Shoot himself?"

"No," the Indian answered. "Your pa's too experienced for that. Someone shot him."

Abbie felt her hand cover her mouth as she heard Whit begin to weep.

"Who?" cried Abbie. "Who would do such a thing?"

"Nate doesn't know who. But he's in a very bad place."

"What do you mean, 'a bad place'?" Corrie demanded. "We've got to get him! Where is my pa?"

"He was hunting in a steep section of Eagle Creek just over the Jenkins Trail Ridge."

"The cliffs below Woodward Knob?" Abbie asked as her eyes widened. She knew the area well, and it was as rough and steep as any in the region.

"Yes," James answered. "He said he was aiming at a deer when he was shot from behind. He was on the edge of the gorge and does not remember if he fell or was pushed over the edge. We found his horse grazing at the top edge, but he was at the bottom. Although the shot didn't kill him, the fall into the gorge should have. But thank goodness he fell into a dense rhododendron thicket. It must have cushioned his landing. I'm sure the man who shot him thought he'd never be found.

"We were able to get down to him. He had gained consciousness and built a small fire. Then he covered himself with fir branches and ground cover. The fire, the cover, and Lilly kept him warm during the night. But he's lost a fair amount of blood and I suspect he's broken some bones. We're going to have to get him out of there. It's hard to move him because of the pain. So, I've come back to ride down to Proctor. There I can get the sheriff and several men to come help us get him out."

"You don't need to do that," Maria said, as she replaced her balalaika in its bag. "I will tell you how we will get him out. He must be strapped onto a padded, flat board, then carried out."

"I agree, Maria. But it will take at least four men to get him out of there. The path is too narrow to carry him. We'll have to lift him out with rope."

"No, it will only take *one* man, James. My brother, Danya, can do it. Come. My bed has a board under the mattress. It will be just right. We will take the wagon."

"Jenkins Trail is not wide enough for the wagon," James said.

"Then we'll have one of our Percheron workhorses pull Nate's sled."

James nodded. "I'll get the sled ready in the barn and bring the bed board."

"Corrie, come help me get one of the workhorses ready," Maria said.

Abbie felt relief rush through her. "Yes, I'm going, too. Whit, can you stay here and take care of Anna and Sarah Beth?"

Whit nodded.

"I want to go, too," Anna cried.

"No, Anna. It's freezin' cold out there. There'll be snow and ice on the trails. Won't be safe for you. And I need ya to stay here with Whit and care for Sarah. We'll be back as soon as we can."

Abbie and Corrie put on their warmest boots, grabbed their long winter coats, and then put on wool hats and scarves before donning lined gloves and walking outside into the chilly air.

Once James and Maria hitched one of her workhorses to the sled, James moved out in front on Nate's horse. As Maria placed a thick scarf over her face, she stood in the front of the sled's bed and took the reins.

"Abbie, you and Corrie hop in."

Once they were beside her and holding on, Maria cried out, "Get up, Matilda. Gettie up!"

The sled surged forward as the large horse leaned against the harness, while James led the way.

7

Descend

After reaching the ridge at Pickens Gap via the main road up Sugar Fork, James guided them off the road, heading north up the Jenkins Trail. As the trail became dramatically steeper and narrower, James stopped.

Maria pulled the reins and called out, "Whoa!"

James said, "Here's where we have to leave the horses and sled. There are too many trees in the path."

Maria asked, "How much farther is it?"

"Not too far. Maybe half a mile."

"We'll have to carry the board and the straps." She moved to the side of the sled and pulled out the bed board, which was two feet wide and six feet long. "James, can you carry this?"

He nodded and easily lifted the board as Maria picked up a sack full of straps. She had an extra blanket around her shoulders for Nate, as well as a medicine bottle she shoved into the pocket of her coat. "Ready."

"Come, we go now." James moved absolutely silently, while the sound of Maria's heavy boots pounded on the snow and ice behind him.

Abbie had been quiet the whole trip, and now as she and Corrie walked behind the tall, dark-haired woman, she tried to fight the growing fear in her heart. For months she had been unable to shake the foreboding she had about her pa. His moonlighting was a constant concern because of its legal uncertainty and the social stigma it would bring down on her and her sisters if their friends discovered it. But those worries paled compared to the ever-present threats from the lumber-company manager, who Abbie knew would just as soon kill a man as argue with him. Abbie not only worried incessantly about her pa, she had begun to have nightmares that would wake her in a cold sweat. And now, her pa had been shot—the fulfillment of all her anxieties. Who did it? What would be next? What could be worse? She tried to put her answers to those questions out of her mind, but could not.

No one said anything until finally they came to the edge of a steep cliff. The sheer sides were precipitous.

"Looks like it's forty or fifty feet down to that ledge," Maria pointed out.

"And the ledge is only a quarter way down to the bottom of the gorge," James added. "Fortunately, he only fell to an outcropping. The brush not only padded his fall, it kept him from falling to the bottom. I don't think he would have survived a fall all the way down."

"Don't look like there's a way down," Corrie observed.

"My father found a narrow path. Maria, you will have to hold on to the bushes and saplings on the way down to keep from falling. Girls, why don't you stay up here? The trail's just too dangerous."

Abbie and Corrie looked at each other. "An angry mob couldn't keep us from goin' with ya," Abbie said.

The man smiled. "I figured as much. But be very, very careful. I don't want us to have to carry more than one person out of this gorge."

It was a struggle as they wound their way down the cliff face. The path was very narrow, and the snow and icy leaves on the sliver of a path made their footing treacherous. Each step had to be carefully placed and before long everyone in the party was panting, both from strenuous effort and terror. Several times Abbie wondered if she should turn around and go back, but she followed Corrie, who bullied forward. She tried to place her feet in James's footprints while Maria followed Abbie.

Without the well-rooted saplings and bushes clinging to the side of the cliff, which she grabbed for stability, she would never have made it. *Not what Pa needs,* Abbie thought. *One of us fallin' and muckin' up the whole rescue.*

At one point Abbie slipped on an icy patch of loose leaves and at the same moment lost her grip on a bush. As she began to fall toward the steep embankment, she screamed but was saved by Maria as she reached out and caught Abbie by the hood of her coat. With her viselike grip and powerful arms, she pulled Abbie back onto the trail. Abbie jammed her back against the cliff as Maria steadied her.

"That was close, little one," Maria said.

Abbie nodded. "Thanks," she muttered as she looked down and felt a chill go down her spine. "I'd've died for sure."

"We're here for each other, Abbie," Maria said.

As they continued to descend, Abbie wondered, *How in the world are we ever gonna get Pa outta this gorge?*

Finally the path leveled out. "This way!" James instructed, and five minutes later they came upon Jonathan and Danya, who were sitting by a small crackling fire next to Nate.

"He's resting now," Jonathan whispered. "He's been in great pain."

Abbie went at once to her father. He was lying on his side, with his ever-loyal Lilly beside him. His eyes were closed and the part of his face she could see above his full, thick beard was porcelain white. His breathing was slow and deep, and she could see the vapor of each exhalation. "Pa," she whispered, as she knelt by him. "It's Abbie. I'm here."

Nate's eyes opened, but his face was stiff. "Punkin, what are you doing here? It's too dangerous."

"Came to getcha, Pa. Maria and Corrie came also. You in a bad way?"

"It hurts so bad I cain't hardly stand it, Punkin."

"Who shot ya, Pa?"

"Reckon we all know who, Abbie. But I caught no sight of him." Nathan groaned.

"Sanders? Was it the lumber-company manager, Pa?"

"Got to think it were, Punkin," he said. "But also gotta admit I didn't see him."

"He's always had it out for us, Pa. Always wanted our property. Everyone believes he's killed men for their property. Everyone, even the sheriff, believes it."

Abbie felt Maria's hand on her shoulder. "We'll worry about that later, Abbie. Right now we need to get your pa to the doctor."

Abbie nodded. "Pa, Maria has some medicine for ya. Can ya swallow it?"

Nate slowly nodded. "I'll try."

Maria reached into her pocket and pulled out the medicine bottle.

"Have him take a big swig, Abbie," Maria instructed. "It's a powerful medicine." She used her teeth to pull the cork from the bottle and handed it to Abbie.

Abbie took it and winced at the strong smell. *This is worse than cod-liver oil,* she thought. She held her pa's head up and lifted the bottle to his lips.

"Drink all you can, Nate," Maria said over Abbie's shoulder. "Three big swallows if you can."

Abbie watched as her father swallowed the potion while making a face, and then she laid his head down.

Nate groaned. "What was *that?*"

Abbie handed the bottle and cork back to Maria.

"Something to make the pain go away," Maria said as she put the cork back in the bottle.

"Tastes like poison," he said as he looked up at Abbie and tried to smile. "You'uns tryin' to poison me?"

Abbie smiled back at him. Even in bad times he always seemed to keep his sense of humor. "Just gettin' ya back for all that cod-liver oil you gave me."

"Weren't me!" Nate exclaimed. "That were your mama."

Maria knelt by Abbie. "Where does it hurt, Nate?"

"'Bout everywhere, Maria. But it's worst down in my lower back and my legs. Never had anything hurt so bad! But I can move my legs, so that's good."

"The pain will be better soon," Maria reassured him, as they gathered around the fire to give the medicine time to work.

8

Rescue

Indeed, Nate's pain diminished within an amazingly short time, and Abbie saw that her father was sleeping.

"That's strong medicine," Jonathan said, leaning forward. "What is it?"

"It's old gypsy medicine. It's similar to the laudanum Doc Kelly mixes up, but cheaper."

"What's in it?" James asked.

"It's a secret mixture of herbs, opium, and some moonshine."

James smiled. "No wonder it works so well and so quickly!"

"I don't know how we're going to get him up the steep path," Jonathan said. "It will be hard enough just to get ourselves up. Maybe we should work our way down this watershed until we get to Eagle Creek and then take the valley road to Fontana. In the meantime, Abbie and Corrie could go up, get the sled and horses, go down the ridge to Pickens Gap, then down Pinnacle Creek Road to meet us on the valley road."

"It will be a long hike for us," James observed, "but much easier than going up the cliff face and certainly safer."

Jonathan nodded. "It would be a much shorter distance to carry him back up the way we came. But I agree with James. It would be both difficult and dangerous. Let's go down valley."

"Danya can do it," Maria said. "He can do it safely. Now bring the board, Danya," Maria instructed.

Danya brought the board, putting it down beside the injured man. Maria put the thick blanket she had been carrying on the board and said to James and Danya, "Now, you two roll him on his tummy. I want to dress his wound."

As they rolled Nate over, he groaned. Abbie could see a small hole in his coat, surrounded by a large patch of dried blood. Maria lifted his coat and the sheer amount of congealed blood made Abbie gasp.

Maria worked silently, peeling his undershirt away from his skin. To Abbie's surprise, a thick poultice covered the wound. She looked at Jonathan.

"It's an old secret Cherokee medicine," he explained, "made up of herbs, sulfur, cobwebs, and lard."

"Cobwebs?" Maria asked.

Jonathan nodded. "They help stop the bleeding."

"It's certainly done that," she said. "Maybe we can exchange recipes."

"Hopefully it will also keep infection out," Jonathan said. "Before I dressed the wound, I looked it over. My guess is the bullet is lodged in his backbone. He's fortunate no nerves were damaged. I think his spine stopped the bullet and spared his internal organs, maybe even his life."

Maria nodded. "Help me move him," she requested as she pulled the layers of clothing down. "We'll need to be careful. Likely the spine is shattered. Don't want to risk paralysis."

James and Danya got on one side with Jonathan and Maria on the other. "Be careful," she warned. They picked him up slowly with one motion and laid him on the board. She covered him with the blanket and said, "James and Jonathan, you hold the head end of the board up while Danya and I put the straps under it."

Abbie stood by watching as Maria directed the operation. Soon her father was bound tightly to the board and the knots expertly tied.

Maria turned to face her brother. "Pick him up, Danya. Put him on your back."

The others watched as the huge man bent down and lifted the head of the board. He slowly rose, lifting the injured man to an almost vertical position as if Nate were a scarecrow made of straw. Then he turned and pulled the board, with Nate attached, onto his back. As he leaned forward, Nate and the board settled to a nearly horizontal position. "We go now," he said.

Jonathan and James looked at each other in disbelief.

"I'll go first," Jonathan said. He pulled out his hunting knife. "I'll clear all the limbs I can."

"I will follow Danya," James said, "and stabilize him if needed. Maria, you walk between the two girls. And I'd suggest you all rope together for safety."

Abbie would never forget that trip back up the side of the rock face. It could not have been done without Danya's immense strength. He used his right hand to hold the board that bore her father, keeping Nate balanced as the board rested on his massive back muscles. With the other hand he would reach out and grab small tree trunks to pull himself up the path. He moved slowly and carefully, placing each foot securely in place before putting his full weight on it. The older Cherokee moved ahead cutting away foliage. It was an arduous task, made only slightly easier by the fact that much of the snow had been stamped down by the party as they descended. However, with each step Abbie felt weaker. She couldn't begin to imagine how Danya was doing it. Finally, she heard someone in front say, "We're here!" and then they were at the top of the gorge.

"Now we'll go more quickly," Maria said.

Danya continued to walk as steadily as he could so as not to jar Nate.

When they reached the sled, Maria said, "Put him inside on the floor." Danya slowly lowered Nate onto the floor of the sled.

After Nate was settled in place, Maria said, "Now, we'll go back to the cabin."

"No, we need to get him to a doctor," Abbie countered. "He's hurt bad."

"In town?" Jonathan said.

"Yes, in Proctor," Abbie said. "Dr. Keller will be there."

"The lumber-company doctor?" James said. "Are you sure?"

"Pa made peace with him before Mama died," Abbie explained. "'Sides, Maddie sends all her patients with bad broke bones to him. He's a good man and has become a friend."

"All right." Maria nodded. "We'll stay together until we are on the Sugar Fork road. Then Jonathan, you, Corrie, and I can go back to the cabin and stay with the girls. James, you and Danya go with Abbie and Nate and help as you can. Come back and tell us as quick as you find out anything. When you get down to the rail by Hazel Creek, you may be in time to catch the afternoon train down to Proctor."

"Yes, we'll do that," Danya answered as James nodded.

"I wanna stay with Pa," Corrie said.

"I need you with me, little one," Maria said.

"I ain't little!" Corrie complained. "Why, I'm nearly thirteen."

"That's why I need you with me and Jonathan," Maria responded.

Corrie nodded and turned to give Abbie a hug.

As Danya and James began to direct the horse down the trail, Jonathan turned to Abbie and said, "The Great Spirit will take care of your father, Abbie." He turned and followed Maria and Corrie toward the ridge leading back to the cabin, as Abbie turned to follow the sled.

When Abbie was able to catch up and look down at her father, still pale, he looked just as her mama did right before she died, leading Abbie to start silently praying.

9

Infirmary

A sudden banging on the door brought Andrew Keller, MD, out of a sound sleep. He always enjoyed his Sunday-afternoon naps and did *not* appreciate being disturbed.

As a longtime company physician for Calhoun Lumber Company, he had volunteered to move to the company's then three-year-old Hazel Creek operation in 1910, where he began to provide medical care for both the company employees and the locals.

The tall man attempted to straighten out his crumpled wavy-brown hair, and rubbed the sleep from his dark brown eyes. Another burst of thumping on the door caused him to jump out of bed.

"All right! Don't beat the door down. I'm coming." He strode over to the front door and as he released the latch he called out, "Who is it?"

"It's me, Dr. Keller. Abbie Randolph. Nathan Randolph's girl."

"Are you hurt, girl?" He threw the door open.

"No, it's Pa. He's been shot. And he's hurt . . . real bad."

"Who shot him?"

"I don't know, but he was shot in the back!"

"Where is he?"

"Coming up the road right now. Mr. Barnes is bringin' Pa in his wagon. Danya, James Walkingstick, and I brought him to town on the company's narrow gauge train that was comin' down valley. Mr. Barnes is drivin' him over here from the depot for us."

"Let me get my coat. We'll need to take him to the infirmary next door."

The infirmary was a small, simple building, sparsely furnished by the lumber company. Dr. Keller used it when he had to, but it had little in the way of modern medical equipment. For X-rays, most laboratory tests, or major surgery, he had to take or send his patients to Dr. A. M. Bennett's clinic in Bryson City.

Keller led her to the white building, then unlocked and threw open the door as he watched the wagon pull up out front. He stared up at the mammoth form of Danya, then said gruffly, "Come along."

Danya lifted up and carried Nate inside, followed by James and Millard Barnes.

"Strong fellow," Keller said to Millard. The storekeeper, in his midthirties, was a short, trim, and fit man. His mild, round face was punctuated with ruby cheeks and a thick white mustache of which he was very proud. His thick brown hair lay neatly combed just above his light blue eyes.

"I've never seen a man like him," Barnes replied.

Abbie and the men sat in the waiting room while the doctor checked her father in an adjacent exam room. James built a small fire in the stove located in the corner of the waiting room. The room quickly grew warm, but Abbie took no comfort from it. Danya and Millard sat beside her on the bench.

After a few moments, Danya began to unfold his massive frame. "Abbie, when are you and Bobby Lee getting married? It seems like a long courtship. In my country a young boy will only court a girl for a few months, six months at the most."

"Hush, now!" Abbie scolded him. "I've not had the time for Bobby Lee that he deserves. Lord knows I dream 'bout what our life'll be like together, and the longer we court the more I long to be with him. But I promised Mama I'd help Pa with the girls and the farm. And right now I'm more worried about Pa than I am about *any* boy."

Danya sat down by her and put his huge hand on her head. "Your pa, he'll be fine. He's one tough man."

"I hope he's strong enough to beat this one, Danya." She took his other hand and held it in both of hers. "I don't know how to thank ya. It woulda taken forever to get Pa outta that gorge without ya. No other man coulda done it. If I live to be a hundred, I'll never forget it."

Finally Dr. Keller came out. Abbie and the men stood up at once.

"Well, I can't tell a whole lot without X-rays," Dr. Keller said, "but I think the bullet is lodged in a vertebrae in his spine . . . the first lumbar vertebrae is my guess. It's a miracle his spinal cord was not severed. And there's no damage to any internal organs as far as I can tell. However, there are the injuries from his fall. Lots of abrasions and contusions. A concussion. Probably bruised lungs and a few broken ribs."

"Will he be all right?" Abbie asked.

"I hope so, but I'll need to keep him here a few days. And when his pain is better, I'd like to take him over to Bryson City. Old Dr. Bennett has a new X-ray machine there."

Abbie nodded.

"What'd you dope him with?" Keller asked.

"Secret gypsy medicine," Danya said, smiling.

"And the poultice?"

"Secret Cherokee medicine," James replied. "It worked good, yes?"

"Yes, they both appear to have worked very well. When we get some time, I'd like to learn more about them."

Danya and James nodded.

At that moment, boots thudded on the outside porch and the door flew open, startling the group as two men burst into the room.

10

Suspicions

The first to burst into the room was a handsome fifteen-year-old boy, thin and lanky with dark hair and eyes.

"Bobby Lee!" Abbie exclaimed. He ran over to her. As they embraced, his father, a tall man with broad shoulders, black hair, and dark eyes, walked into the room, removed his hat, and nodded at Keller.

"Sheriff," Keller said. Even though Zach Taylor was officially a deputy sheriff serving under the authority of the Swain County sheriff in Bryson City, everyone in Proctor and the Hazel Creek watershed called him Sheriff.

"We heard the news from Millard's wife, Etta Mae," Zach said.

"You want something spread in this town," Keller said, chuckling as he looked at Millard, "all you need to do is tell Etta Mae Barnes."

Barnes laughed. "You're right about that, Doc! Etta Mae can spread the gossip faster than a telegraph."

"Can I see Nate?" Zach asked.

"He's sedated pretty heavy right now," Keller responded. "Maybe later."

"Word on the street is he was shot."

Keller nodded. "Single shot to the lower back. The entrance wound looks like a small caliber. My guess would be a .22, a .25, or a .32."

The sheriff turned toward Bobby Lee, who had his arm over Abbie's shoulders. "Abbie, any idea who did this?"

Abbie's mouth tightened as she nodded.

Zach sat on the bench and gestured for her to sit by him. "I think we're both thinking this wasn't an accident, eh?"

She nodded again. "Pa said he thinks it was Sanders. But he didn't see him."

"L.G.? The lumber-company manager?" Zach asked.

"He's a mean and evil man," Abbie said. "You know he has committed crimes in the past and gotten off scot-free. Even you believe he shot and killed Mr. Cable up on Haw Creek. Gunned him down not far from his cabin."

"I'm still investigatin' that one," Zach said. "There was no evidence of a scuffle, so Cable musta known the scoundrel that murdered him. And he was shot right between the eyes with a .22. Sanders is my number-one suspect."

Bobby Lee sat by Abbie and took her hand. "Sanders still blames your pa for the deaths of his sidekick, Reginald Knight, and his brother-in-law, Josiah Simmons, January a year ago."

Abbie squeezed Bobby Lee's hand and added, "Pa says Mr. Sanders has threatened to get back at him any number of times for those deaths. And I, for one, believe him."

"I do, too, Abbie," Zach said.

"But those men ambushed you, Nate, and Danya," Keller said. "Everyone in town has seen the official report from the sheriff in Bryson City and the State Bureau of Investigation. The SBI investigated it completely. Abbie, you and Bobby Lee were there. They could have killed all of you."

"Would have," Abbie corrected.

"It was pure self-defense," Bobby Lee added. "Nothin' but."

The sound of steps running on the boardwalk outside the infirmary turned the group's attention to the door as it slung open. Grace Lumpkin ran in the door panting, her normally coiffured hair a bit disheveled, perspiration beading on her forehead. "Nate?"

"He's all right, Miss Grace," Abbie said as Grace ran over to embrace her.

"Sanders shot him? Can it be?" the teacher said. "That's what everyone's saying."

"We don't know that yet," Zach observed.

"Is he going to make it?" Grace asked Keller.

Keller nodded, as he took out his pipe and filled it with curly leaf tobacco. "He's stable now."

"Can I see him?"

Keller smiled as he lit the pipe. "There's a line here before you."

"I'm serious," Grace implored.

"I know you are," Keller said. "But right now he's sedated and resting. I need to give him some sleeping and mending time . . . alone."

Grace looked down at Abbie. "How'd you find him? And how'd you ever get him out of the gorge? They say it's frightfully treacherous."

After Abbie described the rescue, Grace slowly shook her head. "Sounds to me like there were guardian angels around Nate and you all."

Abbie smiled. "The Petrovas and Walkingsticks were angels for us today."

Keller rubbed the stubble on his chin as he puffed on his pipe and looked Danya and James over from head to foot. "These two scoundrels, well, they don't look much like I've always pictured angels to look." He looked down at Abbie and said, "But maybe you're right, Abbie. Who knows what angels really look like, eh?"

The group laughed.

"Dr. Keller, I'd like to stay with Pa, but I'm plumb worried about my sisters," Abbie said.

"Abbie, I need you—I need all of you—to go your way. The company nurse is coming in to care for Nate tonight. You all best get your rest also."

Grace put her arm around Abbie. "Why don't you stay at my

place tonight, Abbie? It's close and we can come visit your pa in the morning, before classes."

"But I'll need clothes for school."

"You stay with Miss Lumpkin, Abbie," Danya said. "James and I will return and give everyone up valley the report."

"Your sisters could bring some clothes for you . . . maybe for a few days," Grace said.

"I'll be happy to take y'all up to the Randolphs'," Millard said to Danya and James.

"It would save us a long hike," Danya said.

"My horses can get us up there in no time."

"That's so good of you!" Abbie said as she hugged Danya, who seemed embarrassed.

"Y'all get on!" Keller commanded. "I need some peace and quiet in my infirmary."

"Can I visit Pa before school?" Abbie asked.

Keller nodded. "If he ever awakens from Maria's potion. But rest assured, I'll send someone to Miss Lumpkin's if there's any change. You hear?"

Abbie smiled. "Thanks!"

As the group left the clinic, Dr. Keller stared after them. *That's the biggest man I've ever seen in my life. Glad he's on our side.* He took a puff on his pipe and closed the door.

11

Grace

Nate was sitting up after eating a late lunch. Moving around was not nearly as painful as it had been when he arrived at the infirmary only four days earlier. The most uncomfortable part of his treatment was staying in traction most of the day and night, with an occasional bathroom reprieve. Also, having the gunshot wound on his back cleaned and dressed four times a day was a necessary but tedious and irritating process.

The second-best part of his stay was the food. A different family had volunteered to bring each meal, whether it was the Semmeses, Raus, Taylors or Johnsons—or some of the single women, like Nancy Cunningham and Grace Lumpkin. The best part of his stay was the visitors, and of all the visits, after those by his girls, he enjoyed Grace's the best, experiencing her doting and hearing how his girls were doing in her class.

His unexpected feelings for her, which had started several months earlier, had initially been very disturbing to him. The attraction he felt for her seemed traitorous, or even sinful, given his deep love for and devotion to Callie Jean, his childhood sweetheart and wife of more than sixteen years. He had never imagined he could be attracted to, much less begin to love, another woman. But his fondness for Grace grew, as did hers for him. With the halting approval of his girls, and the hearty encouragement of his pastor, he allowed their relationship to slowly blossom. He had no idea where it might lead, but he was finding the journey enjoyable as well as emotionally and spiritually satisfying.

The visits from family and friends helped take his mind off the pain and made the time go by more quickly. This afternoon, after the girls left for home, Grace stayed with him as she prepared and poured tea for them both. Their conversation soon turned to the Randolph daughters.

"You've taught 'em now for two years," Nate observed.

"It's gone by quickly."

"Have you decided if you'll be staying for the next school year?"

Grace chuckled. "I guess that will be up to the School Board."

"Perhaps I can influence them."

"Well, you've certainly influenced me, Mr. Randolph," Grace said, smiling.

"As their teacher, how would you sum up the girls' school year so far?"

"Well, that's certainly a change of subject, sir!"

Nate laughed, then reached out and squeezed her arm. "Seriously, how've they done?"

"Nate, they are all very intelligent. And you know how much I've grown to love each one of them. And . . . I've also grown rather fond of their pa, so my opinion may be a bit biased."

Nate smiled.

"Well, let me start with Darla Whitney. Although Whit's the most emotionally tender of the girls, she's also the most gifted musically. I love when she plays the mountain dulcimer or the flattop guitar. She has an amazing voice—tone perfect and superior to any of the other students by far. Like Abbie, she also enjoys and excels at poetry."

Nate nodded.

Grace continued, "Anna Katherine . . . I think she may be the most intelligent of the girls."

"I believe it," Nate said. "She's very good with numbers—"

"And has a photographic memory. She's special. But as we

discussed before, she has a touch of dyslexia. I think that my and Horace Kephart's tutoring have perhaps helped her more than any of the other girls. She is so observant, and her writing about hiking, nature, and birds and creatures of every kind is superb."

"Corrie?" Nate inquired.

Grace smiled. "Also not one for the books, unless the book is about camping, hunting, travels, explorers, magic, myths, or high adventure. But she's a good writer; that is, if she's writing about a topic that interests her. She's a soul that seems to be designed to be outdoors. I've wondered if she might not be fated to become a travel writer, somewhat like Kep. Lord knows she could not find a better instructor for the craft."

Nate laughed. "She's by far the most daring and outspoken of the Randolph girls and the tomboy of the clan. She can run faster than most boys and loves any sort of games, and she *must* win at all of them."

Grace smiled and took another sip of tea. "She is a strong-willed child, Nathan. May have inherited that from her father, you think?"

Nate nodded.

"She's the quickest of the girls to anger, but is equally quick to be sorry. And she plays a mean fiddle, Nathan."

"Helps her to let her passions escape in a constructive manner," Nate observed.

Grace cocked her head. "Extraordinarily observant for a mountain man. I like that about you, Nathan." After another sip, she continued. "And with all the boys looking her over, you'll need to keep a close eye on her."

"And Abbie?"

"She's certainly the mother hen of the brood," Grace said. "She loves to draw, but her real talent is writing—especially short stories and poetry. She has a lovely style. I just wish I could have written as well at her age." Grace considered her words as she sipped her tea. "She also has a keen sense of humor and a tendency to try to manipulate others, which I've often seen in firstborns. But it's her nurturing nature and innate curiosity, combined with her common sense, that seem to me to be her real strengths. I've often wondered if she might not be cut out to be a nurse or even a doctor."

"A girl doctor?"

"Indeed, Nate. In fact there's a medical school just for women, the Woman's Medical College of Pennsylvania. Actually, I believe all of your girls have the intellect to go to college. I think they'd do mighty fine."

Nate frowned. "There's no money for that, Grace."

"There are scholarships, Nathan. I am willing to help the girls obtain them. And there are plenty of others who can help. Horace Kephart and Kelly Bennett, with their state- and federal-government connections. Amos and Lillian Rowe Frye, the attorneys in Bryson City, with their network. I think we could help each of the girls get a fine education . . . that is . . ."

"What?"

Grace looked down at her cup. "That is, if you will let them."

Nate thought for a moment, and then looked at Grace and took her hand. "I'm pleased with your confidence in my girls. But I just can't imagine any of 'em ever wantin' to leave Sugar Fork, at least as long as the forests and our way of life keep on."

Grace smiled as she swirled her remaining tea. "I think you, Mr. Randolph, will keep Sugar Fork forested in her virgin timber. You and Tom Rau, your neighbor, have successfully fought off the lumber company for over a decade. I have no doubt about your resolve, but . . ."

"But what?"

"Life out here in the mountains is changing, Nate. I, for one, do not believe it will ever be what it was. The girls' way of life will be different . . . likely very different from yours and Callie's."

Nate sighed and slowly nodded. "I think you're right, Miss

Lumpkin." She smiled at him as he squeezed her hand. "I hope you'll be with me along the way."

"Me, too," she said.

He gently pulled her arm, and she fell toward him until their noses were nearly touching. "You smell wonderful," he said.

"You smell like Mercurochrome," Grace said, giggling.

"Well, if I kiss you, will it take your mind off the smell?"

Grace smiled and nodded as their lips met.

12

Order

Even though Nate had been at the infirmary for only five days, because of the persistent pain, several-times-a-day wound packings, and nearly continuous spinal traction, it seemed like an eternity. And he was surprised how much he missed his girls. They came by every day after school, of course, but his heart ached to be with them more often.

He looked out the window to see another swirl of wind blowing the buds that were beginning to fill the few trees surrounding the infirmary. Although the March air outside was still cold, with high temperatures only in the forties, he was warm in the infirmary.

Reba Johnson and Linda Pyeritz, the wives of two of the black lumbermen who occasionally moonlighted on his farm, came by the infirmary a couple of times a day to bring in firewood and stoke the fire in the cookstove, while Dr. Keller visited sick folks up and down Hazel Creek. They and the women from the church saw to it that Nate had plenty of food. "Won't heal if you don't eat," Linda scolded.

Linda always brought along her golden Labrador, Chance. Through the years, Linda had found that bringing Chance to the infirmary always seemed to perk up patients confined there—irrespective of their natures. Nate enjoyed his time with Chance almost as much as he enjoyed Linda's delectable cuisine.

Today Keller was taking Nate in a padded wheelchair on the private company railcar to Bryson City. Gabe Johnson and Rick Pyeritz were pulled from their lumbering duties to help him into the chair, carry him to the depot, and then load him on the train. They both agreed to accompany Nate and Doc Keller to Bryson City. Nate wished Grace could have come, but she was occupied, as she should be, with her teaching.

Nate was astonished by how smooth the ride was. *Probably because the rail line is so new,* he thought. The Southern Railway Company ran the final branch from Bryson City out to Eagle Creek only a few years earlier.

Dr. A. M. Bennett's infirmary in Bryson City was the first in Swain County to have an X-ray machine. The physician looked far younger than his sixty years, and he still saw patients from sunup to sunset. Keller left to see to some business in town while Dr. Bennett examined Nate and performed lab work and X-rays.

After he had run the tests, the physician explained to Nate that his urine specimen showed no evidence of kidney damage, and his complete blood count revealed that his blood loss was not excessive.

"A little liver extract and cod-liver oil every day will build up your blood count before you know it," the good doctor told him. But it was not all good news. "The bullet is lodged in L1, the first and uppermost lumbar vertebrae, just as Dr. Keller thought. It's busted the vertebrae pretty badly."

"Can you get the bullet out?" Nate asked.

Dr. Bennett shook his head. "Would be far more dangerous to try to remove it than to leave it there. It's likely to cause no harm there at all, at least once the bone's healed."

The elderly doctor let the news settle in before continuing. "In addition, your fall broke three transverse processes. They're the little wing bones that stick out from each vertebrae. You're fortunate that the fractures are all on one side of the spine. But the really bad news is that you've collapsed two of your thoracic vertebrae."

"What's that mean, Doc?"

The old doctor sighed. "It means that you're a fortunate man, Nathan Randolph. That's what you are. I've seen this type of broken back disable or paralyze a man for life. You're gonna need to give this some significant time to heal, and other than bein' an inch or so shorter and feelin' some rheumatism in your lower back, likely on a daily basis the rest of your life, you should eventually be fine. You follow my and Dr. Keller's treatment plan and you'll probably not become a cripple."

Nate frowned. "Time to heal? How much time, Doc? I got a business to see to, a farm to run, and five girls to tend to."

Dr. Bennett continued to carefully study the X-rays on the lighted view box. "Nate, I can certainly understand that. But you'll need to not only stay in bed, but in spinal traction most of the hours of the day, for a minimum of six weeks."

"Six weeks!" Nate said. "That's impossible! There ain't no way, Doc! I won't do it! I cain't!"

"You've got no choice, Nate!" the old doctor ordered.

"The heck I don't! I got work to do. Who's gonna do it fer me?" Nate complained.

Dr. Bennett was quiet for a moment as he continued to gaze at the X-rays. He finally turned to Nate, and his voice softened. "Dr. Keller tells me you've hired a couple of gypsies to manage your farm. That true?"

Nate nodded.

"Dr. Keller tells me Gabe and Rick and some of their buddies help you out from time to time. And he tells me your transporting medicines over here keeps you away from the family and farm more than you like."

"Guess Keller's become good enough of a friend now that I can't get too angry 'bout him talkin' 'bout my business over here."

Dr. Bennett smiled as he put another X-ray on the view box. "Keller's got a lot of admiration for you and your family, Nate. I can tell you that. And, of course, my son, Kelly, and I are appreciative of the deliveries you make for us. The medicinal moonshine you bring me for my practice and him for his pharmacy is the highest possible quality. As you know, not all the moonshine in these mountains is safe to ingest."

"Maddie and her partner, Quill Rose, provide quality product, no doubt 'bout that. But the truth is, Doc, if I've gotta be in bed, I'd rather be in *my* bed, in *my* cabin, on *my* home place. There's no way I can wait six weeks to get home."

"The six weeks in traction aren't all. Then you'll need to give it another six or eight weeks after that with no lifting, bending, pulling, pushing, jumping, or chopping. And there'll be *no* riding horses or wagons, or driving that truck of yours, even riding in it, I'll tell ya that right now! Nate, I need to be strict with you about this. This is an order!"

Nate was quiet for a moment, letting the news sink in. "Well, you're right. Danya and Maria are runnin' the farm just fine. And maybe I can get me some help with the deliveries."

The physician turned to face Nate. "I understand the work it takes to run a business and a farm, but if you don't let these bones mend, my friend, then they will collapse further. At the worst, that could paralyze you for life. At the best, you'd be incapacitated real bad. Either way, if'n you don't follow my directions, you'll be wheelchair bound for life!"

Nate looked down and shook his head.

Dr. Bennett had more. "Nate, I'm perfectly serious about this, if you don't follow my instructions to the letter, then you'll be of no use to your girls, your farm, or our mutual business. Period!"

Nate didn't look at him. Several minutes went by as the doctor pulled out his pipe, packed the bowl, and lit it, while the mantel clock kept clicking off each second. It seemed to Nate that time stopped altogether. "What am I gonna do, Doc?" he finally implored.

The doctor took a long draw before speaking. "Nathan, I was born in these hills a long time ago. I know the folks up here. Why,

I've even delivered most of 'em! You know as well as I that when a mountain man goes down, his neighbors will pull together to put him right. They will not let you down. They are not going to let you lose that farm."

Dr. Bennett paused a second and then continued. "Nate, when the Rau barn burned down last winter and Tom Rau got terribly burned, didn't you folks get together and raise another barn for him in no time at all? Wasn't it you who organized the neighbors to take care of him, his family, and his farm?"

Nathan listened, looking down at his feet.

"And when Maddie broke her leg when that durn mule of hers threw her last summer, didn't the men take care of her chores till she was up and about? Why, Dr. Keller even agreed to care for her patients while she was down, didn't he?"

Nate nodded.

"I know what you're thinking. You're wondering if they'll do the same for you and your girls. You're thinking times are tougher now. Am I correct?"

Nate nodded again. He couldn't understand how the doctor could read his mind.

"Nathan, I know the folks out there. I *know* they'll pitch in."

Nate was quiet for a moment and then looked up at Dr. Bennett. "You make good points, Doc. I reckon I'll plan to follow your advice. Don't want to be no cripple."

"I think that's wise," the old man said.

"Doc, can you tell from the X-ray what caliber the bullet was what was used to shoot me?"

"The bullet is lodged in your spine, Nate, so I can't say for sure. But from the size of the bullet, I'm guessing it was a .22 or a .25. Had it been a larger caliber, I suspect you'd either be dead or paralyzed."

Nate's suspicions were confirmed. "Can you tell if the bullet came from a pistol or a rifle?"

"Can't tell that. But my guess is that you were shot from some distance, not close-up, thank goodness. Had it been a close shot, it would have not only shattered your vertebrae, but likely have ruptured your abdominal aorta, and you'd've been a goner in an instant. We wouldn't be having this conversation."

The doctor walked over to his desk, sat down, and began scribbling on a prescription pad.

13

Payment

Dr. Bennett wrote out two prescriptions and handed them to Nate. "Take this to Kelly and he'll mix you up a potion of opium for pain. The second one's for valerian powder. It might be right handy at night to help you sleep."

"I appreciate it, Doc," Nate said. "How much I owe you?"

"Not a penny, for my services or the prescriptions. Dr. Keller's asked us to put it on the Calhoun tab, and even if he didn't, it'd be on me. No charge recorded, no payment accepted."

Nate's jaw tightened. "I take care of my own bills, Doc."

"I understand, Nate. But Calhoun feels he wants to give back to this area. Reckon he'd say if his company wasn't in your valley that you'd not have traveled as far as you had to for that venison."

Nate wasn't sure how to respond to the doctor but felt his anger rising. "Doc, it was likely one of *his* men that shot me. He knows that if'n I'm dead, he'll be able to take my land from my girls."

"I don't know anything about that, Nate. But I'd recommend you accept the gift. And, like I said, if he didn't cover your bill, I wouldn't charge you anyway."

"Why's that?" Nate asked.

Dr. Bennett smiled. "Let's just say I'm happy to exchange my services for yours. That medicinal moonshine not only helps my patients and my bank account, it helps my poker game up at the Fryemont Inn."

"You drink while you gamble?" Nate asked.

"No, sir. But I share my medicinal beverage with the other men," Dr. Bennett said, smiling. "And when I do, it seems to increase my odds of winning."

The sound of boots on the porch was followed by the door opening. Andrew Keller entered, allowing the cool air to swirl in with him. Nate made the mistake of trying to stand and greet his visitor. The pain was nearly unbearable, and with a deep groan he collapsed back onto the wheelchair.

"Nathan, I told you not to stand!" Dr. Bennett roared. "What am I going to have to do—shoot you myself? Or tie you down to that chair?"

"Tell him about it, Dr. Bennett!" Keller exclaimed. He turned toward Nate. "What's a man have to do to keep you down?"

"Sorry," Nate muttered.

"Got the X-rays up for you," Dr. Bennett said, pointing to the view box.

"I can see that. How good are my diagnostic skills?"

The two doctors stepped away from Nate for a minute to confer, talking in low tones as they examined the various X-rays. Finally, they turned to face Nate.

"Maybe he'll listen better to you than to me," Keller complained.

"Doc, how long's it gonna hurt so bad?"

"No way of knowing for sure," Dr. Bennett said. "But I'll tell you this. You move around too much and it'll be longer than if you just obey my orders."

"Your first job is to take care of yourself and that back of yours," Keller said. "If you don't, then your back won't be able to take care of you. You hear me?" Nate was silent as Keller added, "Nate, we've talked, and if you agree to follow our orders, we think it would be safe to release you to go home."

Nate looked at the doctors with surprise.

"But there are two conditions," Keller said.

Nate looked at him suspiciously. "Which are?"

"First of all, I'm going to take you home on the company's narrow gauge up Hazel Creek."

"Doc, I don't need no train! Danya or Rau will come get me in my wagon."

"Nate, you know as well as I do that the road up Hazel Creek is rough. If Maria hadn't had you drugged up and tied down, I'm not sure you would have even survived the trip down Sugar Fork to the train tracks without being paralyzed."

Nate was quiet a moment. He was in terrible pain and wanted it to end as soon as possible. He nodded his agreement. "What's the second condition?"

Dr. Keller smiled. "You let me come and set up the traction equipment in your cabin."

Nate grimaced.

"I'd recommend continuing traction day and night for at least another two weeks, then at nighttime for six or eight weeks after that," Keller said.

"Maybe longer," Dr. Bennett cautioned, "depending upon the follow-up X-rays."

"Nate, that's what it'll take to let the bones set firm enough for you to begin getting around a bit," Keller added.

Nate stared at the floor. He had no idea how he would be able to keep his promises to Cal that he'd keep the girls in church and in school, and keep the farm intact for them. After a moment, he nodded. "I'll do whatcha say. I'll do whatever it takes. I wanna git better, and I want to be home with my girls."

14
___

Homebound

A fter school was out for the day, Abbie walked down to the infirmary for a visit.

After greeting her, Nate asked, "Where's the other girls?" He patted the mattress, indicating for her to sit.

"They're up at Barnes's store. The rumor at school was that Mr. Barnes received a big ol' shipment of new candy and dresses. So, of course, the girls are up there covetin'."

"The Bible warns about covetin', Punkin. Says, 'For all that is in the world, the lust of the flesh, and the lust of the eyes, and the pride of life, is not of the Father, but is of the world.'"

"Well, Pa," Abbie responded, laughing, "they're up there enjoyin' a gaze at the things of the world. But not to worry, no way we can afford any of them goodies."

"Maybe someday," Nate said. "Maybe I'll just surprise you girls."

"That would be nice," Abbie said.

"Well, that reminds me. I *do* have a surprise for you."

Abbie looked curious. "Which is?"

"I'll be comin' home tomorrow."

Abbie's eyes widened as she felt her jaw drop open. Before she knew what she was doing, she jumped to her feet and let out an ecstatic yelp. "Yippee!" She spun around, dancing a few steps of a jig, as she exclaimed, "Pa, me and the girls have been missin' ya so much!"

Nate's grin spread from ear to ear. Finally, Abbie settled beside him. "Doc Keller is going to require that I ride up Hazel Creek on the mornin' train that carries the lumbermen up the valley to do their work."

"I'll need Maria and Danya to help me get you home," Abbie said.

Nate smiled. "Abbie, you're growin' up so quick. I swan, I may need to put a brick on your head to slow ya down. Now, how are you and your sisters gettin' home?"

"Maria's coming to get us. Bet she's already waitin' at Mr. Barnes's store."

"You thank her for me, Abbie."

"I will, Pa. And we'll have the wagon by the Sugar Fork bridge in the morning."

"I love ya, Punkin."

Abbie smiled and nodded. She loved when he called her Punkin; it always gave her a warm feeling inside. She bent over to give him a kiss and turned to pick up her coat. She smiled. "Sleep tight."

Nate laughed. He and his daughter had repeated this ditty almost every night since she was a little girl. He would never forget his usual reply, "Don't let the bed bugs bite."

Abbie smiled. "See you in the morning light."

"Night, night," he said, laughing as she threw her coat on.

"I love ya, Pa."

"Love ya more, Punkin."

15

Confrontation

Maria, Danya, and the younger Randolph sisters were just where Abbie expected them to be, gathered together at Barnes General Store. As Abbie opened the door, she stepped inside and saw the group sitting with the Barneses around a large potbellied stove in the middle of the store.

"Abbie, we've just heard some sad news from England," Millard Barnes began.

"What?"

"Well, I know how much you like the theater, so I thought you'd be sad to learn that the Shakespeare Theatre in Stratford-upon-Avon was destroyed by fire on Anna's birthday, March sixth. The news just came in."

"Well, that is sad. But I've got good news. Pa's gonna get to come home!"

"That is great news! You and I, we will nurse him!" Maria said, as Abbie's sisters jumped up and down in glee. "I am one fine nurse."

Abbie heard the door bang open behind her. Turning around, she saw a short, overweight man whose black hair was greased back. As his dark brooding eyes darted around the room it became as silent as a funeral parlor.

Most of the locals detested the manager of the lumber company, but they had chosen to tolerate him, as they knew he could make their lives miserable if he so chose. He slammed the door behind him and slowly strutted to the center of the room, his thumbs hooked into his belt.

Abbie knew Sanders didn't like the mountain people, and he certainly didn't like anyone whose skin wasn't lily-white. His angry gaze fell on Danya and Maria.

"You gypsies still prowling these parts?" he growled, glaring down at them. Maria just glowered back at him. Abbie could see the fire burning in her eyes as Sanders continued. "Reckon you've been purposefully staying away from me these last couple of months. Shows me you two aren't as dumb as you look."

Abbie spoke up. "Mr. Sanders, they ain't causing no harm. You know they've been helpin' Pa."

Sanders turned his glare toward Abbie. "I think these two have been around these parts long enough. So I reckon it's time for them to leave."

Millard Barnes stood up, his white mustache lifting as he tried to put a smile across his face. "L.G., you know there's no law in these parts against these fine folks being here. 'Sides, their money's just as green and good as yours." Millard chuckled, as he patted Danya on the back.

Sanders stared angrily at him. "Barnes, their money may be as green as mine, but it'll never be as good as mine. Furthermore, Mr. Calhoun has put me in charge of his operation, and I've decided *no* gypsies are allowed. You let one rover in and pretty soon there'll be a mess of them multiplying like rabbits." He turned back to Maria. "So, I came to tell you it's time for your type to get your wagon and get your slimy bodies out of this area. Either that, or maybe you'll bed down in our local jail until I can ship you to the Bryson City jail. You hear?"

Danya kept his head down and Maria remained silent, but Abbie could see she was fuming.

Sanders bent down until his nose was nearly touching Maria's. "Do you or your big dumb brother understand English, you gypsy pig?" he taunted.

Maria started to stand but her brother softly placed his massive hand on her shoulder, easing her back into her chair. Then Danya slowly stood, towering over the small man who was threatening his sister. Sanders pulled his coat back, revealing his pearl-handled .22-caliber pistol.

"You want to speak to my pistol, big man? One bullet through your heart and the sound of you hitting the floor will rock this entire camp! Since you murdered my friend Reginald Knight, and oversaw the murder of my brother-in-law, Josiah Simmons, and got off scot-free, I've been meaning to see justice done."

Abbie gasped as she saw Danya take a step toward Sanders, and she quickly stepped between the men. "Mr. Sanders, you know the sheriff from Bryson came over and investigated," Abbie said. "He even called in the SBI. They declared the whole thing self-defense. My pa, Danya, and Sheriff Taylor are innocent and you know it! *You* hired those men to kill Zach Taylor, Pa, and Danya. If'n it weren't for Danya and my pa, we'd all be dead."

Sanders looked up at Danya, flashing a mocking tobacco-stained smile. "Shame you gotta have a little sissy girl protect you, gypsy. Shame you and her pa had to lie to cover up the murder you committed up on that ridge. You're just lying gypsy slime."

Before Abbie knew it, and without any forethought, her foot reared back and she kicked Sanders in his shin as hard as she could.

Sanders's face immediately turned crimson as he shrieked, grabbed his throbbing leg, and hopped up and down on his good leg. He turned to face her, the veins bulging on his forehead, and in the same instant, she saw his knuckles and the back of his hand coming straight at her face. Before she could react, Danya's massive hand lashed out and engulfed Sanders's, twisting it so that he was spun around with his arm pinned behind his back and was sputtering in pain and rage.

Just then, the door burst open. Abbie heaved a tremendous sigh of relief as Sheriff Zach Taylor and Bobby Lee came striding into the store. Danya released Sanders and pushed him away.

The sheriff quickly approached the group. A smile filled Zach's face. "Sanders, you trying to arm wrestle Danya? Why, I didn't think there was a man in western North Carolina that dumb."

"Just being a responsible company manager, Taylor. Have ordered these troublemakers to leave."

"You playin' sheriff again?" Zach laughed.

"Don't mess with me, Taylor!" Sanders snapped as he rubbed his hand. "You know Mr. Calhoun has me in charge of the morals here in Proctor. I was just asking some of the immoral elements to leave my town."

Taylor looked around with a smile on his face. "Sanders, that's a terrible piece of news. I hadn't heard that Maria Petrova had become an immoral woman. Why, shucks, if that's the case, since I've grown kinda fond of her, I'll just have to throw myself outta town!" He furrowed his brow and looked down at his son. "Of course, if I throw myself outta town, since Bobby Lee here is courtin' Miss Abbie, I guess that'd make the two of them immoral by association." He looked back at Sanders. "Reckon we oughta throw 'em both outta town also?"

Sanders stared fiercely at Taylor, saying, "Ain't you or your boy or this sissy girl I'm worried about. It's this no-good gypsy scum."

Zach nodded. "Sanders, lemme ask you a question. Since when did you get the badge of an authorized officer of the law?"

Sanders was silent.

"If you don't have one, then guess I'm still the law in this store, and in this town, and in this watershed, and this gypsy man and woman got just as much right as you and me to be here, as long as they're law abidin'. So, I 'spect it might be best for you to lemme see to things here, and you go ahead and slither on outta here, ya hear?"

Sanders looked angrily at Taylor and then back at Danya. "I'll deal with you later," he grunted as he turned his scowl back to Zach. "I'll even up with the two of ya. You can take that to the bank." He spun around and stormed out, slamming the door behind him.

Danya walked up to the stove and rubbed his hands over the heat as Zach sat down by Maria. She began to tremble in anger. He could sense she was seething with rage.

"Maria," Zach said, "I'm sorry for that. I'm sorry he's givin' you and Danya so much worry."

"He's the one who's going to be sorry, Zach. I can't believe he said what he did in front of you and my brother."

"He's a fool, Maria."

Maria nodded and finally smiled. "Only a fool would give you or Danya trouble. But I sense he's a dangerous fellow."

Zach nodded and turned to look at Abbie. "I'm glad your pa's better. And I think we all know who the snake is that tried to murder him in cold blood." Taylor looked out the window as Sanders walked away. "I'm just sorry there ain't no proof."

He looked back to Abbie. "But if there's anything I can do, you just say it. You know me and my boy'll do about anything for you and your family."

Abbie was warmed by his kindness. Her mama had always told her that if she was attracted to a young man, to take a long look at his daddy, as that would likely be the kind of man he'd grow up to be. It attracted her all the more to Bobby Lee. She looked at Bobby Lee, who was looking down and shuffling one foot. She could see he was blushing, and her heart began to flutter. She couldn't wait for him to ask for her hand in marriage. *Yesterday wouldn't be too soon!* she thought.

During the trip back to the farm, Abbie and Maria rode in the wagon beside Danya, who was carefully steering around some of the larger potholes in the road.

"I saw the way the sheriff looked at you," Abbie said. "I think others are seein' the eyes he has for you!"

Maria laughed. "Ah? Well, maybe I will let him marry me."

She slapped Danya on the back. "That is, if my brother will let me marry a white man."

Danya smiled. "If you are married to the sheriff, then you'll have someone to protect you."

Maria put her arm around his enormous back. "I think the Lord has already provided that for me in you. And I think that you and Nate are a pretty formidable pair. Don't you, Abbie?"

Abbie laughed. "Miss Maria, there are a lot of women who would want to marry Sheriff Taylor, I can tell ya that right now. 'Specially some of them women over in Bryson City. You're gonna have a lotta competition."

"Ah, maybe I will put a charm on him," Danya said. "Zach will fall in love with Maria because of it."

"Brother, you know the Bible speaks against charms. But . . . perhaps . . . if I don't know." Then Maria let loose a deep laugh that echoed off the trees.

Reckon he can really charm a man? Abbie wondered. *I've heard of snake charmers and bee charmers, but ain't heard of no man charmer. But there's lots stranger things what's happened before in these here mountains.*

16

Homecoming

Before dawn, Abbie opened the cabin door, trying to keep it from squeaking and waking her sisters. *They'll be up soon enough!* she thought. *And Whit can care for 'em till I git back.*

The morning fog was thick, but she could see that Maria and Danya had hitched up her pa's wagon and were waiting by the fence that surrounded the cabin. Abbie ran across the porch yard to them. Danya helped her up onto the seat by his sister and then sat in the back of the wagon. Once they were settled, Maria gently slapped the reins and they moved forward.

The road from the family farm was usually bumpy. But Abbie was surprised by how very smooth it felt as the horse slowly pulled them down their driveway toward the tumbling waters of the Sugar Fork. Maria solved the mystery. "Danya filled the ruts with stone and dirt."

Abbie was amazed and turned to gaze at the mountain of a man who was facing backward, his legs hanging off the wagon. "When did you do this?"

"We worked on it most of the night. Tom Rau, Horace Kephart, Jeremiah Welch, and some of the other men from up and down the Fork all chipped in."

Abbie turned back to face Maria. "He's amazing! He really is!"

෴ ෴ ෴ ෴

The locomotive slowly puffed and strained to push the train cars up the bottom land of Hazel Creek. The caboose, which carried the conductor and Dr. Andrew Keller, was at the front of the train, which ran its route up and down the Hazel Creek valley several times a day, seven days a week, hauling lumbermen and their supplies up the creek for a long day's work and then hauling massive logs down the valley during the day. The train would bring mail to the remote farms located on the creek, although the Randolphs rarely received any.

Once the train was at the top of the spur, Dr. Keller would unhitch his hand-built, gravity-powered, two-man car called a skeeter from the back of the locomotive and then begin the precipitous glide down Hazel Creek, using hand brakes to slow the descent to a manageable speed. If any of the mountain folk needed to see the doctor, they needed only to have someone wait beside the tracks to wave him down as he returned down the track, and he would stop, lift the skeeter off the tracks, and then go tend to their needs. Mr. Calhoun didn't require the good doctor to make such rounds, but he heartily approved of them, and Keller found them highly satisfying.

When he first came to Hazel Creek, more times than not, Keller would make the trip down the line with no one requesting his aid. More than once he had been shot at, although he was never wounded. He was certain the shots were just a warning. *These men are too good of shots to miss!* he thought.

While riding the train up the valley each morning, usually he would walk through the cars and examine the men for signs of hangovers, pneumonia, or the consumption—caused by tuberculosis, which could spread like wildfire through a group of lumberjacks. Fatigued or diseased men could be deadly to a crew working deep in the woods. Today, however, he stayed in the caboose to care for his friend Nate Randolph.

As the train approached the bridge crossing the Sugar Fork, the engineer let out three shrill blasts from the steam whistle and slowly pulled the train to a stop.

As Dr. Keller jumped off the caboose, he was not surprised to see the wagon waiting. "Greetings, Danya!" shouted the doctor.

"Good morning!" Danya shouted back as Abbie and Maria hopped off the wagon.

"Abbie, I've got your pa secured on a backboard. He hated it, but it will make it safer for him to travel up the road. I know the path can be pretty bumpy."

"Not today, Dr. Keller! Danya has it as smooth as ice."

Dr. Keller looked at Danya, who just smiled, then turned back to Abbie. "How about I get some of the men to help carry Nate to the wagon?"

"It won't be necessary," Maria said. "My brother has been waiting for the opportunity to carry Nate."

"I know he's a strong man, but just one slip and Nate could be hurt bad."

Maria now stood in front of the doctor. "Allow him the honor. He will be *very* careful."

"Well, let's have a couple of the smaller men carry him out of the caboose. There's not much room in there for a man as big as Danya."

Maria smiled. "That will be fine."

Abbie stood back as two short, sinewy lumbermen carried Nate on the backboard out of the back of the caboose and then lifted him over the back of the railcar and into Danya's massive arms.

Without even a grunt Danya carried his protesting patient to the wagon and carefully placed him in it. The murmurs from the men who observed this were as respectful as their eyes were wide.

"Abbie," Keller instructed, "I'll have one of the men put the traction setup in the wagon. You all get Nate safely into the cabin and on his bed. I'll be stopping by to check on him on my way down and to set up the traction for you."

"Thanks, Doctor," Abbie said, as she gave him a hug. "Thanks for your care and your carin'."

Abbie bounded up the steps, across the porch, and into the cabin. "Girls!" she shouted. "Pa's home!"

There were squeals from Whit and Anna in the loft. Abbie looked at Corrie and Sarah Beth, who were sleeping in Pa's bed on the ground floor. Corrie stuck her sleepy head out from under the quilt. "Is he really here?" she asked.

Danya's feet stomped across the porch and Abbie cried, "Corrie, Sarah girl! Git outta that bed now! Here comes Pa!"

Danya entered carrying Nate on the backboard, and then slowly and gently placed him on the bed just vacated by his daughters. Nate's voice thundered across the cabin. "Girls, your pa's home. Git down here and give me some hugs!"

Shrieks and laughter came from the girls as they hurried down from the loft. As Maria and Danya untied the straps that secured Nate, the girls swarmed over him like bees on a honeycomb.

"Girls!" Abbie scolded. "Let's get Pa settled. Shoo now! Whit, you and me need to get some breakfast goin'. Corrie, can you and Anna stoke the fire?"

Nate moaned as Danya removed the board from under him.

"Here, here," Maria comforted. "You lie back, and I'll tuck you in."

"Don't need no tuckin' in!" Nate growled. "I need to sit up. Durn board 'bout broke my back." He groaned deeply as he struggled to sit and then slowly situated himself at the side of the bed. His girls were staring. They had not seen their pa in pain like this before.

When he was as comfortable as he could get, he looked at his girls. "Y'all are a sight for sore eyes! Come over here and commence to huggin' on me, but one at a time and gentle-like!"

Abbie watched as he gave each girl a long, gentle embrace, a kiss on the cheek, and a private word in her ear. *He's a special pa!* she thought.

Maria whispered to Abbie, "Danya and me, we'll go now."

Abbie turned to look at her. "No! Absolutely not. You and Danya *must* stay for breakfast!"

Over her shoulder she could hear her pa chime in. "Danya, you either stay for breakfast or I'm gonna have to hurt you."

Danya's laughter rocked the cabin.

17

Books

D r. Keller walked across the street, pausing once to look up at the sky, which was blue enough to scratch a match on. The winter of 1925/26 had been the harshest and most brutal in recent memory, freezing portions of Hazel Creek and the Sugar Fork thick and hard enough to support even horse or oxen as they walked across.

Heavy snows had fallen throughout December, January, and February, even into the first week of March, leaving deep drifts of snow up and down the valley for longer than anyone could remember. The ground froze as hard as marble. For over three months, the sharp, bone-biting frigid cold had swathed the Hazel Creek valley like a heavy wet blanket.

He was glad that winter had finally loosened her grip and allowed spring to arrive and bring her April warmth to the valley. The previous three weeks had finally seen the return of mild weather accompanied by welcomed showers and early spring flowers. Looking both ways, he leaped off the boardwalk and carefully picked his path across the muddy street toward Barnes General Store.

After entering the door, he was greeted by Millard. "Top of the morning, Doc."

"Morning, Millard."

"You saw Nate yesterday?"

"I did. He's been home four weeks and is doing much better. Have him in night traction, which he seems to be tolerating. He's off most of the pain meds and beginning to move around a bit. I'm encouraged."

"Good to hear. By the way, speaking of good news, you hear about Hemingway's new novella?" Millard asked. He prided himself on keeping up on the news from the outside world and would always test his knowledge of current cultural events against Dr. Keller's.

"You mean Ernest Hemingway's *The Torrents of Spring*?" Keller asked.

"Yep," Millard said, sounding disappointed that Keller already knew about it.

"Heard it doesn't come out until next month."

"Well," Millard said, hooking his thumbs into his suspenders as a smile spread across his face under his bushy white mustache. "I received a copy Monday and have begun reading it."

Keller chuckled. "And they call this the wilderness. I swan, folks in Washington, D.C., don't have the book yet, but you do! How'd you pull that off?"

"It's not *what* you know, Doc, it's *who* you know. One of the editors at Charles Scribner's Sons is a close friend. You may have heard of him . . . Maxwell Perkins."

Keller shook his head.

"Pity," Millard said. "He's the most prominent book editor of our time. He edits Hemingway *and* F. Scott Fitzgerald. Rumor is he's working now with a young upstart from Asheville, a kid by the name of Thomas Wolfe. Anyway, he sends me all the newest releases. Not all of them are that good, but this one is . . . least wise what I've read so far. Will be happy to lend it to you when I'm done."

"I'd like that. Now, I came over to see if you received my order."

"Yep. Came on yesterday afternoon's train. Kelly Bennett was able to get everything you needed."

"He used to bring it out himself. Is he too busy to help out us country folk?"

Millard laughed as he picked up a box of bottles and placed it on the counter. "No, sir. I think he and Kep are actually on their way back here from Washington, D.C."

"More of their talk about a national park out this way?"

"Yep, but won't happen in our lifetime, least not in the Smoky Mountains! Dumb idea, if you ask me."

"You ever read Kep's book?"

"Which one? *Our Southern Highlanders*? Or *Camping and Woodcraft*? Hear both of them are best sellers."

"I was referring to *Our Southern Highlanders*."

"The original, from 1913, or the 1922 revision?"

"Son, you ask too many questions!" Keller complained, smiling. "I'm guessing you've read them all?"

"Yep," Millard replied. "I liked his *Camping and Woodcraft* a lot. Helpful book for backcountry campers. Lots of greenhorns swear by it. Why they come by here to buy the supplies he recommends in that book before heading into the Smoky Mountain wilderness. To many of them, it's as important for living as their Bible. However, many folks around here were a bit offended by his depiction of mountain folk in *Our Southern Highlanders*."

"How so?"

Millard pursed his lips and thought for a second. "Some were angered by the book, for the manner he used to describe them and their language and their ways, the way he emphasized feuding and moonshining. Others felt he focused too much on backwoods outlaws and folks living in extreme poverty. Why, most folks are peaceful and live well out here, thank you very much."

"You agree with their criticism?"

"I can see their point, Doc. But, heckfire. Kephart's a writer. Seems to me natural that the majority of his writing would be about our most colorful personalities and traits. And it would likely help sell books, don'tcha think?"

"Guess I'll need to read it to make up my own mind. Now, I best get my supplies and get off to cure the ill."

"Well, let's see here." Millard was comparing the bottles and tubes to Keller's order. "Got your carbolic acid, aconite, nux vomica, eucalyptus, menthol, and asafetida."

He pulled out another small box. "And in this box we've got your phosphate, iodine, cocaine carbolate, lots of Dover's powder opium, Denver's Antiphlogistine, and some chloroform. That ought to about do it, Doc. How about I have a couple of the boys bring the boxes over to the infirmary later?"

"That would be mighty kind. Thanks."

"One more thing, Doc? You have time to take a quick look at Etta Mae? She's laid up in the back." After checking behind him, he leaned forward and whispered, "But Doc, as you know, she's not as sick as she thinks."

18

Natter

Keller smiled, nodded, and then walked behind the counter to follow Millard into the storeroom. In the back he found Etta lying on a small couch, her arm thrown dramatically over her head. He pulled up a stool as Millard stood behind him. "Etta, dear, Dr. Keller is here."

"How may I help?" Keller said.

"Oh, Doctor, thank goodness you're here. My heart is consuming me. It is racing out of my chest. I'm fearful it will stop most any moment."

The physician pulled his pocket watch from its pocket and felt her radial pulse for a full minute. As he suspected, her heart rate was well within normal limits, at about eighty beats per minute. "Any chest pain, shortness of breath, or nausea, Mrs. Barnes?"

"All of that, plus much more. But nothing's worse than these horrid palpitations. Why, when I stand, I get terribly faint." She moved her arm just far enough up her forehead to see him and in all seriousness asked, "How much time do I have, Doctor?"

He smiled, as she had asked him this many times over the years. Without answering, he pulled his stethoscope out from his coat and carefully listened to her heart. Taking the earpieces out of his ears, he looked down at her. "Mrs. Barnes, your heart is fine. I reckon this is more the stress and strain of worry and fret than anything. You've got so very much to be thankful for, Etta Mae. What's so heavy on your heart?"

Tears began to fill her eyes, and she turned her head away. "Oh, Doctor. I worry most about how Millard will do after I'm gone. He's got no sense about business . . . or women."

"Why, I don't believe that at all, Etta Mae," Dr. Keller said, taking her hand into his. "Looky here, he runs as fine a business as there is here in Proctor. And when it comes to women, well, he chose you, didn't he?"

She shook her head. "You don't understand, Doctor. When I'm called to Glory, why he'll likely just marry a silly younger girl who'll waste his money and drive him to distraction. Just a bit earlier a woman came down from the Clubhouse asking for bath powder. He right doted over her. I saw it, Doctor. A painted woman like that would take him and then take all his money. I know it."

Keller smiled. He had seen this type of manipulation before. And his medical opinion was that Millard would have Etta Mae to bother him for many, many years to come. He countered her panic by going with the stream. "Well, maybe you're right, Etta. Tell you what, why don't you and I work together to pick out your successor for Millard?"

Etta Mae's arm fell to her side, and she stared at the doctor, obviously startled.

He continued, "Why, sure! But since you're not up to getting around much in your weakened state, irrespective of what I say, maybe I can assist Millard." Dr. Keller looked around at Millard and nodded. "Why, yes! Millard, you and I can go around and look the single women over."

Dr. Keller looked back at Etta Mae, whose eyes were widened in astonishment. She tried to speak but could not. "Tell you what. First of all, I'll escort him to the Clubhouse for dinner and we can scout around a bit. Then we can go over to Bryson City to seek a spouse. And, if no one's fitting there"—he looked over his shoulder as if checking to see that no one was listening, then leaned forward and whispered in her ear—"he and I could take the train up to Asheville and visit some of the speakeasies there."

As the doctor spoke, Etta Mae's jaw dropped in shock.

"I can see your concern, Etta Mae. But I'm *not* proposing to take him to a blind pig, those low-class dives where only illegal beer and liquor are offered. Not at all. The speakeasies in Asheville, I'm told—having, of course, never been there myself—are high-class establishments that offer food, music, and live entertainment. I'm told they require a coat and tie for men and an evening dress for women. Of course, we'd be hunting for only the highest class of a woman for Millard, just like the one he has right now."

Dr. Keller turned and winked at Millard, who he knew had a dry wit.

"Then"—he turned back to Etta Mae—"when Millard and I find one that might suit him, we can bring her around. You two can talk, and you can see if she'll fill the bill."

Millard picked up on the doctor's strategy. "Doc, I can think of some possible candidates around here. Let's see . . . there's the widow Hankins; she's got some property and she's shaped up real good since she gained a bit of weight. She's got some nice meat on her bones now, if I don't say so myself."

At once Etta Mae broke in. "She will never do. No, no! She's too picky and doesn't like greens. Millard, you like your greens."

Millard nodded. "That's true, Etta Mae. Then there's the new woman at the Clubhouse. Didn't get her name—"

Keller chimed in. "Allie Rogers. Nice lady, I'd say."

"Never!" hissed Etta Mae, glaring at her husband. "She's a painted woman. May even have a disease. Not for you, Millard. Not for you!" Sitting up and turning to Keller she said, "Why, I never . . ."

At that moment, the train whistle echoed across the valley. "That will be the train from Bryson City! Enough of this natter,"

Keller said. "Sorry to have to leave, but . . . Etta Mae, are you well enough to keep a secret?"

She sat straight up. "Why, yes, Doctor. I do believe I'm feeling much better."

Dr. Keller looked over his shoulder and then back before whispering, "Mr. Calhoun's private, luxurious railcar is supposed to be pulled into the depot down by the river this very day by this very train, with Mr. and Mrs. Calhoun making a surprise visit."

Etta Mae gasped.

As Keller stood to leave, he asked again, "Can you keep this a secret for me? No gossipmongering, all right?"

"Oh, yes, Doctor! Why, of course!"

Keller smiled as he walked out of the store. He expected the entire town would know about the Calhouns before his cat could meow.

19

Boss

The train began to slow down as it crossed over a bridge quite familiar to him; after all, he had paid for its construction and helped plan its location. William Calhoun recognized the rushing waters of Hazel Creek as they tumbled and cascaded into the Little Tennessee River just below the trestle.

At fifty-eight years old, he was the founder and president of one of the largest lumber companies in the world, the Calhoun Lumber Company. He was a man of medium height with a broad face and a short beard. Although he spent most of his time in his home city of Philadelphia, he enjoyed getting out to his lumber camps as frequently as possible, even though they were scattered across most of the eastern American wildernesses.

The door to the private Pullman railcar opened, and his personal assistant entered and walked over to the plush sofa where Calhoun sat. "Pulling into the Hazel Creek depot, Boss."

"Thank you, Bernard."

"Shall I awaken Mrs. Calhoun?"

"Yes, that will be fine."

The assistant walked to the back of the car, where he knocked on the mahogany door leading to Calhoun's private bedroom.

Louise Calhoun had developed a migraine headache when the train pulled out of Bryson City that morning. Bernard had administered some ergotamine and opium to her, which would cause her to sleep, but usually resolved her pain and nausea.

She was a very prim and proper woman—tall and spindly—with a strong British accent, long brown hair, and brown eyes. She met Calhoun when he was in England. He was supposed to be there to study, but he actually spent most of his time and his father's money playing the gambling clubs in London. Even though he was from a wealthy, albeit rural, family, which made its money in the lumbering business, the fact remained that he and she came from staggeringly different backgrounds. Although this was initially very alluring to her, she now desperately longed for her home country and culture. Furthermore, she hated traveling away from Philadelphia, especially to the various wildernesses to which he dragged her, all of which she considered uncultured, unsophisticated, and unrefined—in short, uncivilized!

As the train pulled to a stop, Louise stepped from the bedroom. "How is your headache, my lovely?" Calhoun asked.

"Tolerable, William," she replied, looking out of the window at the few buildings surrounding the train depot. "Oh, William, how long will we be in this hideous place? Look, it's positively a wasteland."

"We're scheduled to be here for four to six weeks, but don't judge a book by its cover, dear. This is just the river depot. The town of Proctor is just a few miles up Hazel Creek, a short ride on my narrow gauge. Wait until you see it—it's actually a lovely town. The Clubhouse we're staying in . . . ah, t'would be hard to find nicer accommodations anywhere in western North Carolina."

"I must admit that our suite in the Fryemont Inn last night was far nicer than I imagined it would be. The Fryes were wonderful hosts and the food . . . well, it was shockingly delicious."

"Then you'll *love* the Clubhouse. The owner, hostess, and chef, Nancy Cunningham, and her staff make the Fryemont Inn's kitchen personnel look like beginners. And, trust me, a trip into the forest to admire the earliest of the spring flowers will refresh your heart and soul. I'm expecting the hepaticas, spring beauties, trillium, and several orchids to be out."

Louise's eyebrows arched upward. "Orchids?"

He smiled, knowing she loved the flashy species. "Indeed, lady slipper orchids, showy orchids . . . not to mention the dwarf crested iris, jack-in-the-pulpits, little brown jugs, and scores of violets."

"Harrumph!" she responded. "You're just trying to soften me up. I'm sure I'll detest it here."

As they stepped out of the car and onto the platform of the small depot, L. G. Sanders stepped up. "Greetings, Boss! Welcome to the Smoky Mountains!"

"Greetings, L.G."

"Your wing at the Clubhouse is ready, sir. We have servants hired and trained and awaiting Bernard's supervision. You will find the rooms to be well stocked and completely refreshed."

"Thank you, L.G. If you could accompany Mrs. Calhoun on the narrow gauge, I'd be obliged. I'd like to walk up the creek."

"Yes, sir."

Calhoun looked over L.G.'s shoulder to see his old friend Andrew Keller walking rapidly toward them. A smile broke across his face and he stepped around L.G.

As he leaped up the platform steps, Keller smiled from ear to ear. "It's good to see you, Boss!" The two men embraced and then walked from the platform together.

"Are you ready to come back to Philadelphia and provide for the medical needs of my family and my company's executives, Andrew?"

"William, I'm not a city doctor any longer. Haven't been for over fifteen years. You know that."

"You'd be on the staff of the most prestigious hospital, Andrew. You know how well I'd pay you!"

Dr. Keller smiled. "William, you've always done right by me. But the Smokies are where I'd like to stay, if that will suit you."

Calhoun nodded. "Walk with me up to town, Andrew. Let's catch up a bit."

20

Rude

After a leisurely stroll from the depot and up the lowest reaches of Hazel Creek, they reached the boardwalk at the edge of Proctor. Those passing by greeted the doctor; however, most of them had no idea that the man walking next to him was both their boss and their benefactor.

Abbie Randolph and an older woman walked up to them as they passed the Barnes General Store. Keller recognized Madeleine Satterfield. Maddie, as everyone called her, was a legend in the valley, a popular herbalist, healer, and granny midwife. He hardly knew a person up the various valleys whose birth the sixty-five-year-old had not attended. Her face was deeply seamed and tanned from decades of sun exposure, as she and her old mule, Scratch, made home visits throughout the Hazel Creek watershed. Her short, thin frame was crowned by her gray flyaway hair, somewhat held in place by her bonnet. She immediately focused her deep-set dark blue eyes on the stranger.

"Greetings, Abbie, Maddie," Dr. Keller said. "What are you doing in town today?"

"I came to town with Miss Maddie here. We've come to watch the ten-cent movie."

"What's playing?" Keller asked.

"Charlie Chaplin's *The Gold Rush*," Maddie said, carefully eyeing Calhoun. "Last time I saw it, when it first came out last year, I laughed till my sides hurt. Thought this young lady might enjoy it."

"Oh, Maddie," Keller said, tipping his hat and slightly bowing, "excuse my rudeness. Let me introduce you to a friend." Keller replaced his hat. "Miss Madeleine Satterfield and Miss Abigail Randolph, this is William Rosecrans Calhoun, my boss and my dear friend."

Maddie put her hands on her hips and scrutinized Calhoun from head to foot, while Abbie studied the newcomer. "You related to the man what owns the lumber company?" Maddie finally asked.

Calhoun smiled. "Reckon I am!"

Maddie squinted. "Then you tell him I think he's done some good out here. But, for the most part, his company's destroyin' the land and that ain't no good. Tell him I think he oughta get outta our valley and go somewhere else. Ya hear?"

Calhoun nodded. "I can promise that he's heard your complaint, madam."

She turned on her heels and walked away.

"Nice to meet you!" Mr. Calhoun called out.

"She don't mean to be rude, Mr. Calhoun," Abbie said. "It's just that all of us who live here love our forests and hate seein''em destroyed."

Calhoun's eyes hardened. "But you don't mind the town, or the general store, or the movie theater that the company has provided. Is that true?"

Abbie smiled. "Not sure one outweighs the other, sir. Anyway, pleasure to meet you." Abbie turned to run after Maddie.

Keller sighed. "Abbie and Maddie are like many of the mountain people. They simply do not like change. They resent the land around theirs being clear-cut. But on the other side of the coin, they don't mind the luxuries it has provided. It's a paradox they have trouble explaining and living with."

Calhoun turned to his friend. "Her father the Randolph with all that virgin timber up on Sugar Fork?"

Keller nodded. "Yep."

"Is he willing to sell?"

"I don't think so. He knows he has one of the two or three best stands of virgin wood left in the watershed. Well over six hundred acres. Beautiful land that his father homesteaded."

"Man's a widower, right? And with no male children to help him out, correct?"

"Yes, on both counts."

"Seems like he would be in a position to be bought out cheap. Be rude of him not to consider a decent offer."

"Normal man might. But Nate's a mite stubborn!"

"Well, maybe we can convince him."

"I doubt it. He's awful stiff-necked."

Calhoun smiled. "Andrew, it's a dog-eat-dog world. Haven't you learned that yet?"

Keller laughed. "I guess not. That's why I'm out in this paradise, William. Few of those nasty city ethics out here."

"Well, I'm sure there must be at least a few bad apples out here," Calhoun said.

Keller took in a deep breath and slowly let it out. "Indeed, William, there are."

Now it was Calhoun's turn to laugh as he put his arm around his friend's shoulder. "Maybe I should hire them."

Keller felt his lips tighten as he looked at his friend. "Maybe you already have, William."

"Well, you'll have to tell me about that sometime, Andrew. In the meantime, I'm hoping to enjoy a bit of the wilderness out here and check up on my operations."

"I don't mean to be too harsh, William. Mostly there's good land, good water, good air, and good people here on Hazel Creek and up her many tributaries."

"You're absolutely right, Andrew. That's why I love coming out here. Helps me keep balanced. I'm hoping Louise will agree, as this is her first trip out this way."

As they walked together up to the VIP Clubhouse, Calhoun said, "You need anything out here, Andrew? You know you only need ask."

Dr. Keller nodded. He had expected this question and had been thinking about it for some time. "I'd say I need another doctor, William. Some young fellow who can help me take care of the folks here in Hazel Creek—company personnel, their families, and the locals, most of whom cannot afford a doctor. They have traditional healers, Injun medicine men, and granny midwives like Maddie, but with more folks moving out here, I could use some help."

"Noblesse oblige, my friend. As the Bible says, 'Ask, and it shall be given you' and 'Ye have not, because ye ask not.' In point of fact, I have a dear friend whose son is just finishing his medical training at the University of Pennsylvania School of Medicine."

"Great reputation. If memory serves, it was the first medical school in the thirteen American colonies and the only one for some time."

Calhoun nodded. "My friend's been trying to find a place for the young man, but he's not interested in any of the usual apprenticeships. Turns out my friend is a missionary and thinks his son might be looking for something a little less urban."

Keller chuckled. "Proctor and Hazel Creek might qualify, eh?"

"I'd think so. His name is Chandler . . . Wade Chandler. I've actually already talked to him and he seems willing to come serve out here in the wilderness, although I wonder if his eyes are larger than his stomach, as they say."

"Don't think he'd be wilderness stock?"

"Well, he's been in the big city for a while. He might be used to it, and this wilderness certainly could be a shock to his urban sensibilities. But he's a fine young man and smart as a whip. I think you'll like him, Andrew, although he's awfully wet behind the ears. But tell you what, if you're willing to take him on, I'll pay his expenses to get here, and cover his room and board and salary, at least for the first year."

"Sounds fair to me, William. I'm willing to teach him what I know. Probably won't take very long."

Calhoun laughed. "You're too humble, Andrew. I think the boy's in for a tremendous learning experience. So, I'll send for him. Hopefully he can be out here in the next few weeks, if that will work for you."

Keller nodded as they walked.

"Not only that, Andrew, I'll plan to throw him a welcoming party when he gets here."

"You didn't do that when I came out here."

Calhoun laughed. "I'm much richer now, Andrew. Much richer indeed."

21

Thankful

The girls and Maria cooked a breakfast that would have fed a small army. The heat coming from the roaring fire combined with the smell of applewood-smoked bacon cooking in the frying pan and the laughter from his girls warmed Nate's heart. Even though he had been home nearly a month, he had never appreciated his family or his home more.

"Nate, you sit right there! I'm going to bring your meal to you," Maria called out.

He grimaced as he unhooked his traction unit. "No way, Maria! Dr. Keller took me off daytime traction two weeks ago, so this mountain man's gonna sit at his table in his cabin with his girls!"

Danya, who had just brought in more wood and placed it in the wood box, quickly crossed the room to help Nate walk to the table. Nate knew better than to shake off his help. As he sat at his place, it was obvious he was still in some discomfort.

The meal was set and they all took their places. "Abbie," Nate said, "will you return thanks?"

Abbie nodded and watched as they bowed their heads. "Father in heaven, please continue to heal up Pa. Thanks for our friends Danya and Maria. Thank you for this food—"

"Amen!" Sarah exclaimed, effectively ending the prayer as the other girls giggled and began to eat.

Nate took his first bite of biscuit and sawmill gravy and a smile crossed his face. "Nothin' like my girls' home cookin'!"

The girls all smiled. He could see his compliment was deeply pleasing to them.

After the meal, Maria cleared the table while the girls got ready for school. Nate and Danya went to smoke their pipes on the porch.

After Nate lit his, Danya said, "My sister and I continue to be grateful for you giving us work and allowing us to stay on your land."

"I'm the one who's thankful, Danya. I appreciate y'all's help more than I can say. I appreciate ya gittin' in the early plantin' with the men from town and just keepin' the farm a-runnin'. I just wish I was well enough to do more of the work myself."

As Maria stepped to the door, Nate looked at her and then back at Danya. "You two've been mighty good to me and my girls."

Maria looked down and was quiet a moment. Then in a voice barely above a whisper, she explained, "You've been even better to us, Nate."

Nate cocked his head to the side. "Go on."

"Danya and I have experienced much hatred and prejudice," Maria began. "We have been driven out of every place we have ever been. We have known no friends; we have found no home, until we came here. On Sugar Fork we have found kindness and friendship; here we have been welcomed." She paused a moment. "Here we have learned what it means to be family."

"I appreciate that," Nate said. "It's been the way among our people since our ancestors came over from Ireland and Scotland. It was that way before the company invaded this valley; people knew what it were like to live together peacefully. The Indian, the white man, the negro, the immigrant . . . a good and hardworkin' person was respected no matter the color of his skin or where he came from. Hate didn't really enter this valley until the company came. To my way of thinkin' there's been far more harm than good from 'em. But at the top of the good category, me and my girls count you'uns at the top. We're proud to call you our friends, and we consider you family, that's for durn sure."

As the girls came out to the porch, Nate continued. "The girls tell me that over the winter, you'uns talked about heading out for the summer. You still thinkin' 'bout joining that travelin' carnival again?"

Maria smiled at Nate. "Don't know where you heard that!" She looked askance at the girls who had gathered at the door. "Corrie, that rumor come from you?"

Corrie looked down.

Maria looked back at Nate. "Actually, we received a letter from the owner of the carnival. He offered us a raise if we would return. Me as a fortune-teller, Danya as a laborer. The money was good, but I couldn't agree to be a fortune-teller. My gift is prophecy, and I know fortune-telling is against what the Bible teaches. So we've decided to ask you about staying here longer, to help out you and the girls until you're completely well, or for as long as you'll have us."

Nate looked at her and answered, "It's hard for a mountain man to admit he needs help."

Maria smiled. "You believe God will care for you, yes?"

Nate tried to hide a smile. "Yes."

"I think God sent us to help you."

"I think he did, too, Maria," Nate said, as he took a draw on his pipe. "And if a carnie owner can offer you a raise, maybe I should also."

Maria looked at her brother as the girls squealed in glee. After Danya nodded, she turned back to Nate. "Maybe you would consider an alternative—what they do in the old country."

"Which is?"

"Instead of a raise, how about we work for a small percent of the profit? Hopefully our hard work will increase your profits.

And hopefully we'll make some money so that we can save, and own a place of our own one day. But even more important to us, we'll have a welcoming place to stay and family . . . our family nearby."

Nate thought for a moment and then looked at his girls, who were all smiling and nodding their agreement. He took another puff and looked over the hills. "Well, with these injuries I've got, I'm not sure how much I'm gonna be able to do to keep up my farm and my . . . uh . . . business. But I do hav'ta admit I need some help. And even though money's tight, if'n you two are willin' to stay and allow me to give you a raise, *and* give you some of the profits, then I'd be plumb pleased with that."

A cheer went up from the girls. Maria's smile lit up the entire farm.

22

Visitor

The slim young man seemed almost awkward in his movements as he boarded the morning train in Bryson City.

His height, at six feet three inches, made the passenger seats quite uncomfortable for him. He shook back a thick shock of auburn hair as he glanced at the Bryson City train depot. *I wonder,* he thought, *will this be the last time I see civilization?* Then he laughed. *If you call this civilization!*

As the train pulled out of the station heading toward Bushnell and then on to the Hazel Creek Depot, he settled into his seat, praying no one would come by to sit with him. His long arms and legs would make sharing the small bench seat even more miserable. As the locomotive strained to pick up speed, Wade had time to think back on his childhood in the Republic of Liberia in West Africa. He had been educated in missionary schools there. When he arrived in America to attend college, he could speak French fluently and Latin passably. As a budding writer, he had even been published; several of his short stories and poems had been printed in British and American publications. *As if that will have any merit in this wilderness!* he thought.

While in college he'd become a fair piano player and he excelled at imitating several famous singers. The prior two evenings he enjoyed playing and singing popular songs, as well as some he had composed himself, with the other guests after the astonishingly excellent dinners he enjoyed at the Fryemont Inn. *These skills will be of no value in the backwoods!* he thought.

His mother died of cholera when he was a child and his father remarried a nurse at the mission within a year. Wade had taken a steamer the previous summer to visit them at their mission deep in the jungles of Liberia and to spend a summer of study with the missionary physicians. He deeply loved his father and genuinely admired the doctors with whom he had worked. As a result, he thought he sensed a call to be a missionary—but would it be in the same wilderness in which his father served or another one? *Maybe working in Hazel Creek will help me decide,* he thought.

He also found himself worrying almost incessantly about what his future patients might think of him. Would they have any idea just how well trained he was? Would they appreciate his skills? Would they think that his coming to their wilderness meant he was some sort of medical school failure instead? How would he let them know he graduated at the top of his class, summa cum laude?

I know what I'll tell them! I'll say I was offered an exclusive apprenticeship with a well-known Philadelphia physician but chose to come to the wilderness for a year to serve my fellow man. Of course, that was true—but did it sound too sanctimonious? He smiled. *Probably!*

Maybe, he finally concluded, *I should just be me. After all, that actions always speak louder than words is the lesson my father taught me when I was a young boy.*

When the train pulled past the small depot at Bushnell, a tiny bird on a post caught his eyes. *That's a Hooded Warbler!* He furrowed his brow for a moment as he tried to remember and then his eyes brightened. *Ah, yes! Wilsonia citrina!*

As an amateur ornithologist, he had studied birds on three continents, and even knew most of their scientific names. He had seen pictures of the Hooded Warbler but had never actually seen one in real life before. He smiled. *Well, I do love birds and botany.*

Maybe it won't be as bad out here as I'm imagining. Maybe this will be the adventure of my life.

Then he felt a frown spread across his face. *I'm going to miss my friends. I'm going to miss Philadelphia. And, most of all, I'm going to miss the young ladies. How many will get married while I'm out in this godforsaken wilderness? Why did I ever agree to this?*

As the train chugged on, he pulled a well-worn book out of his day pack and opened up his favorite collection of poems— including his favorite poems by Kipling, Frost, Sandburg, Cummings, and Eliot. But, remembering the warbler, he put it back and pulled out *The Travels of William Bartram.* Reading took his mind off his worries and the concerns of the world. And Bartram, a naturalist who traveled extensively in the southeast colonies of what would become the United States in the late eighteenth century and wrote about the Great Smoky Mountains, was one of his favorite authors. Wade opened the book to a favorite passage:

> *This world, as a glorious apartment of the boundless palace of the sovereign Creator, is furnished with an infinite variety of animated scenes, inexpressibly beautiful and pleasing, equally free to the inspection and enjoyment of all his creatures. Perhaps there is not any part of creation, within the reach of our observations, which exhibits a more glorious display of the Almighty hand than the vegetable world; which excite love, gratitude, and adoration to the great Creator, who was pleased to endow them with such eminent qualities, and reveal them to us for our sustenance, amusement, and delight.*

I wish I could write like this! he thought, as he watched the hills rush by, fully clad in vibrant multihued spring flowers. He felt himself smile. *It is beautiful out here. Okay, Father,* he silently prayed, *forgive me for calling your creation "godforsaken."*

🙠 🙠 🙠 🙠

"Hazel Creek!" the conductor called out as he walked toward the back of the train. "Last stop before Eagle Creek and the end of the line!"

Wade could already feel the train slowing down. For more than twenty miles they skirted the edge of first the Tuckasegee and then the Little Tennessee Rivers. Wade closed his book, gathered his belongings, and made his way out of the car. As he ducked his head to step off the train, he heard his name and turned to see an older man in a plain brown coat approach.

"Dr. Chandler?"

A tall and lanky man with wavy brown hair and brown eyes took his pipe from his mouth as he stepped forward. "I'm Andrew Keller. Welcome to Hazel Creek!"

Wade smiled and firmly shook his new mentor's hand. "Good to meet you, sir."

"If you'll just come with me, I'll have some of the men bring your bags to the Clubhouse, where you'll be staying until we can get you a proper house. Let me walk you up there."

Keller turned to walk down the platform and Chandler almost had to run to keep up with the older man. He was happy that he was in fair shape, and he enjoyed Keller's recitation of the history of the area as they walked up Hazel Creek toward Proctor. Reaching the edge of town, Keller stopped.

"Down there to the left is the mill. Trees are floated down Hazel Creek, or brought down the valley by train. Here they are cut and kiln dried, then shipped to all over the United States and even to Europe. The Calhoun Lumber Company is known to produce the finest hardwood lumber in the world. We'll take a tour down there a bit later, but let me walk you through town and up to the Clubhouse. Nancy Cunningham is waiting to welcome you up there."

In the center of town, Wade's attention was distracted by laughter. He turned to see three young girls spilling out of a general store giggling. They didn't see him until the tallest of the girls almost ran into him.

"Oh my goodness!" she exclaimed. "Please excuse me."

He was struck dumb by her beauty. Her radiant smile was framed by shimmering auburn hair and capped with luscious dark brown eyes.

She continued to look up at him as she demurely cocked her head. "I don't believe I've metcha before. I'm Abbie Randolph."

23

Clubhouse

After a late afternoon solo walk around town, and trying repeatedly to get the vision of Abbie Randolph out of his mind, Wade arrived at the Clubhouse fifteen minutes before six o'clock. Dr. Keller had explained that Mr. Calhoun expected his dinner guests to be punctual.

As Wade walked up the wooden steps leading up to the Clubhouse, by far the most imposing and beautiful building in Proctor, he admired its three stories, with verandahs across the front of the first two floors. Tipping his hat to guests sitting in rockers on the front porch, he approached the heavy oak front door with an ornate brass doorbell mounted in the center just below the beveled-glass panes. Turning it, just like an old-fashioned bicycle bell, would cause it to ring, but Wade just pulled the door open to enter.

A woman of striking appearance walked up to him as he closed the door. "Dr. Chandler, welcome to the Clubhouse. I'm Nancy Cunningham." She was not the spinster he had expected, although short, and perhaps a tad too thin, but crowned with glistening, thick chestnut-colored hair that was so long it almost touched the floor. He had been told her reputation as a hostess and chef had made its way even to the White House in Washington, D.C. Tycoons from around the country relished her hospitality as they experienced the wilderness along with Nancy Cunningham's unique touch.

"It's a pleasure to meet you, ma'am."

"I apologize for not being here when you arrived. Did Dr. Keller get you settled? Is all satisfactory?"

"Oh, yes, ma'am. Couldn't be better. In fact, I'm amazed at how luxurious this place is."

"I guess you expected the backwoods, eh?" Nancy said coyly.

Wade felt himself blush.

"The Calhouns are expecting you and are waiting in their private parlor. Shall I escort you?"

He nodded and offered her his arm as they walked across the large lobby of the Clubhouse.

"The woodwork is amazing. These floorboards must be two to three feet across. I've never seen their like. It's all quite astonishing, Miss Cunningham."

"Please, call me Nancy. The wood is all taken from the finest hardwood in the world. It comes from right here on Hazel Creek."

The overstuffed horsehair chairs sitting in front of a massive stone fireplace looked inviting, while the electric lights gave the room a warm glow. The mission-style furniture and handwoven Cherokee rugs added to the comfort and ambiance of the room.

"I must say, I didn't expect electricity," Wade observed.

"Mr. Calhoun demands only the best for his executives and employees. Why, the town was hardly formed back in 1907, when he had his own power plant built and wires run to every single home and business in town. That was followed shortly by the phone system, again, to every building in town."

"Even the outhouses?" Nate asked, trying to make a joke.

"Believe it or not, even some of the outhouses, sir."

Wade laughed as they walked past the artwork on the walls. Nancy explained each steel or copper engraving and its mythological scene, as well as the various paintings, some on glass and some on canvas, all of which gave the room a museum-like atmosphere. The stuffed elk head above the fireplace and the deer and boar heads above the front windows hinted that her well-heeled clientele were mostly male.

"I've seen nothing this opulent," Wade commented, "even in the finest Philadelphia establishments. At least the ones I've been privy to."

"That's what most of our visitors say."

They crossed the room to enter a private hallway. It was even more brightly lit and painted a light yellow. The oak floorboards, with inlaid walnut and cherry designs, were sanded and polished to perfection. The baseboards and crown molding were intricately carved and spectacular. The walls boasted large oil paintings of dead fowl, rabbits, and fish, *guaranteed to destroy any appetite customers might have brought with them!* he thought. But then Wade's attention was drawn to a spectacular piece of art depicting small bunny rabbits dining on a verdant patch of clover. He stopped to admire it.

"*Bunnies in Clover* it's called," Nancy said. "Painted by one of the most famous watercolorists in western North Carolina. It's my favorite."

"Why's that?" Wade asked, turning to face Nancy.

"I love its innocence. It reminds me of the world as I think it was created to be . . . soft, gentle, kind, luxuriant. No evil, no wickedness, no violence, no brutality. No dread, no guilt, no fear."

"Sounds like the Garden of Eden itself."

Nancy turned to him. "To me this watercolor reflects the potential this wilderness has to offer. But nature and mankind often seem set to destroy the beauty the Creator intended." She looked back at the innocent painting. "What do you see, Doctor?"

He looked back at the watercolor for a moment. "To me it would represent our great hope, our future."

"Which is?" Nancy asked.

"I'll share a quote I've memorized: 'Behold, the tabernacle of God is with men, and he will dwell with them; and they shall be his people, and God himself shall be with them and be their

God. And he shall wipe away all tears from their eyes; and there shall be no more death, neither sorrow, nor crying, neither shall there be any more pain: for the former things are passed away. Behold, he will make all things new. For these words are true and faithful.'"

"Thoreau?" Nancy asked.

"The apostle John," Wade replied, "from the second to last chapter in the Bible."

"A great hope indeed," Nancy said, sighing. "Well, we best get to the private parlor. Mr. Calhoun does not like to be kept waiting."

24

Soirée

"Dr. Chandler, I presume!" boomed a gregarious voice as Nancy led Wade into a lush parlor. "Everyone!" the voice thundered. "Please welcome Wade Chandler, MD!"

Calhoun walked across the room at once and extended his hand. "William Calhoun," he proclaimed. "Good to meet you, sir." Turning to his guests, he announced, "Dr. Chandler is coming to us straight from what I consider to be the finest medical school in the nation. Now he is the newest physician in Proctor, North Carolina." As everyone politely clapped, Calhoun whispered, "Wade . . . uh, may I call you Wade?"

"Indeed, sir."

Calhoun turned to his wife. "Wade, this is my dear wife, Louise."

Louise slightly curtsied. "Doctor, so glad you could join us for the evening!"

"It is my pleasure, Mrs. Calhoun." As she extended her right arm, he bent forward to place a kiss on the back of her white-gloved hand.

"Cut the formalities, you two. This isn't Philadelphia. My goodness, we're in the middle of the eastern wilderness out here," chided Calhoun, who turned to a handsome elderly couple standing beside him. "Wade, let me introduce you to Captain Amos Frye and his wife, Lillian, the builders and proprietors of the famous Fryemont Inn in Bryson City. Besides being a timber baron, as am I, the captain is also a land baron, the owner of the second-best inn in western North Carolina, and a distinguished veteran of the army."

"Indeed," Wade said as he bowed, "we met two nights ago at the Fryemont Inn."

"Our guests enjoyed your singing, Dr. Chandler," Captain Frye said. "Of course, we would disagree with William's assessment of our Fryemont Inn. We consider it the *best* inn of the entire region."

"This young man will soon be able to judge for himself," Calhoun said, laughing.

"However, you kept a secret from me, Captain," Wade said.

"Did I?" Captain Frye answered.

"Indeed. Dr. Keller tells me you and Mrs. Frye are two of the most prominent attorneys in this region. Mrs. Frye, I'm told you were the first female law-school graduate in the great state of North Carolina—from the esteemed University of North Carolina, no less."

"And, I might add," Captain Frye said, "only the second female admitted to the North Carolina bar!"

"If you ever need our services, please let us know, Doctor," Lillian Frye said, smiling decorously.

"Wade," Calhoun continued, guiding the young man by the arm, "these are my friends Harold and Edith Jenkins. Harold is the mayor of Bryson City. He's the political kingpin of this entire county, and his friendship has been of immeasurable assistance and value to my operations out here."

Harold Jenkins stuck out his hand and Wade shook it. "Pleased to meet you, Dr. Chandler. This is our daughter, Blanche. I don't believe you two met when you were in Bryson City. Blanche has recently graduated from Agnes Scott College in Atlanta."

Wade turned to face Blanche Jenkins and felt his eyes widen. Blanche was a twenty-year-old with striking blond hair; a blue-eyed, curvaceous Southern beauty.

"Pleased to meet you, Miss Jenkins," Wade said, unable to pull his eyes away from her. He sensed warmth in his cheeks.

"My pleasure, Doctor," she replied in a soft Southern accent as she smiled demurely.

Wade could not remember a time in his entire life when he had been awestruck by two such beautifully feminine creatures, much less in the span of a few hours! *Are there more like Abbie and Blanche?* he wondered before shaking off the vanity of the idea. Still, he realized that he was seeing his assumptions about life in "the wilderness" being proved wrong, one by one.

Just then two butlers pulled open the massive pocket doors separating the parlor and dining room. Another butler entered the room; standing at attention, he held up a small glockenspiel with three metal bars and played an eight-note tune. "Ladies and gentlemen, dinner is served in the private dining room. Please follow me."

Wade was going to offer his arm to Blanche, but before he could, Dr. Keller extended his. "Miss Jenkins, would you allow the now senior physician in Proctor the honor of escorting you?"

Her smile lit up the room. "Why, thank you, Doctor," she said as she flipped open a small hand fan and stealthily glanced at Wade.

As Dr. Keller and Blanche left the room, he chided himself. *You're too slow!* he thought. *Especially if you let an old man beat you to the punch!* He turned to follow the group into the dining room.

25

Concert

After dinner, the party was served coffee and petits fours. The conversation turned to the condition of the country. Everyone seemed united in disgust over the Jazz Age, as the period had come to be called.

"I think it's frightful the way young women behave," Mrs. Jenkins proclaimed rather shrilly. "They call themselves flappers and, my word, the way they dress is positively indecent!"

"You're exactly right, my dear!" Harold Jenkins said. "Why, they drink and smoke like men, and even with men!"

Calhoun nodded. "Prohibition isn't working. Anyone can get liquor. Why, it's made men like that gangster Al Capone millionaires!"

Mrs. Jenkins fanned herself nervously. "I saw some young people doing that new dance called the Charleston last month at the Grove Park Inn in Asheville, and it was shameful, I tell you! Positively shameful!"

"Not as bad as the one called the Black Bottom," Louise added, shaking her head mournfully. "Why, they shake their derrieres like baboons!"

"You know what they call a group of baboons?" Calhoun asked. Everyone shook their heads.

"Guess!" he instructed.

No one knew the answer except Wade, who kept it to himself.

"*A congress,*" he said as everyone laughed. "I'm not joshing. A group of baboons is called a congress. As fit a name for that group as I've ever heard."

Finally Blanche smiled at Wade and quietly asked, "Do you ever do the Black Bottom, Dr. Chandler?"

Wade laughed. "No, I've never even seen anyone do the dance. How about you?"

"Mercy, no! My parents would positively die if I *ever* did such a thing! However, if you were to find it acceptable, I'd be perfectly happy to have you instruct me."

Wade was even more enticed by the softness of her alluring Southern inflections. He found her charming vocally and stunning visually. The two continued in quiet conversation until finally Mr. Calhoun said, "Miss Jenkins, I've been told by a reliable source"—he nodded toward her father—"that you're an accomplished singer. Would you be so kind as to share a sample of your gift with us?"

"I will, Mr. Calhoun, but only if Dr. Chandler will accompany me, as he is reputed to have done for the Fryes."

Before he could think, Wade nodded his agreement and the two escorted the dinner party to the grand piano in the Clubhouse's splendid lobby. After conferring with Blanche for a moment, Wade began to play, and he and Blanche began their impromptu concert. For their first selection, Wade perfectly mimicked Al Jolson as he and Blanche sang all verses of the popular Broadway musical hit "Carolina in the Morning," while Wade accompanied on the piano.

After they repeated the chorus, Blanche stood by him as their audience applauded and they bowed together. Then they sang "Good Night, Irene" and "Tea for Two." "I'm Sitting on Top of the World" was supposed to be their finale, but a standing ovation and the insistence of the Calhouns led to an encore with Blanche and Wade singing "That Old Gang of Mine" a capella and in perfect harmony.

After the applause died down and the party retreated to its private parlor, Wade escorted Blanche to a chair. As they sat down, she took her silk fan from her purse, quickly flicked it open, and began to gently fan her face. "You and I should go on tour, Wade. Maybe even to New York. Why, I believe we should apply to perform on RMS *Olympic* of the White Star Line. She's the largest ocean liner in the world. We could have a glorious time."

Wade smiled and answered, "Let me know, Miss Jenkins. I'm ready for Broadway or the *Olympic* anytime you say."

When the evening ended, Harold shook Wade's hand, saying, "You must come to Bryson City again, Dr. Chandler. We'd love to have you as our guest and would happily put you up in the best suite at the Fryemont Inn for a few evenings."

"Well, Mr. Jenkins—"

"Harold, son. Just call me Harold."

"Well . . . Harold . . . if it's any nicer than the room with a fireplace I had the last two nights at the Fryemont Inn, it would be a treat indeed."

Blanche added her own invitation. "Please, *do* come," she said, smiling warmly. "We can perform for the whole of Bryson City. We have a lovely theater there. And we'd have some time to get to know each other a bit better."

"I'd like that *very* much. I'll be there when you summon," Wade said. "You can count on it."

Blanche smiled and held her arm out for him to kiss the back of her hand.

Harold winked at Calhoun, saying, "William, I'm going to try to steal this young man from you. Bryson City needs an energetic young doctor. A. M. Bennett is older than some of the mountains around here."

"You keep your hands off him, Harold!" Calhoun said at once. "We're keeping Wade Chandler right here in Proctor! I can guarantee it!"

26

Oneth

Wade met Keller at the company cafeteria for breakfast at four in the morning, along with all the lumbermen, to eat at the executive table and review the schedule for the day. They then walked to the train depot in Proctor just before five o'clock and settled into the caboose. This would be the daily ritual for one or both of them. The lumbermen on the train would work at least a twelve-hour day before returning to Proctor for their dinner meals, showers, and a strictly enforced ten o'clock curfew.

Keller walked with Wade from car to car, introducing him to the men. "If we find a man with a fever or cough, we pull him off the train and he walks back to town, catches one of the later trains, or takes a ride with us on the skeeter later in the morning. Can't have a man spread infection to the rest of the crew. Last year, over on Eagle Creek, tuberculosis spread through one of the camps. The consumption, as they call it, had a powerful effect and nearly shut the camp down. Mr. Calhoun will not allow us to take any risk like that."

After checking the men, the two doctors sat down in the fairly comfortable caboose, which was at the very front of the train. The powerful Shay locomotive, designed for extremely heavy loads on steep grades, was used on the downhill side of the narrow gauge train—thus pushing the train up the valley.

As they made themselves comfortable, Keller said, "Oh, by the way, happy May Oneth."

"Oneth?" Wade asked.

Keller laughed as he pulled a book out of his knapsack and opened it up. "Yep, my father called the first day of each month the oneth. I always think of him on that day." Keller found his place and began to read. Wade had observed that his mentor was a voracious reader, keeping up with all the new books.

"What are you reading?"

"At the house, I'm reading Charles Darwin's new book. Millard Barnes lent me his copy. But on the train, I've been reading this one." Keller showed his young protégé the cover. "It's a book from Germany a friend sent me. A young political radical named Adolf Hitler wrote it from prison. He was convicted of leading a failed revolution in Munich back in November 1923. Anyway, it's his personal manifesto—called *Mein Kampf*."

"My camp?"

Keller smiled. "Nope. *Mein Kampf* is German for 'my struggle' or 'my fight.'"

"Didn't know you knew German."

"Well, reckon there's a lot you don't know about me . . . yet. But yep, I do read German and Latin. Do you know any foreign languages?"

"Some Latin, of course. And French. A smattering of Italian. Is the book any good?"

"Not sure this fellow's thoughts will ever amount to anything."

Wade nodded. "I feel the same way about Darwin."

Keller put his book down. "Did you hear how the Monkey Trial over in Tennessee ended last summer?"

"I'd say so. I followed it closely. Did you?"

Keller shook his head. "As much as I could. What happened?"

"Mr. John T. Scopes was found guilty of teaching evolution in his class. He was fined, but served no jail time. His conviction upheld the Butler Act."

"The what?" Keller said.

"Over in Tennessee, it's unlawful to teach any theory that denies the story of the divine creation of man as taught in the Bible—and illegal to teach that we humans are descended from a lower order of animals. But the whole kit and caboodle is being appealed to the Tennessee Supreme Court."

Keller smiled. "Either way, my guess is that Darwin's writings will amount to about as much as this Hitler fellow's, but they sure do make for interesting reading." He turned back to his reading as Wade observed the passing scenery.

27

Splash

From time to time the train would stop for a crew to disembark.

"What all do they do?" Wade asked his mentor.

"Some of the crew head up the steep hills to cut the remaining massive virgin hardwood trees; most of those left are in the harder-to-reach hollows," Dr. Keller explained. "Others are in charge of hauling the logs down to float down the creek. In other areas the logs are pushed down greased log paths on the mountainside, which, as you can imagine, destroys all the vegetation in their path. Other times, fancy cable systems are set up to bring large logs down to the valley bottom."

"Back there we passed a large corral of oxen and horses."

"The mules, oxen, or workhorses are kept overnight in temporary pens like you saw. They are used to haul the massive logs when the Hazel Creek water is low or the trunks too big. The animals tow the logs to the tracks to be loaded onto specially built railcars and hauled down the valley, but this process is considered too slow and too inefficient, at least compared to a splash dam."

"Splash dam? What's that?" Wade asked.

"The most efficient way to get the logs to Proctor. The men float the logs downstream to a series of massive ponds that are created with temporary log dams called splash dams. They are made of large hemlock logs spiked together with pins made of locust wood and anchored to the creek bed and sides. There's a huge gate in the center of each dam that can be blasted open and when the 'splash' is over, rebuilt to close the dam. The largest of the three splash dams, the one at Bone Valley, is about two hundred and fifty feet across and almost twenty feet high with gates sixteen feet wide."

"That's gigantic!" Wade exclaimed.

"It is. We'll have to stop and look it over. In fact, it's so wide that locals use it for a bridge."

"How often do they do splashes, if that's what you call them?"

"They wait until the ponds are full of water and logs, especially when the creek is high after a heavy rain. Then the gates are blasted away with specially placed charges of dynamite, and a ten- to fifteen-foot torrent of water and logs will tumble and plunge downstream. The dams are opened sequentially, from the top of the valley to the bottom, building a massive torrent to carry the logs all the way to Proctor."

"Hope I'm never near the creek when this happens."

"Why?" Keller asked.

Wade felt his cheeks blush.

"What is it?" Keller said.

"I can't swim," Wade responded softly. "In fact, I'm terrified to be in water. I think it came from nearly drowning when I was a child in Africa."

Keller began to laugh.

"What?"

"Wouldn't matter if you could swim or not. Get caught in a splash and you're dead as a doornail," Keller explained. "But don't worry. Although most folks know when the dams are to be blasted, the company still has large steam whistles at each dam. They blow the whistle with three short blasts, then three long ones, and finally three short ones. It's Morse code for 'SOS.' And it means get as far away from the creek and as high above it as you can as fast as you can."

"I can only imagine what that does to the creek bed."

"The process has virtually destroyed the bank and bottom of the creek, that's for sure. And it explains why we don't find any fish in the lower portion of Hazel Creek: they've all been pulverized."

When the train reached the top of the valley, Keller showed Wade how to unhitch the skeeter from behind the locomotive, and they began their slow descent back to Proctor. In a few minutes, Wade had the hang of braking the skeeter, and Keller was able to sit on the back and orient his young protégé to the surroundings, telling him who lived where and some of the dangers of being an outsider, or as the mountain folks called outsiders, lowlanders or flatlanders.

"Those aren't complimentary terms, son!" Keller commented, then added, "One fact you should know that's potentially lifesaving is that you never, and I mean never, walk into an area you don't know without a local."

"Why's that?" Wade asked, applying the wooden brakes to slow the skeeter around a sharp bend.

"Folks up here are mighty poor. So some of them use their corn to make moonshine whiskey."

"That's illegal! Don't they know about Prohibition, the Volstead Act?"

"Turns out that when Prohibition was passed in 1920, it was a godsend from Washington for some of these highlanders. It's brought more moonshine business than just a few men could handle. So, quite a few folks have built little copper stills, which are hidden up and down the various creeks and branches. It's been said that a good packhorse or mule could only carry four bushels of shucked corn. But that same animal could haul twenty-four bushels of the same grain in distilled form. And the 'shine sells for a whole lot more than corn."

"So, how's that affect me?"

Keller smiled. "You're awfully green, aren't you?"

Wade laughed and nodded. "Guilty as charged."

"Well, if you come across folks working a still and they don't know you, word is they'll just shoot you dead, drag your body into the woods, and bury you where you'll never be found."

"That can't be true!"

"Are you willing to gamble your life to disprove me?"

Wade shook his head.

"Just last year, over near Robbinsville, one of our company men was walking up to visit some folks. He was walking by himself and decided to take a shortcut. Only reason they found his body, shot through the heart, was that a bear must have dug up his grave, and some Cherokees from over this way, the Walkingsticks, found what was left of him."

Wade was silent. Keller could tell that the story had affected him deeply. "Well, young man, start slowing down. We'll stop just the other side of this next bridge that crosses the Sugar Fork. We need to make a visit."

"Who will we be seeing?"

"The Randolphs."

"Will someone meet us and guide us up to their place?"

Keller laughed. "No. We've got permission to use their road to walk up to their place. Besides, Randolph and his girls are churchgoing folk. There won't be any stills on the way up to their place, I can assure you!"

28

Attraction

"Hello! Anybody home?" Dr. Keller shouted as he and Wade approached the Randolph cabin. There was smoke drifting up from one of the chimneys. Dr. Keller could see the wash hanging on a line between the barn and the cabin. As they got closer, a young woman came out of the cabin and onto the porch.

She waved. "Welcome, Dr. Keller!"

Even from the distance, Wade could see her long brown hair glistening in the morning sun and her sparkling smile. She was holding a young child in her arms as three girls and a woman came out to stand behind her.

As they entered the fence around the porch yard, the Randolphs' hunting dog, which was lying under the porch, began to snarl. "Lilly, be quiet now!" the young lady ordered. The dog quieted.

"Don't worry, Wade," Keller said. "Lilly's a Mountain Cur."

"A Cur. Never heard of the breed," Wade said.

"Without Curs," Keller said, "the pioneers would have never been able to settle in these mountains. They're much better for hunting than guarding a house. More bark than bite to them, I tell you."

As they walked up to the cabin, Keller said, "Grace, girls, meet Wade Chandler. He's the new doctor down in Proctor. He'll be helping me care for folks around here for at least the next year."

Grace smiled at him. "Pleased to meet you, Doctor."

"And you, Mrs. Randolph. Your daughters are beautiful," Wade said.

The girls giggled as Grace blushed.

"Sorry, son," Keller said. "This is *Miss* Grace Lumpkin, the teacher at the school down in Proctor. And these are Nate Randolph's girls: Abbie, Whit, Corrie, Anna, and Sarah Beth, the youngest. Nate lost his wife after childbirth year before last."

"Well, I'm plumb embarrassed," Wade responded as he blushed. However, he felt his eyes drawn to the oldest girl like metal flakes to a magnet, causing him to blush even more as she smiled at him and then turned her eyes down. He instantly sensed that they had made some sort of connection, but was embarrassed by the unprofessional feelings he was experiencing.

"My apologies to you all," Wade said as he tipped his hat.

Abbie looked up at him as she smiled and blushed.

"But it's a pleasure to meet you," he said as their eyes locked once again. Suddenly he recognized her as the beauty he had seen in town. "Uh . . . again," he stammered.

"What brings you up here, Grace?" Keller asked.

"I'm up here, as I am most Saturday mornings, tutoring these girls."

"Is Nate around? I came to check on him and bring him a new potion that might help him sleep better."

"That's right nice of you, Dr. Keller. But Pa's away this morning," Abbie said.

"Well, here's the potion. The instructions are on the bottle. I hope it helps."

Abbie walked down the steps, took the bottle, and said, "I'll let Pa know you come by, Dr. Keller." Abbie paused as she blushed slightly and smiled. "It's nice to meet you, Dr. Chandler . . . again."

Wade smiled. *I knew she'd remember me,* he thought as he said, "The pleasure is all mine!"

29

Rebuke

As they walked back to the skeeter, Keller told Wade about Callie's death as well as Nate's being shot and his slow recovery.

"How's the man keep up his farm?"

"Has a lot of help from a gypsy brother and sister he's hired, plus, neighbors and members of their church help out." Keller pointed to a small cabin and gypsy wagon at the edge of the meadow. "The gypsy man he's hired, Daniel Petrov, everyone calls him Danya, and his sister, Maria, live right over there. They've been a great help to Nate. When necessary," Dr. Keller continued, "he hires some of the lumbermen when they have time."

"Guess it's profitable for him. Seems like a nice spread."

"I've found that the typical highlander is land rich and cash poor. Rumors have it that he's also running medicinal moonshine over to Bryson City."

"I thought moonshine was illegal."

"Making it for personal or medicinal use is not. However, transporting medicinal whiskey is something they say is not explicitly covered by the federal law."

"Well, he's got a mighty fine piece of property here, doesn't he?" Wade said, looking across the land.

"Yep, goes right up to the high ridge up there. Between Nate and his neighbor, Tom Rau, they have the finest stand of virgin trees left in these parts."

"Why doesn't Mr. Calhoun buy them out?"

"He's offered a number of times, but Nate and Tom turn him down every time. Nate says this was his pa's farm and he promised his wife to keep it in the family. Reckon he's just stubborn enough to do it."

"It's a long way down to Proctor. How do the girls get there for school?"

"One of the gypsies will usually bring the girls down to town by wagon."

"How's the loss of their mother affected them?" Wade asked.

"I'll tell you, Wade, seems like the death brought those girls even closer to each other. Nothing is going to separate them! And it's made Abbie grow up quicker than most in these parts. She's more of a mother to those girls than she is a sister."

Wade laughed. "How old is she? Eighteen? Nineteen?"

"Only sixteen, believe it or not. A beautiful young woman, wouldn't you agree?"

Wade nodded. "Agreed. Suspect she's an attraction to most of the boys up and down the valley. Does she have a beau?"

"She's been courting Sheriff Zach Taylor's son, a boy by the name of Bobby Lee, for over a year. Most expect them to get married in the not-too-distant future."

"But it must be hard on her," Wade commented.

"What, having a beau?" Keller asked.

Wade smiled. "No. Having to mother her sisters. It's got to be one tough job."

"Well, she's got more character than most any young woman I've met," Keller said. "I wish she didn't have such a hard life, but it's what she promised her mother."

"Sort of rare to find a person like that," Wade commented as he looked back at the cabin. "A good thing to see."

Keller stopped and turned toward him. "How do you mean?"

Wade thought a moment. "Well, I've not been around the block a lot with women, if you know what I mean. I haven't gone out with that many, and maybe it's just the shallowness of those I've met, but it seems to me that some women are beautiful on the outside, and others are beautiful on the inside. But to find one who's both, that seems rare."

"You sound like you're describing my Rebecca," Keller said. "As precious as gold she was. Knew she was the one the moment I laid my eyes on her. I lost her when we were mighty young. Diphtheria took her, took her quick. I've never been attracted to another." Keller sighed and looked at Wade. "You attracted to that young lady?"

Wade blushed. "Well, I can't imagine any normal young man who would *not* be."

The two turned to continue down the road. Finally, Wade said thoughtfully, "I'll be happy to assist you in keeping an eye on that family, Andrew. Sounds like they deserve it!"

"Just be careful who you keep your eye on!" Keller said, laughing.

30

Surprise

Maddie grimaced. "So, you're thinkin' 'bout quittin' on me? You joshin'? Tell me you're pullin' my leg."

"I don't rightly know," Nate said. "The extra money I made from runnin' the 'shine to Bryson City before I was shot has certainly helped me with the bills. 'Course most of it has gone into paying for the truck, the farm help, and the plantin'. Add to it that we're about outta food from what we stored up last winter. So, without runnin' the 'shine for ya, me and my girls are likely to be hand-to-mouth until some crops come in."

"Well, don'tcha forget that the money's kept you from having to sell any of your timber. I know ya promised Cal ya wouldn't."

Nate nodded as he took a puff on his pipe.

"Quill Rose and I have rightly appreciated you making the runs to Bryson for us. That road ain't an easy one to drive—bein' as full of curves and potholes as it is."

Nate smiled. "The Bennetts have appreciated it also, and I 'spect the folks at the Fryemont Inn and boardin' houses have profited mightily from the trade it brings 'em."

"Well, my friend, it ain't bad money for drivin' over there once or twice a week. So why you thinkin' 'bout quittin'?"

"I'm still troubled a mite 'bout the law, Maddie. I talked to Lillian Frye last time I was in Bryson. She does legal work for me from time to time."

Maddie nodded as she lit her corncob pipe.

"Mrs. Frye reminded me it weren't illegal to drink the stuff if'n ya make it. And it ain't illegal to sell 'shine as medicine, if'n it's properly labeled."

"So, what's the problem, Nate? The labels we put on say it's medicinal. You only deliver to the doctor and the pharmacist."

"True 'nough, Maddie, but she says my transportin' the 'shine is a gray area in the law. She says if I get caught, I could possibly go away to the state pen for a few years. I know you believe that the Prohibition is not a righteous law—"

"Yep," she interrupted. "Not obeyin' an unrighteous law, to meet people's legitimate needs, well that's downright righteous to me."

Nate took another puff and thought for a moment.

"Maybe, Maddie. You make it sound virtuous, but the Good Book says, 'There is a way which seemeth right unto a man, but the end thereof are the ways of death.' And given how Sanders has it out for me, I wouldn't want to give him any excuse to put me away and take away my family's land." He was quiet for a moment before continuing. "Also, I wouldn't want him to send my girls away."

Maddie spun her head around as fast as a top, as her mouth fell open. "Send your girls away? How in the devil could he do that? Why we'd ne'er let that happen, I'll tell ya that!"

"According to Mrs. Frye, there'd be no way to stop him. If'n I'm gone, the girls would be considered orphans. And that would leave them and the farm in the hands of my sister in Raleigh and her scoundrel of a husband. Why he'd take the girls away from here and sell the farm to Calhoun in a second, I know it."

"I never even thought of that, Nate." Maddie was quiet for a few moments as she took draws from her pipe; then she looked back at him. "Nate, you gotta do what's right by you and your girls."

Nate nodded.

"You want to make the run today, or you want me to find someone else?"

"I'm a man of my word. Said I'd run for you today, so I will. But—"

"You need to reflect on what to do from here on out?"

Nate smiled. "Not really, Maddie." He turned to face her. "I've pondered it out and I've prayed about it. I think this next run will be my last one fer ya."

Maddie nodded as she looked across the ageless mountains.

31

Confession

"**Y**ou seem more lighthearted, Pa . . . more yourself," Abbie said after breakfast as she hugged him. "That makes me happy!"

It gave Nate immense pleasure to hear it. He did feel as if a ton of bricks had been lifted off his shoulders.

While sitting with his girls the evening before, he announced he would be making fewer trips to Bryson City and spending more time with Danya supervising the farm. The girls clapped in joy.

At the morning service, as he did each Mother's Day, Pastor Semmes recognized all the mothers—including the oldest and youngest and those with the most children—and the longest marriage. Prayers were said for those who had lost children that year and for those mothers trying to conceive. Every mother was given a small bouquet of spring wildflowers and then the whole lot was prayed over and then applauded.

Before he began preaching, as was his habit every Sunday, Pastor Semmes said, "I like to hear God's people testify, and none of us have the right to withhold testifyin' of a blessin' that the good Lord has bestowed upon us. And sometimes we need to confess where we've fallen short."

He paused for impact and then continued. "As the Good Book says, 'Is any among you afflicted? let him pray. Is any merry? let him sing psalms. Is any sick among you? let him call for the elders of the church; and let them pray over him, anointing him with oil in the name of the Lord. Confess your faults one to another, and pray one for another, that ye may be healed. The effectual fervent prayer of a righteous man availeth much.' In any case, this is testifyin' and confessin' time. Anybody that's got a blessin' or needs to say anythin', now's the time."

Nate sat and listened as his neighbors and friends stood up. It was a happy time for most, and he joined in with a hearty amen when Ronald Smith testified how God had healed him from the sick bed in Doc Keller's infirmary.

Finally Pastor Semmes said, "Anyone else?" No one spoke, and the pastor said, "Well—"

Nate suddenly found himself standing. He had not planned this. He was aware that Grace and his daughters were all staring up at him from their pew. Abbie, she was comfortable talking about her faith; and Callie, well, *she* was just plain outspoken when she was alive. Nate had never testified in church.

"Reckon I need to say a couple of things, although I ain't used to speakin' up in church."

He hesitated so long that Reverend Semmes finally leaned forward on the pulpit. "Just take your time, Brother Randolph. We're in no hurry."

Nate felt as if his throat was constricted. "Well, I ain't been the kind of Christian I should be, and I want to say to the Lord and to everybody here that I'm plumb sorry, and it's my intention to be a better servant of the Lord."

Amens rose from all over the room and Nate felt his hand being grasped. He looked down and saw Abbie. "It's all right, Pa."

Clearing his throat, he continued. "I ain't been the kind of pa I shoulda been to my girls. Most of you knew my good wife, Callie Jean. She was as fine a Christian woman as there ever was. So I'm ashamed I ain't done better. But I'm makin' a promise here and now that I'll be a better pa and a better servant of the Lord from now on. And I want you'uns to all hold me to it."

The simple testimony touched the hearts of those in the congregation. After the service, many came to Nate and shook his hand. Finally, when they got outside in the truck and everyone was getting situated in the back, Abbie reached over, put her arms around his neck, and kissed him. "You ain't been a bad pa. You've been a good pa!"

"That's right!" Whit exclaimed.

Nathan Randolph sat there wanting to cry like a baby. Instead, he wiped his eyes with his sleeves and said huskily, "Well, let's get on home."

He started the truck and as he drove away, he suddenly felt a release. He had been heavily burdened by the loss of his wife for more than nineteen months, missing her terribly every single day and night, more than anyone could know. Being shot in the back had robbed him of his manhood, or so he thought, as he had been unable to provide for his family in an active way. He had needed to depend upon others to care for his farm. And even before he'd been shot, he felt forced to run moonshine, for which he felt considerable conviction.

But now all that was gone! As he drove home, he hummed hymn after hymn. The girls smiled and hummed with him. Life to Nate Randolph was good again.

32

Mama

"**I** have a surprise!" Nate said when they arrived home. "I've invited Grace and Bobby Lee to join us for the afternoon."

The younger girls all cheered, but Abbie only cocked her head.

"It's a beautiful May Sunday," Nate said, "and we're ahead on the work. Whit, you and Corrie pack us a picnic lunch, and let's plan to go stay all afternoon at the creek."

"How about beef sandwiches and sweet potato salad?" Corrie asked.

"Along with lemonade!" Anna added.

"You bet," Nate answered. "Off with ya."

All the girls ran inside except Abbie.

"Pa?" she said.

"Ain't any big deal, Punkin," Nate responded.

"Pa, it's Mother's Day. A day to honor and remember Mama's memory. Not a day for another woman."

"I know, Punkin." He put his hands on her shoulders. "But I think it's time to move on. I feel fondly toward Grace, and I think she feels the same. I think invitin' her to be with our family, especially on Mother's Day, is just what's right. Can ya accept my decision?"

Abbie teared up. "Guess I'm just surprised, Pa. Wish you had talked to me about it."

"You're probably right 'bout that, Punkin. I'm sorry. I just want to thank her for takin' such an interest in my girls and teachin' you'uns so good. Reckon you can forgive me?"

Abbie smiled and hugged his neck. "Reckon I can. And reckon I will."

Nate leaned back. "Well, good. 'Cause I'll need you to forgive me for somethin' else."

Abbie raised her eyebrows. "Which is?"

"For not talkin' to ya 'bout invitin' Bobby Lee. Reckon since he's gonna make my Punkin a mama someday, we might just as well celebrate your future Mother's Day and my future as a grandpa. Whatcha say?"

Abbie laughed. "I don't know, Pa. Why don't we just walk down the path one step at a time? After all, he's gotta ask me to marry him. But first he needs to ask you for permission."

Nate smiled and nodded. "Also need ya to forgive me for glancin' at your journal entry this mornin'."

"Pa!" Abbie complained.

"You left it open on the table. What's a man to do?"

"What'dcha see?" Abbie asked.

"I saw your beautiful writin'. Saw where you were practicin' writin' *Lauren Abigail Taylor.* I liked the cursive LAT and ART you had written," he said as he hugged her close. "Liked it a lot, Punkin."

After Grace arrived in her carriage, followed by Bobby Lee on his paint, everyone loaded Nate's truck with the fishing poles and gear and drove to his favorite fishing spot far up the Sugar Fork, a place that had been dammed by natural formations so that the creek was wide and smooth. At the top of the pool was a bend in the creek, and the sand and silt had built up a beach and left a band of water shallow enough for wading.

They ate their lunch and then fished the early part of the afternoon, catching a mess of trout.

Midafternoon, Bobby Lee walked over to Nate. He was more than a bit nervous, for in the mountains, when a boy and girl were courting they had to stay within sight of a parent or adult. That's just the way it was. But Bobby Lee and his pa had met that week with Nate, so his confidence was higher than it might normally have been.

"Mr. Randolph, would it be all right if Abbie and I took a hike?"

Nate smiled and put his arm on Bobby Lee's shoulder. "I think that'd be mighty fine. You take good care of my girl, ya hear?"

"Yes, sir!"

"Abbie!" Nate called out. "Come over here."

Abbie laid down her pole and walked over.

"Do me a favor, Punkin. Take Bobby Lee down the ridge trail and show him Ramp Holler, where Mr. Sanders tried to rustle your walnut tree year before last. Will ya? Then we'll all meet up at home in a couple of hours."

Abbie wrinkled her brow at this very unusual request. "Are you serious, Pa?"

"As a heart attack."

She looked at Bobby Lee and then back at her pa. "It's okay if we be *alone*, Pa?"

"'Spect my friend Mr. Jeremiah Welch will be keeping an eye on you two from a distance. So consider him your guardian angel."

Abbie smiled and looked up at Bobby Lee, who smiled and nodded.

"Then let's go."

33

Names

Far above their heads, the thick branches of the massive trees gently rustled in the afternoon breeze, blocking out most of the sunlight and creating a pleasantly cool atmosphere as Bobby Lee and Abbie entered the forest.

As she cocked her head, Bobby Lee asked, "Whatcha listenin' for?"

"It's an old habit the Walkingsticks taught me, to focus on the sounds of the birds."

"Why?"

"If they're chatterin' playful-like, it means it's all safe ahead. But if they're quiet or squallin', it means danger ahead. They can see and hear things from their perches that we can't down here."

"Then I best walk by ya," Bobby Lee said, taking Abbie's hand. Abbie blushed and smiled.

"I learned somethin' 'bout your name, 'bout *Lauren Abigail* and what it means," Bobby Lee said.

"What?"

"I asked Miss Grace about it and she told me *Lauren* is of Latin origin, and it means 'the bay or laurel plant.' She said the scientific name is *Laurus nobilis*. Like you're noble or royal or somethin' like that. Ain't that somethin'?"

Abbie laughed. "I didn't know that."

"What's more, since we call it sweet bay, and since we use the bay leaf for cookin' 'cause of the special flavor and fragrance it brings, and since you bring a wonderful fragrance to any event you attend, I'm thinkin' your name's a good one."

"I see," Abbie said as they walked deeper into the woods.

"Miss Grace also helped me look up *Abigail.* Turns out it comes from the Hebrew language and was the name of King David's third wife who was, and I quote, 'good in discretion and beautiful in form.' So, I think both yer names fitcha like a glove."

"And your name?"

"Came from General Robert E. Lee himself. My dad admires him a heap. Lee's pa was a Revolutionary War hero called Light-Horse Harry. Lee himself was a top graduate of West Point. What most folks don't know is that President Abraham Lincoln initially asked Lee to take command of the entire Union army."

"He did?" Abbie asked.

"Yep. But Lee turned him down 'cause his home state, Virginia, left the Union. My pa says Lee was loyal to Virginia and he were the shrewdest general in the whole war. Pa says he was a Southern gentleman until the end."

"What'd he do after the war?"

"Pa says he became president of Washington College. It was named Washington and Lee University after he died."

"A man of loyalty, integrity, and shrewdness," Abbie said. "Sounds like the type of man I'd like to marry."

"Even a shrewd one?" Bobby Lee asked.

"Yep!" Abbie exclaimed. "*Shrewd* just means 'wise or cunning.' And Jesus himself taught, 'Behold, I send you forth as sheep in the midst of wolves: be ye therefore wise as serpents, and harmless as doves.' So, yes, I like the idea."

"If you were to marry such a man, I assume you'd wanna lotta children?"

Abbie was quiet a moment. "I've thought about that, Bobby Lee. Watching Mama and some others lose children in childbirth or as young babes was plumb heartbreakin'. But seein' the joy of children and knowin' the Lord calls 'em a gift from hisself, I think I'd like to have a large family. That is, if my husband, whoever he might be, would want the same."

"Hadn't thought of children as a gift," Bobby Lee said, "but . . . makes sense."

After silently walking nearly halfway up to the ridge, they came across a large clearing containing an ancient mountain bog, and stopped to admire the massive virgin hardwood trees surrounding it.

"From my earliest memories, I've enjoyed hikin' in these mountains," Abbie said. "I take my greatest pleasure from bein' in the woods. I've learned the sounds of the birds and can mimic a bunch of 'em."

"Learned by yourself?" Bobby Lee asked.

"Nope," Abbie said, chuckling. "The Walkingsticks taught me and they taught me all about the wildlife. Pa taught me fishin' and huntin', along with Mr. Kep. But it were Maddie who taught me how to recognize all the plants in the woods. She tutored me 'bout which plants are poisonous and which part of each nonpoisonous plant can be used for eatin', seasonin', healin', dyein' clothes, and makin' baskets. Reckon all that'll help me as a wife and a mama."

Bobby Lee turned to face her and took her hands in his. "Abbie, I think you're gonna be a great wife and an even better ma to as many kids as the good Lord gives ya."

Abbie felt her eyes mist up, and she dropped her head.

"Did I say somethin' wrong?" Bobby Lee asked.

Abbie sniffled and looked up at him. "I promised Mama I'd help Pa care for the girls. I need to stay and help him."

Bobby Lee's head turned to the side as he looked down at her. "Any man deservin' of you, Miss Lauren Abigail, would support just that."

Abbie smiled. "Would *you*? Would you really?"

"You bet!" Bobby Lee said. "If'n your pa would allow it, why we'd build a cabin right there on his property. I'd help him and

Danya run the farm. You'd help with the girls till they're all
growed up. And then we'd have a slew of our own."

"I'd like that," Abbie whispered. "In fact, I'd *love* it!" She felt a
wisp of wind begin to blow, and suddenly she felt an uncomfortable memory as she looked over the bog.

"What is it, Abbie?" Bobby Lee asked, looking around.

"I was just rememberin' the day, a couple of years ago, when I
heard Sanders and his crew rustlin' my big ol' walnut tree. In fact,
I was standin' in this exact same spot." Suddenly she took off trotting uphill. "Come on, Bobby Lee! I'll show ya."

Bobby Lee caught up with her as she crouched under a large
laurel bush. She turned and put one finger over her lips. "Shh!"
she warned as Bobby Lee crouched over by her.

"What is it?" he whispered.

Abbie took a deep breath. "Smell that?"

Bobby Lee sniffed and his nose wrinkled up. "What is it?"

"Danger!" she whispered.

34

Boar

A bbie slowly raised her head to look over the ridge into the hollow below and felt her eyebrows arch. "Oh, my goodness. It's a sounder of boar!" she exclaimed in a low voice.

Bobby Lee slowly crawled up beside her and they looked down into the small hollow. A tiny stream flowed out of the base of a huge boulder at the top of the hollow. Rooting in the plants was the group of wild pigs.

"A slew of 'em," Bobby Lee whispered.

"Yep. Russian boar," Abbie answered.

"What's a sounder? I don't know what that word means."

Abbie smiled. She admired a man who could admit when he didn't know something. "It's a family of wild pigs." Abbie pointed toward the largest boar. "I think he's the pa, likely over a hundred and fifty pounds. Rooting behind him are the females. The smallest ones, the ones with the stripes, they're the piglets. I'm guessing they're three to four months old."

"They're *all* huge," Bobby Lee whispered. "The adults must be four to five feet long and two to three feet high at the shoulder."

Their malodorous musk rose up the ridge like a fog, while their coarse, wiry black hair, long legs, and formidable tusks combined to make them a frightening sight. Abbie knew that although boar had a keen sense of smell and hearing, their eyesight was poor.

"Let's scare 'em," Abbie whispered. "On the count of three, let's run toward 'em screamin' like banshees."

"Won't they attack us?"

"Not when we're comin' down on 'em. Also, we're downwind from 'em. We'll scare 'em silly."

Bobby Lee smiled and nodded. "If'n you say so."

Abbie counted and at *three* they both stood, began screaming, waving their arms, and sprinting down the ridge toward the boar, which immediately began to tear through the underbrush down valley, squealing as if they had been shot.

Bobby Lee and Abbie stopped at the bottom of the small hollow, laughing so hard their sides ached and they could hardly catch their breath.

"Nineteen twelve," Bobby Lee said, panting.

"What?" Abbie asked, trying to catch her breath.

"That's when Pa said a shipment of wild boar from Russia was brought to that private game reserve over on Hooper's Bald."

"Really? I didn't know that."

"Yep. Eventually, some of 'em escaped. They dug under the walls and in a few years made their way over here. They're one tough animal!" Bobby Lee explained. "Seen men gored to the bone and dogs tusked to death by 'em, I'll tell ya that."

After catching her breath, Abbie spun around with her arms outstretched. "Bobby Lee, this here's Ramp Holler. It's where me and my sisters have gathered spring onions, what we call ramps, since we were little."

She stopped spinning and pointed to the top of a massive stump. "And that there's all that remains of one majestic walnut tree! *My* walnut tree. The one Sanders and his crew tried to rustle from our family."

They walked up to the stump.

"Oh, my goodness," was all Bobby Lee could say as he looked over the massive stump. "Must be over nine feet in diameter. I've never seen a walnut that big."

"I loved her. Pa said she was the largest remaining walnut tree in the entire Hazel Creek watershed. Me and my sisters counted over three hundred rings there. She were older than these United States themselves."

All of a sudden, Abbie felt sadness sweep over her, as tears began to streak down her cheeks. She turned from Bobby Lee and sat on the stump.

"What is it?" Bobby Lee asked softly, as he sat beside her, his hand on her shoulder.

Abbie wept a minute and then regained her composure. She wiped her tears with the backs of her fists as she gazed up at the forest awning far above their heads.

"Guess this stump reminds me of what I've lost. Mama would come up here with us. This beautiful little valley reminds me of her. It plumb makes me gloomy."

Bobby Lee was quiet a moment as he looked around the hollow. Then he turned to face her. "What if we could turn that sad memory into a happy one?"

Abbie turned to face him. "Whatcha talking about?"

Bobby Lee grinned ear to ear. "Just watch and see."

35

Commit

Bobby Lee reached into his vest and pulled out a small velvet box. He held it gingerly in his left hand for a moment, then he slowly opened the top.

Abbie felt her eyes widen as she recognized the Edwardian wedding ring trimmed in milgrain and highlighted with an intricate fine carved pattern.

"Mama's?" she asked, as her eyes widened.

Bobby nodded.

She knew that the inside of the ring contained the engraved inscription with her mother's and father's initials and their wedding date: *NHR to CJR 08/01/08*. Abbie looked at Bobby Lee in disbelief, tears once again filling her eyes. "Mama's?" she asked again.

Bobby Lee smiled and nodded even harder.

"How'd you get it? I usually keep it on all the time, but I took it off when Pa decided we were all goin' swimmin' this afternoon."

"Guess your pa snuck it outta the house. When I asked him for your hand, he said he'd give his permission, but only if I'd use your mama's ring."

"You've asked him for my hand? Bobby Lee . . ."

He smiled and nodded once again. "Asked my pa, yer pa, *and* the pastor. After each interrogated me, they gave me their permission. So, I need to do somethin'." Suddenly, Bobby Lee knelt in front of her, on one knee. "Lauren Abigail Randolph, with God as my witness, I want to confess my undyin' love for ya. And, with my pa's, and our pastor's, and your pa's permission, I'd like to ask ya to marry me."

Abbie stared at Bobby Lee. She had waited for this moment her whole life. She had imagined it from childhood. She had role-played this moment with her friends and sisters. She had been delighted when other girls shared the joy of their proposals. For over a year now, she had even dreamed about her and Bobby Lee's marriage. The visions she had were delightful. Yet, despite it all, she feared he might never ask her to marry him, and at the same time, she feared he would. Even after endlessly rehearsing this moment her entire life, and even more so the last few months, she was still struck dumb.

"Will ya?" Bobby Lee whispered.

As tears coursed down her cheeks, Abbie felt her head nod.

Bobby Lee smiled, lifted the ring from its box, and gently slipped it onto her left ring finger.

Abbie whispered, "I'll *never* take it off again." As she hugged him, she began to weep again. "Never ever."

After her weeping stopped, Bobby Lee leaned back and pulled a handkerchief from his pocket. "Here," he said as he handed it to her.

"Thanks. That's sweet."

Bobby Lee's eyes softened. "Not havin' had a ma for a few years, and not havin' ever had sisters, and *never* havin' had a girlfriend, I . . . um . . . well, I'm not always gonna be sure what to do at the right time."

"Well, I've never been with a boy. And I ain't got no brothers. So, I'm gonna have to do some learnin' myself. So I guess we'll just have to find out 'bout this marryin' thing together."

Bobby Lee leaned forward, and Abbie felt herself melt into his arms, his embrace, and his soft lips. *This is good*, she remembered thinking. *This is very, very good.*

36

Swimming

In the heat of the midafternoon, Corrie called out, "Pa, I wanna go swimmin'."

"Me, too, Pa!" Whit exclaimed.

"Well, you two just jump right on in. I've got dryin' towels in the truck, although you likely won't need 'em as warm as it is today."

Anna looked expectantly for permission. When Nate nodded and gestured toward the creek, the girls squealed and quickly plunged into the ice-cold creek. They shrieked as they began splashing each other.

Grace sat holding Sarah Beth for a while as they watched the girls laugh and play. "What do you say, sweetheart?" Nate said. "Why don't you and me swim a little bit ourselves?"

"Me?" Grace said.

Nate laughed. "Actually, I was talking to Miss Sarah Elisabeth."

"Ah, good thing," responded Grace, laughing. "I'm not a swimmer."

"This one is. Oughta see her flutter kick when she's being bathed. I think she's gonna be a natural swimmer, just like her mama."

Grace laughed as Sarah Beth looked up at her and grinned. She was nineteen months old now and had curly blond hair and large crystal blue eyes. "Maybe you'll teach me to swim one day, Sarah girl!"

Nate pulled off his shoes and socks, rolled up his pant legs, took Sarah from Grace, and waded out into the water. He held Sarah Beth above the cold water as she kicked, screeching in delight. He looked around and saw all the girls having a good time. *I wish you could be here to see this, Callie. But maybe you can. I hope you can, for these are mighty fine girls you gave me.*

He looked at Grace, sitting on the picnic blanket. She was radiant. *Callie, there'll never be no one to replace ya. No one. But my girls do need a ma. And I long for the company. Pastor tells me he and the Lord are okay with it all.* He looked up at the clear sky above the creek. *I think I feel your pleasure, Cal. I do.*

After a time splashing in the water, Nate called out, "Time to go, girls! We've gotta get home in time to clean these here fish. I'm hungry for some good fried trout!"

Their suppertime was wonderful. They had caught several slab-sized trout that they dressed whole, and the steamy white flesh simply melted off the bones. Abbie made hush puppies, a specialty of hers, and rosemary-seasoned fried potatoes.

Of course, the talk at dinner was about Bobby Lee's proposal and Abbie's acceptance, and then there was lots of discussion about wedding plans. After dinner, Bobby Lee said his good-byes to everyone. Abbie walked with him to the barn. After putting the tack on his paint, he turned to face Abbie.

"I'm glad you said yes," he said.

Abbie laughed. "After nearly two years of courtin', you didn't seriously think I'd say no, did ya?"

"Guess I was just plumb nervous. But now that you've said yes, me and Pa need to come up and talk to you and your pa about setting a date."

Bobby Lee stepped toward her and put his arm around her waist. "And I'll tell ya this right now, Miss Randolph, the sooner the better." He leaned forward and gave her a gentle kiss, which she eagerly returned.

What neither of them noticed was a thin old man with thick, uncombed gray hair, smiling with a toothless grin, looking down on them from the hayloft.

37

Happy

Grace offered to help with the dishes, but Nate bid her farewell so that Bobby Lee could accompany her back to Proctor before dark. After the supper dishes were cleaned, the family sat around on the porch, talking, laughing, and singing until bedtime.

Finally, when the younger girls were all in bed, Abbie came back down and found her father sitting in his rocking chair on the porch. She went over and put her arm around him. "It was a good day, Pa."

"Yes, it was, Punkin."

"Pa, you look better. You look happier than I've seen you in a long time. Is it Miss Grace?"

"I do feel happier, Punkin," Nate said quietly. "Partly it's her, no doubt. We do have mighty strong feelin's for each other. Of course, the prospect of you and Bobby Lee marryin' up is rightly pleasin' to me. But mostly, it's just that since church, I'm feelin' free, as light as a feather."

"That makes me happy, Pa."

"And I'm mighty grateful for you, Abbie. You've had to be a mama to these girls, and only God in heaven knows what it has cost you. I feel like I've robbed you of part of yer childhood."

"No, you ain't . . . . I mean, no you haven't." Abbie corrected herself. "I miss Mama every day but never more than today, on Mother's Day. We all do, but we got *you*, Pa."

"You know, Abbie, a man's only half a man without a woman, and I miss your mama more than I could ever say."

"I know you do, Pa."

"Pastor told me there was only one time during creation that God said his act of creation was *not* good. After he formed the man, he said, 'It is not good that the man should be alone; I will make him an help meet for him.' In other words, God made him to walk the path of life with a woman. I believe that more than ever, Punkin."

"If'n the Lord's given you the okay to move forward with Miss Grace, Pa, then so do I."

"The Lord's given you a good spirit, Punkin."

"I don't mind, Pa, really I don't," Abbie said, and then sighed. "But I might shoulda stood up to confess this mornin' also."

"Why?"

"Because sometimes I find myself gettin' angry at Mama for being gone, and it ain't even her fault. Sometimes I get mad at the girls for just being girls. And once in a while I even get to fussin' at the Lord. I'm right embarrassed to admit it all. That's a wolf I need to quit feedin'."

"A wolf . . . ?"

"That's a story fer another day," Abbie said as her pa put his strong arms around her and pulled her close.

"Guess we both need to do a bit better, don't we?"

Abbie chuckled. "Like Danya always says, 'No limit on better.'"

Nathan laughed. "Amen, Punkin."

The two sat talking for a while and finally Nate said, "Well, we can't go fishin' and havin' us picnics every day. I've got to go to Bryson City tomorrow and pick up a load of fertilizer and seed for the men who will be planting for us this week. It'll be less expensive than buyin' it here in town. Even factorin' in the price of gas, I'll still save a bunch of money."

"It wouldn't be good for your back to load it."

"Bobby Lee's volunteered to come help me. And there're men

at the feed store who will help. 'Course Danya and Bobby Lee can unload it in no time at all once we're home. All I've really gotta do is drive."

"Can I go with ya, Pa? It'd be fun to have a day with you *and* my new fiancé."

"Punkin, it was hard enough for me to get Miss Lumpkin to let him off a day from school. Don't reckon she'd ever go for lettin' the both of you off. No, you best stay here and get the girls to school, and then take care of the house when you get back." He leaned over and kissed her.

"I think things are going to get better for the Randolphs," Abbie said.

"Ain't no limit on better, Punkin. Night night."

"Sleep tight."

"Don't let the bed bugs bite."

"See ya in the mornin' light."

38

Good-bye

The rain pelting the roof of the cabin woke her before dawn. Abbie could hear that her pa was up, so she put on a housecoat and went down the ladder.

Gazing through the window at the strengthening gale, Abbie said, "It's absolutely pourin' cats and dogs. I don't think ya oughta go today, Pa."

"Oh, I reckon it'll fair off after a while, Punkin."

"I'll be happy to fix ya some breakfast," Abbie said, shaking her head, "but I wish ya wouldn't go."

"Gotta get the supplies today, Punkin, to get the best price."

After a big breakfast of eggs, grits, fried country ham, and plenty of redeye gravy, Nate put his oilskin raincoat on and pulled his rain hat on over his head. He came to Abbie, who was sitting by the fire, and said, "What'll I bring ya back?"

"Just you, Pa."

He leaned over, kissed her, and then hugged her. "You take care of your sisters now."

"I will, Pa. Ya get home early if you can. I'll fix a good supper."

"Oughta be back by late afternoon. I'll plan on pickin' you girls up after school. I'll let Danya know to not go get you'uns."

"Ya sure ya won't be comin' just to sneak a visit to the teacher?" Abbie asked, smiling.

"Don't never hurt for a man to check with his children's teacher and see how they're doing. That's what I say."

"And I say that's a pile of baloney, Pa," Abbie said, laughing, "but we'll be keepin' an eye out for ya."

Looking out, he said, "I do believe it's gonna eventually clear off; gonna be a pretty day before all's said and done." He waved and left the house.

Abbie stood in the door frame watching as he ran through the pouring rain to the barn and got into the truck. She listened to the truck labor to start, and then the motor caught. She walked out to the edge of the porch, waving, as he drove away. He waved back and she could see him smiling. She watched until the truck's rear lights disappeared, then sighed, went back in, and started planning the day. Emily Rau would be there shortly to watch Sarah Beth while she and her sisters were in school. She smiled as she thought, *Only three weeks left in the school year! Then we'll be home with Pa all the time.*

39

Downpour

He and Bobby Lee had seen it coming, a huge roiling cloud, wickedly green-black and charged with fury. It wasn't going to clear off after all! They spied the forecurtain of the monsoon racing down the road toward them. The rain was preceded by a clap of earsplitting thunder, and then a violent downdraft of wind nearly blew them off the road. They felt as if they were driving through a waterfall.

"Looks like the good Lord's pourin' water outta a massive heavenly bucket," Nate complained, leaning forward and squinting to see through the incessant sheets of rain, as gusts of wind pounded against the truck's windshield.

"It's what I imagine it'd be like to walk behind Niagara Falls," Bobby Lee observed.

Nate looked at him and laughed. "Where'dcha ever get an idea like that?"

"Was in one of the books Miss Grace had us read. They dug a tunnel through the rock behind the waterfall, and you can sure enough walk out right behind it. They say it's so loud ya can't hear yourself scream."

The wiper blades were beating as fast as they could but weren't keeping up with the torrent. It was as if the gargantuan cloud were dropping all its water at once.

Nate was driving more slowly than he normally would on the

unpaved, pitted dirt road from Bryson City to Proctor. The pot-holes were overflowing with water, making it difficult to judge their depth.

He tried to miss the deep ruts as much as possible, but whenever he struck a deep one, it shook not only his old truck, but also his entire body. More than once the jolt sent knife-like pains down his spine and into both legs. Nate grimaced and wondered if the bullet still lodged in his back might be migrating, as he was having more pain radiating to his groin and legs. *Might have to get the doc to take it out sometime,* he thought.

Suddenly he recoiled in fear as a blinding white streak of lightning struck near the road. He stomped on the brake pedal and the truck skated to a halt as the thunderclap shook the truck.

"I swan!" Nate cried out.

"Lordy be!" Bobby Lee exclaimed. "That was mighty close."

Nate put the truck in its lowest gear, let off the clutch, and slowly pressed the accelerator.

Bobby Lee looked at the back of the truck. "I'm glad you brought that canvas tarp to cover the fertilizer. Looks like it's holding."

"Wouldn't have been profitable for the fertilizer to have just dissolved on the road, eh?"

As they approached the last few bends before the final straightaway leading to the Proctor depot and the road up Hazel Creek, the rain began to slacken and Nate sighed. He was relieved knowing he'd be home soon and with his daughters.

"Hope the storm's not a-feared the girls," he said as he pressed the accelerator and picked up speed.

"Yep, we're roundin' third and headin' home!" Bobby Lee added.

As the truck rounded the curve, the back tires slipped a bit in the mud. Nate let off the gas and turned the steering wheel into the skid. "Whoopee!" he shouted, enjoying the youthful exhilaration he had felt when he first learned to drive.

"Yipes stripes!" Bobby Lee cried out. "Thought we were goin' into the river for sure."

"Not if I have my way," Nate said, laughing, "although it feels like we've driven through one."

Coming out of the curve, Nate was beginning to accelerate when he saw something on the road ahead that forced him to slam on the brakes. Mud flew as the truck veered slightly sideways and then slid to a halt just inches from a three-foot boulder lying in the middle of the road.

Nate let out a sigh. "That was close!"

"Good eyes, Mr. Randolph!"

Nate picked up the raincoat sitting beside him on the bench seat and pulled it on, grabbing his hat and pushing it on his head as he opened the door to inspect the obstacle. Bobby Lee hopped out of the passenger side.

To Nate's surprise, the boulder appeared to have been purposely rolled across the road. The boot prints in the mud were a sure giveaway. His suspicions immediately aroused, he began to turn back to the truck. *I might need my rifle, and quickly. Could be an ambush, a robbery.*

As he turned, a man in a rain poncho stepped out from behind a large tree with a pearl-handled .22-caliber pistol drawn.

"Go ahead and put your hands up," he growled. "One wrong move, Randolph, and I'll stop your clock. This time I won't miss!"

"There's two of us and only one of him," Bobby Lee whispered. "We'll take him. No trouble."

Just then, several large men, rifles ready, stepped out of the woods in front of and behind them. Nate didn't know who they were, but he did know they were big trouble.

40

News

It was four o'clock, and Abbie's worry about her pa was increasing by the minute. It had started when he did not show to pick them up after school. Given the heavy rain, Miss Grace had brought them home in her covered carriage and then stayed around to offer some extra tutoring.

Abbie's worry was only worsened by Anna, who repeatedly asked, "What time did Pa say he'd be back?"

Each time Abbie replied, "He said early afternoon, but you know how it is. It's rained hard most of the day. He may be stuck somewhere, or just havin' to drive slow on that old rutted road. Keep workin' on your homework now."

As the afternoon wore on, five o'clock then six, Abbie became more worried than she wanted the girls to know. She could not help but remember that her father had gone hunting and was shot, but she had to keep a tight rein on herself. She was glad Miss Grace had agreed to stay until Pa arrived.

"There, he's comin'!" Whit exclaimed. "I hear him."

"That don't sound like Pa's truck," Corrie said as they all raced to the door.

Grace and the girls all went out on the porch. The rain had stopped, and as the vehicle drove into the clearing Whit said tightly, "That's Sheriff Taylor."

Something frosty seemed to close around Abbie's chest. She

could not breathe, nor could she move, as the car pulled to a stop and Zach Taylor slowly got out. He closed the door, but instead of coming toward them, simply stood there, looking out across the floating mist that enshrouded the Sugar Fork valley. He did not move for what seemed like hours, and fear ran through Abbie so sharp and biting that she felt she could no longer stand. Her knees felt weak, and she held her hands to keep them from trembling. Grace put her arm around Abbie and pulled her close.

The deputy turned toward the cabin. He was wearing his raincoat and his usual Stetson hat, which he pulled off as he came forward.

"Grace, girls," he said, and then had to clear his throat. "I've . . . I've got some bad news."

"Is it Pa?" Whit cried out. "Has somethin' happened to Pa?"

"Bobby Lee . . ." Abbie whispered as her hand flew to cover her mouth.

Zach Taylor turned his hat around by the brim as he looked down at it. Finally, he looked up with tears in his eyes, and Abbie knew everything at that instant.

"Your pa has had . . . he's had a bad accident. His truck slid off the road and he and Bobby Lee were both thrown from it."

"Is Pa hurt?" Corrie whispered. "Please, Mr. Taylor, he ain't hurt bad, is he?"

"What is it, Sheriff Taylor?" Abbie asked, her voice tight. "You can tell us."

"Girls," Zach said in a voice barely above a whisper, "I hate to tell ya, but well . . . your pa . . . and my Bobby Lee . . . they're dead."

For a moment no one reacted, and then Whit turned and ran to Abbie. Abbie held her tightly as she began to sob. Corrie held Sarah Beth silently. Anna sat down on the porch and began to cry. Grace's grip on Abbie loosened, but she didn't move.

For Abbie, it was as if the world stopped. It was worse, somehow, than when her mama died. At least they had somebody left to care for them. Pa was there. Bobby Lee was there for her. Now there was nobody!

Zach Taylor said, "Miss Lumpkin, I hope you can stay a bit. Some of the church folks are coming over. Tom and Sandy Rau are on their way. So is Pastor Semmes."

Abbie looked up, through her tears, to see Grace nod and say, "Of course I'll stay." She looked down at Abbie as tears streamed down her face. "As long as you need me," she added.

Zach said, "You know, girls, anythin' I can do I will. I'm right sorry to have to tell you this."

Abbie's mouth felt like cotton and she could not speak. She tried, but no words escaped her now paralyzed and dry vocal cords. She wanted to tell the sheriff that she was so sorry for *his* loss. She felt as if her heart had stopped and the air was sucked out of her lungs. She could not have been more shocked or stunned if someone had punched her in the face.

Abbie turned and walked into the cabin. *Pa . . . Bobby Lee . . . my future . . . gone. Utterly dead. Snuffed out.* She walked to the hearth and leaned her head against the mantel. *Nothin' on this earth will ever be the same for any of us ever again.*

She felt unspeakably empty—as if a bottomless dark cavern opened in her heart and a frigid wind began to blow through. She slowly reached up to her grandmother's mantel clock, opened the glass door, and stopped the pendulum. Later she would go to her mama's cedar storage box and pull out the black velvet cloth that would cover the clock for the next four weeks of mourning, but Abbie sensed the emptiness she now felt might never end.

Part Two

THURSDAY, MAY 13

through

FRIDAY, MAY 21, 1926

41

Packard

It was one of those spectacularly beautiful spring days in the Smokies, the time of year that ushered in longer days and noticeably warmer temperatures. Although the risk of a late frost remained, most of the trees along the Sugar Fork were budding out just fine.

Horace Kephart chose to walk the eight miles from his cabin high on the Little Fork to the depot below Proctor so that he would have time to process the shock of the deaths of Nate and Bobby Lee. He deeply enjoyed seeing and smelling the late entries to the spring-flower bloom, and today they were particularly therapeutic.

Since moving to the region nearly twenty-five years earlier, he had learned to love the flowers that told him summer was not far off and that the cold, hard winter was retreating into the past: hairy beardtongue, rattlesnake hawkweed, and squawroot, all lorded over by the glorious flame azaleas.

Nate and Callie Randolph were two of the first people he met in the area. They had readily welcomed him to Sugar Fork, and Nate even showed him the abandoned cabin on Little Fork, a couple of miles above their place, into which he settled. They often provided meals and fellowship for him during the three-year period he was mourning his own losses of career and family.

Years earlier, Kephart had developed a taste and fondness for alcohol, which led to a depression and personality changes that severely strained his marriage. Then a debilitating season of mental illness led his dear wife to take their six children back to her home in Utica, New York. It also cost him his job as one of the nationally renowned directors of the St. Louis Mercantile Library in Missouri, the oldest and most prestigious library west of the Mississippi.

During his recovery, he often remembered the year he spent in Italy cataloging Willard Fiske's enormous collection of Italian manuscripts at the Villa Forini in Florence. He spent many afternoons and evenings taking hikes in the Apennines and Alps, which left him with a yearning for the wild and romantic. This led him to want to go someplace where he could realize the past in the present—what he called *the back of beyond*: somewhere he could step shortly from the railway to the primitive and into a paradise. He wanted to see with his own eyes what life must have been like for his pioneer ancestors of a century or two before.

Kep searched through piles of maps representing every known wilderness in the country, and it was from these that he had picked out the Smoky Mountains, where the narrow valleys directly sprung into mountains with slopes rising at twenty to forty degrees or more. It was here he hoped for healing, for his own rebirth and revival.

The Randolphs had become an anchor for him. Losing Callie had been hard on him. The passing of Nate weighed even more heavily—on every part of his soul. He always loved the Randolph children and now he vowed to increase his efforts to watch over and protect them.

Even though most of the massive virgin trees in his beloved Hazel Creek were gone, cut down in their prime, like Nate and Bobby Lee, the flowers spoke to him of a time when the valley might possibly be resurrected. It could not happen soon enough for him. He also vowed to redouble his efforts in Washington to have his beloved Smoky Mountains declared a national park, and this time he would dedicate his efforts to the memory of his friend Nate Randolph.

As Kephart neared the depot, his attention was attracted to a low rumble coming from the Bryson City road that passed behind the station. He suspected who might be coming based upon a message he received from Bryson City the previous evening. Sheriff Taylor had been kind enough to deliver the note.

Kephart slowly walked down the steps of the depot as a massive car topped a knoll and coasted down the hill to halt nearly at his feet. From the oversized whitewall tires to the perfectly polished metal and chrome to the overstuffed leather seats, front and back, the car practically oozed luxury.

"I'd recognize you most anywhere from your pictures in the newspapers," the plump, mustached driver said. "Horace Kephart!"

"You are indeed correct!" As they shook hands through the open window, Kephart could see the driver's jolly, rounded cheeks, almost a ruby red, and his finely tailored three-piece linen suit. His pearly white teeth stuck out slightly, making him look a bit like Teddy Roosevelt, whom Kep knew well.

The stranger replied, "I'm Luke Earnshaw. This is my dear wife, Candace."

Kephart bowed slightly toward the dainty blond in the passenger seat. She was wearing a light blue silk and ivory lace dress, and she slowly fanned herself. "I'm so sorry for your loss," Kep said.

"Thank you," Mrs. Earnshaw replied.

"I appreciate your sending the telegraph about Nate's untimely demise," Mr. Earnshaw continued. "Your offer to meet us here was most kind. Of course we left Raleigh as soon as we received the dreadful news. As I predicted in my wire to you, it took a couple of full days of driving to cover the two hundred miles, but this red beauty had no problem with the rougher roads, especially west of Asheville, I'll tell you that!"

"Our stay at the Fryemont Inn last night was lovely and allowed us to refresh," Mrs. Earnshaw added.

Kephart took a step back to admire the car that he knew was widely accepted as one of the Three P's of American motordom royalty, along with the Pierce-Arrow of Buffalo and the Peerless of Cleveland.

"I must say, Mr. Earnshaw, I've not seen a Packard since my last trip to testify in front of Congress. Looks to me to be the Twin-Six Touring version."

"I do say, my man! Why, I wouldn't expect a mountain man to recognize such a deluxity."

Kephart smiled at the made-up word Earnshaw used. "I do recognize a beautiful roadster when I see one."

"Have you ever ridden in a Packard?"

"I have. In fact, it was driven by none other than Alvan Macauley himself, the president of Packard."

"You know Mac?"

"Yes. We first met when he became president of Burroughs Adding Machine Company in St. Louis, before he moved the company to Detroit. I assisted him with some of his patent research."

Earnshaw laughed. "Why, Mac and I served together on the board of the National Automobile Manufacturers Association. Candace and I were with him when he was inducted into the Automobile Hall of Fame. He's taken Packard to number one. I wouldn't drive anything else."

"Ask the man who owns one," Kephart said, laughing, quoting the iconic Packard advertising slogan developed by Macauley himself.

"Gentlemen," Mrs. Earnshaw interjected, "Mr. Earnshaw has not driven me out from Raleigh to discuss automobiles. I have important family matters to see to."

"Indeed," her husband replied.

"Again, I'm sorry for your loss," Horace said. "Nate was a good man, a fine father, and a first-rate friend. I will miss him sorely."

"Thank you," Mrs. Earnshaw said. "Although I hardly knew him. Once I left Hazel Creek, he rarely wrote."

"Mrs. Earnshaw—"

"Please call me Candace."

Kephart nodded. "I've made reservations, as you requested, in the Clubhouse. Nancy Cunningham, the proprietor, is expecting you."

"We best go up to the farm first. I'd like to see my nieces."

"Yes, dear," Mr. Earnshaw said as he reached back to open the rear door. "Hop in the back, Kephart. We'll need you to show us the way up to Nate's farm. We've not seen the girls or the farm in several years."

Kephart opened the door and settled into the plush backseat as Earnshaw gunned the car forward and turned up the Hazel Creek road. When they reached Proctor, Kep watched the townspeople staring at the touring vehicle with looks of astonishment and envy. He was sure none of them had ever seen such a sight, except in magazines or the moving-picture show.

Candace turned back to Kep. "We're here to help the girls. I want to be sure they are cared for properly."

"Darling," her husband responded, "we've talked about this a hundred times. The girls are underage. The law requires that they go to an orphanage. There's no other choice."

"Unless we take them in. Luke, we're their only living relations. We could adopt them," she said.

Her husband turned to her. "We can't take them to raise, not with four children of our own. However, the Masonic orphanage in Oxford is close and the fees there are paid by the state, which, I might add, has no trouble taking our money in the form of taxes. We'll be able to visit them, and them us, often. That strikes me as more tolerable than sending them to Nate's distant relatives over in Cades Cove, who are pure primitives, if you ask me."

She nodded and turned to look across the valley.

Kephart listened with interest. He already had a plan for the girls and the farm, but it was not yet time to share it. He knew he had to keep it to himself, while he hoped against hope that the details would work themselves out.

42

Aloof

Maria looked helpless as she surveyed the table. She had warmed and served lunch to the girls from the food brought by friends, but trying to get them to eat more than a few bites was proving futile. They just picked at their food. She turned, almost by habit, to the mantel clock to check the time, but its pendulum was still, its ticktock silenced, and its face draped with a black cloth.

Abbie was glad Maria had insisted that her pa's body not stay in their home, as was the custom and as they had done with her ma's body. Pastor Semmes agreed, so the wake was at the church, a decision Abbie felt was best for the younger girls and their tender senses. They also agreed that the funeral service and burial would be put off until their closest relatives, the Earnshaws, arrived from Raleigh.

The churchwomen had brought more food than the girls could eat in a month. Anything that would keep was stored in the springhouse or smokehouse. Sandy Rau and her girls had been there since the news of Nate's death, but Maria sent them home for the afternoon. They would be back to stay the evening and night, which would allow Maria some time away, to herself. Abbie knew that Maria's heart was broken over Zach's loss.

Whit turned from the table and was patting Lilly's head as the dog whined. "She misses Pa."

Abbie, who was trying to bear up the best she could, walked over by Whit, stroked Lilly's coat, and looked at Corrie. "We'll have to take her huntin'. That'll make her happier."

Whit looked up at Abbie, large tears falling from both eyes. "But what will make *us* happy, Abbie? When will *we* ever be happy again? I'm so sad that I don't know if the hole in my heart will *ever* heal."

Abbie sat next to Whit and pulled her close.

"What will become of *us*, Abbie?" Whit asked.

Corrie was rocking Sarah Beth. She looked out the door. "I hear a car."

Anna leaped up from the table and ran to the door. "It's the biggest car I've ever seen."

Maria stood beside Anna. "Looks like Kep . . . and some other people."

"Are they coming to take us?" Anna asked.

"What makes you think anyone is going to take you?" Maria asked.

"Emily Rau said her pa told 'em the law's gonna make us go to an orphanage," Anna answered, "'cause that's what we are now . . . orphans."

Maria put her arms around Anna. "Not if Maria has anything to do with it, honey."

"It's not the law drivin' that big ol' car," Abbie said as she looked out the door. "It's Uncle Luke and Aunt Candace from Raleigh. Mr. Kephart let them know 'bout Pa. Aunt Candace is Pa's youngest sister. She's our nearest blood kin."

Abbie saw a lanky arm waving to them from the backseat of the car as it pulled to a stop in front of the cabin.

Kephart unfolded himself from the backseat and quickly walked up to the cabin as Corrie put down her baby sister and ran to give him a long hug.

"Am I still your favorite, Mr. Horace?" Corrie asked.

"Always have been, always will be." He returned her hug as he looked up at Abbie and Whit, who had been joined by Maria at the door.

"Your aunt and uncle are here from Raleigh," Kep said as he left Corrie's embrace and walked up to the porch, hugging the older girls and greeting Maria before sitting down on a rocker and pulling out his pipe.

Luke exited the car and quickly walked around to open the door for his wife.

"Quite the gentleman," Corrie whispered sarcastically to Whit, who sniffled and blew her nose.

Aunt Candace walked around the car on her husband's arm and toward the cabin. Whit whispered, "She's got her some fancy britches, don't she?"

"You girls be nice!" Maria softly scolded.

The Earnshaws walked up the steps and stood in front of Abbie, looking her over from head to toe. "You're all grown up, Lauren!" Candace said. "And Darla Whitney, you're becoming a proper woman also. I declare, I haven't laid eyes on you girls in what, six years?"

As she lightly hugged them, Abbie found that she remembered few details of their prior brief visit, other than she had not particularly liked Uncle Luke and sensed he didn't like her or her family.

Aunt Candace turned toward her husband. "You girls remember your uncle Luke, don't you?"

"Faintly, Aunt Candace," said Abbie, "but I was a mite younger then."

In point of fact, the one thing Abbie remembered clearly was her parents being suspicious about Uncle Luke's motives for their only previous visit—misgivings that were amplified when Uncle Luke began asking about purchasing some of the family land, and even more when he began inquiring about their wills.

Wanting to avoid his hug, Abbie said, "We're just servin' lunch. We're havin' roast. Come in for a bite," as she turned and walked into the cabin.

As Uncle Luke entered, Abbie watched him scrutinize their cabin from the rafters to the floorboards. He exuded a disquieting dismay from his eyes, and suddenly Abbie remembered how he criticized her mama and pa for, as he said, "raising girls in such downright horrible circumstances." Her mama had cried on and off for days after the visit. Her pa said Luke would never be welcome back on his farm. *Now, here he is!*

Abbie had the girls arrange three new settings at the table while she served the roast on their finest tin plates. Corrie and Anna Kate poured mugs of cool tea.

Aunt Candace smiled as she commented on the meal. "Abbie, you're a wonderful cook. This roast is delicious."

"It was made by one of the women from our church," Abbie said, suppressing a smile as Uncle Luke glared at his wife. *He don't like her givin' appreciation to someone else. Why, I swan, if'n his eyes was huntin' knives, Aunt Candace would be mincemeat.*

43

Orphans

After the meal, Kep and the Earnshaws retired to the porch while Maria and the girls cleaned the table and washed the dishes. While they were finishing, Kep came into the cabin, walked to the kitchen area, and sat down.

"Gather round, girls," he whispered as he gestured toward the porch. "I don't want 'em to hear us."

Abbie and her sisters gathered close to him, their eyes expectant, while Maria stood behind. The girls had always admired Kep. After all, he made sure that each of them knew how to read and write long before their first day in school. He and Nate had spent countless hours on the porch discussing the ways their wilderness should be defended. Kep talked endlessly about his favorite causes: building an Appalachian Trail through the Smokies and preserving the Smoky Mountains as a national park. Their pa had worried that the government would try to take their family land in the event of the latter.

Kep would stop by on his frequent trips between his isolated cabin high up the Little Fork and his lodging at the Cooper House in Bryson City. He always had his typewriter and folding desk handy so that he could write stories about his wilderness adventures. He wrote a regular column in the *All Outdoors* magazine, which he claimed was the top sportsman's periodical in the country, and *Field & Stream* magazine. It was said the writing earned him a modest living. Kep and their pa would debate, talk, and josh each other for hours. Nate asked only that he never write about his family or his farm.

As Kephart knelt down, Maria whispered, "Horace Kephart, when you first arrived, I wondered if you now had a driver to escort you up and down Hazel Creek. I figured your books and articles must be making you a pile of cash."

Kep smiled and cleared his throat. "From your lips to God's ears, Maria." Then he looked around at each of the girls. "I want you to know that I've been talking with some of the folks up and down the valley. We're all going to be watching over you. The men, led by Sheriff Taylor and myself, are figuring out how to lease your pa's fields to men like Danya or Gabe Johnson to give you the income you'll need. Maria and Danya are willing to stay on as long as you need them. And the ladies, under the supervision of Etta Mae Barnes and Sandy Rau, are sorting out how to keep you fed and clothed. Of course, Grace Lumpkin has agreed to continue your Saturday tutoring and visit frequently during the summer. So you'll be seeing all of us much more often."

The younger girls began to smile and hop up and down with glee. "Girls, shh!" he cautioned as he paused for a moment. Abbie saw his eyes mist. "All of us are going to be here for you'uns. You all will be well cared for. You hear?"

"Oh, Mr. Kephart!" Corrie exclaimed with a hushed voice. "I'm so happy to hear it!"

"Me, too!" Whit and Anna whispered together.

Kep held out his arms and pulled Whit, Corrie, and Anna into a bear hug. Abbie leaned over and hugged his neck.

As he held the girls, he whispered, "Your uncle Luke says he wants to take you girls to the Oxford orphanage not far from Raleigh. He says that's so you'll be close to him. I think it's because he wants to sell the farm, or at least the timber rights."

Abbie stood. "Never!"

"Shh," Kephart cautioned, looking over his shoulder while holding a finger to his lips. He looked at the door of the cabin. There was only the sound of adults talking on the porch. "Your uncle feels you don't have much choice."

Corrie angrily whispered, "I ain't gonna go to no orphanage! He's got that fancy car and lots of money, but he's stingy!"

Abbie stood up. "Mr. Kephart, I promised Mama I'd take care of my sisters and this farm. I'm gonna do both."

Kephart smiled. "I like your spunk, Abbie. Now, I need to check out some things in Bryson City. But Mrs. Frye's got a mighty fine plan that she thinks will help keep you girls here"— Kephart looked at the door and then back at the girls—"and send the Earnshaws packing back to Raleigh with the backseat of their fancy car empty of any of my Randolph girls!"

The girls were all smiling from ear to ear as the gentleman hugged them close.

44

Faithful

After her sisters were asleep, Abbie sat in front of the fireplace trying to write in her journal. There were just no words. Her heart and soul alternated between a vast cold emptiness and a deep, throbbing ache. She felt as if her tear glands were so drained that she'd never be able to spill another tear ever again.

The only word that would surface, again and again, was *why, why, why?* There was no answer, just the awful sound of silence. She let out a long, slow breath as she looked into the remaining flame. *Mama always said,* she thought, *if you want to hear from the Lord, the best way is to look into his Word.*

She put down her journal and picked up her mama's Bible. After considering where to turn, she remembered a passage in the book of Lamentations. *A book about a people who survived weepin', grievin', and mournin'; that's what I need,* she thought. "The third chapter," she whispered to herself. Finding it, she read:

> *And thou hast removed my soul far off from peace: I forgat prosperity. And I said, My strength and my hope is perished from the* Lord: *Remembering mine affliction and my misery, the wormwood and the gall. My soul hath them still in remembrance, and is humbled in me.*
>
> *This I recall to my mind, therefore have I hope. It is of the* Lord's *mercies that we are not consumed, because his*

compassions fail not. They are new every morning: great is thy
faithfulness.

The Lord *is my portion, saith my soul; therefore will I hope in*
him. The Lord *is good unto them that wait for him, to the soul*
that seeketh him. It is good that a man should both hope and qui-
etly wait for the salvation of the Lord.

At that moment, a hymn bubbled out of her heart, and she
began to softly sing:

"Great is thy faithfulness," O God, my Father,
There is no shadow of turning with Thee;
Thou changest not, Thy compassions, they fail not
As Thou hast been Thou forever wilt be.

As her lips trembled and tears she didn't know she had left
streaked down her cheeks, she continued:

Summer and winter, and springtime and harvest,
Sun, moon and stars in their courses above,
Join with all nature in manifold witness
To Thy great faithfulness, mercy and love.

She wanted to continue, but her voice was cut off. *Where's your*
mercy and love when I need it? she prayed silently. *Where's your great*
faithfulness to me? How's it faithful for you to take my pa and my
Bobby Lee?

She tried once again to hum, but no sound would come. It was
as if her last breath had been taken, as if her very life were being
squeezed from her. She buried her head in her arms and began to
sob.

Just then, a sweet voice began behind her. She turned to see
Whit walking up behind her as she softly sang the chorus Abbie
could not:

"Great is thy faithfulness!"
"Great is thy faithfulness!"
Morning by morning new mercies I see;
All I have needed Thy hand hath provided—
"Great is thy faithfulness," Lord, unto me!

Whit knelt in front of her. "Abbie, remember the sermon Pastor Semmes gave us after Mama died?"

Abbie shook her head. "I'm not sure, Whit. I guess I'm not sure about anythin'."

"I hear ya, Abbie," Whit said. "You've had a lotta weight on your shoulders." She pulled up a chair beside Abbie. "If'n I remember right, Pastor Semmes told us that when the storms of life come, it's 'bout impossible to make sense of God or his promises. In the storm, almost nothin' makes sense."

"I think I remember," Abbie said. "Pastor said that when Pharoah threw Joseph in prison, Joseph forgot all about the promises God gave him in his dreams. There was *no* way a man in a dungeon could imagine becomin' a ruler over anythin'."

"That's right!" Whit said, looking intently into her sister's eyes. "Seems like we're in a terrible, horrible poke right now. But Pastor said, 'When you're in between the promise given and the promise fulfilled, don't try to figure out what God's doing.' Don't waste a lot of time with the *why* questions. God'll have to unfold our story his way, Abbie. Maybe in a way we could never figure. Meanwhile, we just gotta take one step at a time. Keepin' our eyes on him, our trust in him, claimin' that there is no storm what will keep God's promises for us from coming to pass."

Abbie nodded. "I hear you, Whit. I just don't know how."

"Oh, sister. I don't know how either, but the Bible says, 'In every thing give thanks.' I don't know if we'll ever *feel* thankful again, Abbie, but in faith we can give thanks."

"Without him," Abbie barely whispered, "there'd be no hope a'tall." The two of them hugged as they dissolved into sobs.

45

Grave

The large branches of the enormous chestnut tree at the top of the ridge seemed to funnel the breezes and cool the air that enveloped the Randolph family grave plot. Danya stopped his backbreaking labor to take a red bandana out of his overalls and wipe the sweat from his brow. He looked down at the flagstone covering Callie's grave, which was next to the flat stones covering the graves of her three little boys, and felt a profound gloominess.

"It's hard ground, isn't it, brother?" Maria said.

Danya nodded. The ground was nearly as hard for him as was dealing with the unexpected death of his employer, benefactor, and friend.

Maria had offered to help with the digging, but he would not hear of it. She was sitting on the stone wall surrounding the small family plot, her jet-black hair was pulled up into a bun, and she looked deeply saddened. Although she was taller than most women, today she looked small and delicate. He knew how, in a short period of time, she had also grown to admire and respect Nate Randolph, considering him a second brother. He knew that her heart was broken for Zach, the man she loved, and the immeasurable loss of his only child. Although Maria had the gift of prophecy, she hadn't been given a clue of the coming death of either. He wondered if she was secretly blaming herself.

He looked back at the pile of soil he'd shoveled out, knowing it would take quite some time to dig the six-foot-deep hole in this hard, rocky soil.

"It's a good thing that you did, Danya."

"But I have much more to dig," he said, gesturing at the shallow cavity in the ground.

"Not the grave . . . although that will be good also. I meant making Nate's coffin. It's beautiful."

"Mr. Barnes was kind to let me work at his side as he made Bobby Lee's coffin."

"Your carving on the sides of both coffins is beautiful."

"Mr. Nate and Bobby Lee will be comfortable on the soft cotton lining you put in their arks and with the small goose-down pillows," Danya said.

"I'm worried about the girls, especially Abbie," Maria said as she gazed across the almost undulating series of tree-clad ridges stretching northward toward Tennessee. "She's lost her mama, her pa, *and* her fiancé. I can't imagine how she's going to handle it all, especially at her tender age. And how will Kep help them keep the farm?"

"I don't know," Danya said as he sighed deeply.

"We have promised to stay on the farm to watch over them," Maria said. "That will help."

Danya nodded and then added, "I will pull our wagon close to their cabin each night. During the days, the girls will have many friends to watch over them. At night, Danya will watch."

Maria furrowed her brow. "I think the lumber company is going to come after them. My guess is that they will do almost anything to get the land."

The sound of someone approaching caused the brother and sister to turn their heads toward the path up the mountain. Two black men approached, walking quickly up the trail.

The larger of the two nodded as he approached. He reached down and opened the white picket gate to enter the small graveyard, while the smaller and more rotund of the men followed, carrying a pick and two shovels across his shoulder.

Danya reached out to shake hands with the first man. "Welcome, Gabe."

Gabe Johnson smiled. "Thought you could use a hand from me and Rick."

"Looks like Rick could use a hand from you," Danya observed.

"I lost a bet," the smaller man explained as he dropped the tools. "Should've never bet Gabe Johnson about Scripture. He always wins."

"I'm not sure the Lord would be happy with the two of you betting," Maria said. "The Bible frowns on gambling."

"We drew lots, Maria," Gabe quickly added. "Lot drawing is acceptable to the Lord. The Good Book says it in both the Old and New Testaments. So, Rick lost. And his duty was to carry the implements."

Suddenly a staccato chatter-burst of sound rang out from inside a patch of nearby rhododendron.

"Sounds like a wren," Gabe observed.

"Nope, that's a white-eyed vireo," Rick countered.

Gabe looked at Maria. "Don't bet Rick when it comes to birds. He can hear a bird sound and tell you the name of the bird, its sex, and whether it's feeling amorous or angry."

Rick smiled. "The white-eyed vireo is a little green bird that is almost impossible to see. It blends with the green leaves and bushes. It's got its own songs, but it can also copy the notes of some other birds. Still, it's a bird you hear more often than see."

"Like me?" came a deep resonant voice from the trees.

The group inside the fence looked toward the west as Maria stood. "Who's there?" she asked.

"Just me," said the bass voice from what now seemed to be the opposite direction. Their heads all whipped around as they turned toward the east side of the graveyard.

The two black men turned to face each other. Rick's eyes widened. "It's the Haint," he whispered.

"It ain't no Haint, Rick," Gabe said. "It's just old Jeremiah Welch." Then he walked to the eastern wall surrounding the small graveyard. "Come on out, old man. You're safe here."

The thin old man walked out of the woods between two large rhododendron bushes. His thick, uncombed gray hair streamed out in every direction, making his head look as large as a bear's. His face was smeared with what could be mistaken for white Pan-Cake makeup, and his eyes were open as wide as saucers. He was unshaven and unkempt, his black clothes hanging like limp curtains from his skinny body. But his ear-to-ear, albeit toothless, smile indicated friendly intentions.

"Welcome, Jeremiah," Gabe said. He smiled as he shook the old man's hand. "I swan. Seeing you like that would scare the ticks off'n a bear. You been followin' us awhile?"

The old man nodded.

"Guess you've been up in the Randolphs' kaolin pit," Rick said. "That clay on your face makes you 'bout the scariest lookin' person in these here mountains, that's for durn sure!"

Gabe added, "Why, you're the only man in these parts less welcome in a white person's home than me, ain't that true, Jeremiah?"

The man smiled and gently nodded.

Gabe turned to Danya. "Rick and I, we dug Callie's grave. It's mighty rocky soil. So we come to help you with the diggin'. You want to help, Jeremiah?"

The old man nodded again.

"That be all right, Danya?" Gabe asked.

"I would be very happy for the help!" Danya said.

Welch bowed slightly and entered the graveyard, walking up to the gypsy. "Danya," he said, "I will help you another way."

"How's that?"

"You will not be the only one to watch the girls at night. The Haint will watch also."

The large gypsy smiled and gently put his enormous hand on Jeremiah's thin shoulder. "Then, my new friend, we will have the night watch together. And now, we dig together."

Maria observed, "Never has a grave been dug by such a set of rejects and misfits! I think Nate would be pleased indeed."

The men picked up their heavy tools and continued their arduous work.

46

Interruption

Sheriff Zach Taylor stared doubtfully into the pot on the cookstove. Sweat was running off his forehead, for it had been an unusually warm day for May, and the cool of evening had only just begun.

There was a sudden knock on the front door. He walked to the door, drew it open, and was surprised to see Lillian Frye dressed in what appeared to be her Sunday best. "Why, Mrs. Frye. What brings you here?"

"Might I enter?"

"Yes, of course," Zach said.

Closing the door behind them, Zach gestured for her to have a seat in his small parlor. She looked down, opened her purse, and pulled out a small handkerchief.

"Zach," she began, "Captain Frye and I took the train from Bryson as soon as Mr. Kephart contacted us about the deaths. To say we're shocked would be a massive understatement." She looked up with tears in her eyes. "I know it's only been three days, Zach, but how are you doing? The only family member I've ever lost is my mother. I can't begin to conceive of losing a child, especially your only child. I can't imagine what you're going through."

Zach suddenly felt a strong rush of emotion as his chin dropped to his chest. "Lillian, I don't rightly know how I'm doin'. Lost the love of my life, my Hannah, only three years ago. Was cancer. Since then it's just been me and Bobby Lee. We both suffered with that loss, for we both loved her with all our hearts. He was growin' up so fast. Don't know if you're aware of it, but he and Abbie were engaged. Woulda been gettin' married soon. Feel like I've lost a son *and* a daughter-in-law."

He felt tears forming in his eyes and his lip tremble. "He was my only child, my only chance for grandchildren, my family's heritage. And now he's gone. Now he's been taken from me, stolen."

He felt the hot tears streaking down his cheeks and wiped his tears with the backs of his hands and sniffled before gathering his composure. "I've just started dinner, Lillian. There's plenty. Won't you have a bite?"

"No, thank you, Sheriff. Miss Cunningham will have dinner ready for Captain Frye and me at the Clubhouse in just a bit. But I did want to come by and extend my sympathies. I understand the funeral will be tomorrow?"

"Yes, up at Nate's church. The ceremony will be for them both. Nate will be buried in his family plot, Bobby Lee in the city cemetery next to his mother."

"The captain and I will be there."

"Thank you, Lillian. But I suspect there's another reason you're here."

"I'm not sure the time's right."

"I'm still the sheriff. If it's county business, consider me on duty for you."

Lillian nodded. "A couple of reasons, Sheriff. But first some background. When I passed the bar exam, many men in Swain County felt it was wrong for a woman to practice law. If it had not been for the support of my dear husband, it would have been a much more arduous path. Nevertheless, obtaining one's license to practice law does not guarantee one will actually do so. So the men who first gave me their business will always hold a special place in my professional heart."

Zach nodded.

"Nathan was one of those men. He and Callie had me handle their legal affairs, limited though they were. I would, at times, bring my daughter, Lois, out on the train to visit the Randolphs on their farm to discuss business. Lois and Abbie became friends. And recently, since Callie's death, when Nathan would travel to Bryson City to make his medicinal deliveries, he would drop by to visit us on the porch of our home next to the Fryemont Inn. During a recent visit Nathan shared with us a concern about his health."

Zach felt himself sit up. "How so? His back?"

"Not really, although it continued to bother him. He was much more concerned about his life—"

"Life?" Zach asked.

Lillian looked back at Zach. "In answer to your question, yes. He was worried that if his life was prematurely cut short, nefarious parties might use his untimely death as an opportunity to have his girls carted off to an orphanage, and then his property would have to be auctioned on the courthouse steps. Of course, he knew that arrangements would be made so there would only be one bidder."

"Calhoun?"

"Or a Calhoun employee. You can lay good money on that. I am suspecting, as are you, that this so-called accident was something else." She looked out the window for a moment and then turned and looked directly at Zach. "So, tell me what you know about the SBI investigation."

47

Investigation

"**N**o one is supposed to know about the investigation!" Zach exclaimed.

"And no one does, Sheriff, except the DA, the SBI, and me. As Nathan's attorney, I was questioned by the SBI. So I want to know what you know."

"As you know, Lillian, I cannot discuss an ongoing investigation—"

"As a member of the bar, and as the Randolphs' attorney, I have privilege. You may tell me what you know. It will stay with me."

Zach thought for a moment and then said, "Nate and Bobby Lee were murdered."

"Murdered?" Lillian exclaimed. "I thought so!"

Zach nodded. "When I heard about the accident, I went straight out thar. It was raining like cats and dogs. But the scene didn't seem right to me. There weren't no skid marks on the road. The car went off the road at a funny angle, and it didn't seem that it had been movin' too fast. Nate and Bobby Lee both looked like they'd been throwed from the truck, Nate one way, Bobby Lee the other. But the windows were up and the doors shut. Jest didn't seem right. Also, there were scratches on both their wrists. Looked to me like they musta been tied up. Near the road was a boulder I'd ne'er seen thar before. It was the durndest thing I'd ever seen. None of it made no sense—not a lick."

"What do you think happened?"

"I had a theory, so to prove it, I called over to the SBI."

"So, the sheriff from Bryson's not involved?"

"Of course he's involved. But he got mad as a hornet when he found out I had called the SBI on my own. Said I shoulda called him first, which is true. But I felt I needed outsiders looking this over. There's just too many connections between the lumber company and politicians in Swain County. No offense intended concerning your husband—I know he's tight in the political circles."

"None taken, Zach."

"Well, it turns out the SBI sent two agents from the Asheville office right quick and they figured out the boulder I had seen on the side of the road had been pushed into and then off'n the road—likely had been used as a roadblock. They think Nate's truck had been pushed right off'n the road, not a-driven off, and it woulda taken more than one man to do it. Besides finding a bunch of boot tracks I had overlooked, they found something else I completely missed."

"What?" Lillian asked.

"What I didn't see was that both of them had been shot from behind and in the head—gangland execution style, if'n ya ask me."

"Shot in the head? How could you have missed that, Zach? Weren't there entry and exit wounds?" Lillian asked. "Bullets to the head tend to be pretty gruesome and obvious." Lillian blushed. "I . . . er, I'm sorry, Zach. That wasn't very thoughtful of me."

"No apology necessary, Lillian. You're right. Except, in this case, the murderer used him a small caliber pistol, likely a .22. The entry wounds were small and their hair covered them. Also, there were no exit wounds."

"Wasn't there a lot of blood?"

"Wouldn't be with a .22. And their hair was brushed to cover over wounds. The SBI fellas say they was carried down the bank and throwed down by the truck—tried to make it look like they were thrown *from* the truck. Of course, them heavy rains wiped out any fingerprints and most of the boot prints."

"Any suspects?"

"The SBI and sheriff are workin' on it. But they've still got them a suspicion about who led the gang."

"It's got to be Sanders," Lillian said. "He's got the motive and the means . . . he's hired hit men in the past, and he's made more than one threat to Nate."

"Everyone knows that, Lillian, and the fact that he owns a pearl-handled .22 pistol, but . . ."

"Correct. Proving it is entirely another matter."

"Not necessarily," Zach said.

"What do you mean?"

"The SBI has them a new way to match bullets what's been shot to the gun that fired 'em. They call it ballistic fingerprintin'. As soon as I can git a court order, I can confiscate Sanders's pistol and let the SBI test it."

"I've not heard of this. How's it work?"

"It's pretty simple. Each gun's got one-of-a-kind scrapes in its barrel. Them scratches leave marks on a bullet when it comes out. So the SBI can shoot a bullet from a suspect's gun into a tub of water. That bullet is compared to a bullet taken from the victim and looked at under what they call a comparison microscope— one compared to the other. If'n they match, they know they've got them the murder weapon."

"When will you get the court order?" Lillian asked.

"Not sure," Zach said. "Judge Hughes seems to be holding up the investigation."

"I'm planning to discuss another matter with the judge. I believe I can speed up the process," Lillian said.

"That would be good," Zach said. "And I think it best that for now we let the Randolph girls continue to believe it was an accident."

Lillian nodded. "But couldn't Sanders potentially harm those girls?"

"Not even a snake like him would try that," Zach said. "He's taken Nate outta the way. That's all he needs to get the property and trees. Ain't no sense him harmin' them girls."

She narrowed her eyes. "I'm not so sure about that. Well, as you continue your inquiry, I'd appreciate you keeping me informed."

Zach nodded. "You said you had a couple of things for me. Anything else?"

"I hate to ask, in the midst of your terrible loss, but I do need your help on another matter."

48

Loophole

Lillian Frye took a deep breath. "Okay, Zach. I'm not sure it's in complete compliance with the spirit of the law, but it's certainly in line with the letter of the law."

"What? I don't understand," Zach said.

"I have a plan to protect those girls and their farm," Lillian said.

"How do you propose doing that?" Zach asked. "Won't the state declare them orphans? Put them under the guardianship of Nate's sister?"

"It's best, for now, for everyone to think that. But I have an idea. A quite clever one, if I do say so myself," Lillian said.

"Consider me curious, counselor," Zach said, leaning forward.

"The last time I saw Nate alive, he and Mr. Kephart were visiting with the captain and me. It turns out that Mr. Kephart, in one of his trips to Washington, learned of an interesting legal case in Virginia that he thought might be of help to Nate in the event of his demise before Abbie would be considered an adult under the law."

"Case?"

"Yes. Apparently a family of boys was orphaned in the Blue Ridge Mountains, out in the Shenandoahs somewhere. Turns out the fifteen-year-old obtained a legal driver's license from the sheriff of their county. Under Virginia law, a person with a driver's license is considered emancipated, recognized as an adult.

Therefore, the state did not have to send the younger boys to an orphanage, as the oldest boy was legally pronounced the guardian of his brothers and the family estate."

Astonished, Zach shook his head. "Lillian, what do the statutes of North Carolina say?"

She smiled. "In this respect, our laws are identical."

"You mean Abbie could be declared an adult—she could be certified as the guardian of her sisters and the family farm?"

"I've been able to discuss the matter with Judge Hughes at our inn, privately, of course, and I should add, he'll be attending the funeral. Anyway, our discussion occurred during a break in his weekly poker game up at the inn, and while, I might note, he was partaking of a medicinal beverage delivered by Doc Bennett. He says it helps calm his nerves as he plays."

"Medicinal beverages bein' legal under North Carolina statute, correct?"

The attorney smiled. "Correct. And, indeed, I was told by the good judge that should I make such a request of the court, the likelihood of successful petition is virtually assured."

"I think I'm realizin' why you might be visitin' me. So how can I help?"

"As you suspect, I need an agent of the law to issue a legal driver's license to one Miss Lauren Abigail Randolph, once she's been properly taught to drive, that is."

"Why, Lillian, she's driven with her daddy since he worked at the livery," Zach explained. "Everyone in Proctor knows she can drive."

"Good enough to get a license?"

"More than good enough. Better than most men out here," Zach added.

"Can you issue her a license?"

Zach felt himself grinning like a Cheshire cat and said, "Does a black bear have ticks? You can bet yer bottom dollar I can! Will get it done before the next new moon."

"Which is when?"

Zach smiled. "Tomorrow."

Lillian laughed. "Thank you, Zach. If you would be so kind as to drop it by the Clubhouse, I'll be sure to deliver it to Abbie when the time is appropriate." Lillian gave him a warm look and a brief smile, then stood. "Well, I must go now."

Zach stood and accompanied her to the door. Before leaving she turned. "I'm so very, very sorry about your loss, Sheriff. I can't tell you how grieved I am for you."

Zach nodded. "Thank you, Lillian."

"Will you let me know if there's anything I can do for you?"

"I will, Lillian. Thanks."

49

Bunnies

The pallbearers for the funeral of Nathan Hale Randolph and Robert E. Lee Taylor stood outside the church waiting for the arrival of the Randolph girls. The men were wearing white shirts and dark trousers, all had on a tie or a bowtie, and all looked more than a little uncomfortable in their formal clothes.

The group, consisting of Tom Rau, Millard Barnes, Jonathan and James Walkingstick, Horace Kephart, and Danya Petrov, slowly shifted their stances under a flawless Carolina blue sky.

"Glad it ain't raining today," Millard said finally. "It's mighty bad to have to put somebody away when it's raining."

"That's right," Jonathan, the elder Cherokee, said. "It's as good a day for it as could be."

"I'm fearful for the girls," James said, almost to himself.

"Why's that?" Kep said.

James thought for a moment and then, in a soft voice, said, "They're a bit like bunnies in clover."

The other men looked at one another for a moment, until Millard spoke. "What in the tarnation do you mean, son?"

James looked across the meadow, which stretched to a broad bend in Hazel Creek that was cutting into a steep bank.

"Just below my cabin in Qualla, there is a family of rabbits that inhabits the rhododendrons and flame azaleas at the edge of the meadow. The male and female seem to be mated for life. I've seen them several years. Each year they have anywhere from three to six kits in each litter. Those little bunnies are born blind and helpless, and they are fed and protected by their parents."

James was quiet for a moment, continuing to gaze across the meadow. "This spring they had five babies. They'd come out of the burrow into the clover at the edge of the meadow to eat. Usually the mother and father would be there to warn them of any predators. But I haven't seen the father or mother rabbit in a couple of days. I'm fearful something got them."

He took a deep breath and slowly let it out. "If neither parent is left, I think it's only a matter of time before the predators start picking the babies off. Maybe a hawk will snatch one, or an owl. Or the bobcat that lives nearby could chase another down. I'm not sure they're going to survive."

"Young bunnies in clover," Millard sighed. "Guess they don't really stand much chance."

No one said anything else until finally Kep looked up and said, "You men ever hear of the old children's stories about Br'er Rabbit?"

The men nodded but looked confused.

"Br'er Rabbit's a character who, according to his creator, Uncle Remus, succeeds through his wits and wisdom rather than through strength. Most people don't know this, but the Uncle Remus stories actually originated with the Cherokee people."

Tom looked surprised. "That a fact?"

"Am I right, Jonathan?" Kep asked.

Jonathan nodded. "But in the Cherokee tale of the Briar Patch, it's the fox and the wolf who throw the rabbit into a thicket. The rabbit, we call him *tsi-s-du,* escapes, but only because of the help he gets from his friends."

"So, I get it. You're saying they'll be all right," Danya said, "with help."

"I can assure you they're gonna get the help they need," Kep said.

"I think maybe their uncle's gonna try to take care of 'em," Millard muttered, "or rather, try to take everythin' them girls got."

"Nate told me about Earnshaw," Tom responded. "Said he's so tight he breathes through his nose to keep from drying out his false teeth."

Millard spoke up: "Nate said his sister ain't that way, though. He believed her to be a good woman. She'll see to it that the girls get taken care of."

"Well, she doesn't need to," Kep said. "I reckon we sure enough can."

"And will!" said Tom.

Millard looked up suddenly and said, "Look. Here come the girls." Everyone turned to look as Maria's and Grace's carriages pulled up in front of the church. They watched the girls get out along with Grace and Maria. Seeing that Abbie was carrying Sarah Beth, he shook his head. "That Abbie, she's got an awful big load to carry."

"She's got resolve," Kep said. "She'll get out of the Briar Patch with a little help."

"These'll be five bunnies what will make it," Tom said. "I can guarantee it."

"Come on," Kep said. "We'd better get in there."

50

Prediction

Andrew Keller was sitting with William Calhoun and his wife on one side and Wade Chandler on the other, toward the back of the church. Wade was using the funeral fan he was handed when he entered the church—it had a picture of an angel guiding two children across dangerous mountainous paths.

"I've been studying the pews as they've been filling up," Calhoun said. "I've been noticing the line on the top of every center pew."

Keller saw that the pews were stained dark walnut, but there was a four-inch section marked by lighter wood all the way from the back to the front. He was using another of the fans, this one with a picture of Jesus talking to a small group of children.

"You know what those marks are for?" Calhoun whispered.

Keller nodded. "There used to be a board all the way from the back to the front dividing the pews."

"What for?"

"Men sat on the right side, women sat on the left. That's not been too long ago, either."

Keller shifted in his seat uncomfortably. The backs were exactly at a ninety-degree angle from the seats, which forced him to sit up straight. "These benches must have been designed for the Spanish Inquisition. I can't imagine sitting in one for a long sermon."

"I expect the Randolph girls are going to have to sell their place to us," Calhoun whispered. "No way they can farm it themselves. With what I'll pay them, they should get enough money to take care of their needs for many years to come. Talk is they're being taken to an orphanage near Raleigh."

"Couldn't the neighbors help them out?" Wade asked softly.

"Two problems with that," Calhoun replied. "Number one, the rumors circulating say the law is they'll need to be placed in an orphanage, at least until they are adults, unless blood relatives take them in. Second, you've got a flawed opinion of people. Most people aren't that good, Wade. Oh, they may help for a few weeks, but then the help will fade off into the sunset; they won't stick with it."

Wade added, as quietly as he could, "I hope you're wrong, Mr. Calhoun. Dr. Keller tells me that the best he's seen of humanity is around here. When somebody's house or barn burns down, everybody rushes over to take care of the folks who lost everything."

Calhoun looked around at the congregation and shook his head sadly. "Here's my prediction. People will help for a few weeks, Wade, but here we're talking about a lifetime. They'll fall off the job like fleas off a dipped dog. I don't for one minute—"

He broke off suddenly and turned to look toward the front of the church. "Here they come. Breaks your heart to see them, doesn't it?"

51

Onlookers

Reverend Willie Semmes was sitting on the front platform. He looked at the small chalkboard on the side of the church. At the top he had written, "The Fourteenth Day of May, in the year of our Lord, 1926." Below were the numbers for the hymns they would sing.

He looked down upon the beautiful hand-carved coffins in front of him. As people arrived, they went to the open caskets to view the bodies and say their good-byes. Some were somber, others cried. Some left mementos beside the bodies, and others knelt to pray for a moment.

Pastor Semmes looked quickly over the congregation, noting Calhoun and his wife, Louise, sitting by Dr. Chandler and Dr. Keller. Sandy Rau and her children, along with Etta Mae Barnes, were in their usual pews, as was Nancy Cunningham.

He was surprised but pleased to see a contingent of Bryson City's finest were in the church, including Mayor Harold Jenkins, his wife, and his lovely daughter. Blanche kept shooting furtive glances at the young Dr. Chandler, who pretended not to notice as he continued to be engaged in whispered talk with Calhoun and Keller. Kelly Bennett, the pharmacist, and his father, general practitioner Dr. A. M. Bennett, were in their Sunday finest. Judge John Hughes sat beside Captain and Mrs. Amos Frye and their daughter, Lois. In another row was the sheriff from Bryson City and several of his deputies, all in their dress uniforms. The sheriff sat by the county clerk, Samuel Robinson.

His gaze then went to the Earnshaws, Candace and Luke. The woman was weeping already, but Luke Earnshaw was as expressionless as a sphinx. A bitterness came over Semmes as he recalled talking to Luke Earnshaw, trying to determine if the man would help the Randolph girls. He was convinced that any help from that quarter seemed unlikely. Mrs. Earnshaw was willing enough, but Luke believed men should rule women, almost as if they were serfs. All that Luke Earnshaw had offered was to try to get the five girls admitted to the Masonic Orphanage in Oxford. In point of fact, as their guardian-to-be, he was insisting upon it.

Semmes scanned the small balcony of the church. Several black families had asked to attend. He saw Rick and Linda Pyeritz, and almost imperceptibly nodded at Gabe and Reba Johnson. Gabe nodded back. Then another figure silently entered the balcony to stand beside Gabe. His face had no paint, but Semmes knew instantly from the gangly frame and disheveled hair that it was Jeremiah Welch. Semmes dropped his eyes so as not to draw attention to the balcony. He knew that the presence of the actual Sugar Fork Haint would unnerve many of the mourners.

A sin eater like Jeremiah was *never* to be seen in public. Sin eaters were social misfits or beggars who made their living via an ancient pagan ritual that was said to have begun centuries before in Scotland and Ireland and was brought over to the Appalachian Mountains. Often among the folks who didn't attend church, when a highlander was dying, someone in the family would hire the sin eater to come to his home. A relative would place a piece of bread on the chest of the dying person and pass a small cup of wine over the body to the sin eater. He would recite an ancient prayer, then eat the bread and drink the wine. It was believed that this ceremony would remove all the sins from the dying person and put them into the sin eater.

Although Semmes had severe difficulties with the theology

Jeremiah represented, he was pleased to actually see him at the service. Semmes heard that Nate had befriended Jeremiah. Now he knew for sure.

As the door at the back of the church opened, Semmes stood up, indicating to the congregation that they should do the same as Zach led in the Randolph girls followed by Grace and Maria.

Abbie was first, carrying Sarah. Zach and the girls sat on the front pew, while Grace and Maria joined the Earnshaws on the second. As the group took their places, everyone remained standing. Only after they were settled did Pastor Semmes nod to the pallbearers, who had entered the back of the church, indicating for them to come in and be seated on the other front pew opposite Zach and the girls. The six men would serve as the pallbearers for both coffins. When they were at their designated pew, Semmes gestured, and everyone sat.

Then the pastor straightened himself, ashamed of his doubts about how the girls were going to make it. *God's able!* he thought. *Nothing is impossible with him. And these church members will help these girls, or I'll scorch their behinds!*

52

Heaven

A bbie sat Sarah Beth beside her on the pew. On Abbie's other side, Corrie sat pressed close, with Whit and Anna flanking them. Abbie sat stiffly, her mind almost paralyzed.

She looked down and saw Sarah Beth smiling, and put her hand lightly on the child's head. *You don't know you've lost your pa,* she thought. *It'll come to you soon enough.*

Abbie remembered the pain she had experienced with the losses of her mother and three brothers. She actually envied little Sarah Beth, who was not old enough to realize the enormousness of what was happening. Even so, Abbie found herself functioning almost unconsciously. She had gone to bed, risen, and eaten without even thinking about it. Today she kept all her tears and fears buried deep in her heart.

She glanced up from Sarah Beth and saw that Anna's face was white and that she sat upright. Looking down, she saw Corrie with her jaws clenched tightly, looking at her hands, and on the other side Whit, who looked exhausted. Whit had cried all night, and Abbie now wished she had sat next to her so she could put her arm around her. Abbie's own lack of sleep made her groggy, and her mind was weary of trying to think of ways that she and her sisters could cling to the farm and try to survive. But even if she could figure that out, she had *no* idea if she would have the energy or drive to do so.

Maybelle Semmes began playing the piano, and the small choir began to sing. The fact that they sang her father's favorite hymns only made things worse. When they sang, memories flooded Abbie's mind. She could remember sitting on their front porch just a week ago singing this with their pa.

What a friend we have in Jesus, all our sins and griefs to bear.
What a privilege to carry everything to God in prayer.

As they sang "Rock of Ages," tears began to fall from Abbie's eyes. She blinked them away fiercely and clenched her hands together until they were white with the strain.

Finally, Reverend Semmes came and stood before the congregation, just behind the coffins. He opened his large black Bible and read, "These are the words of our Lord: 'Let not your heart be troubled: ye believe in God, believe also in me. In my Father's house are many mansions: if it were not so, I would have told you. I go to prepare a place for you. And if I go and prepare a place for you, I will come again, and receive you unto myself; that where I am, there ye may be also.'"

Closing the Bible, Semmes looked out over the congregation. His voice was soft and gentle as he said, "Jesus came to redeem sinners. He's the friend of sinners, and as the song we've just sung indicates, we have a *real* friend in him.

"Jesus made us fit fer heaven by dyin' on that ol' cross. Each of you'uns know how hard his sufferings were: ya've heard of the nails in his hands, the crown of thorns hammered into his head, the scourgin' and the beatin's, the crowd cussin' and a-mockin' him, even his own Father turnin' his back on him. It was the hardest thing any man e'er endured, bearin' the sins of the world—of each of us. But he did much more fer us than jest make us fit for heaven. He made heaven fit fer us. He said that in his house thar are many mansions, and for over two thousand years now he's been gittin' that home ready for each of us who follow him."

His voice grew even softer, and he looked at the five Randolph girls and Zach. "Our departed brother, your pa, has gone on up to live with your ma"—Semmes looked at Zach—"and yer dear son has gone on up to live with yer beloved Hannah." The pastor then looked across his congregation. "They are all in that special mansion with their Lord and Savior. Not a one of us can even begin to 'magine how wonderful heaven's gonna be. I 'spect it's far more excitin', more beautiful, and more glorious than any of us can conjure up in our mind. Whatever ya think about heaven, it's better than that, because it was made by almighty God hisself. The same God what made the beauty of these here Smokies, done made heaven. It don't make no sense it ain't even prettier than here."

Semmes smiled and then said, "The picture lots of folks have 'bout heaven is of a big ol' crowd, millions of people, standing before a throne, liftin' their voices, worshipin' their God and singin' hymn upon hymn for thousands of years without end—while a bunch of little bitty angels are sittin' around on clouds a-playin' thar harps. Now I like hymn sings as much as the next fella, but for ten thousand years? That wouldn't be fer me, I tell ya!"

There were muffled chuckles across the crowd as Semmes continued, "Now, maybe heaven'll have some o' that, but thar ain't gonna be only a new heaven, but Scripture says thar's gonna be a new earth. You think it were beautiful out here before"—Semmes looked down at Mr. Calhoun for a moment—"in the past, you ain't seen nothin' compared to what the new earth's gonna look like. But thar's somethin' else ya need to know 'bout heaven, fer thar's another aspect of our home in heaven that Nate and Bobby Lee are seein' fer themselves right now."

He paused, trying to gather his thoughts. "Let's see if'n I can explain it this a-way. What was the best times the Lord Jesus had on this earth? I think it were when he sat down with Mary, Martha, and Lazarus and ate dinner with 'em, talkin' with them he loved, while sittin' around a fire or a dinner. And think of the Last Supper, how downright friendly that time was. Jesus, he a-washed the feet of the disciples. 'Member how John was leanin' against Jesus with his head right thar on Jesus' chest? You cain't get any more personal than that! Well, I believe that every one of us who loves Jesus, when we go to be with him, we'll have some time jest like that—a time when he'll jest a-look deep into our eyes and speak to us, jest to us. One on one. Private. Fer no one else. And ya know what? We'll be able to talk with him. We'll have us a grand ol' discussion. We'll be able to ask whatever we want. And he'll take all the time we need to answer us. And finally, we'll understand. We'll understand why everything was the way it was. And we'll see that from his perfect perspective, it were all perfect. Ever'thing.

"Well, I believe heaven's gonna be something jest like that. I can imagine Jesus puttin' his big ol' arms around our loved ones and saying, 'Well done, Nate, well done, Bobby Lee. Good job, you two.' I choose to believe that right now our brothers are walkin' and talkin' with their friend and their lord, Jesus. And you can believe this: thar's no place they'd rather be.

"And you'uns may think the Randolph girls have lost their pa. But they ain't—not really. Because when you've lost somethin', you jest don't know where it is, or ya forgot where it were. But we all know where Nate is right now. As true as that is, though, these here girls have now become orphans—at least here on earth. And I'm gonna tell ya this: God hisself takes a very special interest in orphans."

The pastor opened his Bible. "The word of the Lord, as recorded by Moses himself, says, 'Ye shall not afflict any widow, or fatherless child. If thou afflict them in any wise, and they cry at all unto me, I will surely hear their cry.'" Semmes looked straight at Calhoun. "If I were to set out to afflict someone, it wouldn't be no widow or orphan, for God hisself has vowed to take vengeance on anyone who offends 'em. You can mark that down!"

Now Semmes looked over the congregation and said firmly, "Many of you'uns here are members of this church, which was

Nate and Callie's church as well. I charge ya before yer God that these girls are *our* responsibility, and I promise ya, before these witnesses and the Lord God hisself, Abbie, Whit, Corrie, Anna Kate, and you, little Sarah Beth, will never know want as long as I'm pastor of this here church. And if'n I leave, the church itself will be a father and a mother to ya! So help me God!"

53

Outflanked

Zach Taylor was about as comfortable as a fish out of water. He was sitting in the front parlor at the Clubhouse, surrounded by a group that actually seemed to enjoy the little cups of tea and crustless finger sandwiches, all of which made him feel like a sissy.

After Miss Cunningham had served them and the men lit their cigars or pipes, Luke Earnshaw patted Willie Semmes on the shoulder, saying, "Pastor, that was a mighty fine funeral service."

"Thank you, Mr. Earnshaw. Those girls mean the world to me, and Bobby Lee was as fine a young man as there could be. My heart's plumb broken for the girls and for you, Zach."

"Thanks, Pastor," Zach said.

"The graveside service was even more inspirational," Candace Earnshaw added. "Although my legs are still aching from the climb up to and then down from that frightfully high ridge."

"You're not the only one, Mrs. Earnshaw," Grace Lumpkin said. "I may not be able to move tomorrow."

"Me neither," said Lillian Frye. "Reverend, you about walked my legs off."

"It was hard seein' my son laid next to his mama," Zach added. "I've seen other parents bury their kids over the years, more than I want to count, but nothin' hurts like having to bury your own. Nothin'."

"Mrs. Semmes and I know 'bout that type of pain," the pastor commented. "Buryin' Rafe's older brother, our firstborn, 'bout did us in, Zach. Our healin' is *still* going on. And yours will be for a long time, also. We'll be prayin' for ya, but even more important, we'll be here for ya."

"I appreciate that, Pastor, more than you'll ever know." Zach put down his teacup. "But now I need to transition from a grievin' father to the deputy sheriff, if'n that's all right with everyone."

There were nods all around.

"Mrs. Frye and I had a reason to call you together." Zach knew this was not going to be a comfortable discussion, but in his work, he was in this territory often. "Mrs. Frye, the floor is yours."

Lillian put her cup down and began. "I know we all care for those girls like they were our own. I thought we should discuss how they are going to be cared for in the future. I suspect with this many different folks, we'll have a variety of thoughts."

There were fewer nods this time, but Luke gave the strongest one.

"Mr. Earnshaw, being Mrs. Earnshaw is the closest kin to the girls, what are your thoughts?" Lillian asked.

Luke put down his cup and cleared his throat. He looked at his wife. "We're thinking it best to take them back to Raleigh with us—"

"Luke," Candace interrupted, "we've *not* decided this yet—"

"We know of your *real* plans, Earnshaw," Kep chimed in, his eyes hard and narrowed as he glared at Luke. "You want the Randolph land as much as Calhoun himself does."

"That's *not* true!" Luke roared, sitting up as his face turned beet red.

Candace put her hand on his leg, trying to calm him down. "Mrs. Frye, we're most concerned that the girls not be separated, that they remain a family."

"That's good," Lillian said. "I know that to be the final wish of their mother *and* their father."

"As you likely know, Mr. Kephart," Luke said as he calmed down, "the girls are all underage. The law *requires* that they go to an orphanage, if no blood kin will take them in. Isn't that true, Mrs. Frye?"

Zach could see a wry smile on Lillian's lips. "Actually, Mr. Earnshaw, the older girls tell me that they have no interest in going to live with *you* or in an orphanage. And they have no desire to see their farm or its timber rights sold."

"But they're underage!" Luke exclaimed as his face flushed once again.

"No need for anyone to raise their voices," Zach said. "I actually think I can arrange for blood kin to care for the girls—"

"Not those primitive hicks and hillbillies who live over in Cades Cove!" Luke roared. "They're distant, distant relatives. *We're* the girls' closest blood. And *we'll* take them where we dadblame consider best."

"We should take them into our family, Luke," Candace implored.

"Actually," Lillian said, "the girls would prefer to have another relative, a closer kin, care for them."

Luke could not have looked more stunned if he had been thrown off a horse. "But *we're* their closest real blood," he said, the veins in his neck and face bulging.

"You better explain it to him," Willie Semmes said to Lillian, "before Mr. Earnshaw has a coronary."

For the next few minutes Lillian explained the law concerning the driver's license and her petition to Judge Hughes for Abbie to become legal guardian of her sisters and owner of the farm. She then explained about the trust she had just filed that week in the courthouse for the girls, that Reverend Semmes, Mr. Kephart, and she would serve as trustees for the girls, and that the trust should be approved and activated in just a week or two.

Grace then explained how the School Board was going to see that the Randolphs continued to have special tutoring each weekend for the younger girls. "Abbie," Grace explained, "has been given a special exemption by the School Board and will be allowed to graduate from high school in two weeks."

Zach watched Luke as he began to realize he'd been out-flanked. The girls and their farm would be saved from a family takeover. Zach just hoped he could protect them from Calhoun and, in particular, Sanders. He hoped his meeting with the SBI on the following Monday would give him some assistance in that duty.

54

Numb

Abbie felt so weak she could hardly move as she stepped inside their home. She hesitated for one moment, not knowing whether she could even take another step, much less finish the rest of the day.

The funeral was over, as was the steep walk down to the farm from the graveside service underneath the towering chestnut. As if that weren't difficult enough, she, Whit, Corrie, and Maria then traveled to town to attend Bobby Lee's burial, while Tom, Sandy, and Emily Rau stayed at their cabin with the younger girls.

But when they returned home, there was no time to rest, as many folks were at the cabin to greet them. The last of the people coming by to whisper words in Abbie's ear had already been forgotten, as she was too numb to hear or understand any of what they said. She was appreciative, but exhausted in every way. She hoped all of the events of the day were finally over.

"Here, lemme have that young'un." Emily Rau stood before her. She reached down and took Sarah Beth and cuddled her. "I'll change her. You need to go to bed yourself. You're plumb played out. In a bit, me and Ma will take Sarah Beth to be with us in the room across the dogtrot."

"Thank you, Em." Abbie watched as her friend took Sarah Beth and began to change her. Maddie, Sandy, and Maria were cleaning up in the kitchen. Abbie turned to face the other girls. They all had a lost look in their eyes, and Abbie said, "Y'all held up fine, every one of you. I'm right proud. Mama and Pa would be, too."

"What are we gonna do, Abbie?" Whit whispered. Her face was white as chalk, and the tearstains on her cheeks were evident.

Abbie went over and put her arm around Whit. "We'll be all right," she whispered. "You just wait and see."

At that moment, the girls heard the sound of a car. Abbie walked to the door and looked out to see the fancy Packard car pulling up to their cabin. Her sisters gathered behind her as Abbie stepped out onto the porch and watched her uncle Luke turn off the car. Luke, Candace, Lillian, and Kep all got out and walked toward the cabin.

Luke took off his hat as he approached the porch, finally standing at the base of the steps.

For some reason, Abbie found she couldn't speak. After a few awkward seconds, her uncle asked, "Mind if we come in?"

"No," Abbie stammered. "Please come in."

Everyone entered the cabin and had a seat as Sandy and Maria served iced tea. The adults made small talk about the funeral and how nice the arrangements had been.

Abbie noticed that her uncle was quiet. His face looked grim and his mouth taut. He looked almost angry and she felt a pang of fear. Yet an inside voice whispered, *Fear not!*

Then Abbie looked at the hair she'd been twisting around a finger. One of her favorite Bible verses sprang to mind: "Are not two sparrows sold for a farthing? And one of them shall not fall on the ground without your Father. But the very hairs of your head are all numbered. Fear ye not therefore, ye are of more value than many sparrows."

When she looked up, Candace was smiling at her. She said softly, "Girls, my husband and I want to talk to you before we leave."

Abbie thought she knew what was coming, so she stiffened her back and waited.

Aunt Candace began, "We've just had a talk with Reverend Semmes, Sheriff Taylor, Mrs. Frye, Miss Lumpkin, and Mr. Kephart. They have assured us that no one will come out here to take you girls to any orphanage."

"How is that?" Abbie heard herself asking.

Mrs. Frye opened her purse and pulled out a piece of paper. She stood and handed it to Abbie.

"What's this?" Abbie asked as she unfolded the paper. The room was silent, except for the shuffling of Whit and Corrie as they stood behind her and joined her in reading:

State of North Carolina
Operator's License 930955
Name: Lauren Abigail Randolph
Street and No.: Sugar Fork Branch
City or Post Office: Proctor
> The above-named person is hereby licensed to operate
> a motor vehicle until the license is suspended, revoked,
> or canceled.
>
> Signed: Zachary Taylor, Deputy Sheriff
> Swain County, North Carolina
> May 14, 1926

"Is this what I think it is?" Abbie said.

"Yes, of course!" Corrie said. "It's a driver's license."

"How . . . ?" Abbie said, looking at Mrs. Frye.

"As you can see, Sheriff Taylor issued it, and it's official as it can be."

Candace looked sternly at her husband. He sat as still as a statue.

Lillian continued. "The driver's license you have, Abbie, makes you an adult in the eyes of the state. And as soon as I present a certified copy," she said, patting her purse, "to Judge Hughes, you'll be declared the legal guardian of your sisters and the owner of all your father's assets, including the farm and all the land."

"When?" Corrie asked.

"I leave in the morning for a business trip to Knoxville. But I'll be back Tuesday or Wednesday of the week after next and will plan to do it then."

"And," Candace said as she looked even more severely at her husband, "we've been promised that you will be well taken care of. We've reviewed the arrangements and were pleased when Miss Lumpkin assured us that you all will be able to graduate from school and even consider college, if you wish." She paused and smiled at Abbie. "You will graduate this year, and you'll be able to manage the farm."

"But Aunt Candace," Abbie countered, "I don't know how. We have almost no money and what little income we had came from Pa's work—"

"Not to worry, sweetie. Uncle Luke and I are going to put some money into a trust fund for you girls. Mrs. Frye tells us your pa had put away some money at the bank in Bryson City, and we will add our money to that. Furthermore, Mrs. Frye, Pastor Semmes, and Mr. Kephart will be the trustees."

Abbie felt her eyes widen as she looked at Mrs. Frye, who smiled, nodded, and said, "That's correct. Your pa set it up for you from some of the profits of his business dealings. So, when I visit with Judge Hughes week after next, I'll be asking him to declare the trust open."

Whit and Corrie cheered and hugged each other. Abbie stood in stunned shock.

"On top of that," Candace continued, "you girls will get twenty-five dollars every month for the next five years from me and Uncle Luke, and I'll try to send more if you have an emergency."

Abbie could hear her sisters continue to cheer but felt her throat tighten. This amount of money was staggering, almost what the best-paid lumberman would earn for an entire month's work of backbreaking labor. She shot a quick glance at her uncle's face. He looked angry, and Abbie knew that her aunt had forced her husband to contribute financially. As relief continued to flood her mind, Abbie felt tears form. She reached for her aunt and hugged her. Abbie whispered, "Thank you so much, Aunt Candace. We can make it fine on that."

Aunt Candace had been weakened by the struggle; Abbie could see that as she went around and hugged each of the girls while Uncle Luke merely nodded as they prepared to leave.

"You girls write me every week, you hear? And I'll write back. I'll be praying for you every day. The Lord will take care of you. And Uncle Luke and I will be out in the fall to check on you all and the farm."

They all thanked her, and as soon as the door closed behind the pair, Corrie sighed. Her eyes were glowing as she suddenly put her arms around Whit again and cried, "We ain't never gonna go to no orphanage. We're gonna keep ourselves right here."

Abbie walked to the door of the cabin and watched her closest living relatives drive away. *But,* she thought, *even if I have the money, how in the world am I gonna care for these girls and this big ol' farm all by myself? It was hard enough when Pa was here some of the time. It's gonna be impossible without him or Bobby Lee doin' the man's work with Danya!*

55

Conspiracy

After a sumptuous dinner at the Clubhouse that evening, Nancy Cunningham, on the arm of William Calhoun, led the VIP guests down a hallway to two of her private lounges. At the end of the hall, the left-hand door opened to the men's, with the one across the hall leading to the ladies'.

"Nancy," Calhoun said as he patted her arm, "your meal was as astonishing as ever."

"Thank you, sir."

"I would think that with suffrage now being in our past, women's rights would insist upon a lounge in which we could enjoy each other's company."

Nancy laughed. "William, you know that we women have much to discuss together in private." She lifted one finger and wagged it side to side as she cautioned, "And we don't need any male ears hearing of our plans and purposes."

"I see now what's come from giving women the right to vote. By golly, now you'll soon want to boss everything."

"William, that was true *before* suffrage."

"Fair enough!" Calhoun bellowed as he laughed, turned, and entered the opulent lounge. As many times as he had been there, he still found the carved woodwork astounding. *As fine as any in Philadelphia*, he thought. After lighting a cigar and having his personal assistant, Bernard, pour him a bourbon diluted with ice-cold branch water, he settled into one of the overstuffed chairs.

As Judge Hughes entered the private parlor, Calhoun's voice boomed across the room, "Come take a load off, Judge!"

As the judge sat, Calhoun waved over Bernard, who took the judge's bar and cigar order.

"Judge—" Calhoun began.

"It's John, if that's acceptable, Mr. Calhoun."

Calhoun smiled. "Only if you call me William."

"Agreed."

"Well, John," Calhoun said, "let's talk brass tacks. First, tell me a bit about yourself. What caused you to settle out here, Jud . . . uh, John?"

"Our family has been in western North Carolina for four generations. Our home place was a farm not far from Asheville. My father was one of the first attorneys out on this end of the state. I guess I've just followed in his footsteps."

Calhoun nodded as he sipped his drink.

"If I might ask," the judge inquired, "how did you become regarded as the father of the Appalachian hardwood industry?"

"And might I add, humbly, the founder and president of the world's largest hardwood lumber company?" Calhoun said.

The judge smiled and nodded as Bernard held a lit match for his cigar.

"Not much to tell. Like you, I was born on a farm, only ours was in eastern Pennsylvania. My father owned a water-driven sawmill that could produce about a hundred thousand board feet of lumber a year—enough to keep us in food, clothing, and even a few luxuries, like molasses and coffee.

"When I was twenty-six, I left home with my life savings of fifteen hundred dollars—a small fortune in those days—and traveled to Europe to do the whole grand tour. However, I ended up spending most of my time and money in London gambling, I'm afraid to say. When I came back to the US, nearly a pauper, I began my lumber career in earnest. Fortunately, I was much better at starting businesses than I was at gambling. Over the last thirty years, I've acquired several large lumber companies and have expanded operations to most of the forests along the east coast."

"Do you have any businesses besides hardwood?"

"Of course, my friend. I'm deep into industries like coal, gas, electric power plants, local phone companies, and railroads."

"Your interests are certainly diverse."

Calhoun sat up and checked around the room to see that the ears of the other men present were otherwise occupied. He leaned forward and said, "Let's cut the formalities, John. My goodness, after all, we're in the backwoods out here. And I *do* have an ongoing interest in this incredible wilderness."

The judge cocked his head. "The wilderness, William, or her trees?"

Calhoun laughed and sat back as he took a puff on his cigar. "A manager of mine has estimated that when the first of the colonists arrived in this great land it contained over fifty billion trees. And the most amazing of these trees, my friend, are right here in Swain and Graham counties, and none more so than those owned by the five little orphan girls who buried their father today. I think I'd like to help them out. Perhaps you could assist me?"

"How so?"

"Doesn't the law require them to go to an orphanage?"

"Are you versed in North Carolina statutes? Seems an unusual interest for a lumberman."

"Actually, a necessity for a shrewd businessman, wouldn't you agree?"

The judge took a sip of his drink before continuing. "Unfortunately, and this must stay confidential, there are legal moves being made in my court either this or next week to grant the older girl emancipation. Given the statutes and constitution I've sworn to uphold, I'll have no choice."

Calhoun took another puff. After exhaling a circular plume of smoke, he set his cigar in an ashtray, reached into his inside coat pocket, and pulled out a large wallet. "Many judges I do business with have allegiance to another form of legal tender."

The judge seemed taken aback. "Are you suggesting a bribe, sir?"

"Absolutely not, my good man! Never!"

The two stared at each other for a moment.

"Good," the judge said. "If I thought a man was trying to buy my influence, I could make his life as a businessman most difficult indeed."

"As it should be," Calhoun responded. "What I was merely suggesting was that a man as versed in the law and the customs of this area as you obviously are could possibly be available for some private consulting; some well-paid consulting, I might add. After all, I'm used to paying the scandalous fees of Philadelphia lawyers, you know. Perhaps you'd be willing to be of legal assistance to a Philadelphia man who might be looking for ways to obtain more timber property."

"Well, sir, since you put it that way, I may have some information of value to you."

"Not knowing the customs of the mountains, sir, I need you to help me know what such information might cost me."

The judge took a sip and after a moment of thought, nodded. He leaned toward Calhoun and whispered a figure no one in the room could hear, or would have believed.

56

Pitch

When their breakfast was finished, the girls cleaned up the
kitchen. As they finished the dishes, they heard a car approaching. The girls went to the cabin door and stepped out onto
the porch as a Ford Model T Coupe with wire wheels strained up
the road toward their home.

As the car approached, Danya climbed down from the back of
his gypsy wagon parked near their cabin. He had his rifle with him
as he sat on a log by his fire pit. Abbie could see the smoke swirl-
ing up around his coffeepot. She felt safer since Danya had begun
bringing the wagon up next to their cabin each evening. During
the early morning, he would have his horses pull it back down to
his cabin. His and Maria's presence brought the girls great comfort.

As the car drew closer Abbie said, "That's old man Sanders."

"Who's the other man?" Whit asked.

"It's Mr. Calhoun, the owner of the lumber company. Met him
in town a while back and saw him at Pa's funeral. Don't rightly
know why he was there, though."

"What do they want?" Corrie asked.

"I 'spect I know. But we'll all find out for sure soon enough,"
Abbie said.

The two men walked up to the porch. "Miss Randolph, this
here is Mr. William Calhoun. He owns the lumber company."

"We've met," Abbie said.

Calhoun nodded and took his hat off. "I'm glad to see you again, Abbie. Good to meet you other girls. I came to tell you how sorry I am that you lost your father, but it was a very nice funeral, I must say."

"Thank you," Abbie said almost in a whisper. Somehow she was frightened by their visit. She remembered the time Sanders had illegally cut down her walnut tree and how her father had harsh words with him. She knew he had threatened her pa a number of times and had orchestrated their ambush at Pickens Gap, and she had come to believe that he shot her pa in the back over on Eagle Creek. She also wondered if he didn't have something to do with the deaths of her pa and her fiancé. She felt nothing but abhorrence toward him. But for now, she turned her eyes to Mr. Calhoun.

"I'd like to talk to you," Calhoun said.

"Would you like to come in?" Abbie said.

"That's very nice of you. I believe we will."

Abbie and the girls stepped aside to let the men in. Out of the corner of her eye she could see Danya standing next to his wagon with his rifle in the crook of his arm.

The girls followed the men inside, leaving the door open. Abbie offered the men chairs. "Would you like something to drink? We've got some sassafras tea."

"No, thank you, little lady. Let's see. What are your sisters' names?"

"My sisters are Whit, Corrie, Anna Kate, and that's Sarah Beth."

"Again, I'm sorry about the passing of your father and your fiancé." Calhoun shook his head and said, "Very grievous, I'm sure. I imagine it's going to be *very* difficult for you."

"We'll make out," Abbie said firmly.

"I hardly see how. You won't be able to farm this place."

"Our friends are seeing to it. And our aunt and uncle are providing us some money every month."

Calhoun nodded. "I heard about that. Very nice of your folks, I'm sure, but it won't be enough to run a farm as big as this one."

"We'll be fine," Abbie said. "We have folks to help us." She heard the porch creak and knew Danya was just outside the door.

"Is that right? Well, I'm sure you're doing your best. But I tell you what, I've come out this morning to try to help you. You probably know that I've been trying to buy this place for some time."

"I heard Pa talk about it with Mama before she died."

"Well, he wasn't anxious to sell and understandably so, but things were different then. You had your parents to take care of you. Now, I'll tell you what I'd like to do. I've got a very nice house in town just about right for you girls with a little fixing up. I could buy your place, and you could have that one as is and take any of the furniture here you'd like. Your horse and wagon would be kept at the livery as long as you live in town, all on me."

Calhoun went on speaking of how nice it would be for the girls to live in town. "You'd be right there at the school, right there for church. You'd make lots of friends, and you wouldn't have to work at all. There's even a spot for a garden out back that goes with the place. You'll have electricity and a phone, provided by me as long as you live there. Of course, there's running water and an indoor bathroom. Hard to beat that, eh?"

"Thank you, Mr. Calhoun. That's very generous. But I don't reckon we'll be sellin' or movin'."

Calhoun shot a quick glance at Sanders, who said, "Now, looky here. I know you girls would like to stay out here, but it just is not sensible. You simply cannot make it way out here."

"Yes, we can!" Corrie said. "We can make it just fine."

Calhoun said quickly, "Well, you know what I offered your father, I suppose."

"I heard him say what it was," Abbie said. "But he wouldn't take it."

"Well, the price of timber is good right now. I'm prepared to add one thousand dollars to the offer. No, I'll make it two. I'd really like to do something nice for you girls."

Abbie stiffened. She was aware that all her sisters were looking to her and silently begging her not to give in. However, what Calhoun was offering was a small fortune. She took a deep breath, held it during a brief prayer, and then slowly let it out.

She knew what she had to do. She remembered her solemn vow to her parents and to the Lord.

"We promised our parents that the farm would stay in the family. I promised them I'd care for my sisters here. So I have to say no. But thank you for coming out."

As Abbie began to stand, Calhoun indicated for her to sit. "I think I can help you do both."

Abbie looked at him suspiciously. "Do both?"

"Keep the farm and care for your sisters. I think I could offer you a win-win proposition. I'm prepared to make you an offer I'll make no one else in this valley. And I'll only make it once. Are you ready to hear me out?"

Calhoun's steely eyes narrowed as he looked at Abbie.

"I'm listenin'," Abbie said.

"How about I buy just the timber rights for most of your six hundred acres? We could survey it out so that you'd still have a thick border of forest around the farm. We'd only take the trees you can't see from your porch."

"No!" Corrie said. "You can't have *any* of our trees."

Calhoun glared at Corrie. "Your sister, as I understand from Judge Hughes, will have the legal right to make this decision, and I'm prepared to offer five dollars per acre for the rights. That's three thousand dollars. And of course, the trees will all grow back."

"Mr. Calhoun, there ain't many trees growin' in spots up and down Hazel Creek 'cause of the way you've scalped the hills," Abbie countered. "You say the trees will all grow back, but there's not much proof of that now, is there?"

Calhoun nodded. "For you girls we could do some special lumbering. We could take only the larger trees, the ones that are more likely to die anyway, and leave plenty of smaller ones. We could even agree together which trees would be taken and mark them."

Abbie looked at him a moment. "Pa told me that five years ago you paid John Farley nine dollars per acre for timber rights, and his trees weren't nearly as fine as ours."

"Don't negotiate with this snake!" Corrie hissed.

Calhoun ignored her and leaned toward Abbie. "I can see you're a shrewd businesswoman for such a young lady." He rubbed his beard for a moment as he thought. "Of course, I was able to clear-cut Farley's place, which is the least expensive way to lumber. A partial cut will take more time because we have to work around all the trees that will be left. That will cost me a lot more time and labor, but given the rising price of lumber and the size of the virgin trees here, I'm prepared to double my offer. I'll give you ten dollars per acre, and you keep your farm."

"Don't do it, Abbie!" Whit begged. "We can make it without the devil's money."

Calhoun continued. "I know of the promise your father made to your mother. Everyone in the valley admires your grit and your gumption. However, I'm here to tell you, for a fact, that you will *not* be able to keep this farm. You need to listen to me very, very carefully. It will *not* be possible. I cannot tell you why, but I beg you to believe me. I'm serious when I say that I want to give you a way out, a way of luxury, a way of having everything you might ever want. But if you refuse me, then you will be plunging yourself and your sisters into poverty and servitude. I know that's not what you want for yourself or for them."

Suddenly Abbie felt a chill go down her spine. She suspected he was not a man of idle threats. She thought, *What does he know that I don't? And what about me and my sisters' needs? What if Aunt and Uncle don't come through with the money they promised? What if the men who promised to help us farm don't show up? What if Danya and Maria leave? How will we make it?*

Just as suddenly a verse popped into her mind: "The Lord is at hand. Be careful for nothing; but in every thing by prayer and supplication with thanksgiving let your requests be made known unto God. And the peace of God, which passeth all understanding, shall keep your hearts and minds through Christ Jesus."

Instantly a comforting peace settled over her, and Abbie knew what to do. Her father wanted the land to stay pristine, untroubled by human hand. She looked around the cabin at the massive logs her grandpa and pa had hand hewn. She could sense her pa's presence and guidance. She looked back at the lumber baron. "Mr. Calhoun, I want to thank you, I really do. I appreciate your offer, but I won't be able to accept it. I won't be able to sell you the land *or* the timber rights."

Calhoun's face reddened. He apparently was not accustomed to being dismissed. He took a deep breath and let it out slowly. "One last time, young lady. Take my offer or you *will* lose everything, and I mean everything. I have friends who *will* make it happen."

Abbie felt her face chill. She grasped her hands together to keep them from trembling. She now knew that he was *not* bluffing. "Mr. Calhoun, I don't doubt you sincerely believe what you're saying. But my God tells me to 'be strong and of a good courage.' I'll cast my faith and my future on him. So, you best leave my house *now*. Or I'll haveta ask Danya to escort you out."

Sanders leaned forward. "If'n you think the lumbering ox could get here fast enough . . ."

Danya quickly entered the cabin holding his rifle in front of him. He cocked the rifle before Sanders could move.

"I think he could," Abbie said.

Sanders grimaced, looking like a guilty schoolboy.

Calhoun leaned over and whispered to Abbie, "Good thing

he was here. He'll be a witness to the fact that you've decided to put some very sad events in motion. In point of fact, you've just cooked your goose, little lady. You have no idea how big a mistake you've just made." He got up and walked out without another word.

Sanders followed, but stopped at the door and turned around to say, "You think you can hold on to this place, but now it ain't gonna happen. You'd better take the offer Mr. Calhoun gave you. You better take it now, or you will regret it the rest of your life."

He spit some tobacco juice on the floor and then looked back up at the girls. "If you girls don't go running after Mr. Calhoun right now, I can promise you this: one of you'uns is likely to get hurt and real bad." He looked up at Danya. "Maybe even you, you big lump of clay."

Danya said nothing.

Sanders looked back at Abbie. "You'll suffer the same fate of your pa and your boyfriend. I'll see to it myself." He turned and stormed out the door.

The girls ran to the door to watch them get in the car. As soon as it sped off down the road, Corrie and the others turned to Abbie.

"What'd he mean 'bout you suffering the same fate as Pa and Bobby Lee?" Whit asked.

Abbie shrugged, trying to hide her concern.

"Think we oughta let the sheriff know 'bout his threat?"

"I think that's a good idea, Whit," Abbie said. "How 'bout we take the truck to town this afternoon and let him know?"

Whit nodded.

"You done good, Abbie," Corrie said. "That old man Calhoun's trying everythin' he can to buy us off. He's got enough money to burn a wet mule."

"And I hear he's so cheap that when he squeezes a penny, old Abe Lincoln's nose bleeds," Whit said.

"But he ain't gettin' our place," Anna added. "Ain't that right, Abbie?"

Abbie gave her sister a hug as Whit added, "I'm glad you didn't let him talk no more, Abbie. I think he's as evil as Lucifer hisself."

"I don't know about *that*," Abbie said. "But we'll make it, the good Lord willin'."

57

Charming

After Abbie and the girls had finished their Saturday chores, they drove to town to talk to Zach. Upon returning home, and settling Sarah Beth down for her nap, Abbie decided to take a walk to clear her head. She headed down their property toward the Sugar Fork thinking that she could have some time away from the weight of the world she felt was resting on her shoulders.

She sat on a log lying by the branch. She had come here so often over the years that an area of the log was rubbed smooth and served as a comfortable seat. She looked around the small clearing, which was filled with beautiful lush ferns and covered by a high canopy of ancient hardwood trees, and listened to the rushing water as she tried to relax. However, she could not shake the thoughts about Mr. Calhoun's visit and old man Sanders's threats. *As long as Pa was here,* she thought, *we could make it fine. It was hard to go to school and then come home to see that the chores were done, but we done it. My guess is it's gonna be* a lot *harder now.*

She was just glad that Maria and Danya, along with Jeremiah Welch, were on the property to help and watch over them. After the girls met with him, Zach had come up and taken a statement from Danya about the visit from Calhoun and Sanders. She was glad she had him and her sisters as witnesses.

Hearing the sound of a stick breaking behind her, she dropped her Bible and twirled around as she leaped to her feet ready for whatever might be sneaking up on her.

"Miss Randolph," a soft voice reassured, "sorry to have startled you. But you are indeed a sight to behold sitting here in these ferns. What a beautiful spot."

"Dr. Chandler! I swan! You 'bout scared me to death."

"Again, my apologies. I should have called out. I hope you'll forgive me."

"Well, I have no choice."

"You don't?"

Abbie bent over to pick up her Bible, dusting off the leaves. "Nope. The Lord hisself said to forgive."

Wade smiled and Abbie felt her cheeks flush. She had never noticed how beautiful his smile was.

Stop it! she warned herself, but she couldn't. *He's more handsome than I first realized,* she thought.

Stop right now! she cautioned herself again. *You just buried your fiancé . . . and your pa!*

"What are you doin' up here, if'n I may ask?" Abbie said, trying to change the subject.

"Just coming to check on you and your sisters. Especially the toddler."

"Reckon we're doin' just fine," Abbie stammered as she began to walk up the bank toward the road.

"I have no doubt, Miss Randolph—"

"Abbie," she interrupted, surprising both herself and the young doctor. "Um . . . that is what I'm used to, Dr. Chandler."

"Only if you call me Wade," he said, reaching down to offer her his hand.

She looked at it for a moment and then accepted it. As his hand grasped hers, she sensed her heart continue to palpitate and was impressed with his strength as she felt him pull her up the incline. He then tenderly took her arm to escort her up to the road. She felt short of breath as she admonished herself. *Heavens,*

Abbie! He's a doctor for goodness' sakes—and a flatlander. You need to get ahold of yourself. But she couldn't suppress the emotions she was feeling.

"Anyway," he continued, "Dr. Keller told me that Sarah Elisabeth is nineteen months old, and we like to check youngsters at that age. So, since she's almost due, I thought I'd drop by and give her a checkup."

"We don't need no doctor bill," Abbie said.

Wade laughed.

"You laughing at me?" Abbie said.

"No. Not at all. It's just that I have no idea what to charge. Why, I don't even know how to charge. I just wanted to drop by—"

"To check Sarah girl?"

Wade smiled and placed his hand on her arm. "Yes. But even more so . . . her oldest sister." He then looked up. "What a beautiful grove of trees, Abbie. I can see why you like coming here."

"Whenever I would come here with Pa, he'd always sing me a song called 'Spare That Tree.'"

"Can you sing it for me?"

Abbie nodded and began singing in a clear voice:

Woodman, spare that tree! Touch not a single bough!
In youth it sheltered me, And I'll protect it now.
'Twas my forefather's hand That placed it near his cot;
There, woodman, let it stand, Thy axe shall harm it not!

To Abbie's surprise Wade said, "I'll take this one." He walked over to the trunk of a massive tree.

When but an idle boy I sought its grateful shade;
In all their gushing joy, Here too my sisters played.
My mother kissed me here; My father pressed my hand—
Forgive this foolish tear, but let that old oak stand!

Wade walked back to her. Abbie thought she could see mist in
Wade's eyes as they sang the last verse together.

My heart-strings round thee cling, Close as thy bark, old friend!
Here shall the wild-bird sing, And still thy branches bend.
Old tree! the storm still brave! And, woodman, leave the spot;
While I've a hand to save, Thy axe shall harm it not.

Abbie looked intently into his eyes. "I didn't know you felt so
about the forest."

"I do love what forest is left in Hazel Creek," he said, turning
and pointing to the largest of the oaks in the grove. "Bet that oak
is five hundred years old. She's a beaut."

"She reminds me of a poem Miss Grace made us memorize in
school," Abbie said. "It was written by a war hero, a man named
Alfred Joyce Kilmer."

"You remember it?" Wade asked. "I don't know it. I'd love to
hear it!"

"Oh, I don't know. I'm not sure I 'member it, Wade," Abbie
said, smiling.

"Aw, come on, Abbie. I bet you do. Go ahead on. Give it a try
in honor of that queen of an oak over there."

"Well, maybe I can recollect a mite," Abbie said as she faced
the massive old oak.

I think that I shall never see
A poem lovely as a tree.

A tree whose hungry mouth is prest
Against the sweet earth's flowing breast.

Abbie looked back at Wade and felt her cheeks blush. He
smiled and nodded. "It's good. Go on." She cleared her throat and
continued.

A tree that looks at God all day,
And lifts her leafy arms to pray;

A tree that may in summer wear
A nest of robins in her hair;

Upon whose bosom snow has lain;
Who intimately lives with rain.

Poems are made by fools like me,
But only God can make a tree.

Wade was quiet as Abbie walked back to the log and picked up her Bible.

"Well done, Abbie," Wade said in a hushed voice. "Well done, indeed."

Abbie felt herself blush again.

"I like it . . . a lot!" Wade said softly.

"Thanks," Abbie replied. "But I best get back home before the girls get to worryin'."

"I'll walk you up there and give Miss Sarah a looking over."

Abbie felt as if she floated home.

58

Precipice

The girls were eating lunch after church when Corrie straightened up. "There's a horse a-coming." She ran to the window. "It's Dr. Chandler!"

Corrie went to the door as Wade dismounted and came running up to the porch.

"Come on in, Dr. Chandler. You want some potlikker and corn pone?"

"No thanks, Corrie."

Abbie came to the doorway holding Sarah Beth. "Hello, Wade. Did you forget somethin' since your visit here yesterday?"

"No, Abbie. I'm sorry to have to bring some bad news," Wade said.

"What is it?" Corrie demanded. "Somebody sick?"

"No, it isn't that," Wade said. He chewed his lower lip and shook his head.

Abbie indicated for him to sit down at the table as she sat in the rocker near him. "What is it?" Abbie said. "Just come out and tell it."

"Well, the sheriff's gone over to Fontana with a posse, including Dr. Keller, to arrest someone. Anyway, after Dr. Keller left I was reading on his porch and Mr. Kephart called on the phone from Bryson City wanting him. I told him he wasn't there, but he would probably be back late tonight or tomorrow, and I didn't know how to get hold of him, since he's out in the woods looking for someone."

"What did Mr. Kephart want?"

Wade paused a second, looking down as he turned his hat in his hands. "Well, it was about you girls."

"About us?" Abbie said. "What about us?"

"Well, he found out that the taxes on your place haven't been paid since your mother passed."

"I don't know anything about that," Abbie said. "Pa always took care of our business. And Mrs. Frye always helped with our legal affairs. It don't make sense."

"That's what Mr. Kephart said, too. He was awfully aggravated about it. He said Judge Hughes declared the taxes due late Friday afternoon. Mr. Kephart believes the judge chose the close of business on Friday because he knew the bank would be closed, and he must have known the Fryes were going to be out of town. Either one of them could have come up with the money for you girls. Turns out the judge declared that if the taxes are not paid the first thing tomorrow morning, then your place can be bought by the first person who pays the bill."

Abbie felt her face pale. She remembered that her pa had always gone to Bryson to pay their taxes each year and had fond memories of her once-a-year trip with him, at least before her mama died. "Oh dear," was all Abbie could say. "Pa musta not even thought about it this year since he was injured. I could kick myself for forgetting."

"It's all right," Whit said. "You've had a lot on your mind."

"They cain't do that without giving us a chance to pay! Can they?" Abbie asked.

Wade shrugged.

"How much was it, Wade? Did he say?"

"Four hundred and eighty dollars."

"What?" Abbie exclaimed. "That ain't right! That's way more than our taxes. Why, that's more than most men make in a year. That's robbery, that's what that is!"

"Mr. Kephart said the judge put a big fine on top of the actual tax bill," Wade explained.

"We don't have any money like that!" Whit interjected. "Not here."

"But we've got a trust fund!" Corrie said. "How much is in it, Abbie?"

"I don't know. Mrs. Frye was gonna come out and let us know the details once the legal parts were settled. But that's not until next week or the week after. I don't think the money's ours till we hear from her." Abbie's heart was sinking and fear began rising in her.

"We've got to do *something*!" Corrie said. "We cain't let 'em sell our place."

Wade explained, "Mr. Kephart said that L. G. Sanders was there in Bryson City boasting about how he was gonna pay the taxes and penalties and get your place tomorrow for Calhoun. He's saying that if anyone bids against him, he was prepared to raise the roof to get your property."

Abbie felt herself begin to tremble as she stood, only to find her knees were strangely weak. She had to sit and put Sarah Beth down on the floor. She looked at Wade. "I don't know what to do."

"Is there anybody you could borrow from?" Wade asked.

"No, I can't think of anybody that could give us that much money. Not anybody in all of Sugar Fork . . . or, for that matter, all of Hazel Creek."

Abbie felt her eyes filling with tears. *There's no hope!* she thought. *None!*

"I'll bet Aunt Candace will help us," Corrie said. "Don'tcha remember she said she'd help us if we needed it?"

"But she's in Raleigh, the banks are closed today since it's Sunday, and the taxes have to be paid Monday morning—*tomorrow*—

even before the banks open," Whit said. "What are we gonna do, Abbie?"

Abbie had no words to answer. She felt hollow and empty.

"Couldn't we try sendin' Aunt Candace a telegram from town?" Corrie asked.

"The post office is closed until the morning. So that's the earliest you could have a telegraph sent," Wade said.

Abbie wanted to run out of the cabin, into the woods, and forget all her problems. *It's not fair, Lord! I'm just sixteen years old, and I cain't handle all this. Why'd you take my mama and pa away and put it all on me?* This prayer flashed through her mind, but instantly she was ashamed.

"Zach would know what to do," Wade said, "but there's no telling when he'll be back."

"What about letting the pastor know?" Whit asked. "Maybe he could go to some of the folks at our church and raise some money."

"When I leave here," Wade said, "I'll go to the parsonage and let him know. I bet he'll help us figure something out. Then I'll see if someone can open the telegraph office and get a message off to your aunt and uncle in Raleigh."

"Even if you could," Abbie sighed, "the money's got to be at the courthouse in Bryson City by eight o'clock in the morning. Their bank won't be open by then. Money can't be wired by then."

"Maybe Mr. Kephart could help us out," Corrie suggested.

"He told me he's working on some ideas," Wade said.

"I can only hope so," Abbie said as she let out a deep breath.

Wade stood and pulled Abbie to her feet. Before she could react, he took her hands in his. "I'm going back to town. I'll talk to the pastor, try to find the telegraph fellow, and then wait for Zach and Dr. Keller to get back. I'll also try to reach Mr. Kephart again." He stepped back as he looked into her eyes. "We're gonna figure something out, Abbie. We will."

She was still in shock when he turned, stepped out the door, hopped off the porch, and jogged toward his horse. Corrie called out, "Dr. Chandler, thanks for tryin' to help."

"Ah, it's nothing," he called over his shoulder as he mounted. "I'll try to find Zach or Millard or someone. If we can get the money, we'll still have to get to Bryson City in time—even though it's several hours by car on that pitiful road." He spurred his horse and rode away at a dead run.

Abbie walked back to the rocker and sat down. Her head was spinning. Whit came over and stood close to her. "We've got to do somethin', Abbie."

"That's right," Corrie whispered. "But four hundred and eighty dollars. Only God's got that much money!"

"And we don't have any idea how much is in the trust. Oh, dear!" Whit exclaimed.

Sarah Beth began to cry for Abbie to pick her up. Abbie put the little girl in her lap and sang a lullaby their mama always sang to them—just slightly changing the lyrics.

> Hush up, baby, don't say a word, Abbie's gonna buy you a
> mockingbird.
> If it can't whistle, and it can't sing, Abbie's gonna buy you a
> diamond ring.
> If that diamond ring turns brass, Abbie's gonna buy you a
> looking glass.
> If that looking glass gets broke, Abbie's gonna buy you a billy
> goat.
> If that billy goat runs away, Abbie's gonna buy you another day.

Despite the reassuring words she was singing, Abbie felt a darkness and a fear growing in her. She took a deep breath, sighed, and said, "It'll take the good Lord himself to get us out of this, so, let's all pray that God will rear back and give us a miracle."

Whit said, "Abbie, you're always tellin' us we need to depend upon God and each other. Remember? When we're at our weakest, that's when we most need to depend upon God and his strength!"

Abbie nodded as tears began to streak down her cheeks.

Whit whispered, "Abbie, do you remember my favorite verse?"

Abbie shook her head.

"It's Philippians, chapter four and verse thirteen. Remember it?"

Abbie nodded and whispered, "'I can do all things through Christ which strengtheneth me.'"

Whit hugged her close. "Maybe our greatest blessin' will come now that we're at the end of our rope. We can't let go of our hope. It's all we got."

weekend, that's when we most need to depend upon God and his

Abbie shook her head.

59

Dreamer

Midnight came and went. Only Sarah Beth and Anna went
to sleep at their normal times, for the rest of the girls
were tense and restless. Whit slept fitfully on a blanket by the
fireplace. Corrie lay on the floor next to Lilly, who was stretched
out full-length on the floor in front of the fireplace. As she slept,
Corrie's head rested on the sleeping dog's plush black-and-
brindle-colored fur.

Abbie stayed awake, listening to the cacophony of forest
sounds enveloping the cabin. She felt as if she were standing on
the edge of a cliff on a gloomy moonless night. *What will happen
to us?* she wondered as she sat at the table staring down at her
hands folded in front of her.

Abbie had prayed and recited memorized Scripture until she
had no words left in her soul. Whit began moaning and thrash-
ing. *She's havin' another nightmare*, Abbie thought, so she broke
her silence. "Whit, wake up." She shook her sister until she
opened her eyes. "You're havin' a bad dream. Wake up. I need you
to help me think. Sit up."

After Whit stretched her arms above her head, she then
rubbed the sleep out of her eyes and said, "Abbie, it wasn't a bad
dream. It were a good one. I think I know where we can get the
money. I dreamed it."

As Whit wakened, Abbie continued, "Even if we had the

money, I don't think we could get to Bryson City on time unless we started drivin' before sunup. You know how dangerous that road can be. It's got more sharp curves and potholes than a porcupine's got quills. And folks have been robbed on that road at nighttime."

Corrie stirred at the sound of her sisters' voices and sat up.

Suddenly a high-pitched guttural growl sounded from the meadow outside the cabin, causing Abbie and Whit to spin around toward the window. "It's just a bobcat," Corrie said, calmly yawning. "Cain't cause us any harm."

Sleepily, Whit said, "Seriously, Abbie. I think I *know* where the money is."

"What did you say?" Corrie said, standing up and walking over to Whit. "What money?"

"I dreamed 'bout where we can get the money to pay the taxes."

Her sisters stared at her, and Whit began to stand. Abbie said, "What are you talkin' 'bout, Whit? You don't have any money."

"I know where it's at. It was in my dream. And I've had this dream before. I dreamed it before Pa died. And I just had it again. It's gotta be true."

Abbie shook her head. "Whit, you are always having strange dreams."

"No, Abbie! I know where the money is, and I'm gonna get it! It's buried."

Whit's brown eyes were large, and she looked excited. "The first time I had it, I dreamed that an angel woke me up. He was big and strong and glowed bright like the moon. I wasn't scared at all. He took my hand and led me across our meadow."

Corrie looked at Abbie and rolled her eyes.

"We flew down the meadow over by the twin chestnut trees and over by the little pond and I saw Pa. It was like we were hoverin' above Pa. It was like he didn't know we were there or nothin'. He was out buryin' somethin'. The moon was bright, and I saw somethin' else. It was the Haint. He was standin' by Pa."

"The Haint . . ." Abbie said.

"Yes. I saw the Haint and Pa—"

"This *is* crazy!" Corrie exclaimed.

Whit ignored her. "They were both diggin', and Pa was put-tin' somethin' in the ground. I watched him till he covered it up. The Haint went back into the woods and Pa walked to the cabin. While he was walkin' back, the angel flew me home, through the front door, and laid me in front of the fire. The angel smiled at me and then, as Pa opened the door, the angel disappeared right into thin air. I ran up to Pa. He hugged me, Abbie, and I asked him, 'What'd you bury out there, Pa?' He said, 'Just somethin' for hard times, Honey. Go back to bed, and go back to sleep. And don't tell anyone our secret.' That's what he said. And then I had the dream *again*. Tonight. Just now!"

"What's that dream mean, Whit?" Abbie asked.

"I'm not sure," Whit said. "But we prayed about the taxes to-night, and I think my dream is the answer to our prayin'. Maybe the angel was givin' us a message."

"You're crazy!" Corrie said.

Abbie went over to Whit and took her hands into her own. "Maybe this one ain't," she said as she smiled at her sister. Abbie sat down. "Do you remember the Bible story of Joseph interpretin' both the dreams of his fellow prisoners and the dream of Pharaoh?"

Corrie rolled her eyes again but nodded.

"And," Abbie continued, "'member the dreams 'bout Jesus? The Magi were warned in a dream that they shouldn't go back to Herod. And 'member Joseph's dream? When the angel of the Lord appeared to him and told him to take Mary and Jesus and run as far away from Egypt as they could? Corrie, it's true enough that Whit has strange dreams, but she seems so sure 'bout this. Maybe the Lord's a-speakin'."

"I think he is," Whit said, nodding.

"Then," Abbie said, "maybe this dream *is* from the Lord—a dream to save us."

"I think it is, Abbie!" Whit declared. "So I'm gonna dig it up, whatever it is. The rest of you stay here if you want to."

"I'll go with you," Abbie said. "Let's get the shovels."

"I guess we'll all go." Corrie sighed. "Should I wake up Anna and Sarah?"

"No," Abbie said. "Let's let 'em sleep. We ain't goin' too far."

"I agree," Corrie said. "After all, no reason for them to see that we're goin' out in the middle of the night to dig a hole in the ground and make fools outta ourselves."

"Everyone put on a sweater. It's chilly out there," Abbie said, ignoring her sister's sarcasm. Then she called to Lilly. "Let's go, girl. We'll be needin' your protection from that old bobcat."

Whit ran to get the shovels. Abbie said, "Hurry up, girls. It's gettin' late!"

"I think we're all outta our heads," Corrie sighed as she stood.

60

Apparition

Although the moon was waning, its three-quarter light still allowed Whit to run ahead with Lilly as her sisters followed with the lantern and shovels. Whit stopped less than one hundred paces from the cabin, where two massive chestnut trees rose nearly a hundred feet up into the air.

"Pa was right here between these two trees—right smack-dab in the middle. I remember it just as clear as can be. I'm gonna start diggin'!" Whit thrust the shovel into the ground and grunted as she put her weight on it. Abbie thrust her shovel into the ground and for a few minutes they dug together. Finally Abbie said, "There ain't nothin' here, Whit."

"There is, too! We just ain't found it yet."

"I'll tell you what. Since we are all actin' like fools," Corrie said, "let's at least git us a plan. How 'bout we start diggin' toward that tree? If we don't hit anything, we'll go back and start toward the other one."

Taking a shovel, she began to dig. Corrie dug the fastest and soon had a trench about four feet long. She rested a moment and said, "Ain't nothin' here."

"So far!" Whit added. "Here, Corrie, lemme try again. I'll go toward the other tree." She took her shovel and stuck it deeply into the ground. She loosened shovelful after shovelful until her arms felt like limp rags. There was only another trench to show

for her effort. She stopped and dabbed the perspiration from her brow. As she sighed, she said, "I'm not sure there's anythin' here."

Abbie let her shovel fall to the ground and hugged her sister. "It's not your fault."

Then Whit gasped. She pointed behind the girls toward the edge of the forest. Lilly began to growl. Abbie saw a small, dark hooded figure slowly floating toward them without a sound. As it approached, a cold wind blew across the girls, and their lantern suddenly snuffed out.

Abbie felt Whit cowering behind her. "I can't believe we didn't bring a gun or get Danya up," Whit whispered. "Should we hightail it to the cabin? Maybe we can outrun him."

The figure stopped about twenty feet short of the girls. Corrie raised her shovel as Lilly continued to growl. "You halt there, whoever you are! Whatever you are! We'll scream and our friend Danya will be here in an instant."

Abbie put her hand on Corrie's shoulder. "No need, Corrie. He's our friend."

The figure seemed to hover just above the ground and suddenly chuckled. What appeared to be black arms reached up and pulled back the hood. Abbie smiled as she saw the white face of the Haint. "Hey, Jeremiah. You old Haint, you 'bout scared my sisters to death."

"You're real?" Corrie asked, dumbfounded.

"Fear not, Corrie Hannah," the deep bass voice said. "I'm here to help."

"You're the Haint?" Corrie said. "You're real?"

Jeremiah softly laughed. "I am."

Abbie stepped in front of the girls. "Girls, like I said, this here is our friend. His given name is Jeremiah Welch, but most folks call him the Haint."

"Fear not," Jeremiah said again. "I will not hurt you or your sisters." He had a soft, reassuring voice. "Your pa asked me to watch over you. I do . . . every night."

Corrie stepped forward, her hands on her hips. "Some call you Satan hisself."

The deep voice chuckled. "I know. But I'm just an old man, here to help." He turned toward Whit. "I was here when you followed your pa that night."

Whit said in a tremulous voice, "Then it wasn't a dream. It was something real I remembered."

"Yep. Your pa and I would meet right here each month during the full moon. He wanted to protect some of his extra earnings. I he'ped him."

"What do you mean?" Abbie asked.

"He wasn't proud of what he had to do to earn the money, but he did it for you'uns in case he weren't here for you. He and your mama always wanted you girls to be able to keep the farm. This was his way. Some of the money he put in the bank, but some of it he put right here. Maybe it would be better for me to show you. Grab them shovels and follow me."

The girls picked up their shovels and followed the small figure. Abbie shushed Lilly as they followed Mr. Welch.

He stopped a few feet from where they had been digging. He pointed at the ground with a long finger. "There's the small fieldstone your pa placed to mark the spot." He bent over and lifted the stone aside. "Dig here, Whit."

Whit sunk the shovel into the soft ground. On the third time she plunged it into the earth, the blade of the shovel grated against a hard object. "There's somethin' here!" she cried. She knelt and with her hands began to move the dirt from around whatever she'd struck. "It's some kinda jug."

The Haint chuckled.

"Lemme get at it," Corrie said as she fell on her hands and knees and, along with Whit, moved the loosened dirt. Corrie reached down, grabbed the container, grunted, and pulled. "I got it!" she exclaimed. The jug suddenly came loose and she fell over

backward with the large object in her arms. "It looks like a big old molasses jug."

As the girls all crowded around, the jug appeared almost translucent in the moonlight. It had a big mouth with a lid that screwed down on it. The lid was made out of some sort of lead or metal and was frozen in place. Whit tried to loosen it. "I can't get it off. It's too tight."

"Well, break it," Corrie said. "Hit it with the shovel!"

"No, we'll go back in the house. We'll get it off somehow there," Abbie decided. She looked up to see if the Haint would object, but to her surprise, he had disappeared.

The girls made their way back to the cabin and after latching the door behind them, Abbie put the large jar on the table. "It's made outta some kind of stone it seems like. I've never seen anything like it before around the farm. You can almost see through it."

Corrie said impatiently, "Let's get the top off that thing!"

The lid was rusty and after a great deal of effort, Abbie finally yelled, "It moved! I felt it move!"

Once loosened, the top came off, and when it did, Corrie thrust her hand into the jar. She lifted out a fistful of money. Her eyes were sparkling.

"You see!" Whit said. "I told you the money was there."

The girls were all talking at once and pulling the money out. Finally they had cleaned the jar out, and Abbie counted the money as the others watched.

"There's twelve hundred and thirty-four dollars," Abbie said, her eyes wide with astonishment. She felt light-headed. "That's not only enough money to pay the taxes, we probably could buy the entire courthouse."

"I wonder where Pa got all this money," Whit said incredulously.

Abbie knew, but kept it to herself. She turned to Whit and

said, "I reckon that musta been our guardian angel that spoke to you, Whit."

"It musta been," Whit replied.

"No time to dillydally, girls. We've got to get to Bryson City by eight o'clock," Corrie said.

"I don't know that we have enough gas to get that far," Abbie said, "and everything is closed." She thought for a minute and said, "Well, we'll start anyhow. Everybody get ready. We'll get Maria to watch the babies. The rest of us are goin' to Bryson City. Right now!"

61

Deadline

The Swain County courthouse was the most ambitious structure in all of Bryson City. Its four imposing columns reached
up to a hipped roof crowned with an octagonal gold cupola containing clock faces on four sides. The impressive structure overlooked the intersection of Main and Everett Streets, the crossing
of the city's two main business streets.

The sun had already been up a couple of hours as L. G. Sanders
strolled up to the front door. After pulling on it a couple of times,
he stepped back to wait. He heard a noise and turned to see Horace Kephart lighting his pipe with a freshly struck match.

Sanders grinned and walked over. "You might as well go about
your business, Kep. You ain't got the money to pay them taxes for
the girls, have you?"

"No, I don't. I just found out about this whole illicit affair over
the weekend. And since the bank won't be opening up until nine
o'clock, I can't get to my money before then. But don't think I
didn't try. And don't think everyone's not going to know that
you're doing those girls wrong."

"I've been waiting too long to get my hands on that property,
and I'm getting it today. We'll be cutting timber out there before
lunch."

Kephart shook his head. "I'm planning to see if I can get the
clerk to put it off."

"He can't do that. By judicial order, the deadline on those taxes is opening of business today. It's a shame the judge had to add such a high penalty to the taxes. Plumb punitive if you ask me. But I heard he wanted to make an example, so as to warn others to get their taxes in on time."

"Wonder who talked the judge into making the penalty impossible for five little innocent girls to pay?" Kep observed. "Looks a lot like a vulture attacking some little bunnies when no one's around to protect 'em, if 'n you ask me. Ain't right."

"That's your opinion, Kephart. But the facts are these: at opening time today, the Randolphs' clock will stop ticking. This will be the last chance anybody's got to pay the taxes. It goes to whoever pays them. Judge Hughes has so ruled."

Kep's face was gloomy as he shook his head. He had been hoping against hope that Wade Chandler or Zach Taylor would come up from Proctor, bringing money donated by the church folk, or perhaps from some of the store owners, but evidently, Wade had not been able to get to Pastor Semmes, or they did not collect enough money. *If we just had some more time*, he thought.

Samuel Robinson, the county clerk, came strolling down the street. He saw the two men as he walked up and said, "You fellows are here early. You know we don't open until eight o'clock."

"I got business to tend to, Robinson. I got the money right here."

"Well, let me get the door open first, L.G." Samuel unhooked a large ring of keys from his belt, located the correct skeleton key, opened the door, and moved inside. Sanders and Kep followed.

They walked down the broad hallway and then turned into the office with the County Clerk sign on it, and as soon as Robinson unlocked the door, they were inside.

L.G. walked up to the counter and, as the clerk walked around, said, "I'm gonna pay all the taxes and penalties due on the Randolph place. I'm paying on behalf of Mr. William Rosecrans Calhoun and the Calhoun Lumber Company."

"Sam, I wish you'd give me a day," Kep said. "I think the girls have enough money in the bank to pay."

"That's against the rules of the road, Kep!" Sanders said loudly. "Judge made his ruling, ain't that right, Sam?"

Robinson was a thin man with scanty salt-and-pepper hair. He wore a white shirt, a string tie, and a pair of black pants. He looked down at the floor and shook his head. "I'd like to give the girls more time, Kep, but Sanders is correct. Judge Hughes gave me his order on Friday and instructed me to keep silent 'bout it. Couldn't even call folks to help. He said that opening time today is the absolute deadline for the girls."

Sanders reached into his pocket and pulled out a roll of bills with a rubber band around it and placed it on the counter. "I got the exact amount of cash right here."

Robinson looked at Kephart sadly. "I wish I could do something, Kep, but the judge's order is the judge's order." He turned and pulled a receipt book down from a shelf, turned the pages, and shook his head. "The tax bill isn't that much. But this is the highest penalty I've ever seen him charge. The girls could mount an appeal up in Asheville or something. Sure seems excessive. Bet Mrs. Frye could help."

"Too late for that," Sanders said gleefully. "Make me out a receipt, Robinson!" he ordered as he unrolled the bills.

Robinson looked sad as he walked over to his desk, sat down, and opened the receipt book. He started to write when suddenly there was the sound of feet running down the hall. He looked up as the door burst open and Wade and the Randolph girls came tumbling into the room.

62

Close Call

K ep exclaimed, "Abbie, Wade, girls . . . what are you all doing here?"

Every eye was on Abbie as she reached into her coat and pulled out a bunch of bills tied with a string. "I got it here. All four hundred and eighty dollars."

Kep let out a yelp, took off his hat, and threw it up so hard it hit the high tinned ceiling. "Well, bless my soul!" he yelled.

"Where'd you get that money?" Sanders hissed.

Whit's eyes were sparkling. "We got it from an angel. That's where."

"And a Haint," Corrie added, laughing.

"How'd ya get here in time?" Kep asked as he picked up his hat.

"Abbie drove their truck to Proctor and came to pick me up. Then I drove here. I used to race cars in Africa when I was a kid. We made the drive in record time!" Wade exclaimed, smiling from ear to ear.

Sanders glowered at them and then turned to face the clerk. "Robinson, I was here first. I got first claim."

The clerk reached down and pulled his pocket watch out of his vest and studied it a moment. "My watch shows it's five minutes until eight o'clock, Sanders. The judge's ruling was that if the taxes were not paid first thing this morning, their place would become the property of the first person who pays the bill. Given that I'll officially open in five minutes, and given the girls are here to pay the bill, I reckon the judge'll allow them to keep what's rightfully theirs."

Sanders's face turned red as he muttered a few unkind words and then turned to storm out of the room. As he reached the door, a shadow crossed the threshold and he ran smack into the giant of a man filling the door. Before Sanders could react, he was lifted off the ground. Sanders tried to protest, but his voice was muffled by the massive hand that grasped him by the neck, holding him above the floor.

Danya entered the room, his arm extended in front of him, holding Sanders, whose legs were flailing uselessly, as if he were trying to run through the air. The colossal man slowly flexed his arm, bringing Sanders's nose next to his own.

Kep was standing close enough to hear Danya's whispered growl, "We know what you did to my friend Nate and Abbie's fiancé, Bobby Lee. We know how you did it. We know you've murdered other men in the valley. Justice will come to you soon. If I were not a Christian man, I'd squeeze the life out of you this very minute, you worm."

Zach entered the office, squeezing between Danya and the door frame. "Danya, put Mr. Sanders down. I don't want to have to arrest you for murder."

Danya released his grip and Sanders fell to the floor, grabbing his red throat as he coughed and stammered. His face was a deep reddish blue and his eyes seemed to be bugging out of his face. He pointed a shaking finger at Danya and tried to speak, but no words came out.

Danya grabbed him by the collar and slung him out the door. "Get out!" he ordered as Sanders bounced off the edge of the door. Then Danya's massive boot kicked him in the rear, lifting him off the floor and out into the hallway. As Danya took a step to follow, Zach stepped in his way.

"That's enough, my friend. Jest leave ol' Sanders to the law.

Before long we'll have him arrested and cooped up in a cell right in this here building."

Danya stood quietly for a moment, glaring into the hall as the sound of Sanders gasping and coughing down the hall echoed into the office.

"You've done enough," Zach reassured Danya.

Danya nodded and sighed.

Kep turned back to Abbie. "Really, honey, where did you get the money?"

"It's the truth, Mr. Kephart. An angel told me where it was in a dream," Whit said.

"And the Haint pointed to the exact spot," Corrie added.

Kep suddenly laughed. "Well, if that's you'uns' story, then you stick to it!"

Abbie moved up to the desk and began counting out the money. Satisfied she had the right amount, she handed it to Mr. Robinson. At the same time, Whit picked up the wad of bills Sanders had left on the counter and held it out to Mr. Robinson, who smiled at her.

"All items that are lost and found on county property must be kept by me, under lock and key for ninety days. If no one claims it, then it goes to the county. My guess is Sanders will eventually come back for it." Robinson looked up at Zach. "Unless he gets charged with murder, then we might never see him in these parts again."

"Murder?" Abbie said, looking from Robinson to Deputy Taylor. "Sanders? Is that how Pa and Bobby Lee died?"

Zach took Abbie's hand, sat on a bench, and gestured for her to sit by him as the other girls gathered around. "This ain't gonna be easy fer me to tell ya, Abbie." Zach cleared his throat. "SBI thinks your pa and Bobby Lee were murdered."

"Murdered?" was all Abbie could mutter as tears began to streak down her cheeks. She felt Whit's and Corrie's hands on her shoulders. "Sanders killed Pa? Bobby Lee?"

"Yep. We got evidence that'll send Sanders into the arms of ol' Sparky hisself."

"Can y'all really prove it? Can ya arrest him?"

Zach nodded. "SBI done ran tests on the bullets that killed 'em. Sanders's gun done it. He done robbed us both, Abbie. You of yer pa *and* fiancé and me of my heritage . . . and jest fer a bunch of ol' trees on some wilderness property in the middle of nowhere. It ain't fair. It ain't right. But the facts are facts."

Abbie reached out to wipe the tear streaking down his cheek. "I know why he did it, Mr. Zach. But how'd he do it?"

"It's a long story, Abbie," Zach said, "and I'll explain later, when the time's right. But right now, you might want to tell Mr. Robinson thank you."

Abbie stood and hugged Whit and Corrie. "Thank you," she mouthed to Mr. Robinson, who smiled and nodded.

The clock began to strike eight.

"Ah," Robinson said. "The clerk's office of Swain County is *now* officially open."

He quickly wrote out a new receipt and reached out to hand it to Abbie. "The property is legally yours . . . totally unencumbered."

But before she could take the receipt, he pulled it back.

"Assuming you can prove to me you're an adult," he said, smiling knowingly.

Abbie reached down to her pocket, pulled out a piece of paper, and handed it to the clerk.

He examined it carefully a moment and then handed it back. "Looks like an official driver's license to me . . . although it ain't stamped yet."

"It will be. I can attest to it," Zach said.

"Kep, Zach," Robinson said, "my guess is that Mrs. Frye can petition the judge to have the penalty reversed." He smiled, as he saw their surprise. He offered the receipt to Abbie. "Congratulations, Miss Randolph. This was a close call, so be sure that you pay your taxes on time next year."

"Yes, sir," she replied as she took the receipt, folded it carefully, and put it in her coat. She turned to her sisters. "Come on, girls. Let's go home. The farm belongs to us now!"

"Can we go to Bennett's soda fountain first? Please, Abbie. Can we?" begged Corrie.

"If it's okay with Abbie, you girls run on down there and tell Doc Kelly the sodas are on me!" Kep proclaimed.

"Mr. Kephart, it's eight o'clock in the morning!" Abbie complained.

"A little treat and a little sweet couldn't hurt . . . if it's all right with you," Kep said.

"Sure. In fact, why don't Danya, Wade, and I come with y'all?" Zach asked. "'Specially since Kep's buying. Why I haven't had a fountain soda in quite a while."

"Me, neither," Danya said, laughing. "I'll go also. I need a soda to calm my stomach. Sitting in the bed of that truck about scared the wits out of me!"

Abbie's sisters looked up at her with hopeful eyes. Abbie tried to give a frustrated parental glance at the men, but could only crack a smile as she said, "Well, okay. But be careful not to run out on the street. I'll be down in a bit."

The girls ran from the office, quickly followed by Danya, Wade, and Zach, down the hall and toward the front door. Kep indicated to Abbie to follow him into the hall, and they sat on an oak bench.

63

Tainted

"Where'd the money come from?" Kep said. "The church folks? Business owners? Some combination?"

Abbie smiled. "It would be hard for any of the folks on Sugar Fork, or even on Hazel Creek, to come up with that much money in one day, 'specially in the middle of planting season. Lord knows Wade and Pastor Semmes sure tried by lettin' as many folks know as they could. Wade even got a telegraph off to the Earnshaws. But according to Western Union in Raleigh, they're outta town and couldn't be reached."

"Then where'd the money come from?"

"I think you know, Mr. Kephart." She looked up at him, but his face remained stoic.

"I do?"

She nodded. "Some time ago Maria told me about Pa. She told me about him transportin' the moonshine that Maddie and Quill Rose produced. I knew Maddie, Quill, and he were splittin' the profits. I just didn't know how much there was or where he was keepin' the money. And when he died, I just figured the secret died with him."

Kep was silent as he relit his pipe.

"What I don't know was, who was coordinatin' the sales over here in Bryson City. Could it be that you might know, Mr. Kephart?"

Kephart took a puff on his pipe and then slowly blew a circle of smoke into the air above them. "Your pa only sold to the doctor and pharmacy. However, after he sold it, some of it found its way out into other establishments. People would come from all directions to sample the 'medicine' he delivered. Many of the flatlanders would stay at the Cooper House, where I have a year-round room. Others stayed at the Fryemont Inn. I'd see strangers who would show up for a few days, some even a couple of weeks, just to enjoy some medicinal moonshine whiskey before they'd head back to their dry counties. And when the revenue agents stayed at Cooper's, well it made for some intrigue."

Abbie smiled. "Well, Mr. Kephart, findin' the money was a miracle, that's what it was. I 'spected any money Pa left us was all tied up in the trust that Mrs. Frye told us we'd be gettin' one day. So, the money he buried, well, it saved our farm and saved all of us girls from becomin' orphans. I told the Lord on our drive over here I was sorry that we had to use whiskey money. In some ways, it just don't feel right."

"Don't you feel bad about it at all, honey. I know your pa was doing what he thought best for you gals. Y'all were everything to him. And if he had been here, I think he would have used that money to save the farm, same as you did."

"I don't know, Mr. Kephart. Seems like some of it may have been the devil's money. Pastor Semmes might call it 'tainted money.'"

"Only one problem with tainted money . . ." Kep commented, with a look of mischievousness.

"What's that?"

"Tain't enough of it!" he replied as his laughter echoed off the ceiling. Kep took a puff and blew another circle of smoke up toward the ceiling and then looked back to her again. "But this much I also know, Abbie, beyond a shadow of doubt: your pa loved you girls something terrible."

Abbie thought for a moment and then said, "Well, I've said

this before, but this time I really mean it. I'm sixteen years old, will be seventeen next week, and that's practically growed up, so I'm gonna have to act like it now."

Kep smiled and put his arm around her, drawing her close. "You definitely are not a little girl anymore, Lauren Abigail Randolph. You're going to somehow have to put the loss of your mama, your pa, and your Bobby Lee behind you. It's more of a load than most anyone should have to carry. Add to that, you've got a farm to run and a family to raise . . . but you can be very sure of this: every one of the highlanders in Sugar Fork and Hazel Creek will be pulling for you, praying for you, watching over you, and helping in any way they can. We plan to see you little bunny rabbits grow up to live long, healthy lives."

Abbie hugged him back.

When he let go, he said, "We'd better get on down to Bennett's Drug Store before your sisters, Danya, and Wade drink all the soda."

Abbie stood and walked down the hall and out of the courthouse. She felt as if all the worries and weight of the world had been lifted off her shoulders . . . at least for the moment.

64

Trail

Zach Taylor and the new posse he had just deputized that Friday morning were silently walking single file through a thick forest of massive virgin deciduous trees interspersed with mighty hemlocks. Although he was happy to have these men with him, most of whom had dogs in this particular fight, he was fearful that one or more might lose his life trying to subdue the man or men he suspected were ahead of them scouting land for the lumber company.

When he had announced the possible dangers to the members of his arrest party, none had hesitated. He had not expected them to, especially after he explained what the SBI had learned in their forensic investigation into the ballistic fingerprinting of the bullets taken out of Nate and Bobby Lee. Of course, the tale painted by the evidence was no surprise to the deputy sheriff, and he was pleased to finally have the information the sheriff and he needed to take decisive action.

The forest closed into a narrow ravine where the men sloshed through a shallow brook bubbling down the valley, and pushed through the chest-high ferns and into a small gorge with a lush garden of black cohosh, trilliums, angelico, Indian cucumber, and some sort of exotic white orchids, each with a broad fringed pink lip.

James Walkingstick took the lead as the men marched across a low ridge covered with huckleberry, gooseberry, and buckberry, all meshed together by the exasperating greenbrier in such a way that no man would be able to push through it, even Danya.

Thick as the hair on a Mountain Cur's back, thought Zach. The brush was so packed and the thorns so sharp they could tear any clothing a man might wear other than leather or hunter's canvas.

Zach noticed that on the other side of the branch stood a patch of leucothoe, usually a low-growing evergreen shrub, but in this hollow looked to be as thick as marsh grass and nearly ten feet high. He knew from experience that its tough inter-woven stems were impenetrable unless a man was to machete his way through nearly inch by inch. Fortunately, there was a well-traveled animal path they could follow, and it was the likely path of their prey.

The Cherokee bent down and was studying the path when Zach came up behind him. "Find something?" he whispered to James.

The Indian nodded as he pointed to a print in the dirt. "Fairly new boots," James said softly. "The nails are not too worn."

"Looks like one man," Zach said.

James nodded.

"This path," said an aging voice from behind, "goes into one of the roughest and most rugged areas left in the Hazel Creek watershed. That's why the company has not logged up here. But I guess they're scouting it now. This is what we Cherokee call Boar Eater Holler."

Zach glanced behind him to see James's father, followed by Tom Rau. "Boar Eater?" asked Tom.

"Yes," Jonathan said. "The Boar Eater is a type of Haint. It's not a man or a varmint; not even a real animal. But a creature that can capture a mean, nasty boar with its bare hands, break its back over its knee, and then eat it alive."

Zach thought he saw Wade's face blanch a bit as he and Danya brought up the rear.

"Some say it will do the same with a man," Jonathan said. "So, nobody from our people ever comes here, at least no one with a lick of sense."

"I think that's just an old-squaw's tale," James whispered. He put his finger in front of his lips, saying, "From here on, no talking. I'd like to catch our quarry unawares." He gestured and the party silently moved forward.

Almost immediately the men were in a maze of laurel and scrubby rhododendron so thick and interlocked over them that the path began to darken. Zach could not see more than ten to fifteen feet in any direction. *A perfect place to be ambushed*, he thought.

He had heard of men getting hopelessly lost in massive thickets like this and never being found. The air noticeably chilled and the men had to stoop to walk forward through the dark brush single file. He could only hope there was enough room for Danya to pass.

As the undergrowth began to thin over them, he heard a waterfall ahead. James stopped and held up his hand. After listening a few minutes, he gave a hand signal that they were to quickly exit the thicket and fan out in the small valley ahead.

He's also worried about a trap, Zach thought as he heard rifle triggers being cocked. *If someone were in the small valley ahead of us, he could pick us off one by one as we come out.* Even in the coolness of the brush, he could feel sweat beading on his brow, so he rubbed it off. *If'n there were another man hidden in the ravine behind us, we'd all be dead in a few minutes.* He could only hope that James would have picked up that there was more than one man against them, and that the target of their search would surrender peacefully.

On James's signal, the six men quickly moved out of the rhododendron tunnel and speedily fanned out, each with his rifle drawn, cocked, and ready. Spread out in front of them was a U-shaped valley, with perilous cliff walls rising from the primeval valley floor. There was clearly no escape.

"He's trapped," Danya whispered.

Zach could see many massive tree trunks—too thick to crawl over—that had fallen across the small valley floor through the centuries and seemingly blocked the way in every direction. *Looks like some giant pitched these trees pell-mell*, he thought.

A sudden metallic click behind them caused Zach and the men to spin around.

65

Ambush

To the shock of the posse, L. G. Sanders was standing on a tall, flat boulder that was jutting above the thicket through which they had just crawled. He had his Winchester .30-30 rifle cocked and ready to fire, while his coat was pulled back revealing the pearl-handled .22-caliber pistol stuck in his belt.

"Drop your guns, boys. This lever action allows me to fire off two shots a second, so . . . it'd take me . . . ah . . . only 'bout three seconds to stop you'uns' clocks, best I can figure."

Zach slowly bent down, placing his rifle on the forest floor. Out of the corner of his eye, he could see each of his men doing the same.

"SBI's on to ya," Zach said. "And so am I. We got proof you shot Nate in the back a couple of months ago and that ya murdered him and my son. It were a pretty nice job of cover-up you and yer no-good gang tried to pull off there on the road from Bryson, but it jest weren't good enough."

"Well," Sanders sneered, "guess you'uns are trying to railroad me outta Hazel Creek the same way you did my brother-in-law."

"Brother-in-law?" Wade asked.

"Yep. Josiah Simmons, my dear sister's husband." Sanders spit out some tobacco juice. "Difference between him and me is I know how to fight back."

"Don't seem like you're one to fight fair, Sanders," Tom remarked.

"You're just sore 'cause I burned your barn down, Rau. I'm just sorry you didn't burn up in it."

Tom stepped forward, but before anyone could blink, Sanders aimed and pulled the trigger. The bullet exploded into the soft ground just in front of Tom's boots, causing him to jerk back a step as the shot echoed throughout the hollow.

"In case any of you can count, that still leaves me six shells in my magazine. One for each of you is all I need." He snickered. "And I still have old Molly here on my belt. She can finish you off just like she did Randolph and that sniveling snot-nosed boy of yours, Taylor. Cried like a little girl before Molly scrambled his pitiful little brain."

Zach bit his lower lip to try to contain the fury that was bubbling up as he felt his face flush. He knew the other men had to suppress their anger, too, and he prayed each would keep calm. He slowly let out his breath.

"I'm a bit surprised a snake like you would make these public confessions," Wade said, sounding remarkably calm. "With this many witnesses, it'll be easy to see you fry in old Sparky up at the state pen, Sanders. Guess we'll see who's a sniveling coward then, eh?"

Sanders sneered. "You don't really think any of you boys are gonna survive, do you?"

"Even if you kill us all, Sanders, there's only one way outta this holler," Zach bluffed. "And we have men guardin' the exit. There's no escape. If'n you surrender, we can guarantee you a fair trial."

"You're a churchgoin' man, ain'tcha, Taylor? You shouldn't lie. Doesn't God hate lying lips?" Sanders pointed to an outcropping of granite halfway up the cliff. "I've been spying you'uns from up there since you dismounted your horses. I know there's no one down there and so do you."

Danya shifted his weight and Sanders pointed his rifle at the large man. "A stinking gypsy, two grimy Injuns, a mountain hick, a wet-behind-the-ears, black-bag-carrying so-called doctor, and a backwoods lawman. Be a nice set of scalps to have on my belt, eh, Chief Walkingstick? But won't anybody find your bodies up here 'cept the bugs, buzzards, and bobcats. Especially if I herd your horses way up Hazel Creek valley and let 'em go."

Suddenly, Zach saw a subtle movement behind Sanders. Slowly rising up, almost as if floating up from the rhododendron, was a short, thin old man, dressed in a black cowl. His unkempt curly gray hair framed a thin bright-white, kaolin-caked face. As he silently stood, Sanders spit another stream of juice. "Tell ya what I'm gonna do, just to make this a fair fight. I'm gonna count to three. At the count of three, you'uns go for your guns and I'm gonna start shooting."

He cocked the lever on his rifle. "One . . ."

Zach wondered if the other men saw what he did, or if it was just an apparition, his brain hoping above all hopes for a miracle.

Sanders lifted the rifle. "Two—"

At that instant, an abrupt, bone-chilling scream erupted from behind Sanders, causing him to spin around. In an instant his eyes widened, his lips separated as if he was trying to say something, and he involuntarily stepped back and stumbled. Before he could catch himself, he began to fall, discharging his rifle toward the old man as he tumbled backward, his arms and legs flailing helplessly against the thick humid air.

As he plummeted toward them, Zach quickly knelt down, grabbed his rifle off the ground, and cocked the trigger. But when Sanders's head crashed against a sharp rock protruding from the mossy floor, Zach heard a sickening crack and snap and knew Sanders's skull or neck—maybe both—was broken. Sanders collapsed onto the ground like a rag doll.

The elder Walkingstick walked over to the limp body and bent over, placing two fingers on his neck. After a few seconds, he looked at Zach and shook his head. "This snake won't strike anymore."

The men looked up at Jeremiah Welch in amazement and admiration, as the old man checked himself for wounds.

"Any hit you?" Zach yelled up.

The Haint shook his head and began to smile.

"I swan, Jeremiah Welch," Zach laughed. "Seeing you like that 'bout scared me silly. I can only imagine what Sanders musta thought. Bet he wondered if'n he was seein' Lucifer hisself."

Jeremiah continued to smile as his toothless grin spread from ear to ear.

"Well, you interested in comin' down to Proctor with us, Jeremiah? Once I get Sanders's body put up, I'll be treating my posse to dinner at the Clubhouse. We'd be right honored to have you join us . . . that is, if'n you'll wash that mess off'n your face."

The old man's eyes opened; he quickly shook his head and spun around, disappearing into the underbrush without a sound.

No wonder the mountain folk think he's a ghost, Zach thought. As he sat down on a moss-covered log, the men gathered around the body. Zach felt a chill go down his spine as he realized how close he and his men had been to dying, and he to enjoying his final rest next to his beloved Hannah and Bobby Lee. But finally, the reign of terror of L. G. Sanders was over.

Part Three

MONDAY, MAY 24

through

THURSDAY, SEPTEMBER 16, 1926

66

Untimely

"Get along, Scratch!" Maddie hollered at her old, bony gray mule. "I swan, you're actin' more and more bad tempered each day."

"Hello, Maddie."

Surprised by the voice, she looked up to see the young Wade Chandler carrying a black bag and walking down the road toward her.

"Sorry to startle you," he said as he walked up to her.

"Just yellin' at this old mule. I tell ya, if I weren't a churchgoin' woman now, I'd had knocked him on the head long ago."

Wade rubbed the mule's forehead. "Scratch, I'd recommend doing what she says."

"Maybe he'll listen to ya. He don't listen to me." Maddie looked at his bag. "Got'cha a new doctorin' bag?"

"I do." Wade lifted it up to display it. "My father sent this as a gift for graduating from medical school. He shipped it all the way from Africa; had it handmade. Here's my name in gold lettering. Look, right here."

Maddie could see he was quite pleased with the gift. "I see it's got a strap to use as a shoulder bag."

"Yes, ma'am. Makes it easier to tote." He let the bag rest.

"Heard that you're courtin' that Jenkins girl from Bryson."

"Not yet, Maddie, but I think she'd like to. She wants me to move to Bryson and set up a practice over there."

"You gonna?"

"Who knows? I've been here only a few weeks, but I'm liking it—quite a bit."

"Well, I'll tell you this, sonny. I think you're built for these parts. Somehow, I don't think you're gonna like Bryson."

"Guess I'll have to decide, eh? Oh, by the way, thanks for the referral of Mr. Cable. That gash in his leg sure was nasty. All the way to the bone."

"I knew my potions and the good Lord would take several months to heal that slash. Left to heal on its own, it would've left a massive scar, maybe even a cripplin' scar if'n it had shrunk. Not only that, a mountain man wants to get back on his feet as soon as he can."

Wade smiled. "In fact, no sooner had I finished stitching him up, and he woke up from the chloroform, than he was up and walking."

"Did you leave some opium for him?"

"I did. A little. And I told him I knew you'd be stopping by to see him, so I left his recovery in your good hands. When it comes to healing folks, there's nothing like trust. And that family trusts you as long as the day."

"Well, I've been healin' up here since the last century," Maddie said.

"I appreciate your faith in me, as well as your teaching, Maddie. Feels like I've got a lot of learning ahead of me."

"Anyone with a smidge of wantin' to learn can pick up a lot over time."

"I'm finding that to be true."

Maddie smiled and nodded. "And, like Kep always says, 'When the student's ready, the professor will come.'" She had come to like this young man—a lot—and she was not one to take to most physicians.

The noise of an approaching wagon drew their attention. They turned to see Millard and Etta Mae Barnes coming up the road toward them.

"Y'all heading to the party?" Millard called out as they approached.

"I am," Maddie replied. She turned to Wade. "Ya comin'?"

"What party?" Wade said.

"Abbie Randolph's seventeenth," Maddie replied. "They'll be a passel of folks up there celebratin'. That Abbie, she's done a fine job being a ma to her sisters, 'specially in light of her pa and fiancé bein' murdered. Now she's got a farm to run on top of it all, so I brung her a fine goose-down pillow for her birthday. It'll hep her git some rest at night, once she lays down. I hate pluckin' the dratted thing, but the feathers do make fine pillows."

"I don't understand it," Wade said, looking down at his boots.

"Understand what?"

"Nate and Bobby Lee were just murdered. Heck, it wasn't but a couple of weeks ago. How in the world can they be having a party? Isn't there a time for mourning the departed up here?"

Maddie removed her corncob pipe from her mouth, after taking a puff, and then pointed the mouthpiece at him. "You got a lot to learn about these folks, son. One reality of livin' in this here wilderness is untimely death. Another fact is the deep faith they have. They believe with all their souls in the life to come."

"True enough," Millard added. "I've found that the mountain people say good-bye to their dead quickly, and get on with the matters of life: good work, good friends, good food, good music, and good frolics. It's just the way it is out here."

Wade nodded as he considered their wise words. "You know, the Africans where I grew up were the same. But living in Philadelphia, I guess I haven't seen it in a while."

"Like I always say, the city is a good place to be *from*"—Maddie looked around the forest—"and this is a good place to be *at*.

So, how 'bout you join the three of us and we'll go on up to the party?"

"I wasn't invited," Wade said, looking forlorn. "And I've others to see to."

"Well, son, you're invited now," Millard said.

Wade's cheeks blushed, which they did easily. "I didn't know it was Abbie's birthday. I don't have a present."

"That won't make no never-mind to Abbie," Millard said. "I can tell you that she thinks a heap of you. Told me and Etta Mae as much just last week."

"That was a *confidential* talk," Etta Mae protested.

"Etta, you've never had a confidential talk in your life," Millard said, laughing. He looked back at Wade. "Hop up here and ride with us. You can come wish her a happy birthday. It'll mean the world to her. Whatcha say?"

Wade smiled. "Well, then, count me in!"

67

Tradition

The cabin was abuzz with activity as the girls and Maria helped Abbie get ready. Corrie was at the kitchen table ironing Abbie's church dress, while Maria was polishing Abbie's dress shoes. Abbie was sitting in her mother's rocker while Whit, standing behind her, was combing her hair.

"Ouch!" Abbie cried out.

Whit pulled back. "Tryin' to get your hair fixed just right. But this brush is plumb worn out. You need a new one, Abbie."

"When you go 'bout gettin' a new brush, how 'bout lookin' into gettin' a new dress?" Corrie asked.

"Why? What's the matter with my dress?" Abbie asked. "I like it."

"'Cause the fact of the matter is this dress needs replacin', Abbie," Corrie said, not realizing how deeply her words would cut into her sister's heart. "You need a proper one."

All of a sudden, tears formed in Abbie's eyes and streaked down her cheeks as she softly began to cry. Whit came around the chair and hugged her sister. "Now, now. It's all right, sister."

"What's she snifflin' 'bout?" Anna asked.

"I'm sorry, Abbie. I plumb forgot," Corrie said, standing and walking over to be by her sister.

"Forgot what?" Maria asked.

"It's the tradition of sixteen," Corrie explained.

"What tradition?"

"In the Smokies, during your sixteenth year," Whit said as she continued to hold Abbie, "if'n you're a boy, your pa's supposed to give ya your own huntin' rifle or maybe even a horse. For a girl, it's usually a real nice handmade dress."

"Or," Corrie added, "if'n you're rich, then your parents will buy ya a store- or catalog-bought dress like the ones at the Barnes's store. Some parents give the gift at the Christmas before the birthday; others wait until the actual birthday."

Abbie looked up and smiled at her sister. "Corrie Hannah, you've always said you'd marry a rich man. Maybe you'll be able to do the tradition for your children."

"For years," Whit explained as she swept away Abbie's tears with her finger, "Abbie and me have almost swooned over the newest dress fashions in the Sears, Roebuck and Company and Montgomery Ward catalogs. And we've even yearned over the occasional *McCall's* magazine that one of the girls at school would bring in."

"So," Abbie said, sniffling, "my prayer was that Sandy Rau would help Pa in choosin' the perfect dress for me. I didn't think there was any way for him to give it to me this last year, us losing Mama, and Pa crippled up from being shot." Tears began falling down her cheeks again.

"Maria, our sister was hopin' that at this year's birthday, Pa might have finally found a way to give her a dress," Whit explained.

Maria nodded as Abbie leaned against Whit, who held her sister close.

"'Spect Abbie dreamed about her and Bobby Lee a-courtin' in that dress. That right, sister?" Whit said.

Abbie nodded.

"I know you thought he was the most amazing boy in the valley," Maria said as she put her arm around Abbie.

"I'd prefer dreamy, Maria. He was a beautiful young man. I miss him more than I can say. There's an emptiness in my soul that I'm not sure any other will fill. I tell ya, there are times when my soul feels so empty, I just plumb wish I didn't have one."

"Abbie," Maria corrected, "you don't *have* a soul, you *are* one. Your soul has a body. One day the two will be separated, but only until the Lord comes back for us."

"I like that, Maria. I think I'll put it in my journal, if'n you don't mind." Abbie pulled out a handkerchief and gently blew her nose. "But even with him being gone, I need to count the blessin's I've still got," Abbie said, sniffling. "Really, now, if we were to all be honest, we'd have to admit that the Lord has given us everythin' we need. Just maybe not everythin' we might want."

"And just like Mama always said," Whit added, "'God will give us everything we need, and more, so that we can freely give to others.'"

"And it was Pa who always said," Abbie responded, "'If you're not content with what ya have, you'll never be content with what ya want.'"

"Stand up, Abbie. Let's put your dress on." Corrie carefully carried the freshly ironed dress to her sister.

"And your shoes," Maria said, proudly holding up a pair of brightly shining patent-leather shoes.

"You're so pretty, Abbie," Anna observed. "Your beauty would make *any* dress look good."

Abbie blushed as she looked at her sisters and quickly changed the subject. "You'uns are all growin' up so fast!" she said as she slipped the dress over her head.

"We're *all* growin' up!" Whit proclaimed.

Maria handed the shoes to Whit—the nice store-bought shoes her mama and pa had given Abbie for her fifteenth birthday—who bent down and slipped the shoes onto Abbie's feet. "They still fit perfectly, Cinderella! Now, you're ready for the ball. Let's all just hope a new Prince Charming shows up!"

"Pshaw!" Abbie muttered.

"So, Abbie, stand up and turn around!" Maria exclaimed.

Abbie slowly stood and then turned and turned, and then she laughed and began to spin around, her dress and hair flying out as she spun while the girls laughed and clapped. Then she quickly walked over to the hearth. She stared up at the draped mantel clock. It had belonged to her grandmother and had been draped for four weeks at the deaths of each of her pa's parents, for each of her three brothers, and at her mama's death. As of today, it had been draped for only two weeks since her pa's and fiancé's murders. With a deep breath, she slowly removed the black-velvet covering, opened the glass door, reset the hands of the clock, and pushed the pendulum to begin the familiar ticking.

She turned around to her sisters and Maria, who all seemed shocked.

"I know it's two weeks early," Abbie explained. "But I believe Pa would have us shake the dust off'n our sandals and begin our family clock anew. I think he'd want us to have a frolic—in his and Bobby Lee's honor—and I think they'll be laughin' right along with us. Whatcha say?"

Whit, Corrie, and Anna all walked over, nodding their consent as the girls embraced.

"Oh, people are comin'!" Maria said as she ran to the door.

Abbie looked down at nineteen-month-old Sarah Beth as she slept. *I wonder what the future holds for us, sweet baby?* she thought.

Whit stepped back from Abbie and held out her hands. Abbie reached out and took them.

"Abbie, you look *so* beautiful."

Abbie looked down at her figure, which, she had to admit, was filling out very nicely. *Finally!* she thought to herself.

"You don't even need a Doc Warner's corset, I'll tell ya that!" Whit added, smiling.

Abbie blushed but knew her sister was correct. The young girl of so long ago was now long gone, in the span of only a few short and very difficult months.

"Abbie, before long you're gonna have to start thinkin' about courtin' another boy," Whit said. "You know they'll be comin' for ya. So, just between us, which of the boys do you favor?"

Abbie released Whit and waved her away. "First of all, ya know I'll never find another Bobby Lee. Second, ya know I have *no* time for it."

"Seriously, Abbie. Ya've given up everything for us," Whit said.

"Don't be silly, Whit! The Lord chose to take Mama and Pa. He chose to take the only boy I've ever loved. I know he has a plan for us all. But I think his intent for me is to care for you girls, help you find *your* men, and care for this big ol' farm."

"And *I* think his plan for you includes you getting a husband," Maria said. "Remember my gift of prophecy? The Lord's told me you and your husband will become healers. When it's time, the Lord will bring him to you."

"And," Whit added, "ya can't spend your whole life just a-takin' care of us!"

"I promised Mama and Pa that I would." Abbie turned back to her sister and they hugged. "I wouldn't have it any other way."

"Well, I think the Lord will have it another way," Maria said.

"I agree!" Whit added as she released Abbie. "But in the meantime, let's go have us a frolic! I believe this party will be the start of a new chapter for us all. And a happy one at that!"

"And I'll pray that your prophecy is correct, Maria," Whit said as the women embraced.

68

Seventeenth

Before long, Abbie's seventeenth birthday party was in full swing. The lemonade was ice-cold and the perfect balance of sweet and sour. The cake the Johnsons and Pyeritzes brought was delicious, especially with a scoop of the handmade ice cream the Barneses brought up from their store. Danya and Millard supervised the afternoon games, while Sandy and Emily Rau, Grace, Maria, and Maddie ran the kitchen.

Friends from town, as well as from up and down Sugar Fork and Hazel Creek, dropped by throughout the afternoon to eat, visit, play games, catch up on gossip, and dance to the music played by a group of black musicians, including Gabe and Reba Johnson, whom Mr. Barnes hired to play all the mountain songs Abbie loved. Proctor's only photographer, Harve Fouts, who worked for Calhoun, was there to take pictures of the event and the families.

Most of the talk was about the death of L. G. Sanders. The consensus was the valley would be a safer and more satisfying locale with him gone. Dr. Keller relayed that Mr. Calhoun was sending in a new man to manage the operation. Dr. Keller was hoping, as were many in town, that the locals and the employees would find the new man to be much more amenable and acceptable, maybe even a churchgoing man, a family man, and, for a change, a fine company manager. However, given Mr. Calhoun's reputation for profits over people, most doubted that a new manager would be any improvement.

There was also significant murmuring about Judge Hughes. No one understood how he could issue such an unfair and onerous judgment against the Randolph girls. "Had to be Calhoun," Millard concluded. "Musta had the judge in his back pocket somehow or another. He's been known to buy the favors of politicians. Why not a judge?"

"Well, the judge cain't be all bad," Zach said. "After all, he accepted the driver's license I issued to Abbie. Had he not accepted it, the girls would have lost the farm for sure."

"I know," Lillian Frye countered. "And he did approve the trust I set up for the girls. But I smell a skunk in here somewhere. I think we should consider filing a formal complaint with the Supreme Court of North Carolina in Raleigh. They'd look into it, you can be sure. But first, let me talk with the judge and see what I can learn."

After a blessing given by Pastor Semmes, Abbie blew out all seventeen candles, praying a secret wish as everyone cheered. Abbie had never seen so many presents. As folks gathered around her, Abbie sat in front of the presents. Zach knelt beside her, handing her a small present.

Abbie smiled and leaned over to kiss his cheek. She whispered in his ear, "I'm glad you came. I know it must be hard for you."

Zach nodded. "True 'nough. It's only been two weeks since that varmint kilt my son. The house is awfully lonely and my heart's terrible empty, Abbie. But I feel I owe it to you to be here for your birthday."

"Mrs. Barnes told me you and Bobby Lee ordered something for me the week before . . . he passed."

Zach looked around at a blushing Etta Mae. "I was hoping it would be a surprise."

"Oh, Mrs. Barnes didn't tell me what it was. She said it were a secret."

Zach's anger quickly subsided and he turned back to Abbie. "It's kinda personal. You don't have to open it now."

"If it's from Bobby Lee, I'd like to open it first."

Zach nodded. "Bobby Lee thought you'd like it."

Abbie quickly unwrapped the gift, and when she saw it, her jaw dropped as she held up a fancy tortoiseshell brush-and-comb set. Her eyes both misted and brightened as she turned the items around and around. "They are beautiful!" Abbie said in a hushed tone. "They will be perfect for my hair."

She turned to Zach. "They are beyond compare. Ideal!" She hugged his neck and when she pulled away she saw the tears streaking down his cheeks.

After the presents were all opened, Grace Lumpkin sat down with Abbie. "I loved your gift from Bobby Lee," she began. "It's so unlike an average boy!"

Abbie smiled. "He was far from average."

"Like your pa," Grace said. "Obviously he loved you deeply."

"Like my pa did you," Abbie said.

Grace nodded as tears formed in her eyes. She took Abbie's hands in her own. "I'm looking forward to your high school graduation next week. I know that your pa and Bobby Lee would have given anything to have been there."

Abbie's lips tightened as she nodded and dropped her head.

"Abbie, I have some news to tell you. And it won't be easy."

Abbie looked up.

"I'll be leaving next week. In fact, the day after your graduation."

"Leavin'?" Abbie asked, incredulously. "Where ya goin'?"

"New York City."

"For how long? When ya comin' back?"

"I'm not planning to return, Abbie."

Abbie shook her head in disbelief. "Why? Why would you leave us? Why New York City?"

"Not too long ago, I lived there for a couple of years. Moved there when I was twenty-five years old and tried my hand at writing, and I actually made a meager living selling short stories. But I became involved in politics, which disillusioned me quite a bit. I found myself missing the mountains, so I moved back. Then I had the marvelous opportunity to get the teaching job in Hazel Creek and I got to know you, your wonderful sisters, and then your pa. Slowly I fell in love with him." She took a deep breath as she looked across the Sugar Fork valley. "Now with the loss of your pa, I'm sensing it's time for me to move on, Abbie."

"Move on, or escape?" Abbie asked, color rising to her cheeks. "Are you just runnin' from your pain? I know there are times I want to, Miss Grace. But we just can't outrun pain. It'll come chasin' after us."

Grace squeezed her hands. "No, dear Abbie. I'm not running from anything. I'm actually moving to something. I've been given a wonderful opportunity in New York."

"What? What are you going to do?"

"I've been offered a job as a writer for one of the best magazines in New York, *The World Tomorrow.* It's a dream come true for me."

"Where ya gonna live?"

"With a dear friend, Esther Shemitz, at least until she and her boyfriend tie the knot."

Abbie shook her head again in disbelief, as if trying to shake away the surprising news. "I lost my mama, then my pa and fiancé . . . now you? It just seems like too much."

Grace took a deep breath and then let it out slowly. She seemed to be in deep thought for a moment, and then looked into Abbie's eyes. "Abbie, I've lost my ma and pa also. And now the first real love of my life is gone. You're right! At times it seems like too much to bear, the pain seems too deep, too hard. But I've been comforted by a verse I'm trying to memorize."

"Which one?"

Grace reached into her pocket and pulled out a small piece of paper. "I've not learned it all. Let me read it to you: 'Though our outward man perish, yet the inward man is renewed day by day. For our light affliction, which is but for a moment, worketh for us a far more exceeding and eternal weight of glory; while we look not at the things which are seen, but at the things which are not seen: for the things which are seen are temporal; but the things which are not seen are eternal.'"

"Second Corinthians, chapter four."

Grace smiled. "Very good, Abbie."

Abbie squeezed her hands. "Just like the Bible says: all things work together for good, if . . ."

Grace's eyes narrowed. "What do you mean?"

"It's in the Epistle to the Romans, chapter eight and the twenty-eighth verse."

Grace laughed. "I don't have that one in my heart yet. Can you tell it to me?"

"'And we know that all things work together for good to them that love God, to them who are the called according to his purpose.'"

Grace nodded as tears formed in her eyes. "Then that will be my prayer for us: that we would both love God and be called to his purpose for us."

Abbie leaned forward to hug her. "Me too," she whispered.

69

First

As the party was winding down, and most of the guests had
left, Abbie took a moment to sit alone on the porch. She was
looking across the valley when someone came to sit in the rocker
next to her.

"You seem in a daze. Are you all right?"

As she turned and recognized who it was, she felt her eyes
widen and her heart flutter. "Oh . . . uh . . . . hi, Wade. Whatcha
doin' up here?"

"Maddie told me I should come up. Hope you don't mind."

Abbie felt short of breath. "Uh . . ." she stammered, "um, not at
all. I'm delighted."

Wade smiled and Abbie felt a slight shiver of anticipation.

"Didn't mean to disturb your meditation."

"I wasn't meditatin'. I was just thinkin' back on some warm
memories."

"I hope today will be one of them."

Abbie looked back across the valley. "I don't think I'll forget
this birthday for the rest of my life."

"Good. Well, I wanted to wish you a happy birthday and congratulations. I've heard you're graduating from high school next
week. You must be awfully smart to graduate a year early."

"Word up the hollers is *you* graduated from high school at sixteen, Mr. Smarty Pants."

Wade smiled. "I was homeschooled by my stepmother at the mission compound where we served in Liberia. I'm not sure I was so smart, though."

"You finished college at age twenty and medical school at age twenty-three. Sounds pretty smart to me."

"I think I was just blessed," Wade said, looking uncomfortable. "I'm so sorry that I didn't know it was your birthday. I was making rounds when I ran into Maddie. She invited me up. Will you forgive me for not having a gift for you?"

Abbie smiled, blushed, and nodded as she looked down. "Well, Wade, I've forgiven you before; I certainly can again. And your presence here is a gift to me. I just hope you'll forgive me for not invitin' ya. Thanks for comin'."

"You're welcome and you're forgiven." Wade looked across the farm for a moment and then back at Abbie. "Come to think of it, there are two gifts I could give you. You like to read, don't you?"

Abbie nodded.

"And you like poetry," Wade said.

"Both Whit and I do. A lot," she replied.

"As you know, I do, too." Wade reached into his bag and pulled out a well-worn book. "It's not wrapped. But it's a favorite of mine, an anthology of poetry." He handed it to her. "Here, I'd love for you to have it."

Abbie shook her head. "I cain't take that."

"Why not?"

"It's obvious you love this book. Look how it's worn. Miss Grace says that a book that's worn out by one person is like a well-seasoned pan; it holds all its past uses, makin' each readin' deeper and more personal than the last."

Wade held up the book and looked at it fondly. "Miss Grace is right. And I do love this book." He held it out to Abbie. "I want you to love it, also."

Abbie looked at the book and nodded. "I'll accept it, but only under two conditions."

"Which are?"

"First, I'll only take it as a loan. Agreed?"

Wade smiled.

"Second, you gotta quote a poem from it. Don't think much of a man can't commit to memory some Scripture, poetry, and literature."

Wade thought a moment. "I've memorized many. I'll share one by Alfred Lord Tennyson. He was the poet laureate of the United Kingdom during Queen Victoria's reign. It's called 'The Brook' and I'll recite part of it in honor of you and Sugar Fork:

I come from haunts of coot and hern,
I make a sudden sally
And sparkle out among the fern,
To bicker down a valley.

I steal by lawns and grassy plots,
I slide by hazel covers;
I move the sweet forget-me-nots
That grow for happy lovers.

I slip, I slide, I gloom, I glance,
Among my skimming swallows;
I make the netted sunbeam dance
Against my sandy shallows.

I murmur under moon and stars
In brambly wildernesses;
I linger by my shingly bars;
I loiter round my cresses;

And out again I curve and flow
To join the brimming river,
For men may come and men may go,
But I go on forever.

"Well done, Dr. Chandler," Abbie said as she first clapped her hands together and then reached out to receive the book. "Since you met my challenge, I'll accept your book . . . on loan."

Wade smiled. "The next time you get sick, I'll give you a complimentary house call. That'll be my second birthday gift to you."

Abbie laughed.

"What are you laughing about?"

"You give your calls away anyway," she said, still laughing.

"Good point. Then, in that case . . ." Wade's voice faded as he thought for a moment. Suddenly, he took her hand in his. She was too surprised to react. "Abbie, I want to tell you how much I admire you for taking care of your family and your farm . . . and at great personal sacrifice, I suspect."

"Anyone would do the same."

Wade shook his head. "Not anyone. Just a special one. So here's my second gift." He leaned forward, lifted her hand, and softly kissed the back of it.

Abbie blushed.

"First time I've ever kissed a mountain lady's hand."

Abbie looked up into his crystalline blue-gray eyes. A shock of thick auburn hair fell onto his forehead, crowning his thin face, high cheekbones, generous mouth, and the handsome cleft in his chin. She felt her heart flutter as she said, "This is the first time a flatlander has kissed my hand."

Wade grinned. "Well, then, I'm honored. I'm glad I'm the first."

He stood as he released her hand. "I've some calls to make. Will you forgive me if I take my leave?"

Abbie laughed. "A friendship with you sure requires a lot of forgivin'."

He smiled, nodded, and turned to depart. She couldn't help but watch him walk away until he was out of sight.

"You shouldn't oughta let old men kiss yer hand."

Abbie turned to see David Rau standing by her. She had not noticed his approach. At age sixteen, he was mischievous and a prankster, just like his pa, but he had inherited his blond hair and blue eyes from his ma.

"Here's the lemonade you asked me to bring you," he said, holding out a cup.

"Thanks, David." As he sat beside her, Abbie said, "He was just being polite."

"Still, he's *really* old. Must be nearly thirty. And that's old!"

"Twenty-three," Abbie corrected, tilting her head a bit to study his face. "David Rau, I declare, do I detect a hint of jealousy?"

He chuckled as he looked down at his feet. "Nope. Not *a hint* of jealousy . . . *a whole lot* of jealousy."

Abbie laughed. "Well, I appreciate honesty from a man." David had been sweet on Abbie since they were children and would occasionally serve as her protector at school. She admired his Scripture knowledge, but she was irritated that he always beat her at their Bible drills at church. She had always thought, when she was younger, that they might become boyfriend and girlfriend one day, but David had never shown an interest.

"Well, don't matter. He won't be around to do any more kissin' anyway, least ways not around here."

"What do you mean?" Abbie asked.

"Rumor around town is that the good Dr. Chandler is gonna marry Blanche Jenkins over in Bryson City. Suspect he'll be movin' over there to work with Dr. Bennett, who is really, really old."

Why would he lead me on? Was he just a-joshin' with me? Abbie wondered as she felt her face flush with anger. *It ain't right to do that!* Her eyes looked across the expanse of her beloved Sugar Fork valley as she sighed and thought, *When will I see him again?*

70

Stars

Long after her sisters were in bed, Abbie was still sitting on the porch. The excitement of her birthday party and her encounter with Wade wafted through her mind again and again, leaving warm imprints on her memory of the day.

The new moon was three days away, so the waning crescent moon wouldn't rise until a bit before dawn. The Sugar Fork valley was as dark as coal, allowing millions of stars to blaze and glitter in their glory, as bright as diamonds, spreading across the entire sky.

Remembering one of her favorite Ralph Waldo Emerson quotes, she whispered, "If the stars should appear one night in a thousand years, how would men believe and adore; and preserve for many generations the remembrance of the city of God which had been shown! But every night come out these envoys of beauty, and light the universe with their admonishing smile." She looked down at her Mountain Cur. "What do you think of that, Lilly?" However, Lilly was sound asleep at her feet.

"Jack, you like my quote?" she asked her gray tabby, curled up on her lap and purring contentedly.

"Guess everyone's asleep but me." Abbie looked back up at the sparkling canvas spread across the mountain sky as her mind overflowed again with fond remembrances of her party. The joy of it all was balanced by a deep sense of sadness that her mama and pa weren't there to enjoy the day with her. She quickly turned her mind back to the day's wonderment and frolic.

Out of all her happy recollections of this particular birthday celebration, she kept coming back to her unexpected feelings toward Wade Chandler. She sighed as she remembered Wade's kiss and the look in his eyes. *I've been attracted to that man since I first met him in town,* she thought, *and when he lent me his favorite book of poetry and kissed my hand, I knew it for sure!*

She chastised herself. *No way! There's just no way some fancy doctor is gonna fall for a mountain girl . . . especially a Randolph girl stuck up in some high hidden holler. 'Sides, he's in love with Blanche Jenkins—a big city girl and a rich one at that! He was just a-playin' with me.*

"It was just a foolin' thing!" she said out loud. "Why, a man like that would *never* think of a wilderness girl who is only just finishin' high school . . . and not even college educated at that!"

Jack stood up on her lap, stretched, turned around twice, and settled back down as Abbie stroked him.

"'Sides, that David Rau's a real looker. And he's a mountain boy. And he understands me and knows our ways. I've known him as long as I can remember, Jack . . . why since we were both kids."

Suddenly a mellow, muted trill, lasting two to three seconds, sounded from their big chestnut tree. Lilly lifted her head and growled.

"Just the old screech owl, Lilly. You shush up."

Lilly stood up, the hair on her back rising as she continued her growl. Just then, the owl flew out of the large chestnut tree by their cabin, startling Jack into jumping off her lap. Abbie looked up to see a dark figure standing outside the fence surrounding the cabin.

A soft bass voice said, "Fear not."

Abbie instantly recognized the voice and smiled. "Jeremiah Welch, you old Haint. Whatcha doin'?"

"May I enter?"

"Of course."

He seemed to float across the ground, as was his habit, and

came to the porch steps. "I'm just watchin' out for you girls, like I do every night."

"That's sweet," Abbie said.

"It was my covenant with your pa," he said. "I like lookin' after you'uns."

"Would ya've crossed me off your list if Bobby Lee and I had gotten hitched?" Abbie asked, smiling.

"Word in the woods was you'uns were gonna have a cabin raising here on the property pretty quick. That correct?"

"We were."

"Then I'da keptcha in my sites for sure. I kinda liked that boy."

"Me, too."

"I liked when he asked you to marry him."

Abbie's eyes widened. "What? You watched us?"

"Well, your pa asked me to. But I averted my eyes when you'uns kissed. You gotta admit, it were powerful romantic."

Abbie smiled as she nodded.

"You're up late," Jeremiah said.

"Just admirin' the beauty of the night, Jeremiah."

He looked up at the sky. "Stars," he said, almost in a whisper, "the blessed candles of the night, Shakespeare called 'em. To me, stars are the streetlights of heaven."

"Shakespeare? You read Shakespeare?" Abbie asked.

"*The Merchant of Venice* is my favorite. Kep loans me books to read. I liked that one the most."

Abbie laughed. "Ya never fail to impress me, Jeremiah Welch."

"Well," he said, "I hope this delivery will also be impressive to ya." His hand appeared from underneath his cowl, holding a package, which he held out. "Here. It's for your birthday."

"You shouldn't have," Abbie said as she took the box.

"I didn't. It's not from me," he said as he took a step back.

"Who's it from?"

"Believe it or not, your pa."

71

Bequest

Abbie looked down at the brown-paper-wrapped box held together with a piece of twine.

"Please, have a seat, Jeremiah," Abbie said, gesturing at a porch rocker. "Can I pour you a glass of lemonade? We have some left."

"No, thank you. Miss Maria brought me some, along with a piece of cake and a big scoop of ice cream."

"She knows where you live?"

"No one knows that. She just knows I've been watching over you girls real close. Unwrap it, Abbie. Don't keep everyone waitin'," Jeremiah encouraged.

"Everyone? It's just us!" Abbie said, laughing.

"Can two gypsies come watch?" said Maria as she and Danya stepped out of the dark, up to the fence, and into the yard. "Couldn't sleep with the celebration continuing."

"Welcome," Abbie said.

"Open it up!" Maria directed, pointing to the box.

Abbie pulled off the twine and wrapping, leaving a plain box on her lap. The label indicated the box was from Barnes General Store.

"Your pa showed me where he stored it, in a secret place; a place known only to him and me."

"Did he know he wouldn't be here?" Abbie said, tears forming in her eyes.

Jeremiah shrugged. "Don't know. He was mighty suspicious 'bout Sanders. Knew he was up to no good. 'Course, now *we* know he was."

Abbie nodded.

Danya patted her arm. "Abbie, Sanders won't bother you again. He won't be laying a hand on you, your sisters, or your farm. You can thank Jeremiah for that!"

Abbie leaned over to hug the old man. Then she held up the box. "Thank you, Jeremiah. This means the world to me."

She heard sounds coming from the cabin and turned to see Whit, Corrie, and Anna sleepily stumbling through the door. They looked surprised to see the Haint sitting on their porch next to Maria and Danya.

"Y'all know Mr. Jeremiah," Abbie said.

The girls nodded.

"He brought me a gift from someone very special." As they saw the box on her lap, their eyes widened as they scurried to stand behind her.

"Who is it from?" Whit asked.

"Pa," Abbie answered.

"Then open it! Now!" Corrie ordered, as the sisters gathered around her rocker.

"Hurry!" Anna exclaimed.

Her observers grew completely silent as they all leaned forward. Abbie reached down and pulled off the lid. As she recognized the contents, her eyes became as large as saucers and her hands covered her mouth to stifle a gasp.

Lying in the box was the most beautiful dress she had ever seen: a light blue long-sleeve, two-piece outfit with a full-length skirt. The detailed trim work on the bodice was fit for a queen. She couldn't even move. It was as if all her dreams were lying, gorgeously folded, in a Barnes General Store box.

"I can't believe it," Abbie whispered.

"Let's look," Maria said, lifting the dress out of the box to unfold it in front of Abbie, as the men nodded in approval.

"Here, honey. Let's see how it looks." Maria turned the dress around and placed it in front of Abbie.

"Hold it up, Abbie. And turn for everyone to see," Whit said.

Abbie beamed as she held the dress up and then twirled around, smiling up at the stars, and everyone clapped. "You didn't forget, Pa. You didn't forget."

She knew her pa was looking on . . . nodding . . . tears filling his eyes. She could almost hear him whisper, "I love you, Punkin."

"I love you, too, Pa," she whispered.

Tears were falling from her eyes as she declared, "I don't reckon any girl ever had such a birthday! Not on Sugar Fork. Not on Hazel Creek. Not in the Smoky Mountains. Not anywhere!"

72

Allure

They walked up to the Jenkinses' porch, arm in arm, laughing as they settled next to each other on the swinging porch chair. Blanche laid her head on his shoulder and sighed. "I've got to tell you, Wade, I just didn't like it that much! I mean, our dinner at the Fryemont Inn was wonderful, romantic. But the play . . . I've seen better."

"You're kidding! I thought it was terrific," Wade responded. "I had no idea the theater talent here in Bryson City was so excellent. The troupe here is as fit as *any* in Philadelphia, could even match up with some in New York. And I should know, I've seen most of them."

"Don't get me wrong," Blanche explained. "I think Eugene O'Neill is a talented playwright. I just liked *Beyond the Horizon* and *The Emperor Jones* far better."

"Have you seen *Anna Christie?*"

"Oh, of course. It's my favorite O'Neill play of all!" Blanche exclaimed, sitting up and taking Wade's hand in her own. "I can't avoid tears when Mat forgives Anna for being a prostitute after she promises never to be one again. And then, when her dad agrees to them getting married, well, oh my, it is just *too* romantic."

"So, you didn't find *The Hairy Ape* romantic?"

"Not in the slightest. Yank seemed to me to be a brute . . . a mere laborer. He was too common for me. I didn't find him romantic at all. Did you?"

Wade felt his eyes narrow. "I think I identified with Yank. Maybe I'm a bit like him."

"*I* identified with the rich daughter of the steel-business industrialist. In fact, I quite like being a rich daughter, if I don't say," Blanche said, laughing, "But don't worry, sweetheart, I won't refer to you as a hairy ape or a filthy beast, although I do look forward to cleaning you up a bit when you move out of the wilderness."

"What do you mean by *that*?" Wade asked.

Blanche reached out and took his other hand into hers. "Oh, nothing, dear. Other than I just would like to see you closer to me and to civilization. I'm just sick you have to leave tomorrow. Your two days here have just flown by. You should come live here in Bryson City . . . practice here. You know my daddy can arrange it all for you. He's visited with Dr. Bennett. They both like the idea. And, of course, I could see a lot more of my sweetie."

Wade smiled. "It's very tempting. As a matter of fact, I've not done so well with the mountain people. As you know, they're suspicious of strangers and I'm from the North, which to many of them is a cardinal sin. It's the end of July . . . I've only been there three months, but—"

"Not to worry, sweetheart," Blanche interrupted, condescendingly patting his hand. "The townspeople here just aren't like those hillbillies. Totally different, totally civilized."

"I'd just feel bad leaving Dr. Keller. I committed to spend at least a year with him."

Blanche squeezed his hands again. "Don't worry about that, dearest. My daddy and Judge Hughes will take care of that with Mr. Calhoun. They'll buy out your contract, and Mr. Calhoun says he'll have no trouble finding a replacement."

Wade frowned. "You're saying I'm replaceable?"

Blanche smiled and leaned forward. "Not to me, my love. You've given me the best Saturday date I've ever had; in fact, the best date I've ever had. *Ever.*"

As she leaned toward him, Wade was overcome with the

fragrance of her perfume as he felt her arms encircle his neck. She scooted toward him and lifted her head until their noses met. "Tell me you don't have to go back to Proctor tomorrow." She gently rubbed her nose against his and then brought her lips to his.

As she kissed him, he couldn't help but think what a lovely and tempting beauty she was. He loved the sweetness of her taste, the urgency of her caress, and he pulled her hungrily into his embrace. He had never had a serious girlfriend, much less a woman who raised so many confusing and conflicting currents in him: attraction and caution, appeal and concern, magnetism and uneasiness, fascination and apprehension, charm and nervousness, sexuality and trepidation. He wasn't sure of the source of his uncertainty.

As their lips separated, she slowly opened her eyes. "You seem hesitant."

He smiled. "Guess I'm nervous being in the arms of such a gorgeous woman. It's a first for me."

Blanche laughed. "I don't believe that for a moment. A looker like you has likely had a lamentation of swans swooning over you. That's just another reason I'd like to get you away from the wilderness. Won't you move to Bryson City . . . and to me?"

"I will . . ." he replied, leaning forward and falling into her soft kiss once again . . . *think about it,* he thought. *But I don't know. I'm happy with my life in Proctor, even though I've not been there very long. I think I could love you, Blanche. I think. I have no money, certainly not enough to support you in the manner to which you've become accustomed. I don't want to be dependent on your daddy. And I'm stubborn. I hate to be defeated and so far my work out there has bested me.*

Blanche pulled away and smiled. "I can sense you're miles from here. So, do I need to do something to make you think only of me?" She moved her hands down his chest and around his waist and pulled him into the deepest and longest kiss he had ever experienced.

I just don't know. I just don't know was all he could think as he slowly melted into her.

73

Still

Wade removed his bowler hat and used his bandana to wipe the sweat from his face. "It's hot as a firecracker today! I know it's mid-August, and it's supposed to be hot, but this is by far the hottest day I've experienced out here. It feels hotter than Africa!" he said to himself as he looked up the barren trail, which penetrated Bone Valley and began at the confluence of Bone Valley and Hazel Creeks.

Wade had never been in this particular remote valley, one of the highest in the Hazel Creek watershed. A young boy had waved him to a stop as he rode the skeeter down Hazel Creek. "Old Crate Hall's done broke his leg," the boy said. "He's in his cabin up thar at the end of Bone Valley trail. Maddie says she needs you to hep her set it. Best be quick."

Dr. Keller told him that Bone Valley derived its name from the cattle bones left scattered over one of the lower meadows when the large herd froze to death during the dreadful winter of 1888. The valley was originally settled by several Civil War veterans, one of whom was a son of Moses and Patience Rustin Proctor, the first white settlers on Hazel Creek. Two of their sons were killed fighting for the Confederate cause; however, the third son made it back, although barely surviving the arduous trip home.

Keller also warned him to be careful if he ever hiked the valley, as its residents were not known to be the friendliest. Halfway up the valley, he came across the cabin of one Reverend Joshua and, partly to ease suspicions, spent a few minutes talking to the old man, who said he arrived in 1886 and then pastored a small church in the valley until old-age rheumatism made it too diffi-cult for him to carry out his duties.

Finally, Wade found the Hall cabin. He used chloroform to put the old man to sleep, allowing him and Maddie to painlessly set the broken tibia bone. After applying a plaster of paris splint, he instructed the family in caring for the man. Wade promised to return the next day.

Heading down the trail, he suddenly decided to veer off the main path onto what appeared to be a game trail heading south and up the ridge. Knowing that Sugar Fork lay just on the other side of the ridge, and deciding it would be a cooler hike given all the virgin timber that remained there, he took off up the path.

The high meadows and forest revealed a symphony of flowers with an astounding variety of color: pink, red, orange, purple, yel-low, white, and some colors that were hard for him to describe. He recognized some flowers by name, including the cardinal flowers, evening primrose, jewelweed, and meadow beauty. Other finds in-cluded monkshood, mountain mints, and wild asters. Considering each an astounding sighting, he carefully recorded each discovery, its location, and the number of plants in his day journal.

Quite a congregation of birds accompanied his journey, includ-ing many varieties of warblers, along with Eastern Kingbirds and Indigo Buntings. His most surprising find was a soaring pair of golden eagles, as Dr. Keller had told him never to expect to see them in the watershed until the fall.

Then he came across an extraordinary surprise: a small group of three flowers he had not previously encountered: Indian Pink, Dutchman's breeches, and yellow-fringed orchids. He couldn't believe his good fortune as he sat down to draw pictures of each in his daybook.

After finishing and closing his journal, he took a deep breath and admired the forest around him. *It is truly spectacular*, he thought. *Bartram and Wordsworth are right. There's really nothing like nature.*

A troubling thought came across his mind. *Would you really leave this and move to Bryson City?* Then he had an even more disturbing thought: *Do you really love Blanche? Or do you love her money and the fine life her family could afford to give you?*

"You best not think this way, young man," he said to himself. "She's a fine woman and she loves you desperately."

Does she? his conscience asked. *Really? Or does she just love the fact that you're a doctor? Does she admire you, or is she using you? You know*, his conscience complained, *she's just looking for someone to help her climb the social ladder. She's likely to use you until she's done with you and then discard you like so much used tissue.*

"You're wrong!" he told his conscience. "Of course she loves *me*. After all, what's not to love about me?" He chuckled. "That's what I like most about you, Wade Chandler," he said to himself. "It's your humility!" He laughed out loud.

Suddenly, his laughter was interrupted by the snap of a stick in the thick rhododendron brush behind him. As he spun around to look, the bark on the tree next to his head exploded, showering his face with splinters. The report of the rifle shot startled him and he leaped to his feet as another bullet exploded into the mud between his feet.

Wade turned and sprinted up the trail as a third and fourth shot buzzed by his head. Rather than running in a straight line, Wade dodged left and right, trying to weave his way between the trees, hoping against hope they'd protect him from sure death. He was certain the blasts were coming from a high-powered hunting rifle, and he had seen far too many of the destructive wounds these types of rifles could cause.

Dashing across the top of the ridge, he slid feetfirst down into the thick carpet of leaves, falling onto his back. He flipped over to his stomach and then quickly crawled back up to the ridge. Lying next to a large log, he carefully peered back down into the valley. He wanted to be sure no one was following.

About a hundred and fifty feet away, in a small hollow he had not seen from below, he saw three men, their rifles slung over their shoulders, walking downhill. They appeared to be laughing, as one slapped the back of another. Then he saw it: their still. He could see the smoke drifting up from their small cooking fire.

He felt a chill go down his spine as he realized just how close he had come to death. The skin on his forearms turned to gooseflesh as he heard Dr. Keller's warning reverberate inside his skull: *If you come across folks working a still and they don't know you, word is they'll just shoot you dead, drag your body into the woods, and bury you where you'll never be found.*

He quickly scooted backward, stood, and began running down the hill toward the Sugar Fork. Arriving at Kephart's cabin above the Little Fork, Wade was relieved to find the old man sitting on his porch, his writing desk and typewriter sitting in front of him. He was steadily puffing his pipe while his fingers flew across the keys.

"Hello!" Wade cried out as he approached.

Kep looked up. "Welcome, Doctor. Come sit a spell."

As Wade walked up to the porch, a tall man walked out of the cabin. He was thin with a receding patch of short brown hair. "Howdy," he said as he sat on a chair next to Kep.

"Gran, this here's the newest healer in western North Carolina, Dr. Wade Chandler. Wade, this here's Granville Calhoun, a legendary mountain man renowned for his feats as a hunter, fisherman, and storyteller."

"You related to the Calhouns that own the lumber company?" Wade asked.

Gran looked disgusted at the insinuation. "Proud to say there's *no* relation at all!"

"And, I might add, he's legendary because I've written about him," Kep added, laughing.

"Pshaw!" Gran complained, spitting out a line of tobacco juice.

"Gran used to live here in the Hazel Creek area," Kep explained, "but now he's purchased him a building in Bryson City and renamed it the Calhoun Hotel. An original name, eh? Couldn't you come up with something more original, Gran?"

"Good to meet you, Mr. Calhoun," Wade said as he stepped onto the porch, shook hands with the man, and had a seat. "Tell ya what, Kep, about got myself killed just across the ridge."

"Heard the shots," Gran said. "You musta come across the Cable brothers' still."

"That's a fact," Wade said. "They just missed me."

"Not true," Gran responded.

"It's the absolute truth. I came within an inch of my life."

A smile broke across the man's tanned and wrinkled face. "Shucks, son! They was aimin' to miss ya. Any one of them men could shoot a fly off a cow's ear with his Winchester at a hundred and fifty paces. If'n they had aimed at your heart, you'da been dead with the first shot."

Wade looked relieved.

"Anyway, tell you what, Doc," Kep said. "Gran's taking his dogs and heading out on a hunt this evening. I'm heading down to the Randolphs'. How about I walk you down there?"

Wade nodded and looked out over the forest surrounding the cabin. He hoped Gran's and Kephart's reassurances were accurate. But he still suspected that the men shooting at him had every intention of hitting their target. Maybe not. But whether they intended him harm or not, he was delighted not to have been hit.

74

Pup

As Wade and Kep walked out of the woods toward the Randolph home, they saw Maria running full speed from her cabin toward the barn, followed by Danya.

"What in the world?" Wade exclaimed.

"Something's wrong, that's for sure," Kep said. "You run on up and I'll follow as quick as I can."

Wade shoved his doctor bag from under his arm to behind his back and sprinted toward the barn behind Maria and Danya. Once Wade was inside, it took a few seconds for his eyes to adapt to the dark interior. He heard voices coming from an open stall and quickly walked toward it.

As he entered the pen he could see the girls and Maria hovering around something. Danya was looking over Maria's and Abbie's shoulders, along with Whit, who was holding Sarah. Corrie was sitting on the ground with the most pitiful sound of whimpering filling the stall.

"What's going on?" Wade asked. "Who's hurt?" He pushed forward as Whit and Anna separated to allow him to get to Corrie. Lying in her lap was a softly whining, pitifully skinny Mountain Cur puppy. Its head and back had a beautiful cinnamon color, and the dog's oversized paws were perfectly still.

Corrie had covered the puppy with a towel that was blood soaked. Kep ran into the stall behind them as Wade knelt down by Corrie. She was softly weeping and large tears were streaking down her dirty cheeks.

"What happened, Corrie?" Wade asked as he gently stroked the puppy's head.

"Anna and I were doing some wash, and we heard a terrible baying coming from the woods. Lilly lit out and we ran behind her. We found Lilly protecting this little malnourished puppy from a small sounder of young Russian boar that were attackin' him. When we run up, the boar squealed and ran. But one of 'em had gored the pup bad. Anna ran back and got a towel, and we carried him here. I've named him Cap'n Brown, but I don't think he's gonna make it, Doc."

"Is this one of Mr. Rau's dogs?" Wade asked.

"Nope," Kephart said. "I've not seen this puppy, and I think I know all of 'em that are in the valley. Doesn't look like a feral dog. Maybe he came over from Eagle Creek."

"My guess is someone threw him out 'cause his paws are too big," Abbie said. "Looks like he's half-starved . . . and 'bout half-dead."

Wade looked into Abbie's eyes and was moved by her compassion for the pup. "Not if I can help it," he reassured her. "Let me look at Cap'n Brown," Wade instructed as he knelt down, moved Corrie's hand, and slowly removed the towel. To his surprise, the tusk had laid open the dog's abdominal wall, and his intestines had spilled out onto the towel.

"I tried to push his guts back in, but it hurt him too much," Corrie said, still crying. "Can you hep him, Doc?" she asked, looking up at Wade.

Wade nodded. "I'll do my best, Corrie." He looked up. "Danya and Kep, can you help Corrie and me move the dog to the table outside the stall?"

"Anna, can you care for Sarah in the cabin?" Abbie asked.

"I wanna watch," Anna protested.

"I know," Abbie said, "but I need you to take Sarah inside."

Anna nodded.

Abbie looked at Whit. "Would you mind getting them settled, and then bring two lanterns from the cabin?"

"Not at all," Whit said.

"Abbie, I'll need a clean sheet or towel or two," Wade said. "Maria, can you get some soap and two buckets of spring water?"

For a moment, no one moved, then Wade commanded, "All right everyone, snap to." As quick as ants everyone scurried to their duties.

A few minutes later, after setting up his temporary surgical suite, Wade had Kephart hold the chloroform-soaked hand-kerchief over the dog's snout until he was anesthetized. Wade took off his shirt, washed his hands and arms, and then began his careful assessment. As he quickly and expertly examined the pup, he reported his findings: "Skull, eyes, ears, muzzle, jaw are all right." His hand moved down the body. "Good news. No apparent trauma to the neck or back or chest."

He pulled a stethoscope out of his bag and listened to the dog's lungs. "Clear," he reported. Then he inspected each leg and paw. "These are the biggest paws I've seen on such a puppy," he said as he turned to rewash his hands and arms to the elbows.

"Danya, see if you can position him on his back. Girls, you may need to help hold him in position," Wade instructed while washing his hands and arms a second time.

As he rinsed the soap from his arms, he looked over his assistants and patient. "Good job, everyone. Now, girls, if anyone doesn't want to watch me explore the abdomen, now's the time to leave."

To his surprise, Abbie chuckled.

"What?" he asked.

"Since we were little, Pa taught us to hunt and fish. Any one of us can field dress a deer or clean a fish lickety-split. This ain't nothin' for us."

Wade smiled. "Guess this city boy's still got a lot of learning to do." He first took a fresh towel, dipped it in the clean bucket of water, carefully placed it under the exposed intestine, and began the painstaking process of examining and cleaning the wound and abdominal cavity.

"Good news, the intestine is not perforated. That will increase the puppy's chances a lot." He continued his exam. "Diaphragm is intact. Liver, spleen, and pancreas feel normal. Both kidneys are all right."

"Doc, where'd ya learn to vet?" Kep asked.

Wade smiled. "We learned physiology and surgery in a dog lab," he replied. "It turns out the Creator used the same blueprint when he created most of the mammals. So, I'm just doing with Cap'n Brown what I'd do with anyone with the same wound."

Wade shifted position and moved his hand to the lower abdomen. "Bladder's all right." His hand quickly moved around the periphery of the cavity as he pulled out the rest of the colon and small intestine. "I need to run the bowel, check the whole length for any trauma."

His movements were quick and efficient. "Good, no apparent damage. Now, I'll wash the intestines once again and then put them back where they belong." After placing the organs back into the abdominal cavity, he rinsed the cavity with the remaining water and handed the two buckets to Maria. "Can you get two more buckets of water as quickly as possible?"

Maria nodded, took the buckets, and ran out of the barn.

"Why all the rinses?" Danya asked.

"If this puppy's going to live, we've got to be sure no germs are left inside. One of my surgery professors always taught me this: 'The solution to pollution is dilution with solution.'"

As Maria returned, Wade had Danya slowly pour the contents of one bucket, followed by the other, into the abdominal cavity as he swished the fluid around the abdominal organs. "Okay, now all I need to do is clean the skin with iodine and then sew everything shut."

"Wade," Kephart said, looking over the young man's shoulder. "Believe it or not, some 'shine would be a mighty fine antiseptic.

Much better than boric acid or tincture of iodine. Maddie and I've used it for years to much success."

"Are you serious?" Wade asked.

"As a heart attack!" Kep answered.

Wade smiled. "Like I said, guess this city boy's definitely got a *lot* of learning to do. Do you have any?"

Kep smiled, turned to his backpack, and pulled out a pint bottle. "Here ya go, Doc. Bone Valley's finest and purest 'shine—straight from the Cable brothers. Won't a single bacteria survive a drop of it."

"Then I'll give it a try. And after drowning all those bugs, I'll dress and bind the wound and let him wake up."

"And we'll all pray Cap'n Brown gets well quick," Corrie added as she hugged Wade's waist.

Wade looked up and caught Abbie's eyes. In them he saw not only her gratitude but something else, and he felt his heart skip a beat.

75

Yearning

After Kep and Wade said their good-byes and left, the girls, Danya, and Maria were sitting on the porch watching the dusk settle across the valley.

Anna looked up. "Miss Maria?"

"Yes, dear?"

"I'm gonna marry Dr. Chandler when I'm old enough."

As the girls laughed, Corrie said, "That man's gonna marry him that rich, high-society woman from Bryson City. He's got his sights set on Blanche Jenkins, that's fer durn sure. Besides, he ain't got time to wait for you to get growed up."

"Well, I'm 'most eight and a half. Amy Lou Springer, she got married when she was thirteen. That's only four and a half years."

"I don't think he'll wait that long, sweetie," Whit said.

Anna looked at Abbie. "Now that you're seventeen, Abbie, and all graduated from high school, you could marry him *now*."

Abbie laughed. "Corrie's right, Anna. He's courtin' that Bryson City girl. And city people like him don't marry mountain girls, or gals as young as me anyway."

Corrie thought for a moment and then said, "Shucks, all we gotta do is keep him from marrying that woman for a couple of years, till you're nineteen. Then you can git him. Just think, we'd have us a doctor around all the time fer when we get sick!"

The girls laughed as Abbie commented, "He is a fine-lookin'

man, Corrie, but no man like him would take on a herd of girls like you'uns! Reckon I won't get hitched until I get all you girls raised and married off. I ain't got no more chance of marryin' a man like him than a frog's got of marryin' a princess."

"It only takes one kiss," Whit said.

Instantly Abbie recalled a warm collage of breathtaking reminisces—starting with the first time she had seen Wade in town and thought him a prince. Then the time he came to their home with Dr. Keller and thought Grace was their mama. Their visit in the fern bog and the way he drove them to Bryson City to save the farm. And now the way he swept into their barn and expertly operated on Cap'n Brown this very afternoon, saving his life. Abbie smiled and felt her cheeks blush as she remembered him kissing her hand at her seventeenth birthday. Then she shook her head. *You silly girl*, she thought as she chastised herself. *He don't care nothin' for me or my family or Sugar Fork. All he cares about is doctorin' and ol' Blanche Jenkins.*

Whit patted Cap'n Brown's head and said, "I still believe in fairy tales, Abbie. You mind what I say."

As Sarah napped, Abbie and Emily Rau began preparing the evening meal.

"Em, can you begin the corn bread?" Abbie asked. "I'll finish the stew preparation and get the pot over the fire."

"Sure will," Em said as she took the cornmeal container from the shelf. "I'll run to the springhouse to get some milk. You need anything from outside?"

"Nope. Got what I need," Abbie replied as she began to peel the carrots and potatoes. Sensing Em not moving, she looked up to see her standing there with tears coming down her cheeks.

"What, child?" Abbie asked.

"I just miss your ma and pa," Em said, over trembling lips.

Abbie put down her knife and wiped her hands on her apron as she walked around to Emily and pulled her into a hug. "Me, too, darlin'. Me, too."

Emily hugged her back. "And I'm so sorry 'bout Bobby Lee. I *so* wanted to be in you'uns' wedding."

Abbie smiled as she pulled back, stroked Emily's hair off her face, and wiped her tears. "Well, I *so* wanted to be in my wedding, too, Em."

Emily smiled. "It's only two days since the Labor Day holiday, but the cabin seems empty with the girls being at school."

"Yep, it's only their second day back, but I'm missin' 'em also," Abbie said.

Emily nodded and began to walk toward the door before turning back. "Abbie, thanks for keepin' me on. Not sure I could find work elsewhere. I'm appreciative."

"Em, you're worth every dime I pay you. And not only could Sarah girl and I not get along without you, likely the roof of this old cabin would fall in if you didn't come to keep things up around here."

Emily nodded, turned, and skipped out of the cabin.

Just then, Abbie felt a weight like a sack of flour fall across her foot. She looked down to see that their enormous puppy, Cap'n Brown, had plopped down by her. "I declare, Cap'n. If'n you can't find a lap to sit in, you'll find a foot to lie on. It's getting plumb intolerable. You've grown like a worm and your feet are still outgrowin' the rest of you."

She bent over to softly rub his belly, where the scar had healed nicely. His tail happily wagged, thumping on the cabin floor. Finally, she shooed him away. "You get over by the hearth. I'll get Sarah up here in a bit and you can play with her."

Abbie returned to her chores, with the sweet memories of Bobby Lee filling her soul as a soft gust of wind pushed the front door open. She began to sing:

Down in the valley, valley so low
Hang your head over, hear the wind blow

Hear the wind blow, dear, hear the wind blow;
Hang your head over, hear the wind blow.

Bird in a cage, love, bird in a cage;
Longing for freedom, ever a slave,
Ever a slave, dear, ever a slave;
Dying for freedom, ever a slave.

Roses love sunshine, violets love dew,
Angels in Heaven know I love you,
Know I love you, dear, know I love you,
Angels in Heaven know I love you.

And, she thought, as she rubbed the back of her hand against her moist eyes and sniffled, *I always will.* Whenever she thought of Bobby Lee, which was often, her thoughts turned to heaven.

Although she looked forward to eternity there, she felt pulled by her responsibilities to care for the farm and her sisters down here. *Even if I have to do it as an old maid,* she thought. To lift her spirits, she began to sing one of her favorite hymns:

Shall we meet where flow'rs are blooming, ever fadeless, ever
*   fair,*
Where the light of day illumines lives of those who enter there?
Shall we meet our loved companions, on that brighter, fairer
*   shore?*
When this life's great work is ended, shall we meet to part no
*   more?*
Yes, we'll meet beyond the river, where our joys shall never die,
We shall meet our loved and saved ones, in that happy by and by.

The sound of a horse trotting up to the cabin caused her to look up, as she sniffled again and wiped the tears off her cheeks.

76

Invitation

David Rau hopped off his quarter horse, hitched her to the fence, and then hopped over it, before striding over to the porch.

"Hello!" he shouted through the open door as he walked up to the porch.

Abbie wiped her hands and ran to the door. Placing her finger over her lips, she whispered, "Shh! Sarah girl's a-nappin'."

"Can I come in?" he whispered.

"Yes, if'n you're quiet."

As they walked into the kitchen area, David said, "Danya's bringin' the girls up from school. They'll be here shortly."

"How's that new teacher?" Abbie asked.

"Too early to tell. But I've only got one year left and then I'll be free like you."

"Be careful what you wish for," Abbie warned. "I'da loved to have been down there with y'all."

"Gotta get home and help Pa," David said, "but I wanted to drop by and see if you're plannin' to go to the dance and the poke-supper this Saturday."

"Wasn't plannin' on it," Abbie replied.

"You gotta take some time to frolic," David said. "After all, I was hopin' you'd make a pokebag of cake or some homemade delicacies to be auctioned off to the highest bidder."

Abbie smiled. "So, would you plan to bid?"

"Of course I would. Everyone knows that whoever bids for a poke and wins it is entitled to eat with the girl who prepared it and then escort her home."

"What if someone else outbid ya? Would you be happy with him bringin' me home?"

"Hmm . . ." David said as he scratched his chin.

"Even in Hazel Creek, where a lumberman's work brings only a dollar a day, we've seen a pretty girl's poke bid up to ten, even twenty dollars."

"Well, if we don't think it wise to do a poke for you, maybe we can do one for Whit or even Corrie."

Abbie laughed. "I 'spect Whit would complain, but be pleased on the inside. Corrie, she'd be a different story. She'd run away as fast as she could."

"Well . . . would you come to the dance with me?" David asked, timidly.

Abbie continued to peel the vegetables for a moment. "I'm not sure," she whispered.

"Why not?" he asked. "Is it *me*?"

"No!" Abbie exclaimed. "It's me. I'm not sure I'm ready."

"If'n you go with me, I'll give you all my dances. And I'll protect you from the others. 'Specially that new doctor what's got his eyes on you."

"He ain't got no eyes for me, David Rau. Everyone knows he's a-courtin' that Jenkins girl in Bryson."

"I seen him a-eyein' ya at church. Don't tell me he don't find ya attractive. But I'll tell ya this, I'll fight to keep him away from ya. Ya don't need no flatlander lustin' after ya."

"Then in that case, I probably won't go. No need to have you young men a-fightin' over me." Abbie smiled.

"Ya oughta just go, Abbie."

"Why?"

"'Cause you don't never go nowhere. That's why."

"I'll think about it."

"Fair enough," David said as he turned to leave. At the door, he turned back to her. "I miss ya at school."

Abbie felt her face blush, but she was pleased to hear it.

"Here comes Danya and the girls. I best go!"

Abbie followed him to the door and watched as David trotted to the fence, hopped it in a single bound, and bounced up and into his saddle. Pulling up the reins, he spurred his mount around and away.

I do think he's gettin' fond of ya, Abbie, she thought. *And I've always thought he'd be a mighty fine catch fer some young lass. But, in my heart of hearts, I just don't think he's fer me.*

At Saturday's lunch, the younger girls couldn't quit giggling. "What y'all laughin' 'bout?" Abbie finally asked.

"Ain't none of your put in," was all Whit or Corrie would say.

As they were cleaning the table, Danya and Maria knocked on the open door.

"Welcome," Abbie said. "Have y'all eaten?"

"Yes," Maria replied as she put her bonnet on the hat rack. "I'm here to babysit Sarah, and Danya's taking you girls to town."

The girls laughed as Abbie looked surprised. "What's going on?"

"It's your special day!" Anna exclaimed.

"Whatcha mean?"

"She means," Whit explained, "we've all chipped some money in from the allowance you've been givin' us and are gonna take you to Proctor for a day on the town. Nancy Cunningham's plannin' a fancy English tea for us at her Clubhouse. Then we're gonna go to the movin'-picture house to see *The Black Pirate*—"

"It's starring Douglas Fairbanks!" Corrie interrupted.

"Mr. Barnes said it's the first movin' picture ever made in color," Whit explained.

"Then after the movie we're all gonna go to the pokesupper and dance," Corrie added.

Abbie started to protest, but Danya said, "We've all voted on it. And it's settled."

"What's more," Whit explained, "it's what Pa would have liked, and Mama, too. So just get ready to spread your wings!"

Abbie's head swam the whole day. She had put on, for the first time, the new dress her Pa gave her—the first store-bought dress she ever owned—as well as the new shoes her parents had given her for her fifteenth birthday.

All the girls were wearing their Sunday best and had been embarrassed by the catcalls from some of the lumbermen as Danya drove them through town in a fine carriage he had borrowed from the Semmeses. However, once Danya told them to quit, they did so instantly.

At the movie house, the girls enjoyed popcorn and the swashbuckling nautical movie in which Douglas Fairbanks played a nobleman who revenged his father's murder by boarding a pirate vessel disguised as a thieving, villainous rapscallion. The girls cheered for him as on the high seas, the athletic Fairbanks provided a no-holds-barred, rip-roaring, stunt-filled voyage, complete with a one-man takeover of a merchant ship.

After the movie, a walk up to the Clubhouse afforded them a luxurious teatime where they were hosted and served by Nancy Cunningham. After a time to rest on the front porch, the sisters were off to the parade grounds where the pokesupper and dance were to be held in a massive tent set up by the lumber company, courtesy of the new manager, about whom everyone seemed to say good things.

During the dinner, Rafe Semmes won the auction for the pokebag of cake that the girls had baked for Whit to enter. Then the tables were cleared, and the band began to warm up for the dance.

David Rau sat by Abbie during the dinner and with the start of the music, leaned over to claim his first dance with her.

"You're lookin' mighty handsome in your new suit," Abbie said.

"Don't change the subject, Miss Randolph. Do you want to dance?"

Abbie protested. "I'm not sure, David; I'm not a dancer."

"Me neither," he said. "So guess we'll jest hav'ta learn how as we go."

During their second dance, a slower one, he leaned his head against hers. "Ya look beautiful, Abbie. I can't even begin to tell ya how pretty ya look all gussied up. And ya smell good, too."

Abbie felt herself blush and was relieved that the dance ended at that moment.

"I'll go get us a lemonade," David said as he turned, leaving Abbie with her sisters and some of the other girls.

"I think he's fond of you," Whit whispered.

"I don't think it," Corrie added. "I *know* it. He's about to swoon every time he looks at you, Abbie."

"He's sweet," Abbie said. "I've been fond of him since we were kids. But I don't think he's the one for me. And I don't have any idea how to tell him."

77

Waltzing

As the next song began, Abbie felt a tap on her shoulder. She turned and felt a wave of surprise engulf her as she faced Wade Chandler.

"I think this is our dance, Miss Randolph. May a flatlander have the pleasure of your company for this one?"

After her initial surprise subsided, Abbie felt her head nod, and the words from her lips flowed without her even thinking. "How can a mountain girl turn down a dance with the valley's newest physician, flatlander or otherwise?"

Wade smiled and laughed. Abbie felt as if she was going to swoon. His face was soft, gentle, and jovial, his smile gorgeous, his hair beautiful, and his laughter infectious. *Oh my!* was all she could think.

Before she knew it, she was in his arms waltzing around the dance floor. Initially she felt as clumsy as a mule, but he expertly guided her and softly whispered instructions to her, and in no time she relaxed and just followed his lead in their first dance together.

"You look stunning tonight, Miss Randolph," he whispered in her ear. "Lovelier than I've ever seen you. In fact, you look positively adult . . . all grown-up. Not like the young girl you have been pretending to be."

"I'm just me, Wade," Abbie said as they continued to waltz

around the room. She was quite surprised to find that with every step she felt more confident and comfortable both with the dance and being in his arms.

"Well, what I see tonight is a radiant beauty. That's not meant as a false compliment, but as the diagnosis of a well-trained clinician," Wade said, his eyes reflecting joy.

Abbie didn't have any words with which she could answer him.

"Furthermore, Miss Randolph, I'm awfully proud of you," he said as his blue-gray eyes fixed on her.

"For what, Wade? I ain't—I mean, I haven't done anythin' worthy of your compliments."

"The sheriff told me about the rabid bear you shot as it charged you and your sisters a couple of years ago on Thanksgiving Day. He says everyone talks about it."

"Corrie actually killed the bear."

"But not until you slowed it down with your point-blank shot. Kept that monster from entering your cabin, likely maiming or killing one or more of you. Zach says it was one of the largest bears ever shot in the Hazel Creek watershed. Abbie, you're a brave woman. I'm pleased to know you." They made two turns on the floor and he continued. "I'm even more pleased to have you in my arms."

Abbie was overwhelmed and could not speak. She couldn't take her eyes off him as they whirled around; the entire room was a blur and all she could hear were his warm, gentle words. She wasn't able to remember a single one of them, but just how comfortable she felt in his arms. At one time she thought she felt her face burning in a blush, but maybe it was just the affection she felt overflowing from her heart. She wasn't sure why he had asked her to dance, but the few moments flew by and she never wanted the dance to end.

When the music stopped, Wade smiled and bowed and Abbie curtsied. As she stood, the room came back into focus, and she could hear voices and murmuring in the background as he offered her his arm and walked her back to her sisters, who were all clapping in joy.

David was standing next to them, holding two drinks, looking as if someone had punched him in the stomach. He turned and ducked into the crowd.

"Would *not* have believed it had I not seen it!" a voice behind them sneered. "A hillbilly girl actually trying to do a dance designed for a civilized couple. It has to be one of the more comical displays I've seen in some time."

"Blanche!" Wade cautioned.

She nodded her head submissively and then looked up at Abbie. "I'm Blanche Jenkins," she said as she extended her hand.

Abbie looked at the white-gloved hand but did not take it. "I've heard of you. You're the mayor's daughter. Right?"

"Oh, you have some awareness of modern politics. Imagine my surprise! I wasn't sure the news made it out this far into the woods," Blanche said contemptuously.

"Please forgive her," Wade interjected. "She's just not comfortable this far from home."

"Oh, darling," Blanche said as she put her arm through his, "I couldn't be more comfortable. Here I am with the most handsome man in western North Carolina, a wonderful physician and a marvelous singer, dancer, and conversationalist. Oh, forgive me, dearie, I didn't mean to use such complex words in your presence."

Her icy look at Abbie was like a dagger, a weapon a woman can use only on another woman, a bludgeon that only women could intuit.

"But I do hope you enjoyed your first and *last* dance with *my* fiancé, sweetie. In fact, if I see you even looking at him again, I'll be sure my daddy knows all about it. And you do *not* want to cross him. You can be fractious with the lumber-company officials and get away with it. But *not* with me or my daddy. Are we clear?"

"Blanche!" Wade commanded. "That's quite enough now! You are *not* my fiancée. We are *not* engaged." He turned to face Abbie, his face showing pain. "I'm sorry for this despicable behavior, Abbie, but I thank you for the dance. It meant the world to me."

"Abbie," Blanche cooed. "It fits. A common name for a common girl."

Wade spun around and jerked Blanche away. She smiled a counterfeit smile and with a syrupy voice demurely uttered, "The pleasure's all mine."

"What a cat!" Corrie hissed. "That woman's positively evil, Abbie, I'll tell ya that."

As the next dance started, Abbie and Whit took chairs. Abbie felt herself shaking with emotion.

"Don't give her no never mind," Whit said. "She don't know what she's a-talkin'bout."

Abbie wiped the tears streaking down her cheeks. "Maybe she does, Whit. Truth is, I'm a mountain girl. He's a city boy. I've only graduated from high school. He's a doctor. For Pete's sake, I could never win the affections of a man like Wade Chandler. I shouldn't've even danced with him."

Whit grabbed Abbie's hands. "Abbie, you'd be a great catch for *any* man. And that young doctor knows it. Couldn't you see it in his eyes?"

Abbie just gazed out on those dancing. "I've never felt anythin' like what I felt when I was in his arms, Whit. It was magical. It was like dancin' with Prince Charmin'."

"And that's just what Blanche Jenkins saw. She saw the way he looked at ya, held ya, danced with ya. I tell ya what, that man was swoonin' in yer arms and she didn't like it one bit."

"At least I didn't tell her a white lie," Abbie said, a smile breaking out across her face.

"White lie?" Whit asked. "Isn't a lie a lie?"

"No," Abbie explained as she looked at Wade and Blanche walking away, "there's a difference between a white lie and a black lie. A black lie's much worse than the white one. A white one is more . . . disguised."

"What could you say to her that would have been a white lie?" Whit asked.

Abbie looked at the retreating belle. "I could have told her somethin' like, 'It's *so* nice to meet you.'"

The girls laughed.

78

Admission

Rafe and his parents took Whit home, while Abbie, Corrie, and Anna rode with Danya. After Abbie was sure to thank the Petrovas, say good night to Emily, check on Sarah, and say prayers with her sisters, she went to sit on the front porch. She wanted to process the events of the evening.

"How was your first dance?" a voice asked from the dark.

For an instant Abbie was startled, and then she laughed. "Maria?" Even in the light of the three-quarter moon, she couldn't see her until she fell into the light cast by the lantern.

"So how was it?" Maria asked.

"Come, sit. Let's talk."

Maria walked up the steps and settled into the rocker next to Abbie. "Was it enjoyable? Or deplorable? Pleasurable? Or only tolerable?"

Abbie cleared her throat. "I danced almost every dance! Wearin' the dress Pa gave me made me feel like a princess, Maria. Like Cinderella herself."

"Who'd you dance with?"

"Mostly David Rau. But Rafe Semmes danced with me, although it was hard for him to let go of Whit. And then I had a dance with Dr. Chandler."

"Really? Zach says he's engaged to the Jenkins girl."

"She thinks so. But they're just courtin'. Anyway, she's a

beautiful girl, but a wicked woman. I think she has a hard, cold heart; she thinks she has Wade wrapped around her bony finger. For all I know, she may."

"Sounds like you're an admirer of hers."

Abbie laughed. "If so, the feelings are not mutual. She sure didn't like it very much when her man asked me to dance. Maria, he said I looked downright grown-up . . . and beautiful. And he said I was a brave young woman. It was . . . well, it was wonderful. I reckon he's gonna marry that woman, but I'll tell ya this, she's not good enough for him! That's fer sure."

"Sounds like you're jealous. Are you taken with him?" Maria asked.

Abbie sighed. "He's a dreamy man, no doubt about that. But I'm just seventeen years old, and I've got a call on my life to raise my sisters. I'm gonna do it, too! Then, by the time I get all the girls raised and married off, heckfire, I'll be an old, old lady . . . maybe thirty-somethin'!"

Maria laughed. "That isn't old, Abbie. Why, life doesn't really begin until you get some miles under you."

Maria turned to look into Abbie's eyes. "Let me, as a prophetess, share this promise for you, precious Abbie. It comes from the Lord himself, who says, 'And ye shall dwell in the land that I gave to your fathers; and ye shall be my people, and I will be your God. I will also save you from all your uncleannesses: and I will call for the corn, and will increase it, and lay no famine upon you. And I will multiply the fruit of the tree, and the increase of the field, that ye shall receive no more reproach of famine among the heathen.' That's his word, Abbie. That's his promise for you and yours. Believe it. Don't doubt it."

Abbie smiled and laid her head on Maria's shoulder. "I do, and I won't."

"But I think you're going to have to confess," Maria added, chuckling.

"Confess what?" Abbie asked.

"Your dislike and disdain for that no-good vixen."

"Guilty as charged," Abbie said, laughing.

79

Realization

66 "Did you enjoy the pokesupper and dance last night?" Wade asked as he and Blanche walked along the footpath next to Hazel Creek.

"Actually, my dear, I thought it was frightfully primeval. I considered it a dreadful experience and a nightmare of a memory. I can only hope to quickly forget it and I cannot wait to get you back with me in Bryson City!" Blanche exclaimed. "My daddy and Dr. Bennett have completed all the arrangements. You'll be able to fulfill your lumber-company commitment in Bryson City, and once Dr. Bennett dies or retires, you'll be able to take over the old man's practice. Actually, I expect you to improve it one hundredfold."

Wade stopped and turned to face her. "Why are you trying to rearrange my life, Blanche? We're not even engaged, yet here you are acting more like an overbearing mother than someone who might want the best for me."

"Oh, darling," Blanche softly replied, "I *do* want what's best for you. I just think you are much more likely to be happy when we're together. And there's a much greater chance of that in Bryson City than out here in this godforsaken wilderness."

Wade felt his anger bubble up, but took a deep breath, slowly let it out, and then slowly looked around at the spectacular beauty that surrounded them along Hazel Creek as he gathered his thoughts. Finally he looked back into her eyes. "I think we need some more time to get to know one another. I've only been here a few months and I love being out here. I've found this valley to not be godforsaken at all. In fact, I sense his creation more here than any place I've ever lived. I love the work, the people, and the church. That's why I wanted you to attend with me out here. So that we could begin to talk about spiritual issues, not just day-to-day life. So, tell me, what did you think about the pastor's sermon this morning?"

Blanche shook her head in disbelief. "Darling," she sighed, "I've already told you that I find the primitive church out here almost as deplorable a locale as the town of Proctor itself. That church is frightfully old-fashioned and antiquated, while the town is a bit too wild and uncouth. I do believe my life will be so much better without either. But my life would be positively dreadful without you."

"Did you not understand what Reverend Semmes was teaching about seeking first the kingdom of God and then loving others? Do you not comprehend that serving God and then serving our fellow man are the highest and most satisfying callings one can have?"

"Pshaw!" Blanche muttered. "I think *your* first calling should be to serve me, darling. And," she said, smiling up at him, "if you do, I'll make you a very, very happy man."

Wade sighed forlornly and looked across the tumbling waters of the creek. Dr. Keller had warned him the water was running particularly high for September. But what most ruffled his soul was Blanche. The more he learned about her, the more he doubted they had a future together.

"Especially," she continued, "if you don't ever drag me to another hillbilly shack like the one in which you made a home visit this morning. My heavens, what a dreadful place. No running water. No electricity. How perfectly barbaric. What an appalling experience. I can't even begin to understand what you see in these poor pitiful people. They are wholly and absolutely uncivilized."

"Actually," Wade responded, "I find them more civilized than some of the people who claim to be superior in word and deed. Mountain people are truly good and giving, no matter the situation. In addition, they are truly a happy people. To my way of thinking, there's no dollar sign that can be placed on a satisfied soul."

"Happy?" Blanche said incredulously. "I don't see how they could be. Obviously I prefer completely different tastes. I prefer enlightened and elegant, *not* crude and unrefined. Assets and affluence are more to my taste, dearest. What I've witnessed these past few days is perfectly repugnant. No, dreadful!"

Wade sighed. "It's amazing to me that you live so close to these highlanders and yet know so little about them, Blanche. They are a truly remarkable people."

"Oh, Wade, you are *so* idealistic. It's one of the traits I love about you. But reality will be much clearer when you move to Bryson City. It will be better when you get away from the boondocks and backwoods and begin practice in Bryson City. Why, Wade, there you'll have important people for your patients!"

Wade felt the color rise in his cheeks and was surprised by the speed and sharpness of his response as he retorted, "My patients here *are* important people."

Blanche immediately tried to cover her faux pas. "Darling, I'm not saying these folks aren't human. They are. It's just that their intelligence is limited and their ways ancient. Why, I don't even see how they'll make it once the lumber company pulls out."

Wade stopped in his tracks. He could not have been more startled had she thrown cold water in his face. "Pulls out?"

Blanche turned to face him. Looking around to be sure they were alone, she lowered her voice. "I guess you would have no way of knowing this. So you must promise to keep it a secret. Can you promise?"

He nodded, even though he felt as though he were spinning.

"Mr. Calhoun's plans, which are top secret at the moment, are to completely pull out of Hazel Creek and move the town and the company to another watershed. May happen in the next year, or as late as 1928, depending."

"Does anyone out here know?" Wade asked.

"Only you, my dear. And now you see why it's even more important for you to move to Bryson City. And, as I say, when you do, I'm going to make you a very, very happy man."

As she leaned forward to kiss him, he found himself pulling away.

Fishin'

"That ain't fair!" Abbie yelled at Danya, who was sitting next to her on the shore of Sugar Fork, reeling in an enormous trout.

"What isn't fair, Abbie? I'm just a better fisherman than you!"

Abbie scowled. As competitive as she was, she did not like being beaten at anything, especially fishing. "So, we leave Maria and the girls at the farm and I bring you to my best fishin' spot, and you go and catch *my* fish, and don't even say thank you."

"This *is* a great spot!" Danya exclaimed. "The fish are virtually all gone from Hazel Creek due to the lumber company. So it makes sense that the old monsters, like this one, would have found their way up the side creeks like this." He proudly held up the nearly thirty-inch-long trout. "So, thank you!" he exclaimed as he put it in his large creel.

Abbie looked upstream as the ice-cold water from Sugar Fork tumbled into the top of her fishing hole and then downstream, where it plunged down a steep rapid and into Hazel Creek. A dense thicket of rhododendron encircled her secret spot, hiding it from the unsuspecting folk traveling up Hazel Creek or Sugar Fork.

Her pa had shown her the spot, one of his favorites, just as his pa had disclosed it to him. She would come here from time to time, not just to fish, but also for some quiet time away from the world and all her troubles. She particularly liked how she could scout Hazel Creek, the road, and train tracks below without being noticed. It made her feel like a spy or an undercover agent. At that moment she saw two people walking up Hazel Creek arm in arm. She turned back to her fishing hole. "What'dcha think of church this mornin'?" Abbie asked.

"I don't know," Danya replied as he baited his hook and slung it toward the top of the fishing hole. "It was tolerable. Of course, the sermons in your church are *much* longer than the homilies at our church in the old country."

"Tolerable?" Abbie asked, laughing. "Is that all you can say?"

Danya looked confused. "What did you want me to say?"

"You could tell me what you thought of the pastor's sermon. I thought it was one of his best in quite some time."

"What did you like about it?" Danya asked as he reeled his cork toward the center of the hole.

Abbie felt herself break out in an ear-to-ear smile. "It was a glorious message for me. Just what I needed."

"Why? What did you need? If you don't mind me asking."

She looked at him and he appeared befuddled. "The words of Jesus. They were meant for me, aimed right at my heart."

"Which words?"

"Mama had me memorize them a long time ago. But I've not thought about them in so long. Guess I've just been wrapped up in all my troubles."

"Abbie," Danya complained, "you've now lost me. What are you talking about?"

Abbie turned to look at the still, dark water and thought for a moment. "Jesus said, 'Take no thought for your life, what ye shall eat, or what ye shall drink; nor yet for your body, what ye shall put on. Is not the life more than meat, and the body than raiment?'"

Abbie smiled. "Danya, look at those beautiful flowers," she said as she pointed toward the blooms just behind them. "Jesus said, 'Consider the lilies of the field, how they grow; they toil not, neither do they spin: And yet I say unto you, That even Solomon in all his glory was not arrayed like one of these. Wherefore, if God so clothe the grass of the field, which to day is, and to morrow is cast into the oven, shall he not much more clothe you, O ye of little faith?'"

Danya was quiet for a bit and then said, "I think I see your point, Abbie—that we should trust God and then depend upon him to provide for us."

Abbie nodded. "It was just the reassurance I needed, Danya."

Danya reeled his cork back toward the center of the hole as he grinned. "Me, too, Abbie. Me, too."

"If you won't kiss me," Blanche called out over her shoulder as she ran down the bank toward Hazel Creek, "then I'm just going to have to splash some ice-cold water on my face to calm my passion for you!"

"Be careful!" Wade called out. Just getting *near* the white-water rapids was frightening to him. He had cared for one too many near drownings of lumbermen who had tumbled into the roaring waters of Hazel Creek while working the logs. The closer she drew to the fast-moving water, the more alarmed he became.

"You don't *really* care about me, Wade Chandler!" Blanche protested as she worked her way down the bank. "You just care about your practice with these poor pitiful people."

"Blanche! You come back away from the creek! Now!"

She laughed as she jumped down to the edge of the torrent, lifted up her long skirt, and gingerly hopped from boulder to boulder.

"Blanche! Stop!" But no sooner were the words out of his mouth than she slipped. Suddenly one leg shot toward the sky while her head tumbled backward.

৵ ৵ ৵ ৵

At that instant, Abbie heard a scream and her head whipped around just in time to see a woman, in her Sunday best, tumble into the rapids of Hazel Creek below. She leaped to her feet and began to race through the brush.

Blanche's bloodcurdling scream lasted only a second before her head crashed against a rock. Despite his horror of the water, Wade sprinted down the embankment as Blanche's body collapsed into the raging stream.

Jumping to the water's edge, he felt nauseated. "Blanche!" he shouted as he began running down the creek. He could barely hear himself above the roar of the rapids as her body began to disappear below the waves. "Blanche!"

At that instant, out of the corner of his eye, he saw a flash. He turned his head to see a young woman, her long auburn hair streaming behind her, sprinting down the bank, ripping off her boots as she ran and throwing them aside. Once barefooted, she dashed to the creek's edge and without hesitation ran full speed into the surging stream.

"Abbie?" he heard himself bellow as he then screamed, "Abbie! No!"

He ran down the shallows and without a thought about his own terror followed her into the raging water. He wasn't thigh deep in the ice-cold white water before he saw Abbie lower her body and disappear below the surface.

"Abbie!" he shrieked as he frantically struggled against the water to move downstream, hoping against hope that he might be able to see and grab her. "Abbie!"

At that moment, her head popped up as she gasped and sputtered for air. "Wade!" she cried out as she reached for him with one arm, her other arm clutching a limp Blanche.

He secured his downstream boot against an underwater rock and lunged for her, grabbing her wrist just as her head vanished once again under the water. He pulled her arm with all his might, praying she would not let go. With the pressure of the furious current, he felt as if she weighed a ton.

He lowered himself into the frosty water and leaned back with all his strength. He felt he was beginning to succeed when he felt her lurch away, pulled by the unrelenting pressure of the stream, and he realized he might actually be in a losing battle against the violent water.

As he redoubled his effort to pull her out, a guttural roar erupted from his chest. He felt a slight give. *Thank God!* he thought. *I'm finally making headway.* But just at that instant, he realized his downstream boot had slipped free. In a moment, he and Abbie began plunging together into the deadly undercurrent. *Abbie!* was all he could think as his head was pulled under and his body fiercely dragged downstream.

81

Beseech

To his utter amazement, Wade suddenly felt no panic. None. It was as if, in an instant, he accepted his fate.

He now knew he was going to die. He hoped they might find his body and that, perhaps, some kind soul might send his remains to Africa, to be buried next to his mother. He looked forward to seeing her in Glory, hugging her, and strolling with her again hand in hand, just as they had when he was a little boy in Africa.

The vivid memory of their walking together through the lush grasslands of the high plateau of Liberia flashed through his mind, almost in slow motion. He could hear a mission-compound guard following behind them and as he looked back at the tall black man, with his rifle slung over his shoulder, his mother continued to tell him how she prayed every day for his future spouse.

"Every morning, Wade, I beseech God to protect her and to prepare her to be your wife and the mother of my grandchildren." She laughed—oh, how he loved her laugh; it made his spirit soar with its optimism and joy—"How I pray for my grandchildren and that there will be many."

She turned to him and knelt down by him. "Your future wife will have to be a very special woman, Master Wade," his mother told him. "After all, she's going to marry a very, very special young man—my son!"

She smiled and pulled him into a warm hug. He found her soft embrace irresistible; he loved her gentle touch and spirit and adored her laughter, which was contagious and always made him happy. She leaned back and said, "I love you more than you'll ever be able to imagine."

The bright light of the setting sun behind her made her blond hair radiant. She looked like an angel.

"Come here," she said softly. "Let me hug you once again."

Her embrace was warm. He had always loved her scent and would never forget it.

His eyesight began to dim. Then he began to wonder, was this really Africa? Or did he see her beckoning him to join her now from heaven? Was this his past or his future?

At that instant he felt a viselike pressure on his arm, and he was suddenly and forcefully pulled backward out of the rushing torrent. He looked up, sputtering, to see Danya quickly dragging him to shore. To his utter relief, the enormous man also had hold of Abbie! She, too, was gasping and coughing. But she was alive!

Then he saw that Abbie was still tightly grasping Blanche with both hands, gritting her teeth, as the combined weight of the body and water-soaked dress would have been enormous. Nevertheless, Danya pulled the weight of the three of them almost as effortlessly as a massive Percheron would pull an empty wagon as he surged against the overwhelming force of the water.

When they were almost to shore, as Wade felt the river stones scraping against his thighs, he thought he heard Abbie yelling something between coughs. He couldn't make it out for a moment and turned to face her as he fell backward onto the bank. Her back was to him as Danya jerked Blanche's waterlogged body into his arms and sloshed to the shore, placing her in a small area of thick green grass.

Wade felt himself lurching to his feet and stumbling to Blanche's side. Instinctively he knelt down and felt for a pulse. There was none! She wasn't breathing and her face was a mottled bluish purple. Her skin was ice-cold. His first coherent thought was that he couldn't believe he was going to have to pronounce her dead. *Not me! Not now!* he thought.

"Blanche!" Abbie cried out as she fell on her knees across the body from him. "You will not die! You will not!"

She's dead! Wade wanted to yell out. But before he could, Abbie looked up at him. "Wade, save her! I'll pray!" Abbie clasped her hands together, bowed her head, and began to pray.

Wade remembered his training and quickly placed Blanche's arms over her chest and flipped her onto her stomach. He placed his hands on each side of her spine, over her upper back, and quickly thrust downward. A spew of water poured out of her mouth as he grabbed her elbows and leaned back, extending her back, pulling her a few inches off the ground.

He then laid her again on the grass, placed his hands on her back, and repeated the sequence. *Out with the bad*, he thought as he pushed, *in with the good.* "Come on, Blanche!" he commanded as he pushed on her lungs once again.

This time she sputtered. As he pulled her back, she coughed. When he pushed, water, air, and sputum flew across the grass, and she began to spasmodically cough.

Wade looked at Abbie. Tears were streaming down her cheeks. Her smile was radiant; her smile was the same as his mother's. The warm rays of the setting sun, its cozy yellow glow, shone down on her. *An angel*, he thought as she covered her mouth with both her hands. He leaned toward her and pulled her into his arms as she sobbed.

At that moment he knew that his mother's prayers for his future spouse, as well as his own, had finally been answered.

82

Farewell

As Wade looked over the trees between the train depot and the Little Tennessee River, he didn't know whether to be glad or sad, cheerful or gloomy. *In the end*, he thought, *it's probably a bit of both*.

Blanche's parents had arrived on the morning train from Bryson City and spent the better part of the middle of the day consulting with Wade. He assured them again of the full recovery they could expect of their daughter and that it would be safe for her to travel with them back to Bryson City. They then tried everything they could to persuade him to abandon, in their words, his silly obsession with the wilderness, and come experience the fine life they would make available for him, caring for the most upper-crust and significant clientele west of Asheville.

Again and again he thanked them for their offer and their concern, as he reassured them he was certain of his call to remain, at least for now, in the Hazel Creek area. Finally, they seemed to accept his decision.

As the Jenkinses boarded the train, Wade looked over the end of the platform where he could see the rushing waters of Hazel Creek cascading into the river and a horrible thought crossed his mind: *Our bodies could have washed all the way down Hazel Creek and into the river.* For a moment, he found himself second-guessing his decision to finally break off his courtship with

Blanche, but only for a moment. *Blanche and I are as different as night and day, as alike as oil and water. Marry that girl and it'll be nonstop fighting, like cats and dogs, until one of us would be forced to run for cover. Nope, Wade, as hard as this is, it's right.*

A sound behind him caused him to turn and face Blanche as she walked up to him.

"I don't really know whether to love you or hate you," she said hoarsely, as she coughed into a handkerchief. She then looked up with misty eyes, but he knew she could turn the tear spigot on and off as fast as she could transform her mood or activate her Southern charm. "But either way, I'm thankful to you for saving my life."

"If it had not been for Abbie, I'm afraid we would not be talking."

"Well, yes, I'm told she did pull me from those horrid waters, but had you not been there with your medical expertise and your resuscitation skills, I'm afraid my parents would be picking up a cold corpse and a coffin today."

"Blanche, my medical skills were driven by unadulterated dread, but that young woman's persistent prayers for you as I worked were driven by a faith as deep and pure as any artesian spring. She deserves all our gratitude."

"Well, why don't you tell her for me?" Blanche said with untainted disdain. "I need to head back to civilization now. Besides, it's difficult to be kind to a woman who is stealing one's fiancé."

"Fiancé? Blanche, we've *never* been engaged! We were barely courting."

"Oh, Wade, that's part of the problem. We just don't see things quite the same—"

"Stealing? Are you kidding me?"

"Oh, darling. You really don't see it, do you? She's so in love with you that she can't see straight. Are you that blind to the little urchin's attempts to steal your affections? If so, I truly do pity you, my dear." Blanche's cheeks had flushed, but she quickly regained her composure. She stepped close to him, leaning her body into his. "Oh, darling. I can give you so much more than she can. All the finery of life is within our reach, Wade. Come with me. Come now."

The locomotive let out a whistle as the conductor yelled out, "All aboard!"

Wade took her hands into his. "Blanche, one last encouragement from the sermon yesterday morning. I think it will be my life verse, and I hope you'll consider it for yourself."

"Which is?" she asked.

"The words of Jesus where he said, 'Seek ye first the kingdom of God, and his righteousness; and all these things shall be added unto you.' If you seek all those things, you'll miss him. If you look first to him, then *all* these things will be added. Isn't that what you're really looking for?"

"Oh, dear Wade. What in heaven's name are you talking about now? I swan, there's more preacher to you than prince." Her cheeks flushed again and her voice hardened. "Maybe you and that scamp deserve each other. I thought you a man of intellect; now I suspect you are daft or, worse yet, deceived and delusional." She quickly let her annoyance pass and then radiated her most elegant and artificial smile. "You know you're going to miss me like crazy and you'll wish you had never made this mistake. Then you'll come running back for what could have been. Any second thoughts, Dr. Chandler?"

He looked down at his bowler, which he slowly turned in his hands. "No, Miss Jenkins. I sense in my heart this is right, for both of us. In fact . . . I know it beyond a shadow of a doubt."

"Since you're such an aficionado of poetry, I wrote a little verse for this occasion. Shall I share it?"

Wade nodded reluctantly as Blanche cleared her throat.

I think you'll miss me like the dawn misses the day,
I think you'll miss me like the summer misses May,
I think you'll miss me like a long-lost jewel . . .

She tried to laugh as tears ran down her cheeks, and over a trembling lip she finished her poem:

I think you'll miss me, you silly, silly fool.

She leaned up to kiss him.

He turned his head ever so slightly to let her kiss him on the cheek and then stepped back and put on his hat. "I pray the best for you, Blanche," he said as the train slowly began to move.

"Come quickly, my dear!" Mr. Jenkins shouted from the door of a railcar as he gestured for her. "It's back to civilization and culture for us!"

Wade watched as Blanche daintily ran to her father, who helped her up the steps, and then disappeared inside. She smiled, blew him a kiss, and then turned to enter the train car as it slowly chugged away.

He felt as if an enormous encumbrance had been lifted from his shoulders.

83

Fussing

For the two days following her near drowning, Abbie felt progressively worse. Initially she thought she had a head cold, but today her symptoms began to worsen. Her nasal drainage turned from clear to yellow and she began to experience a sore throat and cough, along with body aches and shaking chills, followed by a fever.

"Nothin' an occasional dose of honey and lemon juice cain't care for," Abbie said to herself as she and her sisters began to prepare their evening meal. "That and a bit of willow-bark powder for the muscle aches and fever."

The work of managing the farm that day had been stressful, as Danya and some of the men he hired to work the fields had words. *Managin' my family's hard enough,* she thought, *without havin' to juggle a bunch of independent-minded men who cain't get along!*

The sound of a jar crashing on the floor startled her. She spun around to see Anna Kate standing above a small broken jar of molasses, the liquid spreading into a puddle at her feet. Cap'n Brown dashed over to the spill and began to lick the delicacy.

Abbie slapped her hands. "Shoo, dog! Get away from that!"

"Why cain't he eat it, Abbie?" Anna asked. "It ain't no good to us now."

Abbie lost her temper. "Are you as dumb as a bag of hammers? There are glass shards in there that could kill that fool puppy. Get back! Both of you!"

Anna's eyes filled with tears and her lower lip began to tremble. "Sometimes I hate you, Abbie!" she exclaimed as she turned and ran out of the house.

"You can just keep on runnin', girl! Send us a letter when you get to Mexico! I don't care!"

Whit, who was stirring a pot of soup over the cook fire, looked up at her sister incredulously. "What's wrong with you, Abbie?"

"Nothin's wrong with me!" Abbie exclaimed as she picked up a towel and got on her knees to begin cleaning up the mess. "I just ain't feelin' well and my tolerance is a bit short. That's all."

"That's the understatement of the year," Whit said softly as she walked over by Abbie and began picking up the larger pieces of glass. "I know you're feelin' poorly. Have a seat on the porch for a few minutes. The quiet time will do you some good. I'll finish up in here."

Abbie nodded and walked outside. She was upset with herself. *Lord,* she thought, *it's just too hard runnin' a farm and bein' both parents for a family. I just need some help,* she prayed as she put her face into her hands. *Lord, you tell us that we have not because we ask not, so I'm askin' for some relief. Hep me get well from this cold. Hep me be a better sister to my girls.*

She looked up as she heard the sound of the fence gate opening. Corrie skipped up to the porch. "Finished all the barn chores," she said. "Danya's comin' in a bit. He's agreed to take me to town. I'm plannin' to spend the night with June Satterfield tonight. Bunch of us girls are gonna go to the moving-picture show to see Rudolph Valentino in *Son of the Sheik.*"

"Corrie, it's a school night and school's only begun a bit over a week—"

"We'll not stay out late. You know Mrs. Satterfield won't allow it. I'll just take my school clothes with me."

"When that movie came to Proctor last year, there was a lot of talk. I've heard that the movie ain't good for young girls, Corrie. So I think you should stay home, all right?"

"No, ma'am!" Corrie scowled. "It's *not* all right. I've decided to go, I've arranged a ride, and I'm goin' whether you want me to or not. I'm thirteen years old, and you ain't my mama, even if you think so!"

Abbie's anger erupted again, without her even realizing it was coming. She reached out and grabbed Corrie by the arm. "Young lady, in the eyes of the law I *am* your mama. What I say goes. You hear?"

Corrie jerked her arm away and pushed Abbie's chest with both her arms. "I'm stronger than you and I ain't takin' no for no answer. Danya's comin' to get me and I'm goin'."

Abbie felt her face flush as she pointed her finger at Corrie. "No you ain't! Danya works for me, and if he wants to keep his job, he'll follow my orders not to take yours. Now that's it. That's my final word."

Corrie's face reddened and she slapped Abbie's pointed finger. When she did, Abbie lashed out and slapped Corrie across the face. Suddenly, Abbie's world stopped.

Abbie moaned as she instantly regretted her violence. "Corrie . . ." she whimpered.

Corrie burst into tears. "I hate every bone in your body, Abbie!" she screamed as she ran inside, pushing past Whit, who had just walked outside.

"Corrie!" Abbie cried out. "I'm sorry." She stood and tried to follow Corrie, but Whit blocked her path and placed her hands on her shoulders.

"Just sit down, sister. Best we all cool off a bit. We can all talk about this later."

Abbie let out a deep breath and turned to sit back in her rocker, unable to control the sobs that racked her body. As Abbie cried, Whit pulled a chair up and put her arm around her. "It's all right, Abbie. I know you're feelin' right puny. We'll get this sorted out in a bit."

Abbie sniffled, pulled a handkerchief out of her apron pocket, and blew her nose. "At least you and Sarah girl haven't run away."

"At least not yet," Whit said, smiling. "Not that I haven't thought about it."

Abbie sniffled again. "I know I have, Whit. Sometimes it just seems intolerable. The Lord lets us live in such a beautiful place, but the livin' here's hard, ain't it?"

"Scripture reminds us we'll face trials, Abbie."

"I guess I'm not only feeling sick, but I'm fearful for our Corrie. If only Mama or Pa were here. They could handle Corrie so much better than me."

"We'll pray for your healing, sister. But you need to know that you're doing a fine job with our family and with our farm. And as Corrie grows up, we both need to realize we can't keep her locked up in a room or on a farm."

Abbie nodded. A noise at the door caused them both to look up. Corrie was at the door with a small backpack. "Am I goin' with your permission, or are you gonna make me run away?"

Abbie looked at Whit and then back at Corrie. "Will you forgive me for slappin' your face? I'm sorry, Corrie. I am."

Corrie smiled. "Will you forgive me for slapping you and pushing you? I'm sorry, too."

"I will," Abbie said, nodding. "You can go . . . with my blessing, sister. But be careful. I'll see you after school tomorrow, all right?"

Corrie nodded, hopped down the steps, and ran toward Danya and Maria's cabin.

Abbie began to cough again, a paroxysm that shook her whole body. She winced as she coughed. It felt like knives were stabbing her lungs on both sides. She coughed up the sputa into her handkerchief. When she looked down, what she saw struck fear into her heart. In her handkerchief were clots of bright red blood.

84

Assignment

After Wade walked back to the infirmary from the sawmill below Proctor, where he had diagnosed his first two cases of pneumonia for the fall, the nurse told him that Dr. Keller had gone home ill. Wade walked next door to Keller's home, hoping against hope that he was not napping. The old man was known to be a grizzly bear when unexpectedly awakened. He knocked.

"Come in," said a weak voice.

Wade removed his hat, entered the foyer, and put his bowler on the rack. Seeing Keller lying on a sofa, he entered the parlor.

"You all right?" Wade asked.

As Keller removed the arm that had been thrown over his face, Wade became concerned. "You look awfully pale, Boss. In fact, you look downright puny."

As Keller sat up, he let out a racking cough that sounded painful. Spitting the phlegm into a spittoon, he looked up at Wade with reddened eyes as he blew his nose. "Wouldn't come closer, son. I think I've picked up bronchitis and pleurisy. It's spreading through the men like wildfire. Guess I caught it from one of them."

"You need me to examine you?" Wade asked. "I just diagnosed our first two pneumonia cases among the women. I've asked the nurse to begin a quarantine of men with cough and a fever."

"Good idea. In the meantime, don't come near me. You don't

want to pick this up. It's bad enough to have one of our doctors down. By the way, speaking of pneumonia, can you do me a favor? Can you run up valley for me? I have an assignment for you."

"Happy to. What do you need me to do?"

"Zach Taylor came by. He had been up at the Randolphs'. Says the oldest Randolph girl is very, very sick. Maddie says she has double pneumonia and isn't responding to any of her treatments. She thinks Abbie caught it while trying to save the Jenkins girl."

"Oh my. Bilateral?" Wade said. "That's not good."

"Yep. I know what you're thinking. Case fatality rate is high for bilateral lobar pneumonia, especially if it's pneumococcal. The majority of the folks who get it out here die. Everyone knows that. I think that's what's scaring Maddie."

Wade nodded. "Want me to take some of my serum up there?"

"I don't know, Wade. I know you've been waiting for just the right case to try it on. But it's still too experimental for my tastes."

Wade was silent for a moment. "Andrew, if Maddie's right, then this could be a life-or-death situation."

"Wade, young doctors are always anxious to show off their newfangled treatments. I saw far too many people die of pneu-monia during the Spanish flu epidemic back in '18 and '19. It was terrible. But I've also seen men suffer horrible deaths when given horse serum. You ever see a severe serum reaction?"

"No, sir."

"I have, and it's awful . . . a downright dreadful thing to watch." Keller looked up at his young protégé and continued. "It's bad enough for a doctor to kill an old person with horse serum. Kill-ing a young woman with it would be frightful. Has the serum even been tested in young folks?"

"Not in as many as older adults, at least that I saw."

"I'm serious, Wade. You go off half-cocked and kill one of these mountain folk with some experimental treatment, you'll destroy any trust these folks have with us. You'll run the last decade of my work straight into the ground. Worse yet, if those girls lose Abbie, they're gonna be orphans and you know what that means. You understand me?"

"Yes, sir. I hear you loud and clear."

"One last thing, son. Seems to me you've developed some affection for that girl, correct?"

Wade felt his cheeks flush.

"Well, don't let that get in the way of your professional care. You hear?"

Wade nodded as he grabbed his hat and turned to leave. Before the door shut he heard another paroxysm of coughing.

Fretting

Maddie was sitting in a rocker on the porch, puffing on her corncob pipe. She had left the large entourage that was surrounding Abbie in the cabin. She needed some time to ponder. She and the observers knew that Abbie was severely ill, and they were all worried.

She shook her head as she went over the case again and again. A noise caused Maddie to turn. A drooping Whit, with dark circles under her eyes, walked out the door and sat by her. "She's worsening, ain't she, Maddie?"

Maddie nodded. "Almost by the hour, Whit."

"I thought once the convulsions from the high fever stopped, we might be outta the woods," Whit sighed.

Maddie hadn't worried the girls with her fears when she first arrived the evening before and found Abbie in a full-blown seizure. Meningitis had been her first concern. But a careful exam revealed a fever of 105 degrees, dehydration, and deep congestion in both lungs. Abbie's neck was soft and supple. Maddie knew meningitis stiffened the neck like a board.

"I was pleased when your remedy and our cold-water bath stopped her seizures. And I consider it an answer to prayer that your medicines have kept them away. What'dcha give 'er?"

"Once she was conscious enough to swallow, I gave her a walloping dose of castor oil followed by a treatment of salol and bismuth."

"The seizures 'bout scared me to death," Whit said.

"There's nothin' more frightenin' to see or gives a more power-ful feelin' of helplessness than watchin' a convulsion. I think it's more fearsome even than severe bleeding or the endless diarrhea of typhoid fever."

"When she asked for somethin' to drink, I 'bout cried my eyes out I was *so* happy. I tell ya, I was powerful relieved."

"Me, too, Whit," Maddie said in a voice barely above a whisper.

"Really?" Whit asked.

"Yep," Maddie replied as she took another puff. "Carin' for double pneumonia is worrisome and fretful to any healer worth her salt. Me included."

"With all the treatments you had us doing, it helped take my mind off how sick she is." Whit was quiet a moment. "You think Abbie's gonna make it, Maddie?"

"I don't know, child. You and your sisters can sure continue to pray. I just wish . . ." Maddie took another puff and let Whit fin-ish the sentence for her.

"Dr. Keller would get here. What's takin' him so long?" Whit said, looking down the valley.

"I don't know, honey. I just don't know. But if he don't come soon, I'm a-feared it'll be too late. I think Abbie's nearly on her last leg."

Just then, a sound came from the trail, followed by a man whipping his horse at a full run toward the cabin.

"Who's that?" Whit cried out.

"I declare!" Maddie exclaimed. "It's Dr. Chandler!"

After greeting everyone in the cabin, including the Randolph girls, the Raus, the Petrovas, and Pastor and Mrs. Semmes, Wade explained why Dr. Keller was indisposed. He and Maddie talked in hushed tones as she explained to him her findings and treat-ments; then Wade went to work.

He took Abbie's temperature, and then carefully examined her eyes and tongue, looked into her ears, checked the suppleness of her neck and limbs, palpated her abdomen, measured her liver span, gently pinched her skin, and carefully listened with his stethoscope to her chest and abdomen, front and back.

He then sat back and carefully observed her for a few moments. Her skin was hot and sweaty, yet mottled, with a bluish discoloration. Her skin color and purple lips indicated a severe lack of oxygen. Her body's hunger for it caused her to breathe nearly three times the normal rate, yet her respirations were labored—she was using every accessory muscle of her neck and chest to try to get more oxygen. He picked up her limp hand and examined her nail beds. They were also a sickly blue.

He watched her for a few more moments. A cold terror began to fill his heart as he realized he was examining a woman who had very, very little time remaining.

Finally he stood. "Maddie, Whit, and Pastor, I need to talk to you."

"Go ahead," Pastor Semmes said.

Wade tightened his lips. "In private," he said as he turned and walked out the door.

Once outside, Wade led the group through the fence and under the shade of a large magnolia tree where they sat on a number of logs standing on end.

"Maddie," he began, "how long have you been treating her?"

"A tad over twelve hours."

"Whit, how long's she been sick?"

"She caught a cold on Monday, the day after you'uns saved Blanche Jenkins. Tuesday it worsened fast and I had Maria fetch Maddie last night."

"Anyone else in Sugar Fork sick with pneumonia?" Wade asked the pastor.

Semmes shook his head. "Not that I've heard."

"Maddie, tell me once again how you've been treating her. Try to remember everything."

"I've tried everythin' I know. Got her in a quiet, dark room for rest, and she has plenty of fresh air. The white willow-bark powder and cool-water sponging helps keep the high fever at bay. I'm usin' small doses of morphine to help the cough and to help her rest. I'm givin' her doses of ammonium chloride alternating with sips of wine of ipecacuanha to help her expectoration a bit. She's not takin' as much oral fluids as I'd like. I'll need to push her to take more sweet milk, fruit juices, and custard for energy."

"Did any of the treatments seem to help at all?" Wade asked.

"Worked better when the infection was just on one side. But now that it's moved to the other lung, she's worsenin' quickly."

"What's the gauze on her chest for?"

"When she quit responding to my usual treatments, I was hopeful the Denver's Antiphlogistine would work."

"That the paste you put on her chest?"

Maddie nodded.

"Does it come from Denver?"

"Nope," Maddie explained. "Kelly Bennett actually gets it for Dr. Keller and me all the way from New York City. I spread it across the backs of my pneumonia patients with a large palette knife and then cover it with cheesecloth. I normally peel it off after twelve hours and apply a new dressing, but it's having no effect on Abbie. I think I'll try usin' it every eight hours." Maddie took another puff.

As Maddie continued to explain her treatments regimen, Wade carefully listened, asking questions about medication doses, intake and output, and responsiveness. The more Maddie explained what she had done, the more discouraged he became. He bowed his head for a few moments to think of any other treatment options that might be possible.

Finally, he said, "Maddie, I can't think of anything else you could do. Obviously, she's still alive because of your skill."

Maddie nodded. "Doc, she ain't respondin' no more. You think she has any pus around her lungs? Any infection you could draw off her lungs to help?"

Wade shook his head. "We call that empyema. And if she had it, draining the infection can help, no doubt about it. But I'm sure there's none there. All the infection is deep in the lungs, and it's clogging them up pretty good. Worse yet, I think the infection's spreading to her system."

He turned to Whit. "I'll be honest. She's in real bad shape. She's burning up with fever, she's not getting enough oxygen, she's dehydrated, and she's only responsive to deep pain. All these are very negative signs. It's not good. It's not good at all."

Whit bowed her head and began to silently cry. Wade wanted to comfort her somehow. Maddie walked over to Whit and held her close.

Wade sighed deeply as Whit wept. He felt an overwhelming compassion for her. *I've lost a mother*, he thought. *But I've not lost a mother, a father, three brothers . . . and now, to lose her older sister, her legal guardian, the one who's allowing them to keep the farm . . . I can't begin to imagine.*

Finally Whit lifted her head off Maddie's shoulder, wiped her eyes, and looked at Wade. "Doctor, is there anythin' else to do?"

Wade nodded. "There are two things. One's medical, the other spiritual. The medical treatment is one with a pile of ethical concerns. The spiritual one is of critical, immeasurable importance. Pastor, we will all need your counsel on both."

Pastor Semmes looked from Wade, to Maddie, to Whit, and then back to the young physician. "What?"

"Before I tell you about the medical treatment, which is considered experimental, I'd like to ask you to do three things. My first request is based upon the Scripture. You believe in anointing with oil, Pastor?"

Pastor Semmes nodded. "I have a vial of healing oil with me. Always do."

Wade nodded. "Second, I need you to lead us all in prayer before I treat her; that is, if we all agree my treatment is indicated. All right?"

Maddie patted Whit's arm. "Don't that beat all? A doctor who believes in prayer. I declare, what will we see next?"

Semmes looked at Maddie. "I've never had a doc ask for my help. It's a first for me also, but I'm right pleased to do so."

"The third," Wade continued, "is that I need you to put out a call up and down the valley for the faithful brothers and sisters to pray forcefully and fervently for this very sick young lady. We need to bathe her in prayer from every direction."

"Consider it done," the pastor said. "But what about this treatment? Why is it an ethical issue? Is it illegal?"

Wade took a deep breath and slowly let it out. "It's not illegal, Pastor, but it is experimental. With your permission, I'd like to explain it to everyone inside. Would that be all right, Whit?"

Whit looked from Pastor Semmes, who nodded, to Maddie, who nodded, and back at Wade, the concern in her eyes obvious. "That'd be fine, Doctor."

"Good. Then let's go inside."

86

Faith

Sandy Rau was serving the coffee the Barneses had sent up to the cabin when the small group walked back in. They all gathered around the kitchen table. Wade's lips drew tight as he cleared his throat and began.

"You know how terribly sick Abbie is. You all have seen the incredible job Maddie has done to keep her alive. She's used every tool in her very large bag of treatments. We both now think the pneumonia is so bad it's likely to take her from us."

The girls gasped, and Wade waited a moment to let the news settle in before continuing. "Neither Maddie nor I can think of another herb or medicine or treatment to try, with one possible exception."

"Exception?" Sandy exclaimed.

"What exception?" Maria asked.

"When I was in medical school in Philadelphia," Wade began, "they would send us on various rotations to study with some of the best doctors in the world. A couple of years ago I was assigned to study pulmonary medicine with a famous physician named Jesse Godfrey Moritz Bullowa at the Harlem Hospital in New York City. He is known around the world for his research on a revolutionary new treatment for bilateral lobar pneumonia—"

"Could it save Abbie?" Corrie interrupted.

"Corrie, I don't know," Wade responded as he looked at Abbie. "I just know she doesn't have much time."

"What is the treatment?" Pastor Semmes asked.

"It's called serum therapy and uses a medicine called Felton refined specific antibacterial sera. It's made by injecting the germ—the bacteria—that causes pneumonia into horses. The horses then produce antibodies in their bloodstreams, and antibodies are substances that can fight the germ. They collect the horses' blood, separate out the antibodies, and purify them so they can be injected into patients."

Wade could see from the confused looks surrounding him that he had made the mistake of sharing too much technical medical information.

"Anyway," he continued, "I observed Dr. Bullowa using the serum on a lot of older patients with pneumonia. I've seen people on their deathbeds get the serum on one day and go home well the next."

The baffled expressions turned to joy. "You got some?" Corrie asked. "Can you give it to her?"

"I've got a number of vials of the serum, which I brought with me from Philadelphia."

"Well, son," Tom bellowed, "let's get Abbie cured!"

Wade felt his face tighten and he sighed. "It's not as easy as that, Mr. Rau."

"Why not?"

"Because of the possibility of serum sickness," Wade explained.

"What's that?" Maria asked.

"It's a terrible reaction some patients have to the serum. It can cause extremely high fever; severe joint and chest pain; horrible swelling of the hands, feet, and face; and respiratory failure. On top of all this suffering, it can cause death."

"Anything you can do to make the risk less, Doc?" Maddie asked.

Wade nodded. "Usually we test the sputa a patient is coughing up. That way we know the best serum to give. But there's no way to do that out here. I just have to pick the one I think will work best. Then I'll test it by placing a small drop of the serum into her eye. If there's no adverse reaction, then I can inject a small dose into an arm muscle. Again, if there's no negative reaction, I can inject the full dose into a buttock muscle. The good news is that the Felton's serum I have is the purest made. The risk of a bad reaction with it is much less than with any other sera. So that gives me some confidence, but—"

"But what?" Whit asked.

"This treatment has only been used with older adults. It's not been tried in children or young adults." Wade felt apprehension well up in his heart. "Sometimes a medicine successfully used in older people will have much more severe side effects in younger folks. Pastor, Maddie . . . maybe it was wrong of me to even mention this option. It just might be too dangerous. I'm just not sure I want to experiment with Abbie's life."

Whit reached out and put her hand on Wade's forearm. "Dr. Chandler, she's on the edge of crossin' over the river to Glory. Cain't imagine anythin' you'd do that could make her worse."

Wade put his hand on hers. "Whit, there's a big difference between what the Lord causes or allows and what I do. If I caused you to lose your older sister, I'm not sure I'd ever be able to forgive myself. In addition, if Abbie dies, you and your sisters will definitely become orphans and the company I work for will own this property before you could bat your eyes." Wade swallowed hard, then continued. "In school they taught us that we were to always try to do good and abstain from doing harm. I confess to you, Whit, I don't want to bring more harm to you or your sisters than you've already had."

Whit squeezed his arm. "Me and my sisters, we trust the Lord. We trust that he'll use ya along with your newfangled medicine. Ya do your best, and we'll put our confidence and hope in the Lord. In other words, we have faith in you . . . and in him."

Wade thought a moment and then nodded. "In that case"—he looked at Pastor Semmes—"Pastor, ready to get started?"

Semmes smiled and nodded.

87

Prayer

After Pastor Semmes anointed Abbie with oil and they all
joined him in praying for her healing, he sent Tom and
David Rau to ride up the Sugar Fork and Little Fork valleys, and
Danya to ride down to Hazel Creek, to spread the word about
Abbie and request prayer on her behalf.

Whit watched as the young doctor tested the serum by placing
a drop into Abbie's eye. She was impressed with how gentle he
was with her, and how he softly stroked her cheek with the back
of his hand and whispered in her ear.

After giving her a tiny injection of the serum in her arm muscle,
Whit noticed he gently massaged her arm as his lips moved. No
sound came out, but she was certain he was praying for Abbie. It
wasn't until she saw the tears filling his eyes that she suspected
Wade's feelings for Abbie were far deeper than professional.

When Wade declared each test to be negative, as it showed no
adverse reaction, those gathered let out a sigh of relief, and the
young doctor's confidence and hope seemed to grow.

Pastor Semmes delivered yet another prayer as Wade administered a full-dose injection of the serum into Abbie's body. She
didn't flinch during the injection, nor as he massaged the serum
into her muscle.

"Now, we just need to give it time," he said softly, "and
some prayer." He leaned over Abbie once again and whispered

something in her ear and then turned to the visitors. "If you all don't mind, I'll step out for a moment. I won't be far. Call if you need me."

After crossing the meadow in front of the cabin, he entered the woods and quickly found the spot he was seeking—the old oak lying on the ground, surrounded by a carpet of lush ferns in which he had found Abbie having a quiet prayer time not long after he arrived on the Sugar Fork in May. He quickly located her favorite log and saw a marking that drew his attention. He rubbed it and smiled when he realized the log was showing wear from where she had so often sat. At the base of the log he noticed two indentations. He knelt down to touch them and discerned the depressions had been made by her knees—that this was her private prayer altar—a discovery that brought tears to his eyes. He was certain she wouldn't mind as he placed his knees in her imprints and leaned his elbows on the log where she sat, as he thought about the time he first met her. His first sight of her had taken his breath away, and every subsequent meeting only increased his attraction to her—her guts and gumption, pluck and courage, all balanced by her beautiful smile, gentle ways, soft infectious laugh, and, most of all, her deep spirituality.

He looked at the tree canopy far above and whispered, "Mom, if you can hear me, if you can see me, I think I've found her. I think I've discovered the girl for whom we've both prayed for so many years."

He reached into a pocket inside his vest and pulled out a small book. "This was your prayer book," he said to her. He opened the title page, noticing the dainty and skillful calligraphy with which she signed her name, as well as the date of publication—1892, London, England. "If you don't mind, I'd like to pray from it now."

He turned the book to a page of prayers titled "The Order for the Visitation of the Sick" that he had marked with a small purple ribbon. Laying it on Abbie's seat, he began reading, inserting *Abbie* where the text said *name*:

O Lord, look down from heaven, behold, visit, and relieve thy servant Abbie. Look upon her with the eyes of thy mercy, give her comfort and sure confidence in thee, defend her from the danger of the enemie, and keep her in perpetual peace and safety through Jesus Christ our Lord. Amen.

He closed the small book, lowered his eyes, and bowed his head, softly whispering a prayer he had memorized as a child.

Unto God's gracious mercy and protection I commit thee, dear Abbie. The Lord bless thee, and keep thee. The Lord make his face to shine upon thee, and be gracious unto thee. The Lord lift up his countenance upon thee, and give thee peace, both now and evermore. Amen.

He felt a deep sorrow begin to fill his chest. It was as if these prayers of old were incomplete—inadequate for his spirit to express the uneasy cauldron of distress and tribulation that was erupting within his heart.

"Please, please," Wade desperately pleaded, "bring her back to me again."

88

Dawn

The Raus, Semmeses, and Danya had said their good-byes and left for the evening. They all wanted to stay, but Wade convinced them that they would sleep better in their own beds, while Abbie could rest more comfortably with more quiet and less commotion in the cabin.

As dusk fell, Maria was able to get Abbie to take more fluids by mouth and Maddie announced that her fever seemed to be breaking. Whit was working a spinning wheel while Corrie and Anna were putting up the dishes.

"A good sign!" Maddie said as she gave Abbie another dose of morphine.

After she and Maria applied another chest wrap, Wade walked over to the bed and sat down. He observed Abbie's breathing, then gently brushed her face with the back of his hand. Her eyelids flickered. "Her respiratory rate is slowing and her color is much, much improved." He pulled out his stethoscope and listened to her chest. "Maddie, she's moving air better."

"Maybe she's starting to respond," Maddie said.

"Let's not count our chickens just yet," Wade said as he moved back to a rocker sitting next to Abbie's bed. "A serum reaction can occur at any time. Sometimes, before it hits, the patient seems to get better. This may just be the calm before the storm."

"She's turning," Maria said. "I know it. I can sense it."

"I hope you're right," Wade responded softly.

"I usually am," she said, smiling.

It was nearly dawn and the crowing of Hezekiah, the family rooster, had awakened her before anyone else. The first thing she felt was the warmth of Jack, as the tabby was curled up contentedly next to her. "You're as warm as an oven," she whispered as she sat up and rubbed the sleep from her eyes. She yawned and slowly stretched out her kinked muscles. When Lilly and Cap'n Brown both stood by the fireplace and trotted over to her, she gave each a scratch on the head, which only made their tails beat more quickly and forcefully.

Her tummy let out a loud rumble, and she was surprised by how hungry and thirsty she felt as she ran her fingers through her hair and looked around the cabin. Maddie and Maria were slumped over the kitchen table and were breathing deeply.

A groan caused her to turn toward two rockers. Wade was stretched out on one, his head leaning back, while Whit was sleeping in the other in what appeared to be a *very* uncomfortable position. Whit groaned again and repositioned herself, pulling her grandmother's quilt up and around her neck.

She smiled and slowly stood. Initially she was weak and wobbly, but was able to walk toward her sister and grasp the chair for stability. "Whit," she said in a soft voice.

Whit didn't move. Lilly walked up and licked Whit's hand, causing her to instinctively jerk it under the quilt.

"Whit!" she said again. "Can you help me? I'm thirsty."

Slowly Whit opened her eyes and blinked several times. As she finally began to focus, her eyes suddenly grew as wide as saucers and she sprang up. Her jaw dropped, but no words came out.

"Can I have a bite of something, Whit? I'm hungry," she asked hoarsely.

Tears began to fall from Whit's eyes. In a voice barely above a whisper, she exclaimed, "Lauren Abigail! Abbie! You're up!" Whit quickly stood and grabbed her sister into a bear hug. "You're alive!"

She kissed Abbie's face again and again. "Corrie!" Whit called out. "Come see!" Whit turned to Wade, shook his shoulder, and then turned toward Maddie and Maria, who were beginning to stir, as she shouted, "Doctor! Everyone! Wake up! It's a miracle! God has given us a miracle!"

EPILOGUE

September 16, 2009

66 "That was eighty-three years ago today," Mrs. Abbie said wistfully. "Everyone was dancin' around me and huggin' me and makin' all sorts of bother. It took me a bit to understand just how close I'd been to crossin' over."

"I had no idea today was an anniversary for you."

She laughed, "Doc, when ya gonna learn? There's a lot you don't know 'bout me."

"Well," I said, "I'm learning more all the time."

We had just eaten a picnic lunch on the site of the Randolph farm with several Decoration Day parties—not only our group, which had cleaned the Randolph cemetery, but also one that had been to the Bone Valley Cemetery and another that went to the Bradshaw property—when several musicians began to play mountain songs.

We listened to the old songs until the troupe began to play "Carolina in the Morning." Mrs. Abbie's eyes suddenly brightened, and she began to sing along:

Nothing could be finer than to be in Carolina in the morning
No one could be sweeter than my sweetie when I meet her in the
  morning
Where the morning glories twine around the door
Whispering pretty stories I long to hear once more

Strolling with my girlie where the dew is pearly early in the
 morning
Butterflies all flutter up and kiss each little buttercup at
 dawning
If I had Aladdin's lamp for only a day
I'd make a wish and here's what I'd say
Nothing could be finer than to be in Carolina in the morning!

As the group finished, Mrs. Abbie put her fingers into her mouth and let out a wolf whistle that could have woken the dead and then clapped and laughed as she turned to me. "Not only is that what they played right after Pastor Semmes pronounced us man and wife, it's what he sang to me every morning. Every single morning. I never had a better day than that one," she said.

"Never?" I said.

She smiled. "Doc, I've had some mighty fine ones. Our courtship was fast and furious. Wade visited me every day as I recovered from the pneumonia. Land sakes, took me about two months to feel normal again. I remember our Thanksgiving celebration that year. Maria helped me and my sisters. We worked two days to prepare for it. When the Semmeses arrived they said they could smell our cookin' all the way down at the parsonage."

Mrs. Abbie laughed and then continued. "Well, it sure was a plentiful table. After dinner we enjoyed plum puddin' while the children played four square, hopscotch, or sleeping lions. When dessert was done, we all went outside and gathered around a fire Danya had built. When the fiddles were tuned, we sang songs like 'The Jam on Gerry's Rocks' and 'I'll Take You Home Again, Kathleen.' Of course, there was always a rousin' rendition of 'My Grandfather's Clock' and we all danced to 'Monkey Musk,' allemandin' and promenadin', clappin' and laughin' across the front yard until the last chord. By then everyone was out of breath, even the musicians. Then we finished off the evening with a final course of apples, slices of pie, and cider around the fire. That's when it happened."

She was quiet a moment. When I could take it no longer, I piped up, "Okay, Mrs. Abbie, what happened?"

She smiled. "Thought you'd never ask. Well, that's when he proposed to me. Right in front of God and everybody. Even Jeremiah Welch came outta the woods to be a part."

"How'd Wade do it?"

Mrs. Abbie smiled. "Got down on one knee, took my hand, confessed his love for me and my sisters, said he had sought and received the permission and approval of Zach, Danya, and Pastor Semmes. Then he quoted from a sixteenth-century English poem by Christopher Marlowe. I remember his every line:

> Come live with me and be my love,
> And we will all the pleasures prove
> That valleys, groves, hills, and fields,
> Woods or steepy mountain yields.
>
> And I will make thee beds of roses
> And a thousand fragrant posies,
> A cap of flowers, and a kirtle
> Embroidered all with leaves of myrtle;
>
> A gown made of the finest wool
> Which from our pretty lambs we pull;
> Fair lined slippers for the cold,
> With buckles of the purest gold;
>
> A belt of straw and ivy buds,
> With coral clasps and amber studs:
> And if these pleasures may thee move,
> Come live with me and be my love.

She took a deep breath and let it out as her eyes misted. "I couldn't say a word. I just nodded as he placed this ring on my finger. I couldn't see it clearly 'cause my tears started and wouldn't stop. But he stood and took me into his arms, and then leaned forward and softly kissed me. The kiss went on and on as my sisters and our friends all clapped and cheered; the world seemed to become a blur and I felt like I was spinning just like in our first dance, the waltz . . ."

She took another deep breath and let it out very slowly. Her eyes were sparkling, as she seemed to be gazing into another time.

"Next thing I knew, I was at our wedding, relishing our first kiss as husband and wife. As our lips parted, he looked down at me with eyes that overflowed with love and warmth and desire, as Pastor Semmes said to everyone gathered, 'Ladies and gentlemen, I introduce to you, for the first time, Dr. and Mrs. Wade Chandler.'"

Mrs. Abbie's smile stretched from ear to ear.

"He took my hand and we began to walk down the aisle to the back of the church. It was all decorated up for the holidays and for our Christmas wedding. It was like a fairy tale come true; Whit was right all along. We walked out of that church and into the warm sunshine of the day and the commencement of our wonderful married life together.

"Once outside, we were startled to see five yearling bunnies sitting on the edge of the church lawn. It was as if'n they had been a-waitin' fer us to come out. They looked at us a moment and then scurried off. 'They look happy,' I told him. He turned to me and said, 'Like we'll be.' Then, we kissed again—a long, slow, passionate kiss. It was a fine day." She turned to look at me. "I've never had a better day than that."

"Was Maria's prophecy right about you? Did you have your own children? Did you become a healer?"

Mrs. Abbie gave me that look again and laughed.

"I can tell this is going to cost me another dinner at the Fryemont Inn," I said.

She looked across the meadow and shook her head. "Let's just say that my storytelling is just commencing. The thought of it makes me hungry. I think I want to go to the Hemlock Inn this time. Maybe for their Sunday lunch. It's an amazing spread. That would be mighty fine."

I nodded. "Mighty fine indeed, Mrs. Abbie."

Most of the geographical locations and landmarks mentioned in this book exist or existed; however, the use of their names and functions for the purposes of this book is purely fictional. However, a number of historical characters appear in the book, albeit all used fictitiously, including William Bartram, Dr. A. M. Bennett, Senator "Doc" Kelly Bennett, Granville Calhoun, Al Capone, Charles Darwin, John Farley, F. Scott Fitzgerald, Harve Fouts, Captain Amos and Lillian Frye, Ernest Hemingway, Al Jolson, Horace Kephart, Alvan Macauley, Grace Lumpkin, Maxwell Perkins, Quill Rose, Chief George Sequoyah, John T. Scopes, Esther Shemitz, Henry David Thoreau, Thomas Wolfe, and US President Teddy Roosevelt. All other persons mentioned are the product of my imagination and any resemblance to persons, living or dead, is entirely coincidental.

ACKNOWLEDGMENTS

The writer of historical fiction is always in debt to those who understand, either by having studied or having lived through, the history the author hopes to recount. The same is true for me.

My deepest thanks are extended to Jane Bahnson, Marguerite Most, and Jennifer Behrens, who, as reference librarians at Duke Law School, assisted me in understanding the peculiarities of North Carolina law in the mid-1920s. I'm also grateful to Jennifer Brobst, JD, of the North Carolina Central University School of Law and the North Carolina Association of Women Attorneys for assistance in helping me research Lillian Frye's professional training and practice.

I'm thankful to Duane Oliver, who grew up on Hazel Creek and spent a day with me sharing his childhood memories of the area. His stories, research, and prolific writing about the area served as a wonderful resource for me.

I'm beholden to Horace Kephart. His study and writing of the people in and around Hazel Creek in the early 1900s were an invaluable resource to me. No doubt, those familiar with his work and writing will see his observations unavoidably embedded in these pages. I'm also indebted to Libby Kephart Hargrave for sharing memories and writings of her great-grandfather, as well as reviewing the manuscript for accuracy.

I deeply value the many hours that Barb and Kate Larimore

spent poring over copy after copy of drafts of the manuscript. Thanks also to Annette Finger, Bonnie Happel, Jennifer Brobst, Judy Carpenter, Kim Gunther, Margie Shealy, Ralinda Gregor, Vicki Clark, and Zanese Duncan for additional and valuable manuscript review. In addition, I'm grateful to my friend Steve Dail for advice about early twentieth-century camping, wood-craft, hunting, horses, wagons, and guns.

The seed of this book was fertilized over a decade ago by my first fiction-writing mentor—Gilbert Morris. The idea came initially from Gil, and he reviewed my first drafts of both this book and its prequel, *Hazel Creek*. I gratefully dedicate *Sugar Fork* to him.

Last, but not least, I'm thankful to Holly Halverson for her considerable skills, which have shaped and dramatically improved the initial manuscript I sent her. Thanks also to Valerie Pulver for superb editing and to Jenica Nasworthy and Mia Crowley for excellent proofreading—for catching so many little errors that would have made your reading less enjoyable. Appreciation is due to Jessica Wong for so much assistance in the publication of *Hazel Creek* and *Sugar Fork*. Thanks, Jessica! I'm also grateful for Kirk DouPonce of Dog Eared Design for the cover artwork and Jaime Putorti for the book design.

Finally, I'm indebted to the wonderful people of Bryson City and Swain County, who welcomed me into their community for four years in the early 1980s. I thank and acknowledge them for their love and all they taught a young physician.

Walt Larimore
Monument, Colorado
April 2012

BIBLIOGRAPHY

At Home in the Smokies: A History Handbook for Great Smoky Mountains National Park. Washington, DC: National Park Service, 1978.

Bartram, William. *Travels Through North and South Carolina, Georgia, East and West Florida, the Cherokee Country, the Extensive Territories of the Muscogulges or Greek Confederacy, and the Country of the Chactaws.* Philadelphia: James and Johnson, 1791.

Brown, Margaret Lynn. *The Wild East: A Biography of the Great Smoky Mountains.* Gainesville: University Press of Florida, 2000.

Brunk, Robert S., ed. *May We All Remember Well. Volume 1: A Journal of the History & Cultures of Western North Carolina.* Asheville, NC: Robert S. Brunk Auction Services, 1997.

Bush, Florence Cope. *Dorie: Woman of the Mountains.* Knoxville: University of Tennessee Press, 1992.

Chase, Richard. *Grandfather Tales: American-English Folktales.* Boston: Houghton Mifflin Company, 1948.

————. *The Jack Tales.* Boston: Houghton Mifflin Company, 1943.

Coggins, Allen R. *Place Names of the Smokies.* Gatlinburg, TN: Great Smoky Mountains Natural History Association, 1999.

Dabney, Joseph E. *Smokehouse Ham, Spoon Bread, Scuppernong*

Wine: The Folklore and Art of Southern Appalachian Cooking. Nashville, TN: Cumberland House, 1998.

Duracher, Frank. *Smoky Mountain High: The Consuming Passion of Cecil Brown.* Alexandria, VA: Crest Books, 2007.

Ellison, George. Introduction to Horace Kephart, *Our Southern Highlanders.* Knoxville: University of Tennessee Press, 1984, ix–xlv.

———. Introduction to Horace Kephart, *Smoky Mountain Magic.* Gatlinburg, TN: Great Smoky Mountains Association, 2009, xix–xl.

———. Introduction to James Mooney, *James Mooney's History, Myths, and Sacred Formulas of the Cherokees.* Fairvew, NC: Bright Mountain Books, 1992.

Erbson, Wayne. *Log Cabin Pioneers: Stories, Songs & Sayings.* Asheville, NC: Native Ground Music, 2001.

Holland, Lance. *Fontana: A Pocket History of Appalachia.* Robbinsville, NC: Appalachian History Series, 2001.

Hyde, Herbert L. *My Home Is in the Smoky Mountains: Tales from Former North Carolina State Senator Herbert L. Hyde.* Alexander, NC: WorldComm, 1998.

Kephart, Horace. *Camping and Woodcraft: A Handbook for Vacation Campers and for Travelers in the Wilderness.* Knoxville: University of Tennessee Press, 1917.

———. *Our Southern Highlanders* 1913, reprinted. Knoxville: University of Tennessee Press, 1984.

———. *Smoky Mountain Magic.* Gatlinburg, TN: Great Smoky Mountains Association, 2009.

Kephart Hargrave, Libby. Foreword to Horace Kephart, *Smoky Mountain Magic.* Gatlinburg, TN: Great Smoky Mountains Association, 2009, vii–xiv.

Larimore, Walt. *Bryson City Seasons: More Tales of a Doctor's Practice in the Smoky Mountains.* Grand Rapids, MI: Zondervan Publishers, 2004.

———. *Bryson City Secrets: Even More Tales of a Small-Town*

Doctor in the Smoky Mountains. Grand Rapids, MI: Zondervan Publishers, 2006.

———. *Bryson City Tales: Stories of a Doctor's First Year of Practice in the Smoky Mountains.* Grand Rapids, MI: Zondervan Publishers, 2002.

Lumpkin, Grace. *To Make My Bread.* Chicago: University of Illinois Press, 1995.

Mooney, James. *James Mooney's History, Myths, and Sacred Formulas of the Cherokees* 1900; reprint. Fairview, NC: Bright Mountain Books, 1992.

Oliver, Duane. *Along the River: People and Places. A Collection of Photographs of People & Places Once Found Along the Little Tennessee River, an Area Now Part of the Fontana Lake Basin & Southern Edge of the Great Smokies Park.* Hazelwood, NC: Duane Oliver, 1998.

———. *Cooking and Living Along the River.* Hazelwood, NC: Duane Oliver, 2002.

———. *Hazel Creek From Then Till Now.* Hazelwood, NC: Duane Oliver, 1989.

———. *Mountain Gables: A History of Haywood County Architecture.* Waynesville, NC: Oliver Scriptorium, 2001.

Porter, Eliot. *Appalachian Wilderness: The Great Smoky Mountains.* New York: Ballantine Books, 1973.

Rivers, Francine. *The Last Sin Eater.* Wheaton, IL: Tyndale House Publishers, 1998.

Shields, Randolph. *The Cades Cove Story.* Gatlinburg, TN: Great Smoky Mountains Natural History Association, 1981.

Venable, Sam. *Mountain Hands: A Portrait of Southern Appalachia.* Knoxville: University of Tennessee Press, 2000.

Weller, Jack E. *Yesterday's People: Life in Contemporary Appalachia.* Lexington: University of Kentucky Press (with the collaboration of The Council of the Southern Mountains, Inc.), 1966.

QUESTIONS FOR DISCUSSION

1. Which of the Randolph sisters did you most like? Which one did you most identify with? Why?

2. Abbie and her sisters seemed particularly close to their father. Why do you think that was?

3. Abbie and her sisters hated the damage the lumber company inflicted on their valley, yet they also seemed to enjoy some of the luxuries the company provided (such as community events, ice cream, a movie theater). How do you think they would explain this apparent contradiction?

4. Although the moonshine whiskey was "medicinal," Nate seemed to know it was being used for illegal purposes. Even if what he did was "legal," was it right, especially knowing that people were using the product illegally?

5. At several points in the book, the locals (Maddie and Granville Calhoun, to name two) argued that the Prohibition was either wrong or evil or both. Do you think their arguments were valid? If so, why? If not, why?

6. The characters had a variety of feelings about the impact a

national park might have on their valley. If you lived there, at that time, how would you have felt? Would you have favored the formation of a national park, even if it meant losing your home?

7. Dr. Andrew Keller was the lumber-company doctor. Did the locals trust him or just tolerate him? Why or why not? Explain your view.

8. Why did Wade Chandler come to the area? What do you think he was seeking? Were his motives altruistic or more self-centered? What evidence would you give to support your view?

9. Lillian Frye took advantage of an almost unknown law to help the girls. She admitted she was not following the "spirit of the law," but rather "the letter of the law." Was she right to do this, or not? Why?

10. The Haint, Jeremiah Welch, practiced an ancient tradition called sin eating. Why did the pastor consider the practice "pagan"? With what biblical teaching(s) would this custom clash?

11. How important to Abbie was her spiritual faith? How many spiritual disciplines did Abbie practice? How did these disciplines aid her in both happy and sad times? What spiritual disciplines do you need to develop in your life? How will you do this?

12. Many difficult and bad things happened to Abbie and her sisters during this story. Does God cause bad things to happen? Does he allow bad things to happen? How can God use difficult experiences and circumstances in your life?

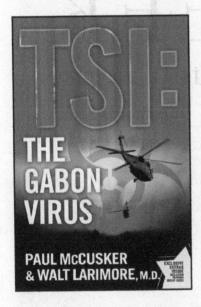
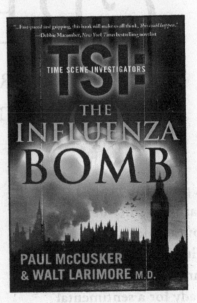